STATE OF DENIAL

FIRST FAMILY SERIES, BOOK 5

MARIE FORCE

State of Denial
First Family Series, Book 5
By: Marie Force

Published by HTJB, Inc.
Copyright 2023. HTJB, Inc.
Cover design by Kristina Brinton and Ashley Lopez
Cover photography by Regina Wamba
Models: Robert John and Ellie Dulac
Print Layout: E-book Formatting Fairies
ISBN: 978-1958035412

The First Family Series

Book 1: State of Affairs
Book 2: State of Grace
Book 3: State of the Union
Book 4: State of Shock
Book 5: State of Denial
Book 6: State of Bliss (Dec. 2023)
Book 7: State of Suspense (Coming 2024)

More new books are always in the works. For the most up-to-date list of what's available from the First Family Series, go to *marieforce.com/firstfamily*

CHAPTER ONE

A persistent banging on the door woke her far too early after a late night. Groaning, she turned over to go back to sleep.

The banging continued.

Her phone rang with a call from her neighbor Janice, three doors down in the condo complex.

"You'd better answer the door," Janice said. "It's the police."

"*What?*"

"The parking lot is overrun with cops and media."

"What do they want with me?"

"You'd know that better than I would."

"Wait until they find out who I am."

"Careers will end, and heads will roll."

"You know it, girlfriend. Thanks for the heads-up."

She got out of bed, put on a red silk robe and took the time to brush her hair and teeth before she made her way downstairs, opening the door to chaos.

"Are you Nicoletta Bernadino?" a stern-looking man asked as he held up a badge.

"I am."

He showed her a piece of paper. "We have warrants to search the premises and for your arrest."

"My *arrest*? For what?"

"You're being charged by the state with engaging in prostitution and solicitation of prostitution. The Feds want you for money laundering."

"Do the Feds know who I am?"

"Ma'am?"

"My son is their boss."

"And who is your son?"

"President Nicholas Cappuano."

The man showed no reaction to hearing the name of the president of the United States. "You'll have to take that up with the FBI, ma'am. Our orders are to bring you in while our team searches your home."

They wouldn't find anything in her house. She wasn't that stupid.

"And your place of business."

Shit. This isn't good.

"I want to make a phone call."

"You'll have the opportunity to make a call after you're booked. If you'd like to change your clothes, I can have a female officer accompany you."

"That won't be necessary." If they were going to arrest the president's mother, then she would put on a show for the media. And how had they known she was being arrested? Her bitch of a daughter-in-law had probably tipped them off. She wouldn't put it past her. It was concerning that mentioning her son hadn't put a stop to this entire farce. Then it occurred to her that maybe he didn't believe her.

"You heard what I said about my son, the president, right?"

"Yes, ma'am."

"You should think about what you're doing while you still have a career to save."

"I don't work for the president, ma'am. I work for the people of the great state of Ohio, and you have the right to remain silent."

THE NEWS of his mother's arrest on misdemeanor prostitution and federal racketeering charges dominated the Monday morning news. President Nick Cappuano stood in front of the TV in the suite he shared with his first lady and watched the madness unfold in Ohio. They'd cuffed her and brought her out of her home in a red silk robe that clung to her considerable curves.

He took perverse satisfaction in noting she looked rattled. Her long dark hair fell in messy waves around her ageless face. People said she reminded them of Sophia Loren. She reminded him of disappointment and neglect.

He wondered if she'd dropped his name yet and then laughed. "Of course she did."

"Did what?" his wife, Samantha, asked as she joined him, dressed for another day in charge of the Metro Police Department's Homicide squad.

"I was wondering if she dropped my name and then decided of course she had."

"No question," Sam said, "but it doesn't seem to have helped her at all. There were a lot of ways they could've arrested her." Eyeing the TV, she said, "They went for a full-impact perp walk, and someone tipped off the media to make sure it was recorded for posterity."

"Probably by someone who thinks her son is an illegitimate president."

Sam sat next to him and rested her head on his shoulder. "I know I've already said it, but I'm sorry again to have brought this down on you."

In a fit of rage toward his mother months ago, Sam had asked their colleague and friend FBI agent Avery Hill to investigate her. Nick had been furious when he recently found out his mother was about to be arrested thanks to that request. However, he'd calmed down after he'd had a minute to think it through. As always, his mother was causing him pain. He wasn't going to allow her to cause a marriage crisis for him, too. No way.

"You didn't. She did. At least we had a heads-up it was coming, which we might not have gotten without Avery's involvement."

"Did they say what she's being charged with?" Sam asked.

"Misdemeanor state prostitution charges and federal money laundering."

"State prostitution charges won't pack much of a punch beyond the salaciousness, but the money laundering is a bigger deal. That's almost always a RICO charge."

"Tell me more about that."

"Under the Racketeer Influenced and Corrupt Organizations Act, RICO charges are invoked when someone has engaged in a pattern of racketeering activity related to an enterprise. So, if she's been laundering money through another company to cover the activities of her bordello, that meets the threshold for a RICO charge."

"Wasn't that what mobsters were charged with?"

"Often. Yes."

"Awesome. So my mother will be lumped in with mobsters and other famous madams."

His personal cell phone rang with a call from his father, which he took, knowing Leo would've heard the news and was calling to check on him. "Hey, Dad."

"Nick... I can't believe this."

"You can't? Really?"

"Well, I can, but it's outrageous. Did you know this was happening?"

"I knew it might be coming, but not when."

"I'm sorry you'll have to deal with this. She's caused you enough hell and heartache in your life. This is the last thing you need right now."

That much was certainly true. He'd spent the last few months trying to convince the American people that he could handle the office he'd never been elected to, and having his criminal mother marched across every screen in America wouldn't help anything. "We're handling it."

"I wish there was something I could do for you."

"I appreciate the call, Dad."

"Check in later, all right?"

"I will."

"I'd tell you to have a good day, but..."

Nick laughed. "Talk later." He ended the call and put the phone in his suit coat pocket.

"What'd he say?"

"He's disgusted by her, as usual."

"What's the plan for dealing with this?" Sam asked.

"I spoke with Terry and Christina earlier," he said of his chief of staff and press secretary. "We'll issue yet another statement that says the president has no relationship with his mother, has never had any relationship with her and will have nothing to say about her arrest."

"I think that's the right way to go. Not that I know anything about these things."

"Thanks to me, you know more about crisis communication than you thought you ever would."

"That's a fact, Mr. President."

Nick held her close for a minute before they went their separate ways for the day. He drew most of his strength from her and their relationship, which was a bright light at times like this, when outside forces threatened to intrude on their sacred bubble.

"I wish there was something I could do for you," she said.

"This helps." He breathed in her familiar lavender-and-vanilla scent, hoping it would rub off on his clothes and stay with him through the endless day. "What's on your schedule for today?"

"More work on the mess Stahl left us. We're reviewing all his old cases and figuring out which ones were investigated and which ones had reports that were total fiction."

"Damn, that's got to be a grind."

"We have to go back to every witness who was supposedly interviewed and make sure they did, in fact, talk to him. Some did and some didn't, so we're asking them all."

"Will that result in overturned prosecutions?"

"Undoubtedly. Malone is still trying to figure out who helped Stahl archive phony reports. He's ruled out the senior officers and is moving on to the IT people who worked for the department at the time the reports were archived."

"What a mess."

"You have no idea. I fear it'll get much worse before we're done."

"So we're both spending today cleaning up messes someone else made for us."

"Good times."

He smiled as he kissed her. "The best of times. I'll see you for dinner?"

"I'll be here. The good thing about working cold cases is we knock off at quitting time."

"I like when that happens. Later, we need to talk about our first overseas trip, which I'm under pressure to schedule. I'd love to have my first lady with me for that."

"Where to?"

"Europe—London, Paris, The Hague and Belgium, to start with."

"Those old places?"

"Yeah, nothing special." Other than their trips to Bora Bora, Sam had never been out of the country.

"Get me some dates, and I'll see what I can do."

"Kiss me again and make it a good one to hold me over."

"All my kisses are good ones."

"Mmm," he said against her lips. "They're the best kisses in the whole world."

SAM SAW SCOTTY, Alden and Aubrey through breakfast and sent them to school with their Secret Service details. Then she went downstairs to meet her agents, Vernon and Jimmy, for the ride to Metro PD headquarters. Her fractured hip was now considered fully healed, and she'd been cleared to drive. But a funny thing had happened on the way to recovery—she'd discovered she liked being driven around the famously congested capital city, and she enjoyed the time she spent with her agents.

Who would've thought it? Not her, that was for sure. However, she'd come to see there were many perks to having the extra time to make calls, review her messages and plan her day before she got to work. Since she'd been so annoyed about having to be driven, she hadn't bothered to mention to anyone that she'd been cleared to drive, even Nick.

Never let it be said that she couldn't change her mind or adapt to new ways of doing things. *Haha*, she thought. She sucked at change, but in this case, she was making an exception to her usual rules.

"Good morning, Mrs. Cappuano," Jimmy, the younger of the two agents, said as he held the back door to a black SUV for her. He was young, blond and handsome.

"Morning." She got into the car, holding the travel coffee cup she'd filled upstairs, while continuing to mourn the diet cola she'd been forced to give up thanks to her cantankerous stomach. Coffee was no substitute for what she really wanted, but she drank the coffee because it kept her from being feral. With hindsight, she should've chosen a job that required little to no interaction with people. That thought made her chuckle.

"What's so funny?" Vernon asked as he drove the car toward the gate. In his late fifties, he was Black, with graying hair that he wore in a close-cropped style.

"I was thinking I should've chosen a career that required no interaction with other people."

After a pause spent probably trying not to laugh, Vernon said, "And what brought this on?"

"I was pondering my need for caffeine to prevent me from ripping the heads off the people I might encounter on any given workday."

"Ah, I see."

Jimmy cleared his throat to cover a laugh.

"You're a character, ma'am," Vernon said with a chuckle.

"So I've been told. A few times, in fact."

"That's shocking to hear." Vernon's sarcasm had won her over. That and the way he looked out for her with almost a fatherly concern had earned him a permanent place in her notoriously picky heart. After losing her beloved dad last October, she found herself looking for him in others and had found a hint of him in the least likely of places.

Vernon was a good guy. He and Jimmy both were, and she believed they would take a bullet to protect her. She prayed it never came to that.

Her phone rang with a call from Darren Tabor from the *Washington Star*, the one reporter she ever spoke to willingly—and even then it wasn't like she relished having to talk to him. "Don't ask me about Nick's mother. I know nothing about it."

"It hurts me that you think so little of me."

And he cracked her up. Sometimes. "What can I do for you on this fine day?"

"I'm filling in a few more things from our recent interview and wondered if you have a minute to confirm some details." She'd given him exactly two hours last week while she and her team were working on Stahl's cold cases and told him to make the most of it.

"I have about two minutes."

"I'll be quick. Double-checking that you're a graduate of Wilson High."

"Yes, but we should note that it's now known as Jackson-Reed." Former President Woodrow Wilson's racist legacy had sparked the name change. The new name represented two important people in the school's history: Edna B. Jackson, the school's first Black teacher, and Vincent E. Reed, who'd served as the school's first Black principal.

"Right, got it. Our policy is to refer to the name of the school when the person graduated."

"Maybe you could say the former Wilson High School in my case, since I fully support the name change."

"I'll do that."

"I also wanted to confirm one of your quotes."

"Which one?"

"'I have three very important jobs—first and foremost as a wife and mother to three young people. Second as the lieutenant overseeing the Metro PD's Homicide division. And last, but certainly not least, I'm proud to serve as the nation's first lady.' Is that correct?"

"Yes."

"My editors wondered whether you might want to play up the first lady part more than you do in that statement."

Sam thought about that for a moment. "The point of this story you talked me into doing was for people to get to know me better, right?"

"That's the goal."

"Then it's important to me that they also know where my priorities lie."

"You're apt to get some pushback on listing first lady last."

"I can handle that." She made a mental note to alert Lilia and Roni in her first lady office, so they'd be ready for anything.

"All right, then. I think we're set."

"This won't be a hatchet piece, right?"

"Sam... And here I thought we were friends."

"We are. For now, anyway."

"You'll like it. I promise. Thanks for giving me the exclusive. That'll never be forgotten."

"I do what I can for the people."

"Happy to be one of your people."

"When did I say that?"

"Have a good day, ma'am."

"If you call me that, you'll never be one of my people." She slapped the phone closed for added emphasis while hoping she didn't come to regret giving the interview Darren had pleaded with her to do.

Vernon drove her around to the morgue entrance at the back of HQ to avoid the media scrum always positioned outside the main door. She'd learned to wait for Vernon to get the door for her, because it mattered so much to him. She would've preferred to do it herself, but she'd compromised on that. See? She was growing up.

"See you in a bit, gentlemen."

"Have a good day at the office, dear," Vernon said, earning him a grin over her shoulder.

It'd taken serious effort to get him to call her anything other than ma'am.

Her partner, Detective Freddie Cruz, was coming toward her as she stepped into the antiseptic smell coming from the morgue. "Morning," Sam said.

"We've got bodies."

CHAPTER TWO

"Bodies as in plural?" Sam asked.

"Unfortunately, yes." Freddie walked with her to the detectives' pit. "We've got a family of six found shot to death in Cathedral Heights. The father failed to show up for work, so one of his colleagues requested a wellness check."

"What do we know about them?"

"Not much yet."

"Let's get everyone on this," Sam said.

Freddie and her sergeant, Tommy Gonzales, rounded up the other dayshift detectives—Green, O'Brien and Charles.

They were about to leave when Captain Malone appeared in the pit. "You're on the situation in Cathedral Heights?"

"Yes, sir," Sam said. "On our way now."

"Keep me in the loop."

"Will do."

"Sam."

She turned back to him.

"I heard it's ugly. Four kids involved. Bring Trulo in as needed."

Nodding, she turned away from him and jogged to catch up with her team, steeling herself for the gruesome scene.

"What'd he say?" Gonzo asked.

"That it's a bad one."

"Aren't they all?"

"Some are worse than others."

While Sam and Freddie got into her Secret Service SUV, the

others headed to their cars. Freddie gave Vernon the address in Cathedral Heights.

"Use the lights, please, Vernon," Sam said.

"Yes, ma'am."

"Anything online about it?" Sam asked Freddie.

He scrolled through his phone. "Nothing yet, but there's a helluva lot about Nick's mother."

Sam sighed. "That's all my fault."

"It's not your fault she was running a prostitution ring, Sam."

"It's my fault that the FBI investigated her."

"Did you work it out with Nick?"

"Yeah. As usual, he's triggered by her, but he was so pissed when I told him I'd asked Avery to investigate her and failed to mention that to him. I haven't seen him that angry in a long time."

"He's not mad at you. He's mad at her."

"And I know that, but the anger was directed at me. It was unnerving."

"I'm sure it was, but at least he had warning this was coming. It might've blown up without a warning if you hadn't gotten Avery involved."

"I guess so. Nick was wondering if she'd dropped his name to the officers when he saw the coverage on TV this morning."

"Of course she did."

"That's exactly what we said."

"She's a grifter, and soon the whole world will see what we've known all along."

"I hope that's how it goes," Sam said. "It's the last thing Nick needs with everything else he's got going on. He's finally making some inroads in convincing people he's a legitimate president, and now this."

"This, too, shall pass. Something else will happen to knock it out of the headlines. That's how these things go."

"I hope whatever knocks it out of the headlines isn't worse than this."

"I'm sure it won't be," Freddie said.

"I wish I could be so confident. It's always something awful. That's one reason I was so glad when he said he wasn't running for president." To Vernon and Jimmy, she added, "That's on the deep down-low, guys."

"Everything is," Vernon said.

"Thank you."

"How's Ang?" Freddie asked.

"I talked to her last night, and she sounded pretty good, all things considered. She said the kids went down easy, and for the first time since Spence died, Jack didn't cry at bedtime."

"Poor kid."

"I hate this for him more than anyone."

"It's so freaking tragic."

Sam's brother-in-law Spencer had recently overdosed on fentanyl-laced pain pills, and the family was still reeling from the sudden, shocking loss. "We've got the preliminary hearing in that case next week." At the hearing, they would lay out the case they'd built against the people who'd produced and sold the lethal medication and hope to see it remanded over to trial.

"Gonzo can take that."

"I'll do it."

"Sam, you don't have to."

"Ang will want to be there, so I'll go with her."

"Sometimes it's all too much," Freddie said with a sigh.

"Just sometimes?"

"Most of the time."

"No one says you have to do this job for the rest of your life, you know."

He shot her a look of pretend offense. "Are you trying to get rid of me?"

"Not even kinda, but there's other stuff you can do besides this."

"I'd be bored out of my mind," he said.

"Probably, but you wouldn't be subjected to trauma on a daily basis or thrust into danger on the regular."

Freddie turned in his seat to study her more closely.

Sam rubbed her cheek. "What? Do I have something on my face?"

"Where's this coming from?"

"Where's what coming from?"

"You saying that I don't have to do this job anymore if I don't want to. Where's that coming from?"

"Nowhere. I'm just stating the obvious fact that you didn't sign a lifetime contract with the department."

"Neither did you."

"No, I didn't."

"Are you speaking for yourself or for me?"

"I'm just saying... You have options. There're a lot of other things you could do that would be better than this."

"I've heard you say—many, many times—that there's nothing better than this."

Sam hated when her own words were used against her. "That's how *I* feel. Doesn't mean you have to feel the same way." She wished she'd never opened the can of worms that had Freddie looking at her like he didn't know her at all, when he knew her better than most.

She'd been out of sorts since they'd arrested the people who'd sold the fentanyl-laced pills to her brother-in-law. That'd been a hollow victory, as many of their victories were for victims' families. Arresting the dealers didn't bring Spence back. In fact, it didn't change much of anything for her sister, their children or the others who'd loved him.

As Sam got out of the SUV and followed Freddie to the front door of a large brick-fronted home with pillars and ornate trim, she hoped it would someday matter to Angela and her children that they'd gotten justice for Spence. Right now, that was cold comfort.

Patrol Officers Phillips and Jestings greeted them at the doorway, which had yellow crime scene tape across it.

"Lieutenant, Detective," Phillips said.

"What've we got?"

"Marcel and Liliana Blanchet and their four children." Phillips swallowed hard as he consulted his notebook. "According to the neighbors, they're Eloise, age twelve, Abigail, age ten, Violet, age six, and August, known as Gus, age four. By all accounts, a loving and well-loved family."

"Any info on what the parents did for a living?" Sam asked.

"He's an OB/GYN and well-known infertility expert. She's a lawyer."

Professions that give us plenty to work with, Sam thought.

"Possible murder-suicide," Jestings added. "The father was found with a gun by his body."

"Give us the tour." Sam pulled on gloves as Freddie and the rest of her team did the same. "Gonzo, you're on photos."

"Got it."

They walked into the house, where the smell of death was nearly overpowered by the scent of potpourri or something else scented. In a big, gourmet kitchen, the wife and mother was on the floor with bullet wounds to her chest and forehead. She'd been a beautiful Black woman with long braids and bracelets on her arms. Sam noticed she was wearing a coat, and bags of groceries were scattered about on the floor. Whoever had done this had caught her arriving home to a nightmare.

The husband, who was also Black, looked to be about six foot four or five. They found him on the floor in an office or study, a bullet wound to the temple and brain matter splattered on a dark wood desk behind him. Next to his body was a nine-millimeter handgun. "After you take photos, bag the weapon and his hands," Sam said. "I want them tested for gunshot residue. While you're at it, bag the wife's hands, too."

While the others saw to her orders, Sam and Freddie followed Phillips and Jestings upstairs, where each of the children had been shot in the head in their beds. The eldest of the four had three obvious wounds. Each of the others had one.

Their innocent faces and sweetly decorated bedrooms reduced Freddie to tears that he quickly brushed away.

That didn't happen to Sam anymore, which was probably cause for concern. She'd never understand how anyone could commit murder in the first place, let alone the murder of innocent children, but for some reason, she felt oddly detached from the brutal scene before her.

"Have you called the ME?" Sam asked.

"They're on the way with two trucks," Jestings said.

The sound of a woman shrieking had Sam and Freddie rushing downstairs, while Gonzo and the other detectives came upstairs to take photos, measurements and notes that would guide their investigation.

A Black woman with gray hair, wearing a red coat, stood outside the crime scene tape demanding to be let in. Another Patrol officer stood in her way.

"This is my family! Let me in!"

"Who are you?" Sam asked.

The woman did a double take when she recognized Sam. That happened far too often lately. "I'm Graciela Blanchet," she said, her chin quivering. "This is my son's home."

Sam and Freddie ducked under the tape and led the woman away from the front door. "Trust me when I tell you that you don't want to go in there," Sam said.

"Are they... Are they dead?"

"Yes," Sam said, making eye contact.

"*All of them?*" she asked in a high-pitched tone.

"I'm sorry, but yes."

The woman crumpled before their eyes.

Only Freddie's quick action kept her from falling to the ground as she screamed the children's names.

Sam watched the scene unfold in an odd state of numbness, as if she were an observer rather than an active participant in what was happening right in front of her.

This reminded her of the Reese case in some ways. In that instance, the father, Clarence, had murdered his wife and three young children and then gone on the lam. She didn't like to remember that horrific case or how it ended in his suicide a foot from her. Maybe that was why she was reacting so strangely to this new situation.

"Are you all right, Lieutenant?" Jestings asked as he approached them.

Sam realized she'd completely checked out to take a trip to a past she'd much rather forget. "Of course. What's the ME's ETA?"

"Ten minutes out."

"Thank you. How about Crime Scene?"

"They're fifteen minutes out."

"Good job, Jestings. Thank you."

The rest of her team came out of the house, each of them seeming undone by what they'd seen. Who could blame them? Sam walked over to them while Freddie stayed with the grandmother. When the other detectives were gathered around Sam, she said, "Please ask for help if you need it after what you've just seen. There's no shame in reaching out to Dr. Trulo at a time like this." She said the words as a rote recitation, knowing they should be said, not because she felt the need for help.

Detective Charles, the newest member of her team, subtly swiped at a tear on her cheek. "I'll never understand how a father can do that to his family."

"It's possible whoever did this wants us to *believe* the father killed them," Green said.

"That's something we need to fully investigate," Sam said.

"*You think my son did this?*" Graciela said with a shriek. "He would never have harmed them! He loved them with his whole heart. He would've *died* for them."

Sam hadn't realized the grandmother was listening to them. "Ma'am, would you be willing to come to headquarters to answer some questions about your son and his family?" Sam asked as gently as possible.

"If it would help."

"It would," Sam said. "It would help tremendously."

"We'll canvass the neighbors," Gonzo said.

"Wait for the ME and Crime Scene, and then find out who their friends were." Sam glanced at the gaggle of bystanders that formed any time a great tragedy occurred. It drove her crazy the way people felt the need to be up close and personal with disaster, as if to assure themselves they were fine. Or whatever weird need motivated them to stand in the cold and stare at a home where murder had occurred. "We'll need some insight from those closest to them."

"On it," Gonzo said. "Will be back to the house when we're finished."

"Come with us, Mrs. Blanchet." Sam led the woman to the Secret Service SUV. "Back to HQ, please, Vernon."

Freddie got in the other side.

"Yes, ma'am."

As the car pulled away from the crime scene, the older woman sobbed softly into a handkerchief that had crocheted edges. Sam was reminded of her grandmother Ella, who'd tried and failed to teach Sam and her sisters to crochet. They'd all sucked at it. The memory would've made her smile at any other time.

"Is there anyone we can call for you?" Sam asked her.

"My other son... Raphael. He's in Richmond."

"If you can provide the number to my partner, Detective Cruz, he'll make the call for you."

With trembling hands, the older woman withdrew her phone from her purse and recited the number, which Freddie wrote down.

Sam appreciated that she didn't have to tell him to wait until the woman was out of earshot before he made the call. He understood such things without having to be told, which was one of many reasons he was the best partner she'd ever had.

"When was the last time you spoke to Marcel or his family?" Sam asked. Time was not their friend in cases like this, and there was no point in waiting to get to HQ to start the interview.

"Yesterday afternoon, and then nothing from any of them, which was why I came by today. It's not normal to go that long without talking to them. The kids and I are in constant touch. They... They taught me to use an iPhone so we could text." She broke down again. "How can they all be gone? My babies. My beautiful babies."

Sam moved to the facing seat and put her arm around the woman, who leaned into the comfort she offered. "I'm so sorry for your losses."

"My son didn't do this. There's nothing that could make me believe that. He was the most devoted, loving husband and father you've ever met. He recently cut back at work so he could spend more time with the kids as they got older and involved in more sports and activities." She took hold of Sam's hand and held on tightly. "Someone *did this* to them. It wasn't him."

"We'll fully investigate every possibility," Sam assured her.

"You should talk to Rory," Graciela said with a bitter edge to her voice.

"Who's Rory?"

"He was one of Marcel's partners in the practice. Rory was furious when Marcel reduced his hours to spend more time with the family. Liliana told me the two men had a screaming fight over it. Rory accused Marcel of being selfish and thinking only of himself."

Sam glanced at Freddie, who was taking notes.

"What is Rory's last name and the name of their practice?"

"McInerny, and the practice is District OBGYN. The other doctor in the practice is Oriana Harvey."

"Who else needs to be notified about their deaths before the names are made public?" Sam asked.

"Oh Lord, Liliana's mother has terrible dementia. She and her sister, Esme, take care of her full time."

"Do you know how we can reach Esme?"

Graciela withdrew her phone again and found the number,

which she recited for Freddie. "I help them whenever I can, which is why I have her number."

"Is there anything else you think we should know?" Sam asked.

She hesitated, as if debating whether she should share.

"Every detail, even the smallest thing, is relevant in an investigation of this sort." She hesitated to refer to it as a homicide investigation until they were sure that Marcel hadn't murdered his family before he took his own life. "If you know something, now is the time to tell us."

"Marcel suspected that Liliana was having an affair."

CHAPTER THREE

Christina and Terry were waiting for Nick when he arrived in the Oval Office by way of the East Colonnade, the only time he made it outside some days.

"We've got the statement ready, Mr. President." Christina placed the sheet of paper on the Resolute Desk, which was clear of all other items.

How was it, with all the problems facing the country and the world, the first thing he had to deal with was his goddamned mother?

Nick scanned the statement. *As we have said many times in the past, President Cappuano has no relationship with his mother and as such will have no comment on her arrest.*

"We figured we should keep it short and sweet so there's no room to read between the lines," Terry said.

"That's fine," Nick said. "You can issue it, Christina."

"Thank you, sir."

After she'd left the room, Terry took a seat in the chair next to the desk. "Are you okay?" He asked as Nick's friend and not as his chief of staff.

"It is what it is," Nick replied. "Or, I should say, she is what she is. She'll never change, and I gave up hoping for a real mother years ago. Thanks to your mom, I know what a real mother is." Laine O'Connor had shown him that time and again since he first met her as a Harvard freshman when Terry's late brother, John, had brought Nick home to Virginia.

"I talked to Dad this morning on the way in," Terry said of retired Senator Graham O'Connor, who'd been an extra father and mentor to Nick. "They're outraged on your behalf."

"Believe it or not, it helps to hear that."

"We know better than just about anyone what an asshole she is."

Nick smiled. "Thanks for the support, friend. It means a lot."

"Is everything okay with Sam? Things seemed tense between you guys the last time I saw her."

"We worked it out. I wasn't happy to be blindsided by my mother's impending arrest, but at least I got advance notice it was coming."

"So Sam asked Avery to investigate your mother?"

He nodded. "She said it happened during a fit of rage over that shitty interview my mother gave."

"Ah, I see. Well, I have to say I don't blame her for being furious about that interview. It was a total hatchet job."

"Anyway, enough about *her*. I'm sure there's real work to be done."

"Plenty of it," Terry said as he stood. "We're due to the morning security briefing in the Situation Room in ten minutes."

Nick grabbed the binder he'd taken "home" the night before that he'd marked with questions and thoughts for the briefing, which he thought of as the little shop of daily horrors. If people knew what really went on in the world, no one would feel safe anywhere. He'd liked it better when he hadn't known such things.

"May I get you something to drink?" Sam asked Graciela when they had her settled in the conference room at HQ. "Water or coffee?"

She shook her head and reached for another tissue from the box Sam had placed on the table. "No, thank you."

"Detective Cruz is calling your son and Liliana's sister. Is there anyone local I could call to come in to be with you?"

"My neighbor Bertie Dawson. She'd come."

Sam wrote down the number Graciela gave her. "I'm going to step out for just a minute, but I'll be right back."

Graciela nodded as if she couldn't care less what Sam did. And who could blame her for not caring? The people she'd loved best were gone forever.

Leaning against the cinderblock wall outside the conference room, Sam made the call to Bertie. "Is this Bertie Dawson?"

"Yes."

"This is Lieutenant Sam Holland with the DC Metro Police Department."

"You're the first lady!"

Sam closed her eyes and prayed for patience. "Yes, I am. I'm here with Graciela Blanchet."

"Why is she with the police?"

"Her son Marcel and his family were found dead in their home a short time ago."

Bertie let out a scream of dismay. "Oh God, no! Not the babies, too. Oh no, no, *no*. Poor Graciela. They were her whole life."

"Is there any chance you might be able to come to our headquarters building to sit with her while we interview her?"

"Why are you interviewing her? She had nothing to do with it."

"She's helping us to gather information we need to begin our investigation. She'll be here awhile and could use a friend, as her other son is in Richmond."

"I'll be right there."

"Thank you."

Sam slapped her cell phone closed but took none of the usual satisfaction from the smacking sound.

Captain Malone came to a stop in the hallway, seeming surprised to see her there. "I heard it was ugly," he said.

She nodded. "I'm back with the grandmother."

Freddie came from the pit to join them. "I made the calls to Marcel's brother and Liliana's sister." He looked pale-faced and drawn after what had to have been horrible conversations. "They're on their way."

"Thanks for taking care of that."

"Sure."

"Update me," Malone said.

Sam took him through the facts of the case thus far.

Malone grimaced. "Christ, four little kids."

"Marcel Blanchet's mother, Graciela is in the conference room. She insists there was no way that Marcel could've hurt his family. By all accounts, he was a devoted husband and father. However, she did tell me that he suspected his wife was having an affair. We'll look into that next."

"Keep me in the loop, and I'll ask Dr. Trulo to check in with your squad."

Sam was about to tell him that wasn't necessary, but she stopped herself when she caught the haunted expression on her partner's face. "Thanks." She'd like to think she'd learned a few things about what happened when emotions got buried on this job. "Let's get back to it, Detective Cruz."

When they returned to the conference room, Graciela was sobbing into tissues. "I don't know what to do. Tell me what I should do."

"We'll walk you through every step, Mrs. Blanchet," Sam said, even though their help would hardly fix the disaster that had befallen the woman. It was all Sam could do for her and the rest of their family.

Sam returned to her seat across the table. "Do you feel up to talking a bit more?"

She shrugged. "I guess."

As the woman dabbed at her face with tissues, Sam scanned her notes. "You mentioned that Marcel thought his wife might be having an affair. What can you tell me about that?"

"Things had been strained between them lately." She wiped away more tears. "I'd noticed it and asked Marcel if everything was all right. He said he started to wonder if she had someone else."

"Do you know if he did anything about that?"

"I'm not sure. We talked about it last week, and I was going to ask him about it the next time we talked."

Sam made a note to ask Lieutenant Archelotta in IT to dump Liliana's phone first. "Prior to this, how would you describe their marriage?"

"Loving," Graciela said softly. "They were crazy about each other from the start."

"Where did they meet?"

"In college at UVA. Marcel went to medical school there, as well, while Liliana went to law school at American. They've lived in the District since they finished school fifteen years ago now."

"Did something change between them recently?"

"Not that I'm aware of, but there'd been tension. Their oldest daughter, Eloise, was an Olympic-caliber gymnast. The demands of her competitions and training put strain on the entire family."

Sam made a note to investigate the daughter's gymnastics situation, especially in light of the fact that she had three bullet wounds while her siblings each had one. "Was there anything else going on that you knew of that might've led to murder?" She still wasn't convinced that this wasn't a murder-suicide, but Graciela's conviction that Marcel never would've harmed his family would have Sam casting a wider net.

"Nothing that I can think of. They're all well-liked by their colleagues and peers. They have a wide circle of friends. I just can't imagine who'd want to harm them."

A knock on the door sounded.

"Come in."

Freddie poked his head in. "Mrs. Blanchet's friend is here."

"She can come in."

Bertie was as round as she was tall. Her Black face was so youthful that only her gray hair gave away her age. The two women hugged.

"Thank you for coming," Graciela said tearfully.

"Of course I came. I'm so sorry for your loss."

Graciela leaned her head on her friend's shoulder. "I don't know what to do."

"We'll figure it out. I'll be with you every step of the way." To Sam, Bertie said, "What else do you need from us?"

Sam went through the usual list of routine questions about the family's closest circle of friends and family, their daily routines and the kids' school information.

After about two hours of questioning, she could see the older woman was beginning to tire. "The medical examiner will perform autopsies, which is standard in a situation such as this, and then we'll release the bodies to a funeral home. You'll need to choose one."

"Green's on Mass Ave handled the arrangements when my husband passed," Bertie said. "They were caring and compassionate."

"That's fine," Graciela said.

Sam made a note of the funeral home owned by Detective Cameron Green's family. "I'll pass that on to Dr. McNamara, the ME." She pushed her business card across the table. "If you think of anything else that might be relevant, or if I can be of any assistance to you and your family, please call me. My cell number is on the back of the card."

"Thank you."

"It's amazing," Bertie said, gazing at Sam as she retrieved the business card from the table.

"What is?" Sam asked, though she suspected she knew what Bertie would say.

"That you're the first lady *and* a police detective."

Sam shrugged. "I had this job long before I was first lady."

"You're setting an amazing example for working mothers."

"Thank you." She didn't mention that she felt guilty all the time for the time she spent away from her children. "I can ask someone from Patrol to give you a ride home."

"That's all right," Bertie said. "I have my car. I'll see Graciela home and stay with her until her son arrives."

Sam walked them out and said goodbye at the main door. When she turned to head back to the pit, Chief Farnsworth was waiting for her.

"Heard you caught a tough one today."

"Horrible."

"Murder-suicide?"

"I'm not fully convinced. We're looking at it from all angles."

"I'm sure you'll do the usual thorough job."

"We'll have to back-burner the Stahl stuff while we work this case."

"Understood." He tipped his head to study her more closely. "Are you all right, Sam?"

She realized the question was coming from her uncle Joe and not her chief. "I'm trying to be."

"But?"

"It's a lot, you know?"

"What is?"

"All of it."

"You didn't take much time off after Spencer died. Maybe you should take a few days."

"No time for that with a new case."

"There's always time for that. Your very capable team could step in for you."

"Hasn't come to that."

"But if it does, take the time. That's an order."

"Yes, sir." He was always looking out for her, which she appreciated.

"Keep me in the loop on the new case."

"I will, sir."

Sam went back to the pit.

Freddie stood when she came in. "Cam is on the way in with cell phones and other electronics. I notified Archie that they're coming."

"Great, thanks. Did they get anything from the neighbors?"

"Some leads on friends. I'm tracking them down now."

"How about doorbell cams or other cameras in the area?"

"They didn't have one, and none of the neighbors' cams covers any part of their house. Archie is working on pulling film from our cameras in the neighborhood." The MPD had cameras positioned all over the District.

Sam took note of the complete lack of animation in Freddie's voice. "Are you all right?"

He shrugged. "Define 'all right' after what we just saw."

"I know. It's horrific."

"Why'd they have to kill the kids, too? Whatever beef there was couldn't have involved them."

"I don't know," Sam said with a sigh. "These things never make sense from the outside looking in. It's hard to say what causes someone to do something like this."

"Are we looking hard at the father?"

"The grandmother is adamant that he never would've hurt his family. By all accounts, he was a devoted family man. I want to talk to the business partners in his practice."

"Did the grandmother say any more about the wife possibly having an affair?" Freddie asked.

"Just that he'd suspected something was up. When Green arrives with the phones, let's prioritize the wife."

"I'll send him and Archie a note about that. According to the next-door neighbor, the wife's best friend was named Kelly Goodson, who lives about two blocks from the Blanchets. The neighbor said they met at the playground when their oldest kids were little."

"Let's talk to her and the husband's medical partners."

Freddie grabbed his coat and followed Sam to the morgue entrance.

Lindsey McNamara met them in the foyer. "Brutal."

"Always is when kids are involved," Sam said.

"Murder-suicide?"

"I'm keeping my mind open to numerous possibilities."

"I'll get started and get you my report ASAP."

"Thanks, Doc," Sam said. "We've called in Dr. Trulo to provide support as needed. If you need it, ask for it."

"I will, thanks."

Dr. Byron Tomlinson, the deputy ME, pushed a gurney with a small body bag on top through the door. For once, he had nothing to say as he nodded and went past them into the morgue.

"Lieutenant!"

Sam turned at the sound of a familiar voice.

Dr. Anthony Trulo, the MPD's psychiatrist, walked toward them at a rapid pace. "I'm glad I caught you."

"Hey, Doc." He'd put her back together more than once after trauma on the job, and she'd be forever thankful to him for his support and friendship. "What's up?"

"I'd like to meet with your team at shift change. I thought I'd include the ME and her team as well."

In the past, Sam would've balked. She would've put the impetus on her team to ask for help if they needed it. But she'd learned they'd never ask, and that could lead to disaster. "I'll make sure everyone is there."

"See you then."

CHAPTER FOUR

As all his days in the White House did, this one passed in a blur of meetings, briefings, decisions and nonstop demands.

Nick sat in his study off the Oval Office, eating a late lunch while he watched Christina's press briefing. She'd no sooner walked into the room than reporters began hammering her with questions about his mother.

"I have a few remarks, and then I'll take some questions. Once again, I'll reiterate our statement from earlier. President Cappuano has no relationship with his mother. While those might seem like handy words to describe the situation, I'd like to elaborate on what those words actually mean."

Nick sat up straighter as he wondered where this was going. Christina hadn't consulted with him about how she planned to handle the briefing. He trusted her implicitly, but as always, the subject of his mother was fraught for him.

"His mother wasn't at his high school graduation. She didn't attend commencement when he graduated from Harvard University with honors. She wasn't there when he took the oath of office as a senator, vice president or president. The only reason she was at his wedding is because she crashed it, and his bride decided not to make a scene that would ruin the day for him. She was escorted from the premises after the ceremony was completed. She has never met his children. President Cappuano has been my close friend for nearly two decades. I have never met his mother, nor have I ever heard him casually speak of her. She is not in his life. As such, he isn't privy to her business dealings, her daily routine or anything else about her. The only time he ever hears from her is when she needs money."

A massive lump formed in his throat, and tears filled his eyes as he listened to Christina's recitation of the facts of his life. The emotional reaction infuriated him. Here he was, the most powerful man on earth, once again being brought low by the woman who'd given birth to him. The scent of Chanel No. 5 still sent him reeling all these years later any time he encountered his mother's signature perfume, which was another thing he hated.

A knock sounded at the door, forcing him to pull himself together so he wouldn't be embarrassed in front of whoever had come to find him.

"Enter," he called.

In walked two of his closest friends—Derek Kavanaugh and Dr. Harry Flynn. Derek served as his deputy chief of staff and Harry as his White House medical director.

"They told us we might find you in here," Derek said.

"What's up, guys?"

"Nothing much," Harry said in a breezy tone. "We just stopped by to say hello."

Nick laughed. If anyone knew what happened to him when his mother crawled out from under her rock, they did. They'd seen the worst of it over the years and had brought him home in a drunken stupor many times in the past after his mother had resurfaced to fuck with him once again. "It's okay to say why you're really here."

"We're just checking on our friend," Derek said.

"And I appreciate it. I'm okay."

Harry looked around the room. "No sign of open bottles of whiskey," he said. "That's a good sign."

"I'd like to think I've proven repeatedly over the years that whiskey doesn't fix anything," Nick said. "It only makes it worse."

"For what it's worth, we're sorry you're dealing with her—again —and we wish she'd go away and never come back," Harry said.

"From your lips to God's ears," Nick said. "But I'll never get that lucky."

"I liked Christina's briefing," Derek said. "It was spot-on."

"Yes, it was."

Nick glanced at the TV to see how things were going in the

briefing room. Despite Christina's blunt recitation of the facts, reporters were still grilling her about his mother's arrest and how he felt about it. "Shit," Nick said. "Do I need to go in there and shut this down?"

"You'd only add gas to the fire," Derek said.

"Don't put yourself through it," Harry said. "Let her speak for you. She's holding her own with them."

Christina kept referring to their earlier statement and her opening comments when asked about his mother. She never deviated from that response during half an hour of intense questioning. "Moving on to other matters, the president had a productive meeting with his gun control task force. The group will soon issue its first report to include a list of action items that can quickly be adopted to make the public safer while protecting Second Amendment rights for gun owners."

As she took a few questions on that subject, Nick breathed a sigh of relief that they'd moved on from asking about his mother. Not that he thought they were done with the topic. The prime-time news shows would focus on all the salacious details, rehashing every interview she'd ever given and every word she'd ever said publicly about her son, the president.

It made him sick.

"What the fuck was she thinking?" Harry asked. "An escort service? Really? She's the ultimate cliché."

"What's that they say about sex selling?" Nick asked.

"Still... It's ridiculous."

Harry's outrage touched Nick deeply. These were his ride-or-die friends, the ones who'd been there for him when he'd been a lowly staffer to a congressman and would be with him to the end. They'd been through everything together.

"Let's talk about something else."

"I'm seeing Roni," Derek said.

Startled, Harry and Nick glanced at each other and then at Derek.

"This is big news," Harry said. "How're you feeling about it?"

"Pretty good," Derek said with a grin. "She's awesome."

"Yes, she is," Nick said. "Sam thinks the world of her."

"That matters," Harry said bluntly, "because she doesn't like anyone."

The three men shared a laugh.

"Truer words have never been spoken," Nick said. "She told me a while ago that she thought something was up with you two."

"Nothing gets by our favorite detective," Derek said, grinning.

It had been, Nick thought, a very long time since he'd seen his friend smile like he was now, telling them his big news. The murder of his wife, Victoria, and the subsequent revelations about her deceptions had nearly brought Derek to his knees. He'd come back from that horrific loss and had stepped up to be an amazing father to their young daughter, Maeve. Nick was so happy to hear Derek was starting over with Roni. However, he still had concerns. "It hasn't been that long since she lost her husband."

"No, it hasn't, and she's expecting their child. We're taking it slow."

"What does Maeve think?" Nick asked.

"She loves Roni, and vice versa. Roni is great with her. It feels good, you know?"

"I'm glad for you," Nick said. "And for Maeve."

"I am, too, Derek," Harry said. "Sincerely thrilled."

"Thanks."

"While I have you two," Harry said, "I've been told by the boss that I need to arrange a wedding party, and I was hoping the two of you would be my best men."

"I'd love to," Nick said, rising from his chair to embrace Harry.

"Me, too," Derek said. "I'd be honored."

"We'd like Maeve to be our flower girl," Harry added.

"She'd love it," Derek said.

"Thanks, guys. I can't believe this is really happening."

"Neither can we," Nick said with a teasing grin. "We'd given up on you until Lilia made an honest man out of you."

"She's the best." Harry glowed with the kind of happiness Nick had wished for his friend for years. "I can't believe how lucky I am to have found her."

"We love you two together," Nick said. "It's a perfect match."

"Yes, it is, and I can't wait for our big day next summer."

Nick would serve as a best man twice next summer, the second time for Terry when he married Lindsey McNamara. Those events would make for better press than his mother being arrested.

His friends stuck around for another few minutes before they left to go back to work. Nick appreciated how they'd taken his mind off the mama drama with their friendship, their news, their laughter. They'd been doing that for him for almost twenty years now, and he'd never been more grateful for their friendship.

He sent a quick text to Sam. *Just saw Derek, and he confirmed your suspicions that he and Roni are seeing each other. By all accounts, very new and taking it slowly, but he looked happier than I've seen him in a long time.*

Sam wrote back right away. *Holy cow! I knew it! Did I call that, or did I call that? I LOVE to hear that he's so happy, but is it ok to worry that it's still a bit soon for her?*

You called it! And he acknowledged the timing isn't ideal, thus the taking things slowly, but he said she's great with Maeve, who absolutely adores Roni, and it just feels good to all of them.

So happy for them. They all deserve nothing but the best.

Agreed. Harry asked Derek and me to be his best men. Gonna be a busy summer.

Of course he did! Busy and fun!

How many more hours until this day is over?

A few, but we'll make it worth it in the end.

Can't wait.

Same. Love you. Stay tough.

Love you, too. I will.

When he tuned back in to what was happening in the briefing room, he heard Christina repeat the now-familiar refrain. "The president has no relationship with his mother, so no, he won't take any calls from her."

"No, I won't."

Nick used the remote to shut off the TV. He had better things to do than listen to any more of that nonsense.

SAM AND FREDDIE emerged into frigid air that had her immediately on alert for ice. The last thing she needed was to fall on her newly mended hip.

Vernon held the door to the SUV for her.

Freddie got in on the other side and gave Vernon the address of where they needed to go.

"Send the others a text and tell them we're meeting with Trulo at four. Everyone needs to be there."

"Done."

Sam watched the world go by through the polarized window. "What's the latest with Nick's mother?"

Freddie checked his phone. "Christina made a statement during the press briefing that's gone viral."

Sam wondered why he hadn't mentioned it when they had texted. Probably because he was pretending that none of this was happening. And then it occurred to her. That was why Harry and Derek had been with him. Because they knew what this shit with his mother did to him. "What did she say?"

As Freddie read it to her, Sam burned with outrage and sadness for her husband, to have the troubled relationship with his mother trotted out for all the world to chew on. "I'm sick over this."

"Christina did a good job of emphasizing what they mean when they say she's not in his life."

"Yes, she did, but it makes me so sad for him. Any time his mother resurfaces, it messes him up for days. He doesn't have the time for that with everything else he's got to think about."

"I'm sorry she's causing him more pain when she's already caused more than enough."

"For sure. It's ridiculous how she continues to hurt him." Sam withdrew the secure BlackBerry she used to contact him and sent a quick message. *Heard about Christina's statement. I like how she tried to shut down the questions, but I'm sorry you had to hear that recitation of all the ways SHE has failed you. SHE never deserved a son like you. WE love you. More than anything. See you soon.*

She left the BlackBerry on her lap, hoping she'd hear from him, and forced her mind back to the case when all she wanted was to go to him. "Tell me about Kelly Goodson."

"From what one of the other neighbors said, Liliana met Kelly when Eloise was a baby. Kelly's son Mica is a few months older than Eloise, and the two have been best friends since they were babies."

Sam ached at the thought of twelve-year-old Mica mourning the loss of his lifelong friend. Murder touched so many people beyond the victims' immediate family.

Vernon double-parked in front of the Goodsons' stately home. The driveway was full of cars, and every spot on the street was taken.

Sam took that to mean that the word was out about the murder of the family's friends. She gazed at the house for a long time, working up the wherewithal to get out, go inside and intrude on yet another family's time of sorrow. She did that all the time, so why was it taking so much out of her today?

"You want me to do this?" Freddie asked, tuning in to her odd mood.

"No, that's okay."

"Sam."

She looked over at him.

"You just went through an awful loss. No one would blame you if it's too much for you right now."

It was too much. It was all too much. The murder of an entire family. Sam's mother-in-law arrested for prostitution and racketeering. Her brother-in-law dead from a fentanyl overdose. But she had a job to do, and damn it, she was going to do it, no matter the turmoil swirling inside her. "Let's do this."

They went up the stone stairs to a door that fronted a screened-in porch. They rang the doorbell. "Can't even hear it from outside," Sam said. "That's my kind of doorbell."

"Does it work?"

She hadn't considered that, so she knocked hard on the door, hoping someone would hear them.

Two minutes passed before the inside door opened, and a man came out, doing the usual double take when he saw her there.

As she showed him her badge, she was so tired of getting that reaction, even if she knew it was part of her life forever now.

He pushed the door open.

"Lieutenant Holland, Detective Cruz to see Kelly Goodson."

"She's not able to see people right now," he said.

CHAPTER FIVE

S am summoned the patience she would need to deal with yet another grieving family. "We understand this is a very upsetting time for her, for all of you, but we need to speak with her. We can do it here or downtown. It's up to her." Sam hated this as much as the man staring her down did, but she couldn't tell him that. "We're not looking to add to your grief. We're trying to get answers for the Blanchet family."

"We heard it was a murder-suicide."

Apparently, people were already spreading unfounded rumors. "The investigation is ongoing. May we please speak to Kelly?"

After a long pause, the man nodded and stepped aside to admit them to the home. "Wait here." He gestured to a sitting room. "I'll get her."

They sat on a sofa to wait. A low buzz of voices came from other parts of the house. On the walls were photos of three children—two boys and a girl, who was quite a bit younger than her brothers. She focused on the older boy, who had dark hair, brown eyes and an impish grin. How sad he must be today.

The man returned with a woman who had the same dark hair and brown eyes as her son. Her eyes were red and swollen.

"Kelly, this is Lieutenant Holland and Detective Cruz," the man said gently. "They want to talk to you about Liliana and the family."

Kelly lowered herself to an upholstered chair that faced them and took a new tissue that the man handed her. Every movement seemed to cause her pain.

"Are you Kelly's husband?" Sam asked the man.

He nodded.

"Your name?"

"Henry."

Sam made a note. "We're sorry to bother you at such a difficult time, but as I'm sure you know, time is of the essence in cases such as this."

"Do you know what happened to them?" Henry asked.

"They were shot."

Kelly let out a whimper of distress that had her husband putting his arm around her.

"As Liliana's closest friend, we were hoping you might be able to give us some perspective on what had been going on with them lately," Sam said to Kelly. "If anything was different or unusual."

"I've been trying to think since I heard the news," Kelly said in a tentative tone, "but I just keep coming back to Marcel. He'd been distant lately. Liliana didn't know why, and she was upset about it. They've always been a very close couple until lately."

"We've been told that he suspected she might be having an affair."

Her mouth fell open, and her expression shifted to outrage. "Told by whom? That's a lie. She was always faithful to him."

"Would you know if she wasn't?"

"We told each other everything. Every. Single. Thing. If she was having an affair, I would've known. She never so much as looked at another man since the day she met Marcel. She was madly in love with him."

Sam took notes as Kelly spoke. "Did she mention any specific problems or challenges they'd been having lately?"

"They took a big financial hit when he scaled back to part time at work. He did that without telling her until it was already done. She wasn't happy about it, because it meant she'd have to take on more at her job. They were juggling a lot with the kids, their activities, Eloise's gymnastics. Money had become an issue for the first time in their marriage."

"We heard that one of his partners in the medical practice was upset about his decision to scale back, too. Do you know anything about that?"

"Rory was furious. Liliana said he and Marcel had gotten into a screaming fight over it, but Marcel was unwilling to change his mind. I guess the partners were as surprised as his wife was when he made the decision without their input."

"What was their relationship like with the partner before that?"

"They were close friends with him and his wife. Had been for years."

"Was the partner angry enough to murder Marcel and his family?"

"Liliana described the argument as vicious. I've met Rory and his wife, Brittany, many times. I can't picture him murdering children, but then again, I can't imagine how anyone can commit murder." She dabbed at her eyes. "It's unfathomable to me that they're all gone."

"When was the last time you saw or talked to Liliana?" Freddie asked.

"We had brunch last Sunday, just the two of us."

"Did she express any concerns or say anything that might be relevant with hindsight?" he asked.

"Just that she was worried about their finances now that Marcel's income would be cut in half. She made a joke about how your lifestyle expands to meet your income, and now that theirs was being cut, she was going to have to figure out how to scale back. She said she never expected to be worried about money at this point when they had two successful careers."

"What kind of law did she practice?" Sam asked.

"Estate."

"With a firm or on her own?"

"On her own. She worked from home so she could be there for the kids. She could've made much more money working for a firm, but chose the sole-proprietor path because it was best for her family. She was shocked when Marcel decided to go part time at his job. She said he knew what a hit that would be for them, but he didn't seem to care. He was very determined to spend more time with his kids and to hell with the consequences."

"Did she have any idea what brought on this sudden desire to be with his kids?" Sam asked.

"Eloise placed first in an important regional meet while he was delivering a baby. He was very upset to have missed that, and it seemed to have sparked something in him that led to the decision. That was what Liliana believed. They'd been mostly not speaking since he told her the news—after he'd already done it."

To Sam, he didn't sound like the kind of man who'd viciously slaughter his children after scaling back at work to spend more time with them. He seemed like the opposite of a man who'd do something like that.

"Is there anything else you can tell us that might be relevant?" Sam asked.

"I'm not sure if it's relevant, but Eloise was beginning to make a big splash in gymnastics. She was very talented, and there was some stuff online that really upset Liliana."

"What kind of stuff?"

"Nasty racist shit that made Liliana want to remove Eloise from competition. She was enraged by it, as anyone who loved Eloise would be. I was enraged by it. People are disgusting."

"Where can we find these posts?"

"I'm not sure, but there's a group on Facebook that might provide more info. It's a local gymnastics community."

"Was Liliana planning to take Eloise out of gymnastics?"

"No, because she knew how much her daughter loved it. But she was angry about the jealousy and vitriol over Eloise's natural talent. She said you never see that kind of thing directed at the white girls."

Filled with disgust on behalf of a young girl she'd never have the chance to meet, Sam took note of the issues Kelly had raised. "Had Liliana had any confrontations with anyone over the posts, that you know of?"

"I'm not sure. There were a lot of gymnastics meets and parents involved. I don't know any of them, but one couple was particularly vicious."

Sam made a note to find those people. "How well did you know Marcel?"

"Pretty well. Our families spent time together."

"How did he strike you?"

"He was the ultimate family man, from what we saw." Kelly glanced at her husband, who nodded in agreement. "He was crazy about Liliana and the kids."

"He struggled with how his work interfered with their family life," Henry said.

"Can you elaborate on how he struggled?"

"His business was unpredictable," Henry said. "Babies arrive whenever they're ready, and often he'd get called away from family dinners, holidays, gymnastics meets, ball games. It was important to him to be there for his patients, too, but as the kids got older, the push-pull became a bigger problem for him. That's why he decided to cut back at work. He said he didn't want to look back and realize he missed all the important things with his kids."

"Were you aware of any other issues either of them was having with anyone?"

Kelly shook her head. "I can't think of anything that would lead to something like this."

"Me either," Henry said, tearing up. "Those kids were so sweet and well-mannered and smart as hell. I just can't believe they're all gone."

"Would it be possible for us to speak to your son, Mica?" Sam asked.

Henry was shaking his head before she finished asking the question. "I'm sorry. I just can't ask that of him today. He's so distraught."

"We understand, but as Eloise's closest friend, he may have insight that will help our case," Sam said.

"We'll talk to him, and if there's anything to be added, we'll get in touch."

Sam knew that was the best she was going to get from them under the circumstances. "We appreciate your insight at this difficult time." She stood to leave and handed Henry her card. "If you think of anything else, even the smallest detail, please call me. My cell number is on the back of the card."

"Liliana would've loved to have met you," Kelly said softly. "She admired you and your husband."

"That's nice to know. Thank you. We're sorry again for your loss."

"We hope you figure out what happened to them," Kelly said.

"We'll do our best," Sam said.

When they stepped outside, the weather had turned dark and stormy, as it so often did in March. Sam zipped her coat, jammed her hands in the pockets and dreamed of her and Nick's upcoming trip to Bora Bora to celebrate their anniversary.

She checked her watch and saw they had time before the

meeting with Trulo. "Let's go see the partner he had the screaming fight with."

NORMAL DAYS at the White House usually passed in a blur of meetings on a vast array of domestic and international concerns. Alliances were tended to and partnerships formed with industry and foreign leaders. Every day was different from the last. Nick faced decisions with enormous consequences for the environment, climate, economy and national security. Sometimes all those things were impacted by a single decision.

It could be overwhelming on the best of days.

Today was not the best of days. Hanging over every minute of the day was the shit show with his mother and her crimes. How much worse would it get before the full picture was known? The pit in his stomach was reminiscent of a childhood spent waiting for her to show up and often being disappointed when she blew him off. He could hear his grandmother saying things such as, "Why do you bother to get your hopes up?" and "She's a selfish cow who doesn't think of anyone but herself."

All of that was true, but she was his mother, and he'd loved her despite her failings. Once out of every five or six times, she'd show up as planned, and they'd spend the day together at the park or ice skating. They'd always hit a toy store and McDonald's, which his grandmother wouldn't let him have. Ice cream topped off their time together.

Those days were the highlights of a childhood short on fun of any kind, except for that which he made for himself with friends, most of whom had since done time in prison.

Before she left, his mother would hug and kiss him, leaving her indelible scent on him. He would fight for days with his grandmother about taking a shower or washing the clothes that smelled like her.

"Mr. President," Jennifer, one of the admins, said from the doorway. "Vice President Henderson is here for your weekly meeting."

"Thank you, Jenn. Give me five minutes and then send her in."

"Yes, sir."

He went into the bathroom that adjoined the Oval to splash cold water on his face and drag himself out of memories he tried hard to never revisit. Nothing good ever came of that. In the past, he would turn to bourbon to numb himself whenever she reappeared out of the ether to turn his life upside down.

Since that wasn't an option now, he needed to buck up and get through this last meeting of the day before he could go home to his family. They always made him feel better, no matter what he was dealing with. He pulled the BlackBerry he used to communicate with Sam from his suit coat pocket and saw the text she'd sent a couple of hours ago.

His spirits sagged when he realized she might get home late.

When he felt like this, she was the only one who could make it go away.

I'm ok, but I'll be better when you get home. See you when we see you, he wrote in reply. *Be safe out there. Your husband loves you very much.*

After he sent the text, Nick stared at his reflection in the mirror. "You're the POTUS," he said. "The fucking president of the United States of America. The leader of the free world. She can't touch you unless you let her."

"Letting her" had always been the problem. He had no control over his reactions to her, and that infuriated him more than anything. At times like this, he was right back in that cramped apartment in Lowell, Massachusetts, with a grandmother who didn't want him and a mother who came and went from his life with no regard for how her long absences affected him.

He took a couple of deep breaths, trying to calm his mind and settle his emotions so he could meet with the vice president and be done with this day from hell.

His five minutes were up, so he returned to the Oval Office just as Jenn brought in Gretchen Henderson.

Nick put a smile on his face and went to shake hands with his VP. "Good to see you, Gretchen."

"You as well, sir."

"Can we get you anything?"

"I'm fine, thank you."

"Thanks, Jenn," Nick said to the admin.

"My pleasure, Mr. President."

He and Gretchen sat on sofas that faced each other. Today, she wore a sharp red pantsuit and had her dark hair up in an elegant twist.

"I'm not sure what to say about the latest headlines," Gretchen said tentatively.

"There's nothing to say. It is what it is, which is what I've been saying all my life where she's concerned."

"I'm sorry you have to deal with it."

"Thank you, but I've learned not to let her get to me. How are things with you? Are you settling in at the Naval Observatory?"

"We are. The kids love it, even if they're not sure how they feel about the Secret Service agents yet."

"I'm sure they'll come to see them as friends before too long."

"I hope so. It's a tender age to suddenly be surrounded by security."

"Yes, it is." He tried to recall the ages of her children. Twelve and fourteen, maybe?

"Anyway," she said, "I asked for this meeting in the hope that we might touch base once a week so I can learn more about how I can be supportive of your agenda."

"I'm eager to have your assistance anywhere you feel you can make an impact. Do you have ideas about where you'd like to focus your efforts?"

"As the nation's first female vice president, I'd like to use my platform to support women in any way that I can, especially working mothers. I was so pleased to hear at the State of the Union that government-assisted childcare is part of your legislative agenda. Finding safe, affordable childcare is a barrier that keeps so many women out of the workforce who might otherwise be pursuing careers."

The comment took him back in time to being in day care as a young child while his grandmother was still working. He recalled the place being somewhat sketchy, but it was all they could afford.

"Mr. President?"

Nick realized he'd spaced out on her for yet another visit to a past he'd rather forget. "I think those matters and other areas affecting women, such as pay equity, would be an excellent use of your platform. The first lady and her team are working on similar issues."

"I'm glad you agree, sir, and I hoped that perhaps the first lady and I might partner on some of these projects. If she's willing, that is."

"As you know, her time is very limited, but I'll certainly mention to her your interest in partnering."

"Thank you, sir. I won't take any more of your time."

He stood to walk her out. "I'll look forward to meeting weekly. Jenn can get you on the schedule."

"That sounds good. I want you to know that I'm here if there's anything I can do to be of assistance to you. We don't know each other very well, but hopefully that will change as we go forward, and you'll come to know you can count on me to have your back. If there's anything I can do for you, please don't hesitate to ask."

"Thank you for that. I appreciate it."

"Very well. I'll see you next week, if not before."

"See you then."

He closed the door and leaned his head against it for a long moment before he returned to his desk, packed up the briefing books he needed to go over before tomorrow and walked out the door to the Colonnade, nodding to the Marine positioned outside the door.

"Have a nice evening, Mr. President."

"You do the same, Sergeant Potts."

A radio crackled to life behind him. "POTUS on the move on the East Colonnade."

His lead Secret Service agent, John Brantley Jr., was probably behind him. On many a day, he walked "home" with Brant. Today, he wanted to be alone with his troubled thoughts.

As he breathed in the fresh air and headed for the residence, he wondered what Gretchen, Sergeant Potts, Brant and the rest of America would think if they knew their president dissolved into emotional despair any time his mother resurfaced to remind him of all the pain she'd caused him. Apparently she wasn't done yet.

CHAPTER SIX

They were still trying to locate the home of Dr. Rory McInerny, who'd recently moved. The office didn't have his new address on file yet. Another call to the office, looking for the second partner, Dr. Oriana Harvey, had reached the practice's answering service. "Dr. Harvey is out of the office for the rest of the week," they were told. "Is there a message?"

"No message," Freddie said as he ended the call.

"Do we have a home address for her?"

"Varnum Street, Northwest, in Petworth," Freddie said so Vernon could hear him.

"Ugh, had to be way the fuck up there, huh?" Sam asked.

"Don't shoot the messenger."

She leaned forward to check the clock on the dashboard and saw it inching closer to three. "Nick will be a mess over this shit with his mother. I need to get home."

"I can take care of Petworth if you want to go."

"That's okay. I'll do this with you, and then we'll get back to HQ for the meeting with Trulo." Both he and Jeannie McBride had recently found themselves in unsafe situations by being alone with witnesses. Sam didn't want him going anywhere alone after that. But she was seriously torn between what she needed to do and what she wanted to do, which was get home to Nick as soon as possible.

"How bad do you think this thing with his mother is going to be?" Freddie asked.

"Hard to say. Could be the tip of the iceberg, for all we know."

Petite, with short dark hair, blue eyes and a serious expression, Dr. Oriana Harvey answered the door of her townhouse with a baby on her hip.

Sam and Freddie showed her their badges and introduced themselves.

She studied their badges and then stepped aside to admit them. "Come in."

They followed her to the kitchen at the back of the house. She put the baby in a high chair and sprinkled some dry cereal on the tray. "Can I get you anything?"

"I'd love some water," Sam said.

"I'll take some, too," Freddie added.

As she filled glasses of ice water for them, Sam looked around at the fancy kitchen with the high-end stove that had a wooden hood above it. She would have no idea how to use a stove like that. The instruction book was probably three inches thick, which meant she'd never open it.

"I assume this is about Marcel and his family." She put the drinks on the table. "I'm in total shock. I spent every day with him and never would've thought him capable of something like this. He adored his kids, or so it seemed to me." She sighed as she sat next to Freddie. "I guess you don't ever really know people."

"So you believe he killed his family and then himself?" Sam asked.

Dr. Harvey stared at her. "I... I don't know. I just assumed... With the news of the lawsuit about to hit the media."

"What lawsuit?"

"Oh God, you haven't heard." She rubbed her temples as she seemed to struggle to find the words. "Four women have accused him of inappropriate behavior. He refused to settle out of court, and the whole mess was about to go public with a trial starting in two weeks."

"What sort of inappropriate behavior?" Sam asked.

Oriana seemed exquisitely uncomfortable. "The kind where he allegedly ejaculated on them while they were under light sedation."   •

After having been through fertility treatment, Sam's stomach turned with revulsion as she imagined such a thing happening to vulnerable women chasing a dream. She cleared her throat. "Do you believe he did that?"

"I believe that four women have remarkably similar stories. Prior to hearing that, no, I wouldn't have thought him capable of such a thing. He'd always been a consummate professional, and his patients loved him. They waited months to see him." She released a deep sigh. "And he was my close friend and colleague. It's just impossible to believe that he'd risk his livelihood, his reputation, *everything* for a cheap thrill. It's disgusting."

"Did the women report the assaults to the MPD?" Sam asked.

"They did, and each was investigated, but since there was no proof, charges were never filed. The women had decided to pursue the matter civilly. And that was about to erupt in a scandal for the ages. When I heard the news, I assumed Marcel snapped and decided to spare them all the shame."

Sam was reeling after hearing about the lawsuit and realizing it was more than possible that Dr. Harvey's theory was exactly what had happened. "While I understand that assumption, our job is to fully investigate every possibility."

"Including that they were murdered?"

"Every possibility," Sam reiterated. "Can you tell us where you were last night?"

The question shocked the doctor. "*I'm* a suspect?"

"Everyone is at this point in the investigation."

"I... I was here with my husband and daughter. I got home around seven and didn't leave again until this morning around seven thirty to go to the office for a couple of hours. We have cameras and a security system here at the house that records comings and goings."

Sam glanced at Freddie, who would take care of getting a warrant for her cameras. Even with her permission to view the cameras, they would still get the warrant to cover their asses. "We've heard that Marcel and your other partner, Rory, had a somewhat major disagreement recently. Is that true?"

The doctor folded her hands on the table and then stared at them. "We were very upset with him for cutting back on his practice, at a time when people are canceling with us because of him, even though his calendar has remained booked solid. That he cut back without consulting with us first was the part that infuriated us the most."

"Would you say that Rory was angry enough to harm Marcel?"

"God no. He thought of Marcel as a brother. The argument was intense, but they were like family to each other. Rory was as angry as I've ever seen him, but he loved those kids like they were his own." With tears in her eyes, she added, "As did I."

"Prior to these latest issues, how would you describe your work relationship with Marcel?"

"It was excellent. We've been in practice together for seven years and worked very well together. We helped each other out when one of us had outside obligations. We covered for each other. We were close friends as well as colleagues. Him making a major change like that without discussing it with us first was out of character, to say the least, as were the things his patients accused him of. We were deeply disappointed about all of it. I was especially upset with him cutting his hours, because he knew how challenging everything was for me since I had my daughter. Not to mention the lawsuit was heavily affecting Rory and me while leaving him relatively unscathed."

"Wouldn't you want him to cut back until the lawsuit was resolved?" Sam asked.

"He was booked solid with appointments more than a year out. His proven track record of success was what brought most of our patients to the practice."

"Was this the only thing that was out of character for him lately?"

She thought about that for a minute.

Sam wanted to tell her to hurry up as she noticed the clock on the stove moving toward three thirty.

"He'd been unusually harsh in his comments about Liliana lately."

"How so?"

"He said she expected too much from him, was always on him for missing things with the kids, but when he decided to cut back on his work, she freaked out about the financial implications. He was angry with her for putting him in an impossible situation."

"And he told you this even though you were also upset about his decision?"

"It came out during the argument with Rory. He said everyone expected so much of him, and he couldn't seem to make anyone happy. We asked who he meant by everyone, and he said Liliana had been making him feel like shit for missing so much with the kids. But he said she certainly enjoyed the lifestyle his income provided."

"She worked, too, though, right?" Sam asked.

"She did, but he made most of the family's income. She worked around the kids' schedules, so her hours were somewhat limited."

"Did Marcel indicate what his plan was for continuing to pay the family's bills on half his regular income?"

"Not to us." She got up to get something from a cabinet and returned with baby food and a small green spoon.

The baby lit up at the sight of the spoon, sparking the old familiar yearning in Sam that hit at the strangest of times, like now when she had a million other things to think about, including the three children who'd made her a mother.

"What else can you tell us about his relationship with Rory?" Sam asked.

"As I mentioned, they were like brothers. They'd been friends since med school, and their families were close, but he was very upset about Marcel making a decision that impacted all of us without even talking to us first, especially when his lawsuit was having a much bigger impact on us than it was on him. It was all over the local infertility groups online, and people were canceling with *us* but not him."

"Can you think of anyone else who might've wanted the family dead?"

"Everyone loved them. The kids..." Her eyes filled as she shook her head. In a whisper, she said, "They were beautiful."

Sam put her card on the table and gave the usual spiel about calling if she thought of anything else that might be relevant. As she went through the motions, she felt like she was wading through quicksand, unable to find her usual groove.

"Thank you for your time," Sam said.

"I really hope you figure out who did this," Dr. Harvey said.

"We'll do our best."

"If I may... It was very nice to meet you, although I wish it had been under different circumstances. My husband and I are supporters of you and your husband."

"Thank you. We appreciate it."

Back outside, they got into the SUV, and Sam asked Vernon to take them to HQ.

"How're you making out?" Vernon asked, glancing at her in the mirror.

"The usual frustrating bullshit at this point in any investigation," Sam said. "Everyone loved them. The kids were beautiful. No one can think of any reason someone would want to kill them. Yada, yada, yada."

"The lawsuit is an interesting twist," Freddie said. "Didn't see that coming."

"Me either." It was a very interesting twist that she couldn't work up an ounce of enthusiasm over. Feeling overheated in the car, she unzipped her coat and rested her head against the cool window.

"Are you okay, Sam?" Freddie asked in a low tone.

"Yep." What the hell was wrong with her? She lived for this stuff, but she couldn't seem to find the groove she needed to oversee a complex investigation. Was it because of the crap with Nick's mother? Possibly. Even though they'd made up, their argument over her asking Avery Hill to investigate his mother had rattled her. The uneasiness of an unusually harsh encounter with Nick remained as Avery's investigation blew up into a scandal Nick and his team had to deal with.

She knew better than anyone how even a mention of his mother affected Nick and worried that when the dust eventually settled, as it always did, he would blame her for bringing this down on him.

But it was more than that.

Something was off inside her, and she couldn't say what it was. While she had a minute, she texted her sister Tracy. *Have you talked to Ang today? How are they doing?*

Sam had liked it better when Ang and the kids were staying with them at the White House so she could see them every day. However, she respected Angela's decision to return to their own home, where she could work on putting her life back together after her husband's sudden death.

Maybe it was Spencer's death and the senselessness of it all that had her by the throat. He'd often gotten on her nerves with his big opinion of himself, but he'd loved Angela and their kids with all his heart. No one could deny that. Sam gave Angela credit for pushing forward when Sam would've been catatonic if she'd lost Nick.

People said you found a way through it when things like that happened. She wouldn't find a way through losing him. No way. The thought of it was enough to wreck her. And why was she thinking about that? How could she not after a loss like that had struck so close to home? She'd never admired her sister more than she had in the last few weeks as Angela made the adjustment to being a widow and single mother to two young children with a third on the way.

Her phone chimed with a text from Tracy. *Talked to her earlier. Jack didn't want to go to school this morning, but they worked through it and got him there a little late. She said he had a good day. Ella is getting molars, so she's miserable, and Ang is feeling nauseous. Mom is there now and making dinner.*

I'm glad Mom is there helping.

She's staying with them for a little while.

That's good.

I think so, too. How are you?

New case. Parents, four kids murdered. Staged to look like murder-suicide, but I'm not convinced.

Jeez, Sam. Don't know how you do it.

Someone's gotta.

How's Nick holding up with the mother shit?

Okay, I guess. Anxious to get home to him. Gotta meet with Trulo first. Tough crime scene earlier. Mandatory shrinking.

Glad you're getting that support. Don't be difficult about it.

What? Me, difficult?

Tracy replied with laughing emojis.

It's not that funny.

YES, IT IS. Call me later.

Maybe I will. Maybe I won't.

That got her an eye roll emoji that made her snort with laughter.

"What's so funny?"

"Tracy rolling her eyes at me."

"That happens so often in the course of a day, I'm surprised you still find it funny," Freddie said dryly.

Vernon coughed to cover a laugh.

Jimmy laughed out loud.

Sam glared at Freddie. "This shall be remembered at annual review time."

"I'm scared."

"Good. You should be." The banter with him and the laughter with her sister and the agents helped to take the edge off an awful day. She'd had a lot of awful days on this job, so it was hard to say why this one felt different. Something was wrong when she was looking forward to a session with Dr. Trulo.

"Is it weird that Liliana's best friend, Kelly, didn't seem to know about the lawsuit?" Sam asked.

"I wondered that, too. I'll circle back with her to ask if she knew."

"Yeah, let's do that, and if she did, ask her why she failed to mention it to us."

"If she knows, she was probably trying to protect his reputation."

"Understandable, but remind her this is no time to hold back."

"I'm on it."

Sam put her head back against the seat and closed her eyes, thinking through the parts and pieces of the case, such as it was thus far. It was a muddled mess of images and details and things that didn't add up, which only added to her frustration. Her dyslexia was bad enough when she tried to read something. She didn't need it making her own thoughts into a mess, too.

The car came to a stop, which startled her. Somehow she'd managed to doze off, which was also not like her during a workday.

Freddie gave her a curious look as they walked into the morgue entrance. They were running late for the meeting with Trulo, or she would've stopped to see Lindsey. Following voices to the conference room, they found the rest of the squad already seated around the table, along with Lindsey, Byron and two of the techs from the ME team.

"Sorry we're late," Sam said as she and Freddie took the last two seats.

"We just started," Dr. Trulo said with a warm smile for Sam. "Thank you all for being here at the end of a long, difficult day. Most of you have been doing this long enough now that you've seen a few things, but it's always worse when kids are involved. Or at least that's what officers have been telling me for almost thirty years.

"This is an opportunity to talk about it as a group, while

knowing my door is always open to you on an individual basis as well. Day or night, I'm here for you. If there's anything you'd like to say, this is a safe space to share your feelings. Nothing you say here or in individual sessions will impact your career within the department in any way. You have my word on that."

After a long moment of silence, Trulo said, "Would anyone like to start?"

More silence greeted the question.

"Not sure what there is to say other than crime scenes like that are the worst," Gonzo said.

"It makes you wonder what kind of world we live in where someone could shoot innocent kids in their beds, in the place they're supposed to be the safest."

"That's a good point, Sergeant," Trulo said. "How do you feel about that, Detective Cruz?"

"Same as Gonzo. It makes no sense that whoever did this killed the kids, too. Like, what could they have possibly done to anyone?"

"Nothing," Detective Green said. "They didn't do anything to anyone. They were collateral damage."

"Are we thinking the father did it?" Detective Charles asked.

"I'm not a hundred percent sold on that theory," Sam said.

"He had gunshot residue on his right hand," Lindsey said.

"That's new information," Sam replied as she glanced at her friend, "but I'm still not convinced. Everyone we've talked to said he loved his wife and kids more than anything."

"You'll answer all the questions about the case in due time," Dr. Trulo said. "For now, let's focus on how you're feeling as people rather than as detectives."

"My mother was murdered when I was six," Detective Charles said.

The room went completely still as all eyes shifted to the young detective.

"I witnessed it from a closet. A man I'd never seen before forced his way into our apartment and shot her in the chest. I think she was dead before she hit the floor. He never saw me and was gone as fast as he'd come. I was so scared he'd come back that I stayed in the closet for an hour before I worked up the courage to go to her. She was already cold.

"I knew that meant she was dead because we used to watch *Law & Order* together. She said I couldn't tell anyone that she let me watch that, because I was too young. It was her favorite show, though, so we watched it. Her killer was never caught. I became a cop because her favorite show was *Law & Order*. It's different, though, when it's real people who've been killed, and well, I just wanted you guys to know why it means so much to me to be here. Even on days like today, I wouldn't want to be anywhere else."

"Neveah," Sam said. "I'm so sorry."

"Thank you. It was a long time ago now."

"She'd be so proud of you," Dr. Trulo said.

"I hope so."

"Thank you for sharing your story, Detective," Dr. Trulo said.

"My grandfather was a pharmacist," Detective O'Brien said. "He was killed in an armed robbery in his store. They wanted drugs. He wouldn't budge, even when they said they'd kill him if he didn't give them what they wanted. I was eleven, but I never forgot the detectives who worked his case, how much they cared about us and him, even though they'd never met him. I'm here for him and for other victims of senseless crime who count on us to get them answers."

"I'm so sorry, Matt," Sam said.

"Thanks. Like Neveah said, it was a long time ago."

"But you never forget," Gonzo said.

"No, you don't," Matt said.

"Thank you for sharing, Detective O'Brien," Dr. Trulo said. "We're sorry for the loss of your grandfather. The Blanchet family and the others you encounter in your work are lucky to have you working on their behalf. I won't keep you any longer, because you have important work to do, but I'm here if I can help. Please don't hesitate to ask for it if you need it."

"Thanks, Doc," Gonzo said as he led the exodus.

"Was it something I said?" Trulo asked Sam when only the two of them remained.

"Shut the door, will you?"

CHAPTER SEVEN

Dr. Trulo reached behind him to push the door closed. "What's up?"

"I'm not sure," Sam said. "I'm off my game."

"How so?"

She shrugged. "Can't find my mojo. We caught a hot new case, and I just feel... numb. I saw those kids... dead in their beds, took note of the facts and went on with my day. I want to know who killed them, but I'm not feeling the usual rage on behalf of my victims. It's weird."

"How much time off did you take after your brother-in-law died?"

"This isn't about him."

"Are you sure?" Before Sam could reply, he said, "No one I know has ever been murdered except for people I've worked with here. I've never had a close family member killed that way, thank God, or even a friend or acquaintance. I've been extraordinarily blessed to avoid that hell."

Sam wanted to ask what his point was, but she'd learned to let him get to it on his own.

"You, on the other hand, have lost your father, your brother-in-law and one of your detectives to murder, all within the last couple of years. You're still getting over a major injury. That's a lot by anyone's standards. Now, add to it your husband has gone from the Senate to the White House, and you've taken in three children, all while juggling multiple jobs. I'm surprised you haven't gone numb long before now."

"I don't like being numb to the job."

"No, you wouldn't care for that at all."

"So what do I do?"

"You can power through, like you always do, or you can take some time away."

"I can't take time away when we have six new bodies in the morgue."

"Sure, you can. Your very competent team can handle the investigation." He got up, came around the table, took the seat next to her and turned to face her. "You know what happens when we push the boundaries of what we can handle?"

"What?"

"We make mistakes. Big mistakes." After a pause, he said, "I don't want to see that happen to you, Sam. I also don't want to see you burn out to the point where you can no longer do the job."

That possibility struck a note of fear in her, which was a relief. At least she wasn't numb to the possibility of screwing up her career.

"So what do I do?"

"Take some time off. Hang out with your sister as she adapts to widowhood. Be there for your kids, her kids. Take care of your husband as he deals with this new thing with his mother."

"How much time?"

"As much as it takes."

"Maybe after we close this case."

"There'll always be another case, Sam, another reason to keep powering through when you know something's not right."

Sam couldn't deny the truth of that. "I don't know how to step back. This job... It's..."

"All-consuming."

"Yes, it is."

"There's no shame in admitting you need a break. No one would blame you if you took one."

Sam laughed. "Sure, they would. They'd say I was getting special treatment, that I can't stand the heat, that—"

"Sam," he said with a kind smile. "Who cares what they say? You know the truth. I know the truth. Joe and Jake would understand. Your squad would happily step up for you the way you always do for them. Who else matters?"

He had a knack for cutting through the bullshit to get to the important stuff. "No one, I suppose."

Since he'd made his point rather convincingly, he stayed silent to give her space to work it through in her mind. She'd learned during previous times of crisis that he liked his patients to find their own way through the swamp rather than him doing all the work.

"So it's just that simple? Take some time off?"

"It can be that simple."

"What about the case?"

"Put Gonzo in charge, or maybe give Cruz a shot at leading an investigation. He's ready by now, isn't he?"

"Yes, but—"

"No buts, Sam. You're as human as the next person. If you need a break to get your head straight, take it."

For the first time she could remember, her heart wasn't in the job. The good doctor was right. She would be no good to anyone until she figured out what was making her feel this way. That she could walk into a house with six murdered people, four of them children, and feel nothing was proof she had a problem.

"What do you think?" Trulo asked.

"I don't know what to think, as I'm in unprecedented territory here."

"It happens to the best of us."

Sam took a minute to gather her thoughts. "It has been a lot since my dad died, and finding out that Conklin knew all along who shot him and why. Stahl's trial, taking in the twins, Nick's new job, Spencer's death."

"I'm honestly surprised this hasn't happened before now," Trulo said. "I've been keeping half an eye on you from a distance— and not in a stalkerish way."

Sam laughed. "I see how it is."

"I care about you, kid. Lots of us do. You're an absolute superstar in this department."

"I don't know about that."

"I do, and it's true. No one gets the job done the way you do, but even superstars have their breaking points."

"How could I look at those kids, dead in their beds, and feel nothing?"

"By asking that question, you're proving you felt something. It just wasn't the usual level of outrage."

"I suppose."

"Talk to Malone. Tell him how you're feeling and that I recommend a break. See what he says. I'd be happy to put something in writing to him, if that would help."

"No, thanks. I don't want a paper trail on this."

"Understood. Let me know how I can help."

"You already have. Thank you."

"You can thank me by taking care of yourself, my friend."

AFTER TRULO LEFT the conference room, Sam went straight to Malone's office, fearing she'd lose her resolve if she didn't do this right now. She knocked on his open door.

"Enter."

Sam closed the door and leaned back against it.

"How'd it go with Trulo?"

"Good. I think it helped for people to talk about it." She pushed off the door and took a seat in his visitor chair. "Did you know Charles witnessed her mother's murder when she was six?"

"I did know that. The case is unsolved."

"Don't tell me it's one of Stahl's."

"No, it was one of Joe's actually. He busted his ass trying to get answers, but it never happened."

"Is that why he was so protective of her?"

"That's one of many reasons. He stayed in touch with her and was a mentor to her when she decided to pursue law enforcement."

"That sounds like him," Sam said.

"Where are we with the new case?"

Sam updated him on what they'd learned thus far.

"So you're not feeling it as a murder-suicide?"

"I'm not sure yet. Lindsey reported residue on his right hand, so he either killed the others, or someone wants us to believe he did."

"Let's treat it as a homicide until we can prove otherwise."

"That's the plan, but I was wondering..." *Here goes nothing.* "How would you feel if I made Cruz the lead on this one?"

Malone tipped his head to study her, his expression somewhat incredulous. "Why?"

"It's been brought to my attention by Dr. Trulo that I may need a brief leave of absence to deal with some personal matters."

"Is everything okay?"

"I'd like to think so, but the evidence is pointing to some concerns in light of recent events that might not have been dealt with properly."

Malone sat back in his chair with his hands crossed over his abdomen. "Spencer."

"Among other things."

"You think Cruz is ready to lead an investigation of this magnitude?"

"I do."

"How will Gonzales feel about that?" Malone asked.

"He'd still be in charge. We'd give Cruz the lead as a training opportunity."

"It's fine with me. You know best what Cruz can handle, and I like the idea of giving him the chance to lead an investigation."

"I'll talk to them before I leave."

"Do you know how much time you're planning to take?"

"Not yet, but I'd keep you posted, if that's all right. Might just be a day or two to reset."

"Last I checked, you have something like three months of accrued leave on the books."

"Is it that much? Even after I was out with my hip?"

Malone typed something into his computer. "One hundred and eight days."

"Wow."

"This info can be found on your pay stub, you know."

"What pay stub?"

"The one that's sent to your email every two weeks."

"Oh. I'm a bit behind on my email."

He grunted out a laugh. "No kidding. Really?"

"I'll get caught up on that while I'm out."

"Don't worry about it. Take the time you need. The job will still be here when you're ready to come back."

"Have you ever felt numb to something that should be

seriously upsetting? Such as four dead kids in their beds?"

"Occasionally. It happens."

"What did you do about it?"

"Therapy helped."

"Did you see Trulo?"

"I have. He's damn good at what he does, as you know."

"Yes, I do."

"This job asks a lot of us, Sam. Sometimes it asks more than we've got to give it. When that happens, it's right to ask for help and take a step back for a minute."

"That's what Trulo said."

"Take the time. Do the work. Come back when you're ready."

"Thank you, as always, for the support," Sam said as she stood to leave.

"Thank you, as always, for making me look so good."

Smiling, she said, "I do what I can for my people." She left his office and went to the pit, asking Gonzales and Cruz to come into her office. "Shut the door."

"What's up?" Freddie asked.

"It's been brought to my attention that I might be suffering some ill effects from losing Spence and my dad and a few other recent things. Dr. Trulo has recommended I take a break to deal with these things, and Captain Malone has concurred."

"Oh," Freddie said, seeming stunned.

If she were him, she'd be stunned, too. It wasn't like her—at all —to let the job get to her this way, which was proof that something was up.

"It's been decided that Freddie will take the lead on the Blanchet case with Gonzo's supervision."

"*What?*" Freddie asked, his eyes going wide.

"You're ready," Sam said. "You've been ready for quite some time now."

"I agree," Gonzo said. "You've got this."

Freddie sputtered. "But I... Are you sure?"

"Positive," Sam said. "I'll be a phone call away if you need me, and I'll want to be kept in the loop about what's going on."

"I, um, okay."

Sam wanted to laugh at his stuttering replies but knew he wouldn't appreciate that. "I have every confidence in you, Detective Cruz."

"Thank you, Lieutenant. I appreciate the opportunity."

"I guess I'll just go home now."

"If you need anything," Gonzo said, "you know where to find us."

"Yes, I do, and that makes all the difference."

After they left, she powered down her computer, grabbed her coat and phones off the desk, locked her office and headed for the morgue exit, eager to get home to her family.

BEFORE HE LEFT the West Wing for the day, Nick stopped at Christina's office.

Surprised by his sudden appearance, she jumped to her feet. "Mr. President."

"Don't do that."

"I, uh, I can't help it."

"Try." He sat in her visitor chair as she returned to her seat. "Long day, huh?"

"Yes, it has been, but I think we're staying ahead of it."

"I wanted to thank you for what you did in the briefing room today."

"Oh, well, I was hoping I hadn't gone too far."

"You didn't. You did an excellent job of telling the story of my life in a way that makes it clear she's not part of it."

"I've known you long enough to have seen the toll it takes on you when she rears her ugly head. Are you holding up okay?"

He shrugged. "I tell myself it is what it is, but she never fails to crawl under my skin."

"I hate that for you. We all do."

"Thanks. You should go home to Tommy and Alex. This place will still be here in the morning."

"I was just getting ready to go. Angela insisted on having Alex. Tommy just picked him up."

"Ang is trying to get back to normal, and she adores Alex."

"She's wonderful with him, but I worry she's got enough to deal with without another little one underfoot."

"She'd tell you that Alex keeps Ella entertained, so it's a win-win."

"I suppose so. I can't imagine what she's going through."

"I know. It's awful and so tragic."

"I think all the time about 'there but for the grace of God go I,' you know?" Christina said.

"I'm sure it strikes close to home."

Tommy Gonzales's battle with opioid addiction following the senseless murder of his partner, Detective Arnold, had been brutal for him and everyone who loved him, especially Christina.

"We got so lucky," she said softly. "So, so lucky."

"Thank goodness for that."

She nodded.

"I won't keep you any longer," he said. "Just wanted to thank you for having my back."

"Always."

They'd met as young congressional staffers. He and Sam considered her and Tommy family. "Having you, Terry, Derek and Harry by my side in this surreal new reality makes all the difference for me. I hope you know that."

"We do, and we're so damned proud of you."

"That means a lot. Thank you. Now go home. That's an order."

"Yes, sir, Mr. President."

He gave her a playful scowl as he left her office and headed for the residence with Brant walking beside him. "Another day in paradise, Brant."

"Yes, sir."

"Have you heard anything about the situation with she-who-shall-not-be-named?"

"A friend in the FBI mentioned there may be other charges forthcoming. I'm sure you'll receive a briefing on it as soon as the information is solid."

"I'll look forward to that," Nick said in a tone laced with sarcasm.

"I'm sorry you're dealing with this, sir."

"I'm sorry, too."

Brant walked him to the top of the stairs. "Have a good evening, sir."

"You do the same, Brant."

One of these days, Nick wanted to get to know his lead agent better, but today wasn't that day. As he walked the red-carpeted hallway toward their home away from home, he pulled his tie free and released the top two buttons on his dress shirt.

He stopped outside Scotty's room and watched his son's lips

move as he typed something on his laptop. Nick hoped he was doing homework. He gave a light knock on the door.

When Scotty looked up and saw him there, his adorable face lit up with a big smile that made Nick's terrible day seem like a long time ago. "There you are. I was just about to come looking for you."

"You know you can. Any time you want."

"I know, but I was trying to get this stupid essay finished before dinner so I could have the rest of the night free."

"That's a good plan. What's the essay on?"

"NATO."

"Ah, a worthy subject."

"Did you know that an act of war against one NATO nation is an act of war on all of them?"

"I did know that."

"Duh, you kind of have to know those things."

Nick laughed. "It does help to understand such things."

"I can't imagine how many things you need to understand to have that job."

"Luckily, I'm surrounded by an amazing team of people who do a lot of the understanding for me and make me look good every day."

"They might be awesome, but you're the guy out front."

"Which is so much fun on days like this."

"I'm sorry your mother is horrible."

"So am I."

"It makes me mad when people hurt you and Mom."

"Thanks, pal, but we don't want you taking on our battles."

"Too late. We're family. Your battles are my battles."

That Scotty could touch his heart so profoundly, even after all the time they'd spent together, never failed to amaze him. "Love you, buddy."

"Love you, too."

"Let's see what's for dinner."

"I need ten minutes to finish this."

"Take your time, and I'd be happy to read it for you when you're finished."

"That'd be cool. Thanks."

"You got it."

CHAPTER EIGHT

Nick went into the bedroom to change into his favorite Harvard T-shirt and sweats. He exhaled a deep breath, thankful to have survived this day mostly intact, even if his emotions were still all over the place. He was about to text Sam to ask when she might get home when she came into the bathroom, where he was leaning against their double sinks with his phone in hand. "There's my gorgeous wife."

She came to him and wrapped him up in her love, holding him just right and filling him with a powerful feeling of homecoming. There was nothing she could've done that would've meant more to him. When she finally pulled back some time later, she looked up at him, studying his face, probably looking for signs of despair. "How're you doing?"

"Hanging in."

"Christina did an amazing job with the briefing," Sam said.

"Yes, she did."

"Still, it's not the easiest thing to have made public."

"I tell myself it has nothing to do with me."

"And yet..."

"Yeah."

"I hate her for continuing to hurt you this way."

"Don't waste the energy. She's not worth it." He tipped her chin up and kissed her. "Let's go find our Littles and have dinner with the kids."

"Give me five minutes to get changed."

"Take your time. I'll run upstairs to get them."

"Invite Celia to come for dinner."

"Will do." He kissed her again and left her to get changed while he went upstairs.

The door to Celia's suite was open, and the sound of little voices made him smile as he approached. "Knock, knock."

"Nick!" Alden ran for him, with Aubrey in hot pursuit.

Was there anything better than a greeting like that from his Littles? He lifted them both into his arms and kissed them until they were giggling madly. "Did you guys have a good day?"

"It was Michael's birthday at school, so we had cupcakes," Aubrey said.

"Yum. That sounds fun."

"They were red!" Alden said.

"Even better." Nick put them down. "Grab your stuff. It's dinnertime." To Celia, he said, "Sam and I would love for you to join us for dinner, if you'd like to."

"That'd be fun. I'll be down in a few."

Their social secretary and close friend Shelby Faircloth Hill came into the room and received the same greeting from her son, Noah, as Nick had from the twins. He toddled on chubby legs to get to his mother.

Since Shelby was heavily pregnant with her second child, she bent to hug her son but didn't lift him. "How's my big boy?"

"Mama."

"Are you guys free for dinner?" Nick asked.

"In fact, we are. Avery is out of town."

Nick suspected Avery was in Ohio dealing with his mother, but he'd talked about her enough for one day. "Come down to eat with us."

"Thanks. We'd love to, wouldn't we, Noah?"

"Mama. Dinner."

"Yes, my love. We're going to have dinner with Alden and Aubrey."

They were his favorites. Hell, they were everyone's favorites.

A few minutes later, with the people he loved best gathered around the dining room table for a dinner of chicken, potatoes, stuffing, green beans and corn, Nick felt like he could breathe again for the first time since the news had broken about his mother that morning.

Being with Sam, their kids and their loving extended family more than made up for the deficiencies of his childhood. These people and many others would do anything for him, and that meant so much to him. But underneath it all, lurking as she had from the beginning of his life, was the woman who'd given birth to him and then treated him with reckless disregard ever since.

Nick had learned that he could find the love of his life, build a family with her that filled him with joy and ascend to the highest office in the land, but his mother would continue to haunt him.

NICOLETTA SAT in a crowded jail cell, waiting for something to happen. She wasn't sure what, but no one seemed to care that she was the mother of the U.S. president, which was concerning. How could that not count for anything? They'd asked if she had a lawyer, but she didn't know anyone.

They'd said someone would be appointed.

That was probably the hang-up, waiting for the lawyer.

A man in a suit appeared outside her cell. He was handsome, with gorgeous caramel-colored hair, golden eyes and cheekbones she would kill for. "Who are you?"

"FBI Special Agent-in-Charge Avery Hill."

He had a cultured Southern accent that was to die for. She'd always had a soft spot for a Southern gentleman.

"What do you want?" she asked.

"Have they called an attorney for you?"

"They said they did."

"I'll speak to you when your attorney arrives."

"About what?"

The agent tipped his head. "The charges you're facing."

"Did my daughter-in-law send you?"

"Who's your daughter-in-law?"

"As if you don't know."

"Enlighten me."

"The first lady!"

"Of the United States?"

"Is there another first lady?"

"Well, each of the states has one, unless the governor is a woman. Then they have a first gentleman."

"What does that have to do with me?"

"You asked if there was another first lady."

She hoped her scowl told him what she thought of his sassy comment. "Do you know my son?"

"The president? Yes, I know him."

"Did he send you here?"

"No, ma'am. I don't work for him. Well, technically, I do, but there're a lot of layers of bureaucracy between him and me."

"Do you know *her*?"

"Who do you mean?"

"His bitch of a wife."

"Yes, I know her. She's a lovely person."

"No, she isn't. I know she's behind all of this."

"How so?"

"I don't know, but I'm going to find out. When I do, I'm going to ruin her."

"You're not threatening the first lady, are you? Because, as you can probably assume, I'd have to do something about that as a federal agent. If you're threatening her, that is."

"I never threatened her, but don't tell me she isn't a hateful bitch."

"Okay, I won't."

"You DC people are all in bed with each other. It wouldn't surprise me if you told me you were having an affair with her."

The handsome, sexy man became even more so when he smiled. "If you know anything about your son and his wife, it's that neither of them is having an affair with anyone, because they're madly in love with each other."

Nicoletta couldn't believe her gorgeous, smart, successful son had married a shrew like her. "What do you want, Agent Hill?"

"I was just checking on when you think your attorney might arrive."

"I'm here." A short, balding man in a cheap suit came rushing over to where Agent Hill stood. A man like him should never stand next to someone like Agent Hill. Looking at the two of them was like watching the sun eclipse the moon.

"I'm Roland Ducharme from the public defender's office, Ms. Bernadino." To the agent, he said, "May I have a moment alone with my client?"

"Of course," Hill said. "I'll be in the interrogation room when you're ready. I'm sure you know the drill."

"I do. We'll be along shortly."

After Agent Hill walked away, Roland glanced around to make sure no one who mattered would overhear him. "Ma'am, you're in a heap of trouble."

WHEN AVERY ENTERED the room the police had assigned for his use, he sent a quick text to Shelby. *Might be here overnight. Sorry.*

No problem. We'll be fine, but we'll miss you.

I miss you guys, too. How are you feeling?

Big like a whale, heartburn so bad it's like I'm on fire and the usual nightly flatulence.

I'm very sorry to miss that. I look forward to it all day.

Her laughter emojis made him smile. *You're sick in the head.*

Love you and Noah. Tell him Daddy said good night.

I will. We love you, too.

I'll call you when I get to a hotel.

If I don't answer, I'm dead asleep.

Should I just call in the morning, then?

That might be better. We had dinner with S&N and just got home. I'm so tired, I might fall over.

Don't do that. Get some rest. Make sure you set the alarm.

Already done.

Good. Sweet dreams.

You, too!

He wanted to tell her what a bitch Nick's mother was, but he'd never put that in writing. But what a piece of work she was. Of course, he'd heard the stories about her and had seen her in action during several TV interviews that'd cast a negative light on the son she claimed to love with all her heart. Meeting her in person had confirmed that she was every bit as vile as she seemed. No one needed a mother like her.

It made him sad for Nick to have to deal with her shit right when he was beginning to make inroads in convincing the American people to accept him as their president.

From what their investigators had unearthed, Nicoletta had been a busy, busy lady, dabbling in everything from prostitution to drugs to money laundering. And that was just what they'd found thus far. He'd be surprised if she didn't spend a big chunk of time in prison.

The president's mother.

It was almost too much to be believed.

His phone rang with a call from Shelby.

"Avery!"

"What's wrong?"

"I think there's someone in the house."

His entire body went rigid with shock and fear. "Shelby!"

He heard a struggle, Noah's sharp cry, and then the line went dead. For a second, he couldn't remember what he was supposed to do at a time like this, and then his training kicked in. He called his deputy, George Terrell.

"Hey, what's up?"

"My... My family, George. Shelby called to say someone was in the house."

"I'm on my way, and I'll call the cavalry."

"George."

"I'm on it, Avery. Hang tight. I'll be back to you as soon as I know anything."

After the call ended, Avery stood in the generic interrogation room that looked like all the others he'd seen during his career. A million things ran through his mind as he contemplated what was happening at home. Had someone come for him and been disappointed to find only his wife and son? Would he ever see them again?

He'd never felt that kind of panic as he ran from the police station, past the astonished officers he'd recently met and spoken with. He jumped into the government car that had met him at the tarmac and ordered them to get him to the airport as fast as possible. On the way, he kept trying to call Shelby, but the phone just rang and rang.

When he ran toward the government plane that had ferried him to Cleveland earlier, the two Air Force pilots who'd flown him there chased after him. He wasn't sure where they'd come from, but he didn't have time to care.

"Agent Hill?"

"I need to get back to DC right away."

"Yes, sir. We'll have you airborne as soon as possible."

His heart raced from anxiety and exertion as he tried to call Shelby again. The call went straight to voice mail.

· · ·

"WHAT DO YOU WANT?" Shelby asked the woman with the sunken green eyes, wild brown hair and track marks on her arms. Shelby figured her to be in her midthirties, but it was hard to tell for sure.

She pointed a gun at Shelby. "Where's Agent Hill?"

"He's not here."

"I can see that. Where is he?"

Shelby tried to keep herself together as she debated whether it was in her best interest to tell the truth or make the woman believe that Avery might be home at any moment. She chose the latter. "He's on his way home."

"When will he be here?"

"I'm not sure."

Her phone rang and rang. She ached when she imagined what he'd be going through, knowing they were in danger.

Noah cried so hard, his little body shook.

"Shut him up, or I will."

"You'd hurt an innocent child?"

"He's nothing to me."

The nonchalant way in which she said that terrified Shelby. There was nothing she wouldn't do to protect Noah and her unborn child.

A man came into the room, looking as unkempt as the woman. His teeth were as yellow as his eyes. "Where is he?"

"Not here."

"I can see that." To Shelby, he said, "Where is he?"

"On his way home." That there were two of them truly terrified her. "What do you want?"

"We want to talk to him. Shut that kid up."

"He's due for his bottle. I need to go downstairs to get it."

"We'll go with you."

Shelby's legs felt like rubber as she went downstairs with Noah in her arms, trying not to drop him. She shouldn't have been carrying him. He was too heavy for her in the third trimester, but when that woman had appeared in her bedroom, Shelby had reached for her son and held him tightly to her chest.

She held him with one arm as she prepared the bottle he had only at bedtime now. Her hands were shaking so hard, she could barely function. Would they kill her and Noah if they didn't get what they'd come for? And how had they gotten in? They must've already been there when she got home, but how was that possible? She'd set the alarm when she left for work. Hadn't she? They'd overslept and had been running late. Had she forgotten? When she got home, had she disarmed it? Why couldn't she remember?

When tears flooded her eyes, she refused to let them blind her. She used her sleeve to mop them up. Noah needed her to stay focused, so that's what she would do. By now, Avery had sounded every alarm available to him, and help would be on the way.

She went into the living room she and Avery had put together piece by piece over the last year and sat on the brown leather sofa he'd wanted. Had she ever told him that he'd been right about the sofa? It was gorgeous and held up perfectly against the shenanigans of a toddler.

Shelby wanted to scream from the outrage of strangers in their home, of a gun pointing at her, Noah and their unborn child as she fed Noah his bottle. In this position, it would be so easy for the man to shoot them. The bullet would hit Noah first, a thought that would've brought her to her knees had she been standing.

"Call your husband. Find out when he'll be home."

"My... My phone is upstairs."

To the woman, he said, "Go get it, and hurry up about it."

"Fuck you, Willy. I don't work for you."

"Move your ass, or I'll shoot you in it."

Shelby watched the scene with a sense of surreal disbelief. Was this really happening, or was she having one of the vivid dreams that'd been part of both pregnancies?

The woman returned with Shelby's phone and handed it to her.

"Call him. Tell him his family's life depends on him getting his ass home right away. Put the call on speaker."

Shelby found his number first on her list of favorites and made the call.

"Baby," he said, sounding distraught. "Are you all right?"

"There're some people here to see you. They said to tell you my life and Noah's depends on you getting home soon."

"I'm two hours out."

"Okay."

"Are you..."

"We're fine," Shelby said with a defiant look for the man named Willy.

"For now," Willy said, "but your old man needs to hurry home before someone gets hurt."

His words struck terror in Shelby's heart, but she refused to let him see that. She tightened her hold on Noah, who'd dozed off while drinking his bottle. She'd do whatever it took to protect him and the baby.

CHAPTER NINE

S am and Nick had just finished tucking in the Littles when her phone rang with a call from Dispatch. Technically, she didn't have to take it because she was on leave, but apparently, no one had told the dispatchers that.

"Holland."

"Lieutenant, we received a call from Agent Hill letting us know that his wife and son are being held hostage in their home."

The words took a second to register, and then she was on her feet, running to the bedroom to unlock her bedside table, where she kept her service weapon.

"Agent Hill is on a flight home from Cleveland, and we've dispatched our Special Response teams to assist the FBI, but he said you'd want to know."

"He was right. Thank you." Sam slapped the phone closed and put on her shoulder holster with trembling hands that didn't want to work the way they were supposed to.

"What's wrong?" Nick asked from behind her.

Sam spun around. "Shelby and Noah have been taken hostage in their home. Avery is on a flight back to DC. Our Special Response teams are assisting the FBI. He asked Dispatch to notify me."

Nick looked stricken. "I want to go with you."

"You can't. I'll keep you posted." She kissed him quickly and then ran from the room, grabbing her coat from where she'd left it, slung over a chair, when she got home. *Shit*, she thought as she descended the stairs. *I need to notify the Secret Service.* She'd promised Nick she'd never again leave without a detail, and she intended to keep that promise.

At the bottom of the stairs, she ran into Nick's lead agent, Brant.

"I need a detail," she said. "Right now."

"Yes, ma'am. Give me one minute."

"I have less than a minute."

"Understood." He walked away and ducked into a room down the hall.

While she waited, Sam forced herself to breathe, hoping she could calm down and get her emotions in check. The numbness from earlier was long gone, replaced by a searing ache in her chest for Shelby and Noah, whom she loved with all her heart.

Avery must be out of his mind.

She flipped her phone open and called him.

"Are you at the scene?" he asked.

"On my way. What do you know?"

"Two people were in the house when she got home."

"How'd they get in? Don't you have an alarm?"

"We do, but she must've forgotten to set it when she left this morning. That happens sometimes. Sam... I can't lose them. I just can't."

She'd never heard him sound so undone. "You won't."

"I have no idea who these people are, but they're asking for me."

"Could be anyone tied to a million cases over your career. Don't drive yourself crazy trying to figure out who. We'll take care of it."

"Please..."

"I love them, too, Avery. I'm on it."

"Thank you. I'm two hours out."

Sam could hear the fear in every word he said. "I'll keep you posted."

"Okay."

She slapped the phone closed. "Brant!"

He came out of the office with two agents so young, one of them still had acne. "These are Agents Quigley and Wright. They'll accompany you to Adams Morgan."

"I want lights and sirens."

"Yes, ma'am," Quigley said.

She'd have them kill the sirens when they got close, but there could be no more delays. Her phone rang, and she took the call from Freddie.

"Did you get the word about Shelby?"

"I'm on my way."

"I am, too. What do you know?"

"Only that there're two people in the house with her."

"I'll see you there."

Sam appreciated that he didn't get emotional or ask her how she was feeling or anything else she'd find irritating at a time like this.

"Don't hold my door," Sam said to the agents. "Just get in so we can go."

"Yes, ma'am."

They left the White House grounds with lights and sirens flashing, which of course would attract media attention, not that she gave a flying fuck about that with Shelby's and Noah's lives on the line.

Tension had every muscle in her body tight to the point of pain as she imagined what Shelby was going through with her home under attack from strangers. This was every law enforcement officer's greatest fear, that someone they encountered on the job would seek retribution in the most personal way possible.

If there was one good thing about Nick being president, it was that her family was protected by the finest security in the world.

"Kill the sirens a few blocks out," Sam told the agents.

"Yes, ma'am."

She wanted to tell them to quit calling her that, but she knew that was a losing proposition. It'd taken weeks to scrub the ma'am out of Vernon and Jimmy.

Thinking about that was better than worrying about what Shelby was dealing with. And Noah... God, Noah... He was so perfect and adorable and...

Sam couldn't think about him, or she'd lose her composure.

The entire block was lined with emergency vehicles and dark FBI sedans.

Without waiting for the agents, she got out of the SUV and

sprinted toward the hub of the action, nearly colliding with Avery's deputy, George Terrell. "What've we got?"

"Two individuals inside with Mrs. Hill and Noah. One of them has a Glock and is waving it around with no regard for who might be looking in the window."

"Do we have snipers?"

"On the way."

"Is that the plan?"

"It would be if we were certain there was only one gun."

"What's plan B?"

"We're working on that now with your SWAT commander."

"They're very important to my family, too," she reminded Terrell.

"Yes, I'm aware."

"How can I help?"

"Due to your personal relationship, you should probably let us handle it."

"Yes, I probably should, but I'd like to be involved. Please."

She'd added the *please* out of desperation.

"Sure. Whatever you want."

"Thank you, George." Sam followed him back to the group of law enforcement officers, who were huddled over a map of the townhouse.

"Mrs. Hill and her son are here," one of the officers said, pointing. "Suspect number one, a male, is in the room with them and has the Glock pointed at them."

Sam bit back a gasp.

"Suspect number two, a female, is in and out of the room. We haven't been able to ascertain whether she's armed."

Sam wanted to scream at them to do *something*. Anything.

Freddie came up behind her and put his hands on her shoulders.

She wanted to shake him off but never would.

Over the next few minutes, the MPD officers and FBI agents agreed on a plan to go in through all windows and doors at the same time and neutralize the suspects.

"Can we warn her?" Sam asked, concerned for Shelby's fragile state.

"No, ma'am," one of the MPD tactical officers said. "We wouldn't want to chance tipping them off."

"How long will it take to get everyone into position?"

"A few more minutes."

Sam spent that time with her eyes glued to the window where she could see the man holding them hostage. He was talking with his hands, waving the gun around. Shelby would be terrified. Sam was terrified for her—and Noah, who was hopefully sleeping through the nightmare.

"Are we sure that snipers wouldn't be more efficient?" Sam asked Terrell.

"What if we miss? He's got a gun pointed at them."

He was right, and Sam knew it, but she couldn't seem to speak around the enormous lump in her throat. So she nodded to acknowledge what he'd said. While she waited, memories of Shelby and Noah ran through her mind, starting with the day she and Nick had met the petite woman who'd become one of their closest friends, Sam's Tinker Bell. After she'd planned their wedding and become a close friend, they'd wanted to keep her in their lives, so they'd asked her to help with Scotty when he'd first come to live with them.

She and Noah—and Avery—were family to them.

"Keep breathing, Sam," Freddie said quietly. "They'll be okay."

Of course, he had no way to know that for certain, but she appreciated his confidence.

The smashing of glass startled her, and she'd known it was coming. She couldn't begin to know how shocked Shelby would be. Everything happened fast. Sam held her breath until she heard both suspects had been neutralized, and then she ran for the door. "Let me in," she said to the officer at the door. "She's my family."

The officer stepped aside.

Sam bolted toward the room where they'd been held.

Shelby was still on the sofa, holding Noah as she sobbed uncontrollably.

Sam went to her, put her arms around her and held on tightly. "It's over. You're safe." She kept one arm around Shelby while she called Avery. "They're safe."

"Oh, thank God. Tell Shelby I'll be there soon."

"We'll transport them to GW." Sam decided that was necessary because of Shelby's advanced pregnancy. "We'll meet you there."

"Tell her I'm coming."

"I will."

"And I love her." Avery's voice cracked on a sob. "More than anything."

"I'll tell her." She closed her phone. "Avery's coming, and he loves you more than anything."

Shelby was sobbing too hard to speak.

Sam took Noah so the paramedics could tend to Shelby. Holding Noah in her arms, Sam followed the paramedics outside.

"Ma'am?" the pimply Secret Service agent called to her.

"I'm going with her. Follow us."

"But—"

Sam turned her back on him, handed Noah to a paramedic, followed him into the back of the ambulance and took Noah back. Thankfully, the little guy was sleeping through all the trauma. He'd be sad to miss the public safety vehicles, though. He was obsessed with his toy police cars and fire trucks.

"How is she?" Sam asked the paramedics as they drove to the George Washington University Hospital.

"Her vitals are good, but we want to get her on a fetal heart monitor ASAP."

Sam hoped and prayed that the baby was safe and that Shelby would recover from the horrible shock. As she fished her phone out of her pocket she realized she didn't have the BlackBerry she needed to call Nick. So she called the White House switchboard.

"This is Mrs. Cappuano. Can you please put me through to the president?"

"I'm sorry, but I can't do that."

"This is Samantha Cappuano. I want to talk to my husband."

"Do you know how many calls we get every day from people claiming to be Mrs. Cappuano?"

"Please. Our friend was taken hostage. I need to get word to him that she and her son are safe. He'll be senseless with worry for them. I don't have the BlackBerry with me."

"I'll pass along the message."

"Please make sure that you do. It's urgent. Tell him to call me on my regular number."

"Yes, ma'am."

By the time she hung up, Sam thought she had the woman convinced that it was really her. She sure as hell hoped the woman delivered that message, or there'd be hell to pay at the White House.

. . .

Nick was relieved to get the message from Sam about Shelby and Noah and was heading to the bedroom to call Sam when Brant appeared in the hallway.

"Commander Rodriguez has asked for a minute. He says it's urgent."

Lieutenant Commander Juan Rodriguez was one of the military attachés assigned to Nick. They were the holders of the so-called "nuclear football" codes.

With the kids tucked into bed, Nick called Celia to tell her he needed to go to the office for a minute, but the kids were in bed.

"I'll turn on my monitor and keep an eye on it."

"Thank you, Celia."

"No problem."

He headed downstairs to the first floor and was surprised to find Commander Rodriguez waiting for him at the foot of the stairs, dressed in street clothes.

"Mr. President, I'm sorry to disturb you."

"That's all right, Juan. What's going on?"

"I'm not sure, sir."

Nick had never seen the man so rattled.

"Could we go to the Situation Room?" Juan asked.

The request only put Nick more on edge than he already was. "Of course."

Nick, Juan and Brant took the elevator down to the basement room that was the most secure space in the building. Brant keyed them into the room and gestured for Nick and Juan to go in while he waited outside. As soon as the door closed, sealing the two of them into the room, Juan turned to Nick.

"I heard something, and I don't know if it's true."

"Okay..."

"Wilson is planning something."

Nick had inherited Army General Michael Wilson as chairman of the Joint Chiefs of Staff from former President Nelson. The Joint Chiefs were made up of the top officers in all the services, and they served as the principal military advisers to the president. "What do you mean?"

"That's the thing. I'm not sure. A friend at the Pentagon told me that Wilson has been holding high-level meetings all week, but no one knows what's on the agenda. He said there's talk—and this is the part that could get me court-martialed in any number of ways, so you didn't hear it from me..."

"I would never give you up," Nick said, his stomach churning as he waited for the other shoe to fall.

"People are saying he's trying to organize a military coup."

His stomach went from churning to free fall.

"From what my friend has heard, Wilson and other members of the Joint Chiefs are concerned about taking orders from an unelected president who could declare war on behalf of the United States without a mandate."

Nick took his customary seat at the head of the table. The president's seat. "I don't know what to say."

"I'm sorry to have to tell you this, but I thought it was my duty to inform you."

"I'll never forget that you've taken a great personal risk to warn me, Juan."

"I couldn't let them do this to you without at least warning you."

"What should I do?" As the commander in chief, that he was asking a Navy commander for that kind of advice was humbling to say the least. But Juan had become a friend in the last couple of months, and Nick trusted him, especially now that he'd taken a considerable risk to warn him.

"Get your inner circle together and fire the Joint Chiefs. You'll also want to convene a military tribunal to try them for numerous charges, including possibly treason."

"Jesus." Nick was wholly unprepared to deal with something like this, which of course the Joint Chiefs knew. He picked up the receiver on the conference room table and pressed a button that connected him to the staffer who remained on duty in the West Wing twenty-four hours a day. His team took turns taking the overnight shifts.

"This is President Cappuano. Please contact Vice President Henderson, Secretary of State Sanford, Attorney General Cox, Defense Secretary Jennings, Mr. O'Connor and Mr. Kavanaugh and ask them to meet me in the Situation Room immediately."

"Yes, sir."

He put down the phone, his mind spinning with potential implications. With the exceptions of Cox, who had a reputation as an honest, decent man, and Jennings, who'd already earned Nick's respect, he'd invited only the people he'd appointed—those who were loyal to him.

The headlines would be brutal, even more so than the coverage of his mother and her crimes.

"You should go, Juan. I don't want you caught up in this." Nick stood to shake his hand. "Thank you."

"Yes, sir, Mr. President."

"Juan..."

"Yes, sir?"

"Please be careful. It's possible you're being watched."

"I understand, sir."

After Juan left the room, the phone on the conference room table rang with a call from the switchboard.

Nick picked it up. "Yes?"

"Mr. President, the first lady called again to tell you she's on her way to George Washington Hospital with Mrs. Hill and her son now."

"Thank you."

"She also asked that you call her on her regular cell number."

"Can you please make that call for me? I'll give you the number." The Situation Room had no cell service.

"Yes, sir."

"Did she ask to speak to me when she called?"

"Yes, sir, she did, but we get calls every day from people claiming to be her and asking to speak with you. Our policy is to put none of them through."

"We'll need to establish a code or something she can use to get through when needed."

"I will speak to my supervisor about that, Mr. President."

"Thank you."

"Please hold for your call."

Nick was treated to a recording about White House tours. He learned that the forty-five-minute tours were on a first-come, first-served basis and were arranged through congressional representatives and senators. He recalled fielding requests for White House tours through John O'Connor's office when he'd been John's chief of staff. That seemed like a hundred years ago now, when it was just over two years.

He needed to call Graham to come in, too. He would know how to handle this situation.

Nick put the phone on speaker so he'd hear Sam if she picked up the call and went to the doorway to speak to Brant. "Please send someone to pick up Senator O'Connor in Leesburg. Get him here as quickly as possible."

"Yes, sir."

"Nick?" That was all it took to calm him—one word from Sam. No matter what fresh hell was about to descend upon him, he would always have her. That gave him the kind of comfort he'd never had before he had her.

"How are they?"

"Shelby is badly shaken, and Noah is sleeping through it all. I'm staying with them until Avery arrives in about an hour."

"Is the baby okay?"

"They've got her on a fetal monitor, and the doctor said everything seems okay."

"That's a relief. Do you know who the people were?"

"Not yet. We're waiting for more info about them, but they were asking for Avery."

"Give Shelby and Noah all my love when you can."

"I will. How are things there?"

"I'm in the Situation Room."

"Ugh. That says it all, right?"

"You know it. Not sure how long I'll be, but I'll be up as soon as I can."

"I'll be waiting for you."

"Love you, babe. So glad our Shelby and Noah are safe."

"Yes, thank God. Love you, too."

Nick called the switchboard and asked them to notify Senator O'Connor that he'd sent a car for him.

"Yes, sir."

As he put down the phone and sat back in his chair to wait for his team to arrive, his heart went out to Avery Hill. Once upon a time, Nick wouldn't have imagined the day would come when he'd feel for the guy who'd once fancied himself in love with Sam. But once Avery had gotten past that nonsense, Nick and Avery had settled into friendship in support of Shelby, whom they both loved.

The threat to Avery Hill's family was a threat to all of them, and Nick would do whatever he could to ensure the safety of their friends.

Thinking about supporting them was better than dealing with the shitstorm that was about to unfold in his fledgling administration.

CHAPTER TEN

S till holding Noah in her arms, Sam sat by Shelby's bed while her friend slept. The doctors had given her something to calm her, as there was some concern about raised blood pressure. Or at least Sam thought that's what they'd said. So far, the news about the baby was good, which was a huge relief. Shelby was forty-two, so her pregnancy was considered high risk even without the recent threat to their safety.

Sam fought through exhaustion so she could stand watch over the woman who'd become one of her closest friends. When the nurses had brought a gown for Shelby to put on, Sam had asked if they had a pink one, which Shelby was now wearing.

She hoped her friend, who loved pink almost as much as she loved her husband and son, would appreciate that attention to detail. Was it only a few hours ago that Sam had met with Trulo and Malone and agreed to take a leave of absence from work?

That felt like weeks ago after the events of this evening.

Noah stirred and let out a squeak of protest at being held so tightly. He raised his head, saw Sam and gave her a gummy grin, displaying six adorable baby teeth.

"Shh, Mommy is sleeping," Sam whispered.

"Is he awake?" Shelby asked.

They were the first words she'd spoken since they arrived at the hospital.

"He is," Sam said. "Do you want him with you?"

"Yes, please."

Sam transferred the little guy to his mother's arms.

As Shelby held him close, tears rolled down her cheeks.

Sam stood and put her hand on Shelby's shoulder. "You're safe. Everything is all right."

"Keep reminding me."

"I will."

"Avery..."

"He's on his way. Should be here any time now."

"Do you know who they were?"

"Not yet, but don't worry. Everyone is on it. Just rest. That's what you need now."

"I was so scared, Sam. Not for me so much as Noah. I was afraid they'd hurt him to make a point or something."

"You kept him safe. That's all that matters."

Shelby took a deep breath and let it out slowly, the sound of sobs still echoing in her breathing. "Thanks for staying with me."

"Of course I stayed with you."

A rush of activity outside the curtain preceded Avery's arrival.

Sam had never seen him so disheveled or wild in the eyes as he rushed into the room and all but fell on top of Shelby and Noah.

Avery and Shelby sobbed as they clung to each other.

"Dada," Noah said.

"Yes, buddy, it's me. I'm here. I'm here."

Sam stepped out of the cubicle to give them a minute alone and found Freddie waiting in the hallway.

"How is she?" he asked.

"Seriously rattled, which is to be expected. She'll be better now that Avery is here."

"What the hell, Sam? How did this even happen?"

"I don't know. I'm sure the FBI is all over it. You can go home. I'm leaving soon, too."

"Call if you need anything."

"I will. Thanks for being there tonight."

"Of course. She's... Well, you know."

"Family. She's family."

"Yes." He glanced at her tentatively. "So, you're really taking a leave of absence?"

"A short one."

"I think it's a good idea. You should've taken more time when Spence died."

"That's been pointed out to me by others, so for once, I'm doing what I'm told. Something is off inside me. Not sure if it's that, but it's definitely something."

"Then you're doing the right thing. But are you sure I should be the lead on the Blanchet case?"

"I'm positive, or I wouldn't have assigned it to you."

"Shouldn't Gonzo do it?"

"He could, but we agree that you're ready for this. We want to give you the opportunity. Unless you don't want to."

"I do. I want to. I just… I hope you're right that I'm ready."

"You are, and you have been for a while now. If you weren't my partner, you probably would've had more responsibility before now. In that way, I've been holding you back."

"Don't say that. It's not true. The only reason I'm any good at this job is because of you."

"Nice suck-up. It'll be remembered at annual review time."

"I mean it."

"I know you do."

"Am I allowed to consult with you as the case unfolds?"

"I'd be disappointed if you didn't."

"I'm afraid I'll mess it up somehow."

"You won't. Gonzo will be watching."

"Okay, then…"

"Do what we always do. Follow the leads wherever they take you. Do the legwork. Pull the threads. Talk to the people. Draw your conclusions. You know the drill."

"I'll do my best to make you proud."

"You make me proud every day." She squeezed his arm. "How's Elin?" His wife had recently suffered a miscarriage.

"Better. I think. It's hard to tell. We'll go a whole day without tears, and then the next day is a disaster."

"That sounds about right. It's apt to be that way for a while."

"Good to know it's normal."

"It is, and I'm sorry you're finding that out the hard way. The good news is you'll both feel better with some time. When you're ready, you can try again."

"I guess. We'll see."

"Don't let the grief distract you from the goal, Freddie. You and Elin are meant to be parents. I'm sure of that."

"I hope you're right."

"When have you known me not to be?"

He rolled his eyes. "On that note, don't disappear on me, you hear?"

"Like you wouldn't know where to find me if I did. Start with the other partner in the medical practice tomorrow. Rory. Ask him about the screaming fight. You know what to do."

He nodded. "Just for the record, though, it won't be as much fun without you."

"Of course it won't."

Predictably, he groaned. "That was a softball."

"And I hit it out of the park. Go home. Get some sleep. Thanks for coming."

"Are you going home?"

"As soon as I get a chance to talk to Avery."

HE COULDN'T STOP TOUCHING their faces, kissing them, stroking their hair, breathing in their familiar scents. Avery had feared he'd never see them again, and now that they were back in his arms, he might never let them out of his sight again.

Shelby hugged him so tightly, he could barely breathe, but who cared about breathing when the love of your life was back in your arms after fearing she might be killed? And Noah... The little guy was teary-eyed because his parents were. Fortunately, he'd never remember this horrifying evening.

He and Shelby would never forget it.

"It's okay now, love," he whispered to Shelby. "I'm here, and you're both safe."

Her body shook with sobs that enraged him. Someone tied to him had done this to her. To them. He would make them pay for that.

Avery stayed with them until they finally settled into a restless sleep. Only then did he disentangle himself so he could start to figure out how his family had nearly met with catastrophe.

Sam waited for him outside the cubicle. "How are they?"

"Distraught but sleeping." He rubbed at the back of his neck, which was tight with more tension than he'd ever experienced. "What do you know?"

"Not much. There was a man and a woman. He had a gun. We

couldn't tell if she did, too. They're in federal custody, so George will know more than I do."

"Thanks for being here with her."

"I wouldn't have been anywhere else. Since you're with them now, I'm going to head home."

"Okay."

"Let me know if there's anything I can do."

"I will."

"I'll check in tomorrow."

He nodded and went back into the cubicle to be with his family. How would he ever leave them again for any reason? His phone rang, and he took the call from George. "Who are they?"

"Remember the Farmington case about seven years ago?"

"No way. Did they get parole?"

"Apparently, and their first stop was your house."

"Holy Christ." They were a couple of drugged out scumbags who'd been caught up in a federal investigation Avery had led into the trafficking of illegal guns. He felt sick knowing they'd been in his home and threatened his wife and son. A wave of nausea overwhelmed him. He bent at the waist, trying to breathe through it.

"We're booking them on the new charges now and will get them before a judge in the morning. I expect their parole to be immediately revoked."

Avery searched his memory bank for the people involved in the home invasion back then. He recalled wild hair and eyes, a deranged sense of entitlement, a desire to live in a country without a government, without laws or rules. That's who'd held his wife and son at gunpoint.

He thanked George for the info and ended the call. Avery stood next to the bed where Shelby slept with Noah in her arms. He leaned over the bed rail to kiss her forehead and then her cheek. "I'm so sorry, darlin'. I'm so damned sorry."

THE DOOR to the Situation Room opened to admit Attorney General Reginald Cox. At about sixty years of age, Cox had retained the muscular build of the football player he'd once been at Auburn University. He had wavy blond hair that had begun to go gray and sharp blue eyes.

He shook Nick's outstretched hand. "Mr. President."

"Thank you for coming."

"Of course. What can I do for you, sir?"

"I've summoned several others, but before they arrive, I have an important question for you."

"Sir?"

"Since you were President Nelson's attorney general, I need to give you an out if you aren't willing to defend my government against a possible military coup."

Cox's face went flat with shock. "A military coup."

"That's right."

"By whom?"

"The Joint Chiefs."

Cox blinked in disbelief.

"I'm giving you the chance to resign right now if you don't feel equipped to handle this situation."

"I, ah..." Cox pulled himself together and made eye contact with Nick. "I don't wish to resign, sir."

"And I can count on you to defend the Constitution of the United States in this matter?"

"Yes, sir."

Nick breathed a sigh of relief that his top law enforcement officer would have his back. After having inherited Nelson's cabinet, he was never certain of who among them he could trust. This incident had brought home the fact that he was going to have to have that same conversation with every one of Nelson's holdovers. Any refusal to uphold their oath of office would result in them being fired.

When Derek and Terry arrived, he took them aside to fill them in on what Juan had told him, while keeping his source confidential.

"*What?*" Terry asked on a long exhale.

"Holy shit," Derek added. "What's the plan?"

"I'll confront the Joint Chiefs with the information I've received and go from there. I expect I'll be demanding their resignations and turning them over to Cox for prosecution and to Secretary Jennings, who will handle the military portion of the program."

"The Joint Chiefs could be charged with treason," Derek said in disbelief.

"Yes," Nick said.

"Did your source say why?" Terry asked.

"I assume it's because I'm unelected, and they might have hoped to force a special election."

"Damn," Terry said.

Even with some time to absorb the information Juan had given him, Nick still felt the same sense of disbelief that he saw in Terry's stunned expression. "I've spoken to Cox. He's assured me of his fealty to me and to the Constitution and is prepared to do what needs to be done."

"This is going to be..." Derek gave him a wide-eyed look. "The biggest story in the world."

And Nick had thought his mother's arrest would be the biggest story of the day. That had nothing on this.

Secretary Tobias Jennings arrived next. Tall and silver-haired, with a serious expression that rarely ever became less so, Jennings had been running the Pentagon for five years.

Nick shook his hand and asked him the same question he'd posed to Cox.

"Sir?" Jennings's brows furrowed ever so slightly. "What are you asking?"

"It's come to my attention that the Joint Chiefs may have been planning a coup to overthrow my government, and I'd like your assurances that you can do what needs to be done to defend the Constitution in this situation."

For the first time in their acquaintance, Nick saw Jennings's expression shift from serious to shocked. "That's not possible."

"I assure you it is. The Joint Chiefs will arrive at any moment. I need to know I can count on you to handle this appropriately."

After a long pause, Jennings said, "Yes, sir. You can count on me."

"You're sure?"

"Yes, sir."

"Thank you."

"I'd like to say for the record that I had no knowledge of this," Jennings said, "and if I had, I would've brought it to your attention, Mr. President."

"That's good to know."

The others began to arrive, beginning with the vice president, Secretary of State Sanford, Joint Chiefs Chairman General

Michael Wilson and the other members of the Joint Chiefs of Staff. Graham was the last to arrive and took a seat at the table.

Secretary of State Jessica Sanford apologized for the formal red gown she wore. "I was at a dinner with my senior staff," she said as the scent of her Chanel No. 5 wafted across the table and added to the nightmare of this day for Nick. His mother's scent hit him like the usual fist to the gut any time he encountered it.

With far more important things to attend to, he shook that off as best he could and stood at the head of the table, hoping he conveyed command and authority. He would need both to get through the next few minutes. "Thank you all for coming in. It's been brought to my attention that the Joint Chiefs of Staff are plotting to try to remove me from office." As he spoke, he watched Wilson and noted when his gaze darted to Admiral Goldstein, the Navy chief, who had the good sense to look down at the table. That single look between the general and admiral confirmed that Juan's information was solid.

Secretary Jennings looked to Wilson for an explanation.

"Before you say anything, General, please be aware that you have rights." Nick looked at Cox, who seemed exquisitely uncomfortable as he reminded the nation's highest-ranking military officers of their rights in this matter.

Nick watched the scene play out with a feeling of detached disbelief even as he realized that future history books would cover this moment in detail. Never in the nation's history had the Joint Chiefs conspired to overthrow a president's administration.

"Do you understand these rights as they've been explained to you?" Cox asked the generals and admiral.

Each of them said, "I do."

"General Wilson," Nick said. "Were you and the other Joint Chiefs planning to overthrow my administration?"

Wilson hesitated, his gaze encompassing his colleagues. After a long, pregnant pause, Wilson said, "I'd like to speak to my attorney."

Nick gestured to the others. "Is there anything any of you wish to say?"

The others, looking as shocked as Nick felt as their military careers and lives as they knew them came to an end, shook their heads.

"In that case, you're relieved of your commands, effective immediately. General Cox, please take these men into custody."

"Yes, sir, Mr. President."

The FBI was brought in to conduct the arrests of the Joint Chiefs.

Watching that happen was surreal to Nick.

That none of them objected or declared their innocence told him that they were all in on it, which was unbelievable. How could none of them say to the others, *Hey, this might not be the best idea we've ever had*?

When each of them had been led from the room to be processed by the FBI, Nick sat back in his chair. "What do we do now?"

"You'll need to make a statement." Graham seemed as shell-shocked as Nick felt. "Right away. Tonight."

To Terry, Nick said, "Let the media know I'll be making a statement in the press room in thirty minutes."

Terry left the room to see to Nick's order.

The rest of the people gathered around the table seemed to be waiting for Nick to break the silence. "This is an unfortunate turn of events, but we'll press on with the job the American people expect us to do on their behalf. New chiefs will be appointed, and our national defense will remain strong and devoted to the defense of the Constitution."

"That's what you need to say in your statement," Graham said. "Exactly that."

"I'll take this opportunity to remind our service members stationed around the world that you're our commander in chief," Jennings said. "I'll make it clear that anyone unwilling to follow your orders should notify their chain of command so they can be dishonorably discharged."

Nick appreciated the secretary's loyalty to the Constitution, even if he might not fully support Nick as his commander in chief. "Again, I'd like to remind you that if you feel uncertain about continuing to serve my administration, you may submit your resignation at any time, with my thanks for your service."

"That won't be necessary, sir," Jennings said. "It's my pleasure to continue serving you and my country as secretary of Defense."

"Thank you, Mr. Secretary. I'm sure you have things to see to, if you'd like to go do that."

"Thank you, Mr. President." Jennings exited the room, leaving Gretchen, Jessica, Graham and Derek remaining.

"What the hell just happened?" Graham asked.

"I'm sorry about this, Mr. President," Gretchen said. "It's outrageous and unconscionable."

"Yes, it's both those things," Nick said. "It's been that kind of day around here."

"What can we do for you, sir?" Derek asked.

It still rankled to hear one of his closest friends call him sir, but he appreciated the respect, especially considering recent events. "I could use some help crafting the statement."

Derek reached for a pad and pen on the table, since outside electronic devices were prohibited inside the Situation Room. "Let's do it."

CHAPTER ELEVEN

As Sam and her detail approached the White House, they passed a line of FBI SUVs leaving the complex. "What's going on?" she asked the agent who was driving her.

"I'm not sure, ma'am."

He pulled up to the door, and another agent opened the SUV door for her. "Why was the FBI here?" Sam asked him.

"I don't know, ma'am."

Inside, Sam asked the first person she saw, Harold, one of the White House ushers, where she might find the president.

"I believe he's still in the Situation Room, ma'am."

Sam had decided that room was her least favorite in the White House because it required Nick's presence far too often for her liking. "Will you please get word to him that I'm home?"

"Yes, ma'am. Right away."

"Thank you, Harold." Sam trudged up the red-carpeted stairs to the residence, overwhelmed with exhaustion after the long, difficult day. She looked in on the twins and Scotty, all of whom were asleep, before heading for her and Nick's suite to change into pajamas. She was on the sofa with a glass of wine in hand when Nick came in, looking as stressed as she'd ever seen him.

Had something happened with his mother?

"I've got two minutes to tell you what's going on before I tell the rest of the world."

His hastily spoken words further spiked her anxiety, which was already out of control after the situation with Shelby. *What now?*

As he told her about Juan and the Joint Chiefs of Staff, she almost couldn't process what he was saying until he called it an *attempted bloodless coup d'état*. That she understood. She put down the wineglass, stood and went to him, wrapping her arms around him. "I'm so sorry, Nick. You must feel so..."

"Betrayed. I feel betrayed."

"And rightfully so. What will happen to them?"

"They'll be arrested and charged with plotting to overthrow the government of the United States, treason, sedition and numerous other things. Whether or not a case can be made that will stick remains to be seen."

"Wow."

"It's going to be the biggest story to ever come out of this White House, and I'll be smack in the middle of it, right where I don't want to be."

"This is no reflection on you."

"Of course it is, Sam. My top military officers were plotting to remove me from office. It's a reflection of what they think of me and my presidency."

"Or maybe it's just a reflection of their own craven desire for power."

"Either way, the fact that it's happening on my watch is humiliating."

"Don't be humiliated. You had nothing to do with it. You were asked to serve your country when Vice President Gooding fell ill. You stepped up to fill that position and the presidency when Nelson died. You're doing what was asked of you, which is all anyone can do."

"Maybe I should say that when I share this news with the world in..." He checked his watch. "Six minutes."

"Do you want me to come with you?"

"Nah, you're all ready for bed."

"I can change in two seconds. Wait for me."

"Hurry."

She ran into her walk-in closet, grabbed the first dress she saw, which was a rich navy blue, and put it on. Then she went into the bathroom, quickly applied the bare minimum of makeup before twisting her hair and pinning it up. Before she left the bedroom, she grabbed her diamond engagement ring and slid it on over the matching band. She took two seconds to tell Celia that she and Nick were heading downstairs for a bit.

Celia wrote back to let her know she still had her monitor on for the twins.

Thank you so much! Sam replied.

"Three minutes," Nick said when she came out of the bathroom. "Not bad."

"I like to think of myself as low-maintenance."

"You're super low-maintenance," he said, kissing her, "and I love you for that and a million other things."

She wiped lipstick off his bottom lip and took his hand as they left the room. "I love you, too. Remember what we always say—if we have each other, they can't touch us."

"Thanks for the reminder. I needed it after this day."

"And here we thought your mother's shenanigans would be the headline."

"Is it weird that I'm suddenly nostalgic for this morning, when I thought she'd be my biggest headache of the day?"

"It's very weird, but I won't tell anyone."

When he laughed, she was glad she'd come with him. He needed her, and she wanted to be there for him the way he always was for her. Holding hands, they walked to the briefing room and entered to find a crowd, even though it was nearly ten p.m.

I guess when the president himself says he's got something to say, they show up, Sam thought as she nodded to Vice President Henderson, who followed them onto the small stage at the front of the room.

Nick gave Sam's hand a squeeze before he released it and stepped up to the microphone. "Earlier this evening, it was brought to my attention that the Joint Chiefs of Staff were planning to try to overthrow my government in a military coup d'état."

A gasp went through the room.

"Upon receiving this information, I requested the Joint Chiefs report to the White House along with several senior members of my team, including Vice President Henderson, Secretary of State Sanford, Attorney General Cox and Secretary of Defense Jennings. When I relayed the information I'd been given to the Joint Chiefs, they didn't deny it. As a result, I have relieved them of their military duties, and Attorney General Cox has ordered the FBI to arrest them and charge them with crimes against the United States of America. It should go without saying that this came as a huge shock to me, to Vice President Henderson, Secretary Jennings and the rest of my administration. I'm saddened by their deceit and their treasonous behavior. And I don't use that word lightly. These actions were nothing less than treason, and with the help of the Justice and Defense departments, a full investigation will be undertaken, and the people involved in this plot will be held accountable.

"Secretary Jennings plans to communicate with all members of the military, inviting them to begin separation if they feel they're unable to serve their commander in chief with loyalty as well as fealty to the Constitution and all it stands for. Anyone who wishes to separate from the military will be dishonorably discharged with no further benefits or privileges.

"This is a heartbreaking day for our democracy, but we'll go forward from here, confident in the knowledge that our government is legitimate and working on behalf of the American people every day. You have my word on that. When former President Nelson asked me to take the place of the ailing Vice President Gooding, I did so with the full knowledge that I might be called upon to take President Nelson's place should the need arise. The Senate confirmed me with the full understanding that I would be the next president if President Nelson died in office. The fact that I am now the president is exactly what the framers of the Constitution intended when they dealt with the matter of presidential succession. Frankly, I'm tired of the words 'illegitimate president.' In the eyes of the Constitution, I am entirely legitimate. I'll take a few questions."

"Mr. President, how did you find out about the alleged plot?"

"From a confidential source."

"What did the Joint Chiefs say when you confronted them with your knowledge of the plot?"

"Chairman Wilson asked for his lawyer. The others had no comment, but none of them denied participating in the plot."

"With our top military officers allegedly focused on a plot like this, is our country safe?"

"Our dedicated military members around the world are standing watch tonight and every night to ensure the safety and protection of the United States and its citizens. No one should be concerned about our national defense nor convinced that there're weaknesses due to the actions of a few people who had an overinflated sense of their own power. Our country is as strong now as it was earlier today, before we knew about this nefarious plot."

"Mr. President, by anyone's estimate, this hasn't been a good day for you or your administration."

Way to state the obvious, dickwad, Sam thought.

"Can you tell us how you felt when you learned of the plot and also when you heard your mother had been arrested?"

Sam wanted to smack the reporter. Since she couldn't do that, she stared at him with intense focus, hoping she was making him uncomfortable.

"It was a tough day from beginning to end. When I heard about the plot among the Joint Chiefs, I felt disappointed more than anything. That these decorated military officers would risk their positions, reputations, pensions and freedom to get rid of me wasn't a good feeling, to say the least. But as I have since I took the oath of office, I moved quickly and efficiently to do what was in the best interest of our country and the American people. That's what I'll continue to do for as long as I hold this office. To reiterate what Christina told you earlier regarding my mother, I have no relationship with her, so I can't speak to her arrest or the charges. That's all for tonight. I'll update you again tomorrow."

Other reporters yelled questions at Nick that he ignored. He reached for Sam's hand and led her out of the room.

Vice President Henderson followed them.

"You handled that as well as possible, Mr. President," Henderson said.

"There was no precedent for it," Nick said. "That's for sure."

As she had on previous meetings, Sam picked up the same unsettling vibe from the vice president. The woman was strikingly gorgeous, with shiny dark hair, dark eyes made up to "pop" and lips covered in bright red lipstick that would look cheap on a lesser woman. On her, it was classy. Sam wished she knew why she'd taken an instant dislike to someone who'd never done anything to her, but her gut rarely steered her wrong. It was telling her she wasn't to be trusted. If that was true, Sam could only hope they'd find out why sooner rather than later.

"You've had a long day," Sam said to Nick. "Let's get to bed."

"See you tomorrow, Gretchen."

"Yes, sir. Nice to see you again, Mrs. Cappuano."

Sam should tell her to call her by her given name, but she didn't. "You as well."

"Frosty," Nick said when they'd walked away from Gretchen.

"What?"

"You with her."

"I was perfectly polite."

"Exactly. That's not like you."

"I'm offended."

"No, you're not," he said with a chuckle. "What's your beef with her?"

"I don't know, but it's something. You think she knows?"

"Nah, she doesn't know you well enough to pick up on that. But I do."

"I don't want to be right about her."

"I don't want that either. I have enough problems as it is. But she did mention she'd like to work with you on some of your signature issues supporting women and working mothers."

"Hmm, I'll take that under consideration."

"You do that."

They went upstairs to the residence, greeting the Secret Service agents, ushers and butlers they passed on the way.

"Do you think they're all talking about my military commanders plotting to oust me from office?"

"If they are, they shouldn't be working here."

"I don't know about you, but I've had more than enough of this day," Nick said.

"Right there with you." She hadn't even told him about the Blanchet case, the numbness or the leave of absence. "Any one of the things that happened today would be more than enough on its own. For all of it to happen in one day makes me want to run away."

"Take me with you," he said.

"Always."

Inside their suite, he pulled off his tie and unbuttoned his shirt. "You know what sucks?"

"Are you looking for a list? Because it's gonna be a long one."

"One thing in particular."

"What's that?"

"That if I wanted to run away, which I do, I can't. I'm trapped in a way I never have been before, even when I was VP."

"I know it may not give you much solace, especially after a day like today, but it's temporary. This whole situation is temporary."

"Three years feels like a lifetime on a day like today. Did that really happen? The Joint Chiefs plotting to remove me from office?"

She went to him and put her arms around him inside his unbuttoned dress shirt. "It happened. You dealt with it. You'll move on from here and stay the course."

He returned her embrace, holding her as tightly as he could, as if drawing strength from her.

Sam wanted to tell him about the leave of absence, but he'd had enough for one day. That would keep until tomorrow. Before she put her phone on the charger, she texted Avery to check on Shelby and Noah.

They're both sleeping, thankfully.

How about you?

Trying to come down from the adrenaline-fueled panic attack.

Sorry you guys went through such a scary thing. Do you know who the people are?

Unfortunately, yes. The scum of the earth. We're very lucky. That's all I can say.

I'll check in tomorrow. Try to get some rest. Keep telling yourself everything is fine until you start to believe it.

I'll try. Thanks for everything.

Love you all.

Back atcha.

When she joined Nick in bed a few minutes later, he put aside the briefing book he'd just opened and let it fall to the floor with a loud thud that made them laugh.

"The Secret Service will think we're under attack in here," Sam said.

"I don't want to think about them or anything but you."

"I'm down with that."

They met in the middle of the king-sized bed, arms and legs entwined, lips joined in a slow, lazy kiss that made all the stress of the day melt away like it had never happened. It'd still be there in the morning, but for right now, they could pretend the rest of the world didn't exist.

Nick rolled them so she was under him, his body molded to hers as he devoured her with his lips and tongue.

She loved him like this, a little wild and unhinged after an insane day and ready to work it out with her. And, oh, how she was there for that after the day she'd had. No one could erase the hard drive of her always busy mind like he could. When they were together this way, she focused only on him and the all-consuming desire that never failed to take her by surprise, even after all this time.

He created a fever in her with his lips, tongue and hands.

She reached for him only to be rebuffed because he wanted to tend to her.

Her moan of frustration made him laugh. "All in good time, my love."

"Hurry up about it."

"You know what happens when you rush me."

She let out an annoyed huff and felt his lips curve against her inner thigh. "Quit laughing at me," she said.

"My love is so very entertaining."

"I'll show you entertaining."

"What will this show entail?"

"Nick!"

When the bedside phone rang, he dropped his head to her abdomen. "Motherfucker."

Sam wanted to cry.

Nick reached across her for the phone and answered with a testy "Yes?" After a pause, he said, "Put him through." He gathered her into his embrace, whispering, "It's the AG. I have to take this."

"No problem," she said, even though she didn't mean that. Her body hummed with arousal and throbbing desire that would go unsatisfied for now. She focused on the low tenor of his voice and not so much on what was being said as she drifted between wakefulness and sleep.

The conversation droned on, so long that she dozed off and came to when Nick kissed her awake. "Sorry about that."

"It's okay."

"No, it really isn't okay, and I'm truly sorry."

"It's not your fault. Is everything okay?"

"I suppose it will be when the dust settles." He kissed her cheek and then her lips. "Now, where were we?"

"Can we move to the main event? I'm tired."

"We can continue this tomorrow if you'd rather."

"No, I wouldn't rather." She ran her fingers through his hair. "You left me hanging over here."

"Blame the AG."

"We hate the AG."

"We hate everyone."

"Except the kids…"

"Except for them."

Smiling, he kissed her as he smoothly used one hand to remove his boxer briefs.

As he slid into her, Sam released a sigh of happiness and contentment. "Mmm, best thing to happen all day."

"This might be the *only* good thing that happened today." His chuckle made her smile. "Well, Scotty's essay on NATO was pretty good, too."

"NATO is not allowed in this bed."

"Thank God for you," he whispered against her lips as he picked up the pace. "This makes all the bullshit worth it somehow."

"Yes, it certainly does."

CHAPTER TWELVE

F reddie arrived home to loud music coming from the second bedroom, where Elin had installed a small gym. He put his service weapon, cuffs and other work stuff into the bedside drawer and went to see what she was up to.

He nudged the door open, trying not to startle her. The sight that greeted him made his mouth go dry. Dressed in skintight workout clothes, she was bent in half, her perfect ass in the air.

She glanced in the mirror, caught his gaze and smiled. "Hello, dear. How was your day?"

"It just got much, much better."

He was so relieved to see her true smile for the first time since the miscarriage. For a few days, he'd feared that neither of them would ever smile again. But they were bouncing back, just as their friends and family had told them they would.

Elin stood upright and used a towel to wipe the sweat off her face. Then she crooked her finger for him to come to her.

He took a few steps so he was right in front of her and waited to see what she'd do.

She went up on tiptoes to kiss him.

Freddie put his hands on her hips. "You're not doing too much too soon, are you?"

"Nope. Just stretching. Feels good." She wiped her face again. "I told the gym I'd be back to work tomorrow."

"Are you sure you shouldn't take a few more days?"

"I'm sure. I read that getting back to a regular routine helps."

He wanted her to have more time to rest and recover, but that decision had to be up to her. "Guess what?"

"What?"

"Sam made me the lead on a huge new case today."

"Wow. That's amazing. Are you going to be the boss of her for a change?"

"Ha! No, she's taking a short leave of absence."

"Why?"

"She thinks maybe she came back too soon after Spence died."

"Oh, yeah, I can see that." She turned off the music. "I was going to make something for dinner."

"How about we go out?"

"I wouldn't say no to that. Let me just grab a quick shower."

"Take your time."

"Freddie."

He'd been on his way out of the room, but he turned back.

"You can stop looking so worried. I'm okay."

"That's all that matters to me."

"I know, and you've been wonderful. I couldn't have gotten through it without you. But I want to try to get back on track now."

"Whatever you need, love."

"I need you to stop looking at me like I might break. I won't. I promise."

"I love you so freaking much."

"That was almost a *swear*, Freddie Cruz," she said in a scandalized whisper.

"Just speaking the truth."

"I love you, too. We'll be okay, and in a few months, we'll try again, and we'll keep trying until we get it right."

"I'm here for the trying, any time you'd like."

Her bright smile was the best thing he'd seen in days. "I'll keep you posted."

While she went to shower, he retrieved his notebook from the drawer and placed a call to Kelly Goodson. "This is Detective Cruz from the MPD, circling back with another question for you."

"Of course. Whatever I can do."

"Were you aware that Marcel had been sued by four former patients for sexually inappropriate behavior while under his care?"

"*What?* No. I knew nothing about that."

"You said Liliana spoke to you about everything."

"She did, but she never said anything about that. Although..."

"What?"

"About a month ago, she started to seem really different, but I never could get her to tell me why. I wonder if that's when she found out about it."

"How did she seem different?"

"She was distant, distracted, not available to hang out the way we always did. That kind of thing."

"And that was unusual for her?"

"Very. When I say we were *best friends*, I mean that our friendship annoyed our husbands because we preferred each other over them sometimes. But I suppose it makes sense now that I know what was going on with them. She would've been mortified. How could he have done such a thing?"

"I don't know, but the lawsuit was going to court later this month."

"How can their deaths not be related to that?"

"We're investigating every possible scenario."

"You know, earlier, when we talked, all I could think afterward was that it couldn't have been a murder-suicide because Marcel was crazy about Liliana and the kids. But now that I know their lives were going to be blown to bits because of something he did? Maybe he did do it."

"Thank you for your insight. I'll be back to you with any other questions I have."

"No problem. I'm so sick over the whole thing. Whatever I can do to help."

After they said their goodbyes, Freddie sat on the bed thinking about what she'd said as the hair dryer went on in the bathroom. If he was still single, he would've gone to talk to Rory McInerny now rather than waiting for the morning. But since he was married to the stunning Elin Cruz, who was feeling better after their heartbreaking loss, he'd call it a night and take his wife out to dinner.

"BABE, YOU HAVE TO EAT SOMETHING," Cameron Green said to Gigi Dominguez. "You're freaking me out."

"I'm just not hungry."

"But your body needs nutrition. How about a protein smoothie? Do you think you could handle that?"

"I could try."

He kissed her cheek. "I'll make one." He'd brought her to his place after hers had been invaded by his ex-girlfriend, Jaycee, who'd threatened Gigi and sexually assaulted her before Gigi had shot and killed her.

Cam wasn't sure which part of the nightmare was causing the greatest amount of distress for Gigi, but it didn't matter. She'd taken to his bed several days ago and had barely left it since, except to use the bathroom and shower.

His phone chimed with a text from Gigi's partner, Dani.

How is she?

Same. I'm getting worried. She's not interested in eating. I'm going to try a protein shake. If that doesn't work, I'm out of ideas.

I'll bring you one from the place she likes. Be there shortly.

Thanks, Dani.

No prob.

Dani had been a lifesaver since the events with Jaycee. She'd come every day, bringing something she thought Gigi might like, from chocolate to fruit to bagels to her favorite salad. All of it was in the fridge, waiting for Gigi to show some interest.

Cameron was sick with guilt over what'd happened to her. He felt like he'd somehow brought the hellish events into her life by deciding to end his relationship with Jaycee. But everyone, even Gigi, kept telling him it wasn't his fault. He'd had every right to end a relationship that was no longer making him happy and to start a new one with someone who made him happier than he'd ever been.

He knew they were right, but still he blamed himself.

Dr. Trulo had come to the house to meet with them, and Cameron had talked to him about the guilt. Trulo had done what he could to help Cameron deal with those feelings, but it was a work in progress. He kept coming back around to the fact that Jaycee wouldn't have known who Gigi was if it hadn't been for him. She would've had no reason to break into Gigi's home, to hold her hostage, to viciously assault her or force Gigi to do something she'd never done on the job—end a life to save her own. And now Internal Affairs would be investigating the use of her service weapon, which was the last thing any police officer needed.

The whole thing was unbearable.

They had a huge, complicated new case he should be thinking about, but the only thoughts on his mind were centered on Gigi and how to get her through this ordeal.

It was a good thing Jaycee was dead, or he'd be tempted to kill her himself and to hell with the consequences. Her mother had also been killed by SWAT after she'd taken Jeannie McBride hostage. Two of the closest people in his life had been traumatized because of his ex. He was having a very hard time living with that.

Dani texted. *I'm here.*

Cameron went to open the door for her.

"Hey," she said as he stepped aside to admit her.

"Thanks for coming."

"No problem." Tall, blonde and gorgeous, Dani was the sort of woman he'd always been attracted to until the first time he'd seen Gigi and realized he'd been very wrong about what he found attractive.

Because she was on duty, Dani wore a radio on her hip that crackled with traffic. "I can't stay." She handed the smoothie to him. "Tell her I was here, and I love her."

"I will. She'll appreciate the smoothie."

"Tell her she can thank me by drinking it."

"I'll tell her."

"Are you okay, Cam?"

"I won't lie. I'm struggling with my part in this."

"You had no part in it. If we have to tell you that for the rest of your life, we will."

"Wouldn't you feel responsible if you were me?"

"Maybe, but I'd listen to the people around me who were telling me the truth and absolving me of responsibility for something I didn't do."

"I keep picking over every minute I spent with Jaycee, looking for signs she had this level of evil in her, and there was nothing. I would've seen it."

"Yes, you would have, and she clearly kept that side of herself hidden from you and others, who are also expressing shock at what she did."

He hadn't heard that. "What're they saying?"

"Just that the Jaycee they know never could've done such a thing. That kind of stuff."

"They didn't know her. I didn't know her."

"You knew what she wanted you to know—and so did they."

"I guess."

"I've got to run. I'm stretched thin tonight with a long to-do list before my tour ends."

"Thanks for bringing the smoothie."

Dani surprised him when she kissed his cheek. "Be kind to yourself, Cameron. No one blames you for this, especially Gigi."

With that, Dani departed.

Cam waved to her from the door, then closed and locked it and shut off the outside light. He took the smoothie up to Gigi, who was lying on her side, staring at the wall. "Dani came by and brought your favorite smoothie."

"That was nice of her."

"She said you can thank her by drinking it. And she said she loves you."

That got a small smile from Gigi, who moved to sit up and take the drink from him.

Cameron took the paper off the straw and stuck it in the top of the cup.

Gigi took a tentative sip and then another. "That's so good."

Cam breathed a sigh of relief that she was consuming something.

"My girl knows what I love."

"We all want you to feel better."

"I'm working on it."

Cam sat on the edge of the mattress. "Do you want to talk about it?"

"Not really, but I know I need to."

"I've heard that helps," he said with a smile.

As she continued to sip the smoothie, she seemed to be collecting her thoughts. "The thing I can't stop thinking about was whether I could've done something other than kill her. I keep going over it and trying to find another way out that doesn't end with her being dead."

Cameron stroked her pretty face. "You saved yourself, which is what anyone would've done in that situation. She wouldn't have let you leave alive."

"No, she wouldn't have, but I can't stop thinking about firing that shot, the sound it made when it hit her or the expression on her face when she realized she was going to die." Gigi shuddered. "I really wish that hadn't happened."

"I wish the whole thing hadn't happened, but like everyone has been telling us, this was on her, not us. She's the one who came into your home uninvited, pulled a knife on you, did other unspeakable things to you and forced you to defend yourself."

"I know there was nothing else I could've done, but still... I'll never forget that."

"The reason you feel this way is because you have such a kind and loving heart and could never hurt someone the way she tried to hurt you. I'd be worried if you weren't upset about it. But... You have to take care of yourself as you work through this. You've got us all so worried about you."

"I'm sorry about that. I've just felt too sick to eat anything." She held up the smoothie. "This is tasting good to me, though."

"Dani to the rescue." Cameron tucked a strand of her dark hair behind her ear. "I'm so sorry this happened. I'll be sorry forever about this."

"I'll never blame you, in case you're worried about that."

"That makes me a very lucky guy."

"We're both lucky, and we can't let her come between us or she wins, even from the grave."

For the first time in days, Cameron felt like he could lean in and kiss her.

Her hand came to rest on his face, cold from the smoothie.

He startled.

She laughed, and he felt the tension inside him finally ease a bit. If she could laugh, maybe they'd survive this.

"What'd I miss at work today?" she asked.

"Nothing much." She didn't need to hear about the murders of six people, including four innocent children.

"I got an email that my IAB hearing is next week."

"It's routine."

"Still," she said, "it's my first time with Internal Affairs."

"You'll be fine. You'll tell the truth of what happened and be back on the job as soon as you're ready."

"I really hope so."

.   .   .

NICOLETTA SAT IN HER CELL, staring at the cinderblock wall on the far side, waiting for something she now realized wasn't going to happen. Her son wasn't going to fix this for her, and by now, the FBI had searched her office.

Her stomach knotted. That rat-faced lawyer certainly wasn't going to save her, and she sure as hell wasn't built for prison.

She had to get out of there.

Rising, she went to the bars. "Hello? Is anyone there?"

"Shut up, you old bitch," a woman said from across the aisle. "People are trying to sleep."

Nicoletta ignored her. "Is someone there?"

A sheriff's deputy approached her cell. "What do you need?"

"I need to get out of here. I have things to do."

"Don't we all?" the woman across the aisle said. "What makes you special?"

"Your arraignment is scheduled for the morning," the deputy said. "You can tell it to the judge then."

"But I need to use the restroom."

The deputy pointed to the toilet bowl in her cell. "That's your restroom right there."

"I can't do that in front of everyone," Nicoletta said with outrage.

"Then I guess you'll have to hold it."

The deputy walked away, leaving her to her misery. She turned, eyed the bowl with trepidation and wished she had this day to do over so she could've put on something more comfortable than her red silk robe, which was starting to feel slimy.

She went to the bowl, turned, lifted her robe and hovered above it before she wet herself. Her thighs burned from the effort to keep her skin from connecting with the toilet. In the corner of her cell, a camera was trained on her. She wondered if there'd be video of the president's mother peeing in a jail cell posted online before morning.

This was all his bitch wife's fault. Nicoletta had no doubt about that, and when she got out of here, she would make her life a living hell, if it was the last thing she ever did.

CHAPTER THIRTEEN

The morning headlines on the TV news channels summed it up:

JOINT CHIEFS PLOT TO OVERTHROW CAPPUANO ADMINISTRATION.

Coverage was feverish on all the morning shows, and pictures of the highest-ranking military officers in the country in orange jumpsuits had sent the media into a feeding frenzy the likes of which Washington hadn't seen since Watergate.

Sam came out from the bedroom wearing the white silk robe Nick had given her for Valentine's Day last year and sat next to him on the sofa.

"Morning," he said.

She kissed his cheek. "Morning. How bad is it?"

"About as bad as it gets. Plenty of people are calling the Joint Chiefs courageous patriots for trying to do what needs to be done, including the former secretary of State."

"And I'm sure plenty are outraged over their disrespect for the Constitution."

"Seems to be evenly split."

"I'm sorry, Nick. It's such a terrible betrayal."

"Yes, it is, but all I can do is carry on and do the job and hope for the best."

"No one would blame you if you called out sick today."

"Can the president do that?"

"I would think the president can do whatever he wants."

"That would just cause more speculation that I'm not courageous enough to show up after my military tried to overthrow me."

"I suppose it would add to the chatter."

"Why aren't you getting ready for work?" he asked.

"I, um, well... I'm taking a small leave of absence."

"What? Why? When did that happen?"

"Yesterday."

"Start talking, Samantha." He hated when she kept stuff from him, even if it was because he was having a hellish day. "And don't leave anything out."

"We caught a new case yesterday. Parents and four kids shot to death in their home. From what we've learned, they were a nice family with successful parents, lovely kids. A gun was left to make it look like the dad did it. It's probably a case of murder-suicide, but we're treating it like a possible homicide until we're sure. Or, at least my squad will be doing that."

"Without you."

She nodded. "After we left the crime scene yesterday, I realized I was feeling off."

"How so?"

"I was numb. I had no reaction to seeing four young kids dead in their beds. It was just another day on the job. No big deal. And when I asked Trulo why that might be, he said it could be because I didn't take enough time off after Spencer died." After a pause, she added, "You know how I was hell-bent on finding the person who sold him the laced pills."

"And you didn't take any time to grieve."

"Something like that, although I didn't think I would grieve him the way I did my dad, since we weren't particularly close."

"Sure you were. He was married to your sister for eight years, and she truly loved him. He was the father of your niece and nephew and part of your family. You were close to him."

"You know what I mean."

"I do. You didn't *love* him the way you love Mike, but you were still close to him."

"Something like that. It sort of threw me to realize that might be what was going on."

Nick put his arm around her. "You've had a rough few months, babe. I'm not surprised it finally caught up to you."

"I kind of am."

"Because you always power through, but everyone has their limits, even a superwoman like you."

"I hate having limits."

Nick laughed as he put his arm around her. "Of course you do." She rested her head on his chest.

"What're you going to do with your free time?"

"I have no freaking clue."

"You can come to work with me."

"Um, as appealing an offer as that is..."

Nick lost it laughing, which pleased her greatly. Keeping things light for him where she could was her most important job as first lady.

"How about I visit you at some point?"

He gave her a squeeze. "I'll look forward to 'some point' all day."

FREDDIE ASSEMBLED the squad in the conference room. He was so nervous that he'd been unable to eat that morning, which anyone who knew him would find unbelievable. But he'd never been put in charge of a case before, and he wanted to make Sam and the other brass proud of him.

On the way into work, he'd heard the news about the Joint Chiefs and had been flabbergasted and distressed for his friend, the president, who must be reeling from the treachery. Freddie wished there was something he could do for Nick, but right now, he needed to keep his focus on the case. He'd call Sam after his shift to update her and see how they were doing. Yesterday had been one hell of a day for all of them.

Deputy Chief Jeannie McBride and Captain Malone joined the group.

"I've asked Dr. McNamara and Lieutenant Archelotta to brief us," Freddie said. "They'll be here shortly. In the meantime, let's go over what Detective Carlucci accomplished overnight."

"Can we talk about the headlines this morning first?" O'Brien asked. "What the actual fuck with the Joint Chiefs? Has anyone talked to Sam?"

"Not yet," Freddie said. "I'm sure they've got their hands full with that, and we have six bodies in the morgue that require our attention today." That was something Sam would say. He wanted to keep the focus where it belonged, like she would've done. "Back to what Carlucci uncovered."

"She ran the family's financials and found they were running low on money," Detective O'Brien said. "Most of their accounts had balances below fifty dollars, except for the primary joint checking account, which had three hundred. The balances were much lower than usual. Carlucci went back about six months and found their average balance then was between fifteen and twenty thousand."

"So cutting back on his medical practice had caused immediate financial pain," Freddie said. "Were there any unusual expenditures over the last few months?"

"Not that she saw," O'Brien said. "Just the usual sort of household expenses, some transfers here and there to other accounts, some jointly held and others belonging to one or the other of them. Routine stuff."

"Carlucci also did a deep dive on the parents' social media as well as that of the oldest daughter, Eloise," Green said. "She couldn't find active accounts for the younger kids. The father didn't have much of a social presence except through the practice, which posted frequently with photos of new babies that received a lot of likes and comments. The mom posted about her kids mostly and a few memes here and there about stuff she found funny. She posted press coverage of Eloise's meets and a few articles about her as an Olympic hopeful.

"Eloise posted about gymnastics competitions. There were quite a few posts of her with medals, and Carlucci noted an unusually high number of people clicking the angry response to those photos. Dani made a list of the people who gave the angry-face response. She found that most of them were gymnasts of the same age or their parents."

"So the parents of other gymnasts were giving Eloise the angry emoji?" Jeannie asked. "That's screwed up."

"It's bad enough the other competitors were dissing her," Malone said. "But the parents..."

"I think, after we talk to the father's other partner in the practice, we start there," Freddie said. "Do you all agree?"

"I do," Green said as the others nodded in agreement.

"Gonzo? You're good with this plan?"

"It's your investigation, Detective Cruz. You're the boss."

If they'd been alone, Freddie would've told his friend to cut the crap, but since they weren't, he split the gymnasts' parents' names between himself and Gonzo as well as Green, O'Brien and Charles. "Let me know if anything pops."

"Will do," Green said as he headed out with the more junior detectives.

"Let me know if I can help," Jeannie said.

"Same," Malone said. "Crime Scene is still at the house. I'll let you know if they find anything useful."

Lindsey McNamara came in with a cup of coffee in hand. "Sorry I'm late. We just finished the last of the autopsies. I emailed the report to Sam."

"She's out for a bit," Freddie said. "Can you forward it to me?"

"Is everything okay?" Lindsey asked.

"Yes," Freddie said.

Lindsey withdrew her phone and tapped on the screen. "Sent the report to your email."

"Thank you."

"We've had a number of people tell us that certain things Marcel Blanchet had done recently were wildly out of character for him," Freddie told Lindsey. "Is there anything medical that could've caused that?"

"Sure, any number of things. I can do some further testing on him before I turn the bodies over to the funeral home."

"That'd be great. I'm not sure there's anything to it, but I'm following a hunch."

"It's a good thought and definitely worth further examination. I'll keep you posted."

"Thanks, Doc."

Archie came in looking harried and frazzled, per usual. His IT unit was one of the busiest in the department. "It's been slow-going on the devices, but we're making headway. We focused first on the parents' phones as well as the older two kids who had phones. I should know more later today."

"Thanks, Archie."

"I heard Sam is taking a leave," he said. "Is that true?"

"It is." Freddie could tell Archie and Lindsey, both friends of Sam's, wanted more info, but they'd have to get it from her.

"Please keep Detective Cruz in the loop," Gonzo said to Archie. "He's leading the investigation in Sam's absence."

"Okay." Archie gave them both a curious look before he left the room.

"Let me know if you have any questions about my report," Lindsey said. "They all died of gunshot wounds. Eloise was the only one of the kids shot more than once, and as I've already reported, the father had gunpowder residue on his right hand."

"Thanks for the info."

"Are you looking at it as a murder-suicide?" Lindsey asked.

"We're keeping an open mind," Freddie said.

"Sounds good. I'll let you get to it."

"Have a good day," Freddie said as she left the room. To Gonzo, he said, "It's not my place to explain where Sam is, right?"

"You handled that just right. They're her friends, and they'll reach out on their own."

"That's what I figured. Let me take a quick look at the autopsy reports, and then we can hit it."

"Sounds good, boss."

"Cut that out."

Gonzo laughed. "Why would I do that when it makes you so uncomfortable?"

"This whole thing makes me uncomfortable."

"It should. It's a big deal to oversee a homicide investigation. A lot of people are counting on you."

"No pressure much."

"You can handle it. You're ready, or Sam wouldn't have put you in charge."

"She should've put you in charge," Freddie said.

"She wanted to give you the chance, and I agree it's time."

"You'll make sure I don't screw it up?"

"You won't need me to do that. You've got this, Freddie."

"Thanks for the vote of confidence. I need it."

"Which is why we're giving you the chance to build your confidence. You know what to do. You've been training for this moment for years now."

"I had no idea this moment would arrive so soon."

"Sam is thrusting you out of the nest and making you spread your wings."

"You think she's okay?"

"She will be. In time."

AFTER THE KIDS left for school and Nick went downstairs to work, Sam wasn't sure what to do with herself. The White House staff took such good care of everything for them that there wasn't laundry to fold or any other mundane tasks to keep her mind busy.

Her closet could use straightening, but she didn't feel like tackling that project today.

So she poured another cup of coffee, took it to the sofa and turned on the TV to see what was going on with the Joint Chiefs story.

Former Secretary of State Martin Ruskin was doing an interview on one of the morning shows.

"If you ask me," he said, "the Joint Chiefs have done a patriotic thing by trying to force a special election."

"You would say that," Sam said, "after Nick fired you for cavorting with Iranian bimbos."

"How we find ourselves in this situation is unfathomable," Ruskin said. "That a man only elected once to the Senate now holds the most powerful position on earth is something that should terrify every American."

Sam wanted to throw things at the TV.

"An argument could be made that President Cappuano has every right to hold the office after the Senate confirmed him to be vice president," the female commentator pushed back. "If President Nelson and the Senate had faith in him, shouldn't that be enough for us?"

"It's not enough," Ruskin said, sputtering with outrage. "The American people deserve better."

"How does the fact that he fired you as secretary of State play into your animosity toward him?"

Ruskin gave her an incredulous, how-dare-you-ask-me-that look. "That has nothing to do with it."

"Right," Sam said. "Sure it doesn't."

"The man is incompetent and has no business serving as president."

"Recent polls show that more than fifty-five percent of Americans approve of the job he's doing as president, an approval rating that's somewhat unprecedented in modern polling. What would you say to them?"

"I'd tell them to look behind the curtain," Ruskin said. "He's got a polished exterior, I'll give him that, but underneath the surface, is anything there? I don't want to wait until one of our enemies is attacking us to find out he doesn't have the chops."

Sam was outraged listening to him. She found the BlackBerry and texted Nick. *Ruskin is going off on you. Someone needs to shut him up.*

He texted back a few minutes later. *We're working on a statement to tell the public how and why he was released from his SoS duties. We haven't spelled out the details yet. Gonna do that now.*

Good call. I'm glad you're on it.

Don't worry about me, babe. I can handle the heat.

I do worry about you, and I hate people. Especially Ruskin.

Haha, down, girl. What are you up to?

I'm watching daytime TV. I hear this is what people do when they don't have jobs.

You could always spend some time in your office downstairs... If you want to, that is.

I plan to stop in to say hello later.

Excellent. Don't forget to come by here, too.

I won't. xo

Her other phone rang with a call from her sister Tracy. "Hey, what's up?"

"Thought you'd like to know my baby girl got into Princeton."

"What? Oh my God! That's amazing news! I'm so proud of her."

"I am, too. When I think about where she was not that long ago... And now this."

"She must be thrilled."

"She is, but for all the wrong reasons, of course."

Sam laughed. Brooke wanted to transfer from the University of Virginia to Princeton in the fall so she could be with her Secret Service boyfriend, Nate, while he served as the lead on Elijah's detail. "Nate's a great guy. He's worth turning her life upside down so they can be together."

"I hope so."

"He's good people. We all like him."

"That matters to her—and to me. Are you at work?"

"Nope. I'm home."

"Thought you caught a big new case yesterday."

"We did. Freddie is taking the lead."

"Why? What's going on?"

"It was determined that I didn't take enough time off after Spence died, and I might not be in the right frame of mind to effectively do the job."

"Determined by whom?"

"Trulo and myself."

"Really, Sam? You took yourself off the job? Have you been abducted by aliens or something?"

Sam laughed. "Nothing quite so dire. Just a strange feeling of numbness and detachment from the case of the moment had me wondering what might be wrong. So I'm taking a short break."

"To do what?"

"That's what I'm trying to figure out. So far, watching daytime TV isn't working out so well. I got to watch former Secretary of State Ruskin talk about how Nick has a shiny exterior, but there might not be anything under the surface."

"He's a bitter son of a bitch. Don't listen to him. He nearly got us into a war with Iran."

"Nick's team is drafting a statement to tell people that, but I hate to hear someone talk about him like that."

"They're talking about the person who holds an office they all wish they could occupy. They're not necessarily talking about your husband."

"I suppose that's true."

"It is true. How about we take lunch over to Ang and see how she's doing?"

"That's the best offer I've had all day. See you there around twelve thirty?"

"Sounds good."

"I'll ask my friends the butlers to whip up something yummy for us."

"Yay, can't wait. See you there."

CHAPTER FOURTEEN

S am showered, got dressed in jeans and a sweater and then called the chief usher, Gideon Lawson.

"Good morning, Sam," he said, pleasing her with the use of her first name.

"How do you know it's me?"

His soft chuckle came through the phone. "The call is from the residence, and I happen to know you haven't left for work yet."

"In other words, you're running a very elaborate spying operation."

"'Spying' is such a strong word for observing."

"I see," she said, smiling. She liked this guy. "I was wondering if you and the kitchen wizards could whip up a little picnic to go for three people and a couple of kiddos."

"We can take care of that for you. Any special requests?"

"My sisters will want salad, and I've been thinking about that chicken salad sandwich I had last week for days. The kids would love some chicken and mac 'n' cheese."

"Got it. We'll have it ready for you at noon."

"You're the best. Thank you."

"Not working today?"

"I'm taking a day off. Maybe a couple of days. We'll see."

"Good for you. Enjoy the break. See you at noon."

"Thanks, Gideon."

"Always a pleasure."

How lucky were they to have such great people to call on for anything they needed? Everyone who worked at the White House was so nice and gracious. They made living in the most famous house on earth such a fun experience. She would be honest and say she hadn't expected it to be quite so amazing when they moved in, but the staff had made them feel truly at home there, and she would always appreciate the effort they made every day.

She went downstairs and stopped short when she realized Vernon was waiting for her. "Whoops. I knew I forgot something."

"I was wondering where you were."

"I'm taking a brief leave of absence from work."

"Everything all right?"

"Apparently, I didn't take enough time after my brother-in-law died." She shrugged. "So I'm taking a short break."

"I see. For what it's worth, I think that's a good idea."

"It's worth a lot coming from you," Sam said with a warm smile for the agent who'd become a friend. "I'll be heading to my sister Angela's house a little after noon."

"Sounds good. We'll be ready."

"Thank you."

"My pleasure, ma'am."

Sam left him with a playful scowl for the ma'am, which made her feel a hundred years old, even if she'd heard it every day since Nick became president. She walked toward her East Wing office, thinking that she probably should've told Lilia that she would be stopping by.

Oh well, she thought. *Incoming...*

THE RECEPTIONIST'S eyes nearly popped out of her head when she saw Sam come into the suite. She stood so abruptly that she nearly spilled her coffee. "Mrs. Cappuano. How nice to see you!"

"You as well. Are you new?"

"I am. I'm Kaitlyn. It's so nice to meet you."

Sam shook her outstretched hand. "Likewise. I'm going to pop in to say hello to Lilia."

"She'll be thrilled to see you."

"Hey, Sam," Roni Connolly said as she came into the office.

Sam gave her friend a quick hug. "You look wonderful," Sam said, noting that Roni's pregnancy was starting to show.

"Thanks. Nothing fits anymore, but otherwise, I'm doing well."

"I was going to say hi to Lilia. Want to join us?"

"Sure," Roni said, following Sam to Lilia's office.

Her chief of staff lit up with a surprised smile when she saw Sam, making Sam realize she needed to come by more often.

"Mrs. Cappuano," Lilia said. "How nice to see you."

"It's Sam, and it's nice to see you, too."

Roni closed the door as Sam sat in one of Lilia's plush visitor chairs. Everything Lilia touched was classy, even her office chairs.

"What brings you by on a workday?" Lilia asked.

"I'm taking a bit of time off," Sam said. "Things have been intense lately."

"Indeed," Lilia said. "I'm glad you're taking a break. How's Angela?"

"Doing okay, I guess. Tracy and I are going there at lunchtime to check on her."

"I think of her all the time," Lilia said with a sigh.

"Me, too," Roni said.

"Thank you. She's lucky to be surrounded by an amazing group of family and friends."

"Please let her know we're thinking of her," Lilia said.

"I will. So what goes on here?"

"We're working on some social media posts for you and fielding media requests about the situation with Nick's mother."

"We have nothing to say about that," Sam said.

"Which is what we've been telling them," Roni said.

"What's the latest with her? Have you heard?" Sam asked.

"Just that she's awaiting arraignment," Lilia said.

"I love that she spent the night in jail," Sam said. "Does that make me a bad person?"

"In light of the president's history with her, I would say that makes you human," Lilia said.

"Agreed," Roni said. "Whatever happens now, she deserves it."

"How crazy is the thing with the Joint Chiefs?" Sam asked tentatively.

"It's big," Lilia said. "And unprecedented. The West Wing is on fire. The primary goal today is to assure the rest of the world that the Cappuano government is intact and that the perpetrators of this scheme will be punished."

Sam grimaced. "I can't believe this happened."

"It's disgusting," Lilia said. "I hope they all go to prison for the rest of their lives."

"That'd be good," Sam said, "but will it happen?"

"People are saying it should," Roni said.

"On both sides of the aisle?"

"Surprisingly, yes," Roni said. "The Constitution is very clear on presidential succession. Your husband was confirmed by the Senate to be the vice president. It's that simple."

"And that complicated when the president died," Sam said, "and the unelected vice president became president."

"Yes," Lilia said, "but there's no question of who the president is or who the president should be. They had no right to do what they did."

"Won't it make people wonder, though?" That concern had been on her mind since she first heard about the Joint Chiefs' scheme. "When the nation's top military officers basically have no confidence in the administration, why should regular people?"

"It's apt to have a bit of a ripple effect at first," Lilia conceded, "but his polling numbers are exceptional since the State of the Union, and with both sides deriding the actions of the Joint Chiefs, he should be fine."

Should be fine wasn't enough for Sam. "This kind of thing was why I was so glad when he decided not to run." She could trust these women with her true thoughts. "I hate that people are gunning for him when all he's doing is the best he can in an enormously difficult situation."

"He's doing great," Roni said, "and regular people see that. What the Joint Chiefs did is a betrayal of their oaths to defend the Constitution. Trevor, Christina and the communications department are doing an excellent job of keeping the focus where it belongs—on them and what they did."

"That's good. It's just so stressful. Everything is so stressful." Sam looked up in time to see them exchange glances. "Don't do that. I'm fine. I swear. It's just a lot."

"Yes, it certainly is," Lilia said with an empathetic expression.

Sam spent the next hour discussing pending commitments, social media posts and other first lady details, including the upcoming National Association of Police Organization's TOP COPS keynote speech they were writing for her to deliver in May.

"Did you get the email I forwarded about you officially being nominated for a TOP COPS Award?" Lilia asked.

"I saw something about that. I still wish they'd pick someone else."

"It's a huge and very well-deserved honor," Roni said.

"If you say so," Sam said, already embarrassed about the attention that would come with the award.

"We say so," Lilia said with a smile.

"I appreciate all you guys do for me."

"It's our pleasure to support you," Lilia said.

"How are the wedding plans coming along?" Sam asked Lilia.

Her face flushed with a rosy blush. "Very well. While you're here, I wanted to ask if you might be an attendant on behalf of Harry, who said, 'Please ask Sam because she's like a sister to me, and you love her, too.' If I promise to keep dress fittings to a minimum and prohibit any sort of inane games at the shower, would you consider it?"

"Lilia," Sam said, amused and touched. "I'd be honored." She would also be an attendant in Lindsey and Terry's wedding, while Nick was Terry's best man. Nick was right when he said it was shaping up to be a busy summer.

"Thank you. I can't believe the president and first lady will be in my wedding party."

"Believe it. We love you, and we love Harry. We're thrilled to be part of your big day. I trust you'll tell me what you need when you need it?"

"I've got you covered, as always."

"Thank God for you."

A few minutes later, Sam and Roni got up to leave.

"Roni, could I have a quick moment?" Sam asked.

"Of course. Come in." She led Sam into her office, which featured an antique typewriter on a shelf and several awards that Sam took a closer look at.

"Those are from when I worked on my college newspaper."

"Very impressive." Sam turned to her friend. "Derek told Nick you guys are officially seeing each other, and I just want you to know that I think it's wonderful."

"Oh, thank you," Roni said with a small smile. "It's all so strange, you know?" She placed a hand on her pregnant belly.

"Everything has changed since Patrick died, and it's probably way too soon, but..." She shrugged. "Derek makes me smile again."

"I love that for you. For both of you. You've been through so much."

"It's made it easier for me to open this door, because he understands what I'm going through like no one else in my life ever could."

"I'm so glad you have that kind of support."

"He's been great, and my Wild Widows have, too. It's amazing how all these new people have come into my life, and a few I thought would be there forever have kind of faded away."

"People don't know how to handle a loss like yours."

"Too bad for them. How do they think I feel?"

"That's right. I'm glad you're surrounding yourself with people who can show you the way forward. Derek is a wonderful guy, and Maeve is just delightful."

"I'm madly in love with her."

Sam hugged Roni. "I'm so happy for you, and I wish you guys all the best."

"Thank you for the good wishes. I fear that some people might not understand what I'm doing with Derek so soon after losing Patrick."

"They don't need to understand. As long as it works for you, that's what matters."

"That's what I tell myself. And it's really nothing more than very close friendship at this point."

"You're doing great, and I'm proud of you for surviving something that would've wrecked most people."

"It did wreck me, and it continues to. From what my widow friends tell me, it always will. But Patrick wouldn't want his death to ruin my life, so I'm trying not to let that happen."

"Good for you. Keep me posted on how it's going with Derek."

"I will. Thanks for caring."

"I really do. About both of you and Maeve."

"Thanks, Sam."

"We'll talk again soon."

"Look forward to it."

. . .

SAM LEFT the East Wing feeling as if things were under control there thanks to her wonderful colleagues. Without them, there was no way she could've continued in her job with the MPD while serving as first lady. Thanks to social media, she was able to look active and engaged in the job even when she wasn't. Not really, anyway.

She followed the now-familiar path to the West Wing, where she was always greeted with reverence. It would've been amusing to her anywhere else, but it was just another reminder of how much their lives had changed.

"Is he free?" Sam asked the admin outside the Oval.

"Yes, ma'am, he is. Go right in."

"Remind me of your name."

"It's Ginger."

Oh right, she should've remembered her from his VP office. "Thank you, Ginger."

"Of course, ma'am."

It was a ma'am kind of day. That's what she got for staying home from work.

Sam gave a quick knock on the door to the Oval Office and then stepped inside, closing the door behind her.

Nick looked up from what he was doing, and the pleasure that overtook his expression would probably be the single best second of her day. As he got up from the Resolute Desk to come to her, Sam was amazed at the butterflies that still invaded her belly any time he was near.

"Hello, Mrs. C," he said, kissing her. "How's your day off going?"

"Not bad. How's your day from hell going?"

"Could be worse, I suppose."

Sam smiled and reached up to caress his face. "Anything I can do to make things better?"

"You already did just by walking through that door."

CHAPTER FIFTEEN

Nick held her so tightly, it should've hurt, but it didn't.

"I was about to grab a bite to eat. Want to join me?"

She had about forty-five minutes until she needed to leave to meet her sisters. "Sure."

Nick extended his hand to her and then led her through his sitting room off the Oval Office into a private dining room.

"I had no idea this was here," Sam said.

Nick held a seat for her at the table and then leaned in to kiss the side of her neck. "That's because you're never here at lunchtime."

"I'm sorry for that," she said as he took a seat next to her.

"What? Why?"

"I'm never here to have lunch with you."

"That's fine, Sam," he said with the smile that made her life complete. "I rarely get to eat in here anyway."

"Do you have time for it today?"

"Nope, but I'm doing it because I want a few minutes with my gorgeous wife."

"How're you holding up?"

"I'm fine, all things considered. My mother was arraigned earlier and held without bail since she's apparently a flight risk. It seems the judge saw right through her BS."

"Well, that's good, I guess. At least she can't start a dumpster fire if she's in jail."

"That was my thinking, too, although it's still hard to believe my mother is in *jail*."

Roland, one of the White House butlers, came into the room with a tray that he placed on the table. "Hello, ma'am. I heard you'll be joining Mr. President for lunch."

How did they seem to know everything without being obtrusive? It was their special gift. "You heard correctly, Roland."

"What can I get for you?"

"How about a tossed salad with grilled chicken, Italian dressing on the side." She could have that and a little something with her sisters, too.

"No onions, right?"

Sam smiled. "That's right. Good memory."

"It's my job to remember what you prefer, ma'am."

"You do your job very well."

His smile lit up his face. "My pleasure. I'll be right back."

"Certain aspects of White House life don't suck," Sam said.

"No, they don't."

"Go ahead and eat while we wait for mine."

He took the cover off his plate, which had a turkey club and curly fries that he covered in ketchup.

Sam stole one of them and popped it in her mouth before she could think of all the reasons why she shouldn't. The first one was so good, she had a second and then a third.

Nick pushed his plate closer to her to give her easier access.

Sam pushed it back toward him.

He pushed it halfway back.

She took another fry and gave him a glare.

He laughed. "Eat the fries, babe."

"I can't. They go straight to my ass."

"I love your ass, and mine is the only opinion that matters. I vote for more ass."

"No more ass. There's more than enough."

"Never enough."

"What are you hearing from the honeymooners?" she asked of Elijah and Candace.

"He texted me about the Joint Chiefs and said it was an outrage. I asked if he's been going to class, and he said they do come up for air every now and then."

Sam laughed. "They must be so happy to be back together."

Candace's parents had had the twins' older brother, Elijah, charged with statutory rape when he was seventeen and she was fifteen. After not having had any contact for three years, they'd recently reunited after her eighteenth birthday and surprised everyone by getting married.

"I think they're deliriously happy. He said he's looking forward to seeing us for spring break."

"I can't wait to have them home."

Roland returned with another tray and set Sam's lunch on the table with silverware rolled into a cloth napkin. "I took the liberty of bringing some of the iced tea you like, too, ma'am."

"You're spoiling me rotten, Roland."

Roland grinned and placed another plate on the table with the chocolate chip cookies she and Nick had gone crazy over when they'd first had them. She'd told the butlers to keep them far, far away from her after the first indulgence. "For you, Mr. President," he said with a wink for Sam.

"Well played, Roland," Nick said.

"Please let me know if I can get you anything else."

"Thank you," Nick said.

"Yes, thank you, Roland," Sam said. "I'll call you when my clothes don't fit anymore."

"We can get you some new clothes, ma'am."

Sam and Nick were still laughing when he exited the room.

"Such a nice guy," Nick said.

"They're all so nice."

"They make it fun to live here."

"Yes, they do," Sam said as she put the smallest possible amount of dressing on her salad. "But those cookies will be the death of me."

"What a way to go, though." He reached over to put his hand on top of hers. "I had no idea how much I needed this until you arrived and showed me."

"Glad to be of service."

"It's amazing how I can be having the shittiest day in the history of shitty days as the first president ever to have his Joint Chiefs try to unseat him. And then you walk in, and it's like none of that matters. There's only you."

"You do know how to make a girl swoon, Mr. President."

He took back his hand so he could feed her another fry.

"It occurs to me that maybe I should cut back at work so I can be here for you like this more often," she said hesitantly.

His hand froze as he was in the middle of eating a fry. "What?"

Sam shrugged. "I'm just saying... You're kind of trapped in hell here, and if it makes things better for you to have me around, then maybe I should be around more."

He ate the fry, but his gaze never left her face. "You would hate that."

"Not as much as I hate you being stressed."

"I'm always going to be stressed, whether you're here with me or not, and I'll be extra stressed if you're unhappy, which you would be without your job."

"Maybe not."

"What is happening here?"

"I'm not sure."

"Do I need to be worried?"

"Not at all."

"Right... You're saying you'd rather spend your days at the White House than at work, and I'm not supposed to worry?"

"I don't want to add to your plate. It's already full to overflowing."

"I'd push the rest of it aside if my wife needed me, and she knows that."

"She does know that, but you need to keep your eye on the ball here."

"I'm an incredibly accomplished multitasker, as my wife also knows."

Sam smiled at the sexy innuendo. "Yes, you are, but I'm working out some things in my mind about the job. I've got to figure that out before I decide anything."

"Where'd this come from all of a sudden?"

"I don't think it's sudden. It's a bunch of things kind of coalescing into this existential sort of crisis. Stahl trying to kill me twice, Arnold dying, the ongoing war with Ramsey, my dad dying, Conklin sitting on info that would've solved my dad's case, the injustice we've uncovered with the cold cases, my broken hip, Spencer dying..." When she glanced at him, she saw him watching her intently. "All combined, it's taken some of the shine off the place for me. It happens to other people on the job all the time."

"But not to you."

"No, never to me. In fact, I used to scoff at people who'd say they were burned out. Like, how can you burn out on a job that's so much fun?"

"You're the only person who thinks the murder beat is fun."

"I'm not the only one. People who do my job are a different breed. We're wired differently. We cope differently. It's how we can do it in the first place without going crazy from what we see every day. There's, like, a shield that protects us from the emotional fallout, and lately, I've been feeling like my shield has gone missing. Dr. Trulo is the one who said Spencer's death might've been the thing that finally made that happen."

"I can see how that might be possible. Can you?"

"Yeah, I see it."

"You were like a woman possessed trying to get answers for Ang and the kids. You didn't take one second to *feel* the loss of someone you cared about."

"No, I didn't. I tried to keep that separate from the case, and then once we figured out what'd happened, it overtook me like a tsunami. Angela's husband is *dead*. Jack and Ella's father is *dead*. Spencer is *dead*. She's having another baby. It's all so... big."

"Yes, it is, and it also forces you to think about what you'd do if it happened to you."

Sam put her hands over her ears. "Don't even say that."

He tugged on the arm closest to him. "I don't expect anything to happen to me, but your sister losing her husband gives you a front-row view of what it would be like. That's all I'm saying."

"You may be right about that," Sam said with a sigh. "I keep reliving the hours in the hospital, when it became clear he wasn't going to survive. That's the part I can't get out of my head."

"It's your biggest fear come to life right in front of you."

"Is it terrible for me to admit that part is the most upsetting to me?"

"Of course not. We all know you cared about Spencer and appreciated how good he was to Ang and the kids."

"I did, and he was."

"I think it's perfectly normal to put yourself in her shoes and to wonder how you would cope if it happened to you."

"I refuse to ask myself or anyone else that question. I'd never survive it."

"You would."

"I wouldn't."

"Yes, you would, just like I would if the worst happened to you. It'd be ugly, but we'd find a way through because we have kids depending on us, just like Ang does."

Sam shook her head. "I honestly don't think I could go on if you were gone."

"You could, Sam."

"I wouldn't want to."

"Neither would I, but we'd do what needed to be done for our kids."

"Can we stop talking about this?" Sam pushed the remains of her salad aside. "It makes me sick to think of anything happening to you."

"Likewise, love, but it could be why you're feeling odd, no?"

"I suppose so." She forced a smile so he wouldn't worry about her. "I'm sure I'll shake it off in no time."

"Take the time you need to feel better. They'll get by fine without you for a while."

"Freddie is in charge of his first case."

"Oh wow, that's exciting."

"I can't wait to watch him shine."

I'M A TOTAL SCREWUP, Freddie thought as he and Gonzo chased after the father of one of Eloise's gymnastic rivals. The guy had taken one look at them, identified them as cops and run off. *I also need to get back to the gym right away.* They'd had no luck locating Rory McInerny at his new home—or he'd chosen not to answer the door—so they'd decided to speak to the Cortez family while they were in the area.

Freddie's legs burned from the effort to keep Pascal Cortez in sight as they pursued him through the McLean Gardens neighborhood as curious onlookers watched from the sidelines. While he ran, Freddie reviewed what they knew about Pascal. His daughter Lacey was a competitive gymnast. Cortez and his wife, Gia, had commented on Eloise "coming from nowhere" to win all the big competitions that year.

Sam would've had him run a check on the guy before they showed up at his house. He'd failed to do that, and now he was chasing someone who could be a violent criminal, for all he knew.

But he and Gonzo were gaining on him.

With a burst of speed, Gonzo came from behind Freddie and did a dive tackle, taking Cortez down to the pavement with a sickening-sounding thud. Thankfully, they were all wearing a lot of clothes in deference to the cold. Otherwise, both men would've lost some skin.

"This is police brutality!" Cortez screamed as Gonzo cuffed him.

"I wish I had a dollar for every time I heard that," Gonzo said. "I could retire early." He hauled the man to his feet and marched him several blocks to where they'd left their car.

"I want a lawyer."

"That's another one we never hear. Right, Cruz?"

Freddie, who was still trying to catch his breath, nodded. "You know it."

"You can't talk to me without a lawyer present. I know my rights."

"Have you had them read to you a time or two?" Gonzo asked.

That shut him up.

After Gonzo had loaded him into the back seat of his car, Freddie went to the front door of Cortez's house and rang the bell. A young girl came to the door.

"Is your mom home?" Freddie asked through the storm door.

She held up a finger and then closed the door.

Freddie wondered if she was Lacey.

The inside door opened to reveal a dark-haired woman with purple circles under her eyes.

Freddie showed her his badge.

She opened the storm door.

"Gia Cortez?"

"Yes, that's me."

"I'm going to need you to come downtown with me, my partner and your husband, who's in our custody."

"What's this about?" she asked, her eyes rounding with shock.

"We'll talk about it when we get there."

"I can't leave my children home alone."

"Is there someone you can call to stay with them?"

"I... Um... I can ask my neighbor."

"Why don't you do that?"

When she started to walk away, Freddie followed her into the kitchen, where she placed the call to the neighbor, asking her to come stay with the kids.

"I'm not sure how long I'll be gone," she said with a wary glance at Freddie. "Can you come now?" After a pause, she said, "Thank you so much." She ended the call. "She'll be here in a minute."

"Great."

"Am I under arrest?"

"Have you committed a crime?"

"No!"

"Why did your husband run from us?"

"He, um... I'm not sure."

Freddie could tell she was lying. "It'll take us all of five minutes to find out why he ran, so you could save us that time by just telling me."

"There might be a warrant for his arrest."

"For what?"

"He... He left the scene of an accident."

"Why did he do that?"

"Because our insurance had lapsed, and he was afraid of getting arrested." As her eyes filled, she looked away from him. "We've had some financial issues."

"Mommy, what's wrong?" The girl who'd answered the door came into the kitchen.

Gia reached for her. "Nothing, honey. Mommy and Daddy have to go take care of something. We'll be back in a little bit. Mrs. Gersh is going to come stay with you and the boys."

The girl gave Freddie a wary glance.

Mrs. Gersh's arrival gave him an excuse to get out of there while Gia got her kids settled.

On the porch, he gave Gonzo the one-minute signal.

"Not sure why the guy ran from us," Gonzo said. "He's not in the system."

Interesting, Freddie thought. He'd left the scene of an accident and had gotten away with it, but he didn't know that. He filled Gonzo in on what the wife had told him.

"Ah, that explains it. Funny that we never would've known about that if she hadn't told us."

When Gia came out of the house, Freddie got her settled in the back seat next to her husband.

"What's this about, Pascal?" she asked tearfully. "And why are you bleeding?"

"These cops attacked me."

"Don't forget to mention the part where you ran from us," Gonzo said as he pulled the car into traffic.

"We want a lawyer," Pascal said.

"Who would you like us to call for you?" Freddie asked him.

"How should I know? I've never needed one before."

"I'll notify the public defender's office, but they're pretty backed up. It's apt to be tomorrow or the next day before they can get to you."

"We can't wait that long!" Gia said. "We have children."

"I'm sorry," Freddie said, "but once you've requested an attorney, we can't speak to you in any official capacity until you're represented. Should I call the public defender's office?"

"No!" Gia said. "We haven't done anything. We have nothing to hide."

"If you rescind your request for an attorney," Freddie said, "hopefully we can get this taken care of sooner rather than later."

The comment was met with a stony silence.

"Pascal! Tell them we don't need a lawyer. We haven't done anything!"

"There was the accident…"

"That's not what this is about," Freddie said.

"Then what?" Gia asked. "What do you want with us?"

"We'll talk about that back at headquarters," Freddie said. "If you rescind your request for an attorney."

"Fine," Pascal said. "No lawyer."

"Pascal—"

"Shut up, Gia."

CHAPTER SIXTEEN

They passed the rest of the ride in silence. When they arrived at HQ, they brought the couple in through the morgue entrance and straight to an interrogation room.

Freddie started the recorder in the center of the table. "Detective Cruz and Sergeant Gonzales with Pascal and Gia Cortez in reference to the Blanchet case."

Gia nearly levitated out of her seat. "We had nothing to do with that! We barely knew them!"

Gonzo placed printouts of Facebook posts with their comments highlighted.

Gia: *Where did this girl come from all of a sudden, and how is she allowed to outshine girls who've spent years in this program?*

Pascal: *I'd like to know that, too.*

Another post showed Eloise on a podium with two other girls. Eloise was in the center with a gold medal, while two other girls were on either side of her, one with a silver medal, the other bronze.

Freddie pointed to the silver medalist. "Is that your daughter?"

"Yes," Gia said, "but what—"

"And is that your comment about your daughter being 'robbed' by someone who 'doesn't deserve' the accolades?"

Gia stared at the highlighted comment. "I, um... Yes, I wrote that, but I was just saying what everyone is thinking. Look, other parents said the same thing!"

"We're talking to them, too."

"Blanchet killed his family," Pascal said. "It was a murder-suicide."

"That hasn't been confirmed," Freddie said.

"Well, we didn't do it," Gia said. "We didn't like them, but that doesn't mean we killed them. You aren't accusing us of that, are you?"

"Where were you the night before last?"

"We were home!" Gia's voice took on an almost hysterical edge. "With our children. We didn't even know where they lived until we saw the report yesterday about them being found dead."

"How did you feel when you heard they were dead?" Freddie asked.

"Horrible!" Gia said. "We felt horrible, like any decent people would."

"Were you glad Eloise wasn't going to be a threat to your daughter's aspirations any longer?" Gonzo asked.

"We were sad that four children were murdered," Pascal said in a low tone, as if he was trying to contain his rage. "We weren't thinking about gymnastics when we heard that news."

"Really?" Gonzo asked. "You never gave a thought to your daughter's rival being eliminated?"

"We didn't," Gia said. "We were shocked and saddened to hear of such a senseless crime. Lacey was devastated to hear Eloise was dead."

"Were they friends?"

"Not outside of gymnastics," Gia said. "They went to different schools."

"And Lacey considered the girl who'd been winning all the competitions a friend?"

"Yes, she did."

"Does she know what you thought of Eloise?"

"We had nothing against her personally," Gia said.

"I find that hard to believe," Gonzo said. "Your posts would say otherwise."

"We were upset with the *situation*," Gia said. "Eloise started gymnastics *two* years ago. Lacey has been in the program since she was three. She's put in the time and the work. It wasn't fair."

"So let me get this straight," Gonzo said. "Eloise was newer to the sport, so she didn't have the right to excel at it?"

"That's not what I said!"

"Isn't it? Didn't you just say she didn't have the right to win because she'd only been competing for two years rather than ten?"

"I didn't say she didn't have the right. I said it wasn't fair."

"Who decides what's fair?" Freddie asked.

Gia gave him an incredulous look. "How is that even a question? Someone who's put in ten years of hard work versus someone who hasn't?"

"But was it Eloise's fault that she was more talented?"

Gia's expression hardened. "She wasn't more talented. That's not true. Lacey was the most talented girl on their team. Everyone said so."

"Until Eloise showed up and ruined everything?" Freddie asked.

"What are you accusing us of?" Gia asked, giving her husband a nervous look.

"Did you kill Eloise and her family to get them out of your daughter's way?"

"*What?*" Gia said on a shriek. "Did we *kill* them? No, we didn't kill them!"

"When we get the security footage from the Blanchet's home, will we see you on it?" Gonzo asked. It was a good bluff since there was no security footage from the home.

"No!" Pascal said. "We've never been anywhere near there."

"Uh," Gia said on a stammer, "I have. I was there. Once. Two weeks ago."

Pascal spun around in his seat to look at his wife. "What the hell were you thinking?"

"I wanted to talk to Mrs. Blanchet, mother to mother," Gia said, seeming embarrassed.

"About what?" Pascal asked.

Freddie appreciated him asking the questions for them.

"Just about how things work in our club," Gia said.

"And how did that go over with Mrs. Blanchet?" Gonzo asked.

"She asked me to leave and to quit being a racist asshole," Gia said.

Freddie wished he could give Mrs. Blanchet a high five for the spot-on comment.

"It wasn't a racist thing," Gia said. "It's not about that."

"You're sure about that?" Gonzo asked. "Because it kind of feels racist to us."

"It's not! We aren't like that! We love everyone."

"Except Black girls who humiliate your daughter in competitions she was supposed to win?" Freddie asked.

"That's a vile thing to say," Gia said, her eyes shooting flames at Freddie.

"The truth hurts, huh?" Gonzo asked.

"Is that all you dragged us here for?" Pascal asked. "To ask if we're racists who killed an entire family because their daughter beat ours at gymnastics?"

"Pretty much," Gonzo said. "We've seen flimsier motives for murder than this one."

"We didn't kill them," he said. "And unless you have proof that we did, we'd like to leave now."

Gonzo looked to Freddie to make the call.

"You're free to go," Freddie said, "but stay local and available in case we have follow-up questions. And here's a pro tip. The next time we ask whether you were ever at their house, don't lie."

They got up and left the room without another word.

Freddie followed them out. "Pascal, before you go, there's the matter of the hit-and-run you were involved in."

The couple stopped walking, but they didn't turn back.

"If you'd like to make a report about your involvement in the accident, we won't charge you for leaving the scene," Freddie said. "You can take care of that in the lobby. The officer at the desk can help you complete your report."

Their backs stiffened as they proceeded forward.

"I'll make sure they file the report," Gonzo said.

"Thanks."

Freddie went to the conference room and added the info they'd gotten from the Cortezes, which wasn't much, to the murder board. He sat at the table and stared at two photos of each victim —one from when they were alive and the other from their autopsies, noting that Eloise had been shot in the forehead, face and neck, unlike her siblings, who were shot only in the forehead. What did it mean that Eloise was shot multiple times? In light of their conversation with the Cortezes, Freddie wondered if this whole thing would come down to a rivalry between two young gymnasts. But try as he might, he couldn't make the leap to something like that being a motive for murdering an entire family.

"How's it going?"

Freddie startled at the sound of Captain Malone's voice behind him. "Okay, I guess." He filled the captain in on what had transpired with the Cortezes. "They were the most vocal in their disdain of Eloise's success in gymnastics, so we figured they were worth a conversation. After the father ran from us, they insisted they had nothing to do with it, even if they did resent that Eloise had come to the sport recently and knocked their kid off her throne."

"Why'd the dad run?"

"He'd left the scene of an accident and assumed there was a warrant for his arrest. We're making him file a report on the accident before he leaves."

"Do you believe they had nothing to do with the murders?"

"They adamantly deny any involvement. I don't know what to believe. If you look at the evidence we have so far, the father lost his mind, killed his family and then himself. Maybe the truth is as obvious as it seems." Freddie ran his fingers through his hair. "It's just that the grandmother—the father's mother—was so certain that was something he'd never do. She was adamant. He loved his family more than anything. He cut back on his work schedule to spend more time with them."

"He was also facing a lawsuit filed by four women accusing him of inappropriate conduct while he was their doctor." Archie handed a printout to Freddie. "That's the archive of his email. I've highlighted the parts that are relevant to the lawsuit. Three weeks ago, he spent twenty thousand dollars to retain an attorney to fight the lawsuit."

"We knew about the lawsuit, but the twenty K could explain why they were short on money." Freddie read the email exchanges between the doctor and his attorney, in which Marcel adamantly denied ever doing anything improper with a patient. "I wonder why that didn't show up in the financial report Carlucci put together."

"Could it have come from the practice?" Malone asked.

"I suppose," Freddie said.

They're trying to ruin me, Marcel had written to the attorney. *And why? All I ever did was take care of them during complicated fertility treatments. None of them ever expressed any sort of discomfort or unease to me at the time. This comes as a complete shock to me.*

"If he was facing professional ruination, would that give us a motive for a murder-suicide?" Malone asked. "I want to know why the women didn't try to file criminal charges."

"They did." Archie produced more paper that he handed to Freddie. "The allegations were investigated by SVU, which chose not to bring charges because there was no evidence of improper behavior. It was the women's word against the doctor's."

"Who investigated for SVU?" Malone asked.

"Ramsey," Freddie replied.

"Of course," Malone said. "Is this all the documentation of the investigation?"

"Everything I could find," Archie said.

"Great work as always, Archie," Malone said. "Cruz, go talk to Erica Lucas and find out what she recalls about this investigation. I'd rather not have to talk to Ramsey about it if we can avoid that."

SVU Sergeant Ramsey was currently out on bail awaiting trial on felony charges after he rammed Sam's Secret Service vehicle with his car.

"Yes, sir." Freddie headed upstairs to the SVU offices and was relieved to see that Erica was there. "Hey, Detective Lucas."

"Hi there. What's up?"

"You heard about the Blanchet case."

"Murder-suicide?"

"We haven't determined that for sure yet, but we understand the father was investigated for potential sexual assault claims made by patients."

"Let me look." Erica fired up her computer. "I heard it was a tough crime scene."

"Always is when kids are involved."

"Yeah, for sure." She did some more typing. "I can see that Ramsey investigated and found there wasn't evidence to support criminal charges."

"We have his report, but do you remember anything about the investigation?"

"I can't say that I do. Are you looking at that as a possible motive?"

"We're not sure. We were hoping to avoid having to ask Ramsey."

Erica grimaced. "Don't blame you there. I heard he's preparing to file a lawsuit against the department for his son's death."

"That doesn't surprise me." MPD sharpshooters had killed

Detective Ramsey's son, Shane, after he took a woman hostage in a local park. They'd tied Shane Ramsey to numerous rapes and murders before the incident that had led to his death. "He can sue all he wants. That was a clean shot."

"You and I know that, but you can't tell him." She glanced up at him. "How's Sam doing since her brother-in-law passed?"

Freddie knew Sam considered Erica a friend. "Between us?"

"Of course."

"I think she's struggling a bit. She's taken some time off, which she didn't really do after he died."

"That sounds like a good idea. I'm not sure how she or her husband function with so much coming at them all the time. This latest thing with the Joint Chiefs is just insane."

"It really is, not to mention his mother and all of that."

"She's disgusting."

"Always has been, from what I hear. Well, thanks for checking for me. If you think of anything, you know where to find me."

"Will do. Give Sam my best when you talk to her."

He nodded and headed back downstairs, planning to track down Rory McInerny next and then talk to the women who'd sued Marcel Blanchet.

WHEN SAM ARRIVED at Angela's, she and Tracy were already seated at Ang's kitchen table with hot beverages in front of them. Sam recognized the decaf herbal tea that Angela drank when she was pregnant and grimaced. If there was one good thing about her inability to conceive, it was that she didn't have to give up the caffeine that powered her days.

Sam put the bags of food she'd brought with her on the counter. "Lunch, compliments of the White House."

"Yummy," Tracy said, opening bags to investigate.

"There's coffee, Sam," Angela said. "I just made it."

"Don't mind if I do," Sam said, helping herself.

"What're you doing here in the middle of a workday?" Angela asked.

"Taking a little time off."

"Since when?"

"Since yesterday when I realized I needed a break."

Out of the corner of her eye, she saw Angela glance at Tracy, who shrugged.

"From what Trulo tells me, the death of your husband has affected me more than I initially thought."

"When did you have time to even think about it when you were relentlessly chasing down the people who sold him poisoned pills?" Angela asked.

"Exactly. Call it a delayed reaction, not that I wasn't devastated over it from the beginning."

"I know what you mean," Ang said. "You were so caught up in *why* it happened that you didn't have time to fully feel it."

"Yes, something like that. You know how much I love being shrinked, but I had to admit that the good doc was on to something when he pointed that out to me. So, I'm taking a break right as we caught a new case with six victims, including four kids."

"I heard about that," Tracy said. "Who could do that to their own kids?"

"We're not convinced it was him. His mother insists he would never harm them, that he loved them more than life. Who knows what really happened? My team is on it, and they'll figure it out. Freddie is leading the investigation."

"How exciting for him," Tracy said as she doled out salads and little rolls stuffed with chicken salad.

"He's ready," Sam said. "With me out of the way, he'll have a chance to shine on his own."

"I'm sure he'd rather shine with you than without you," Angela said with a small smile.

"He's nervous, but he's got this. Anyway, enough about me. How are you and the kids doing?"

"We're coping, figuring out a new routine and muddling through the days. We miss him, though. Poor Jack cries every night, but some nights it's not as bad as others."

Sam's heart ached for her sweet nephew, who'd been so close to his dad. "I wish there was something we could do for him."

"He's starting with a counselor next week."

"That's good," Tracy said. "That'll help."

"I really hope so," Angela said. "I'm as sad for him as I am for myself. It's just so hard to see him upset every day."

"I could come over at bedtime and read to him and snuggle him until he goes to sleep, if that would help," Sam said.

"You've got your own kids to snuggle," Angela said.

"I'd do it for Jack in a second."

"I know you would, but we have to find our own way through this one step at a time. From everything I've read, this acute stage won't last forever." She took a sip of her tea. "I've been thinking about calling Roni."

"She'd love to hear from you," Sam said. "And I was going to invite you to grief group at HQ tomorrow night."

"I'll go with you," Tracy added. "Mike will babysit."

"I'd like to go," Angela said. "I need the support of other young widows and people who've been through similar tragedies to help me find my way forward."

"I've met Roni's Wild Widows group," Sam said. "I think you'd love them. They're so resilient and optimistic."

"I could use a little optimism."

"Roni would love for you to reach out to her," Sam said. "She's offered several times now."

"I know, and I appreciate it. I just wasn't ready. It's starting to set in now... that I have to raise three kids on my own, and it's just... It's overwhelming."

"Of course it is." Tracy placed her hand over Angela's. "But you'll never be alone. I hope you know that."

"I do, and I appreciate you guys and everyone who's stepped up for us so much. But at the end of the day, it's me here alone with what will soon be three kids. I just never imagined my life looking like this."

Sam wanted to wail at the sheer injustice of it all. An injured back had led to a pain pill addiction that Spencer had been forced to feed illegally after doctors cut him off. He'd gotten pills laced with fentanyl that had ended his life suddenly and shockingly for everyone who'd loved him. Sam would never forget that horrifying morning at Camp David, when Angela had rushed into their cabin, screaming that her husband wouldn't wake up. She could barely stand to think about it, even if she'd have to one day testify about it in court. That day was a long way off. Hopefully, she'd feel more ready to fight for justice on behalf of Spencer, Angela and their family by then.

"We'd give anything for this not to have happened to you," Tracy said tearfully.

"I know, and I'm so, so thankful for you two and everything you've done for me and the kids. I'll be all right—and so will they. It's just going to take some time."

"We're here for whatever you need, whenever you need it," Sam said. "If you want me to come at bedtime for Jack, I'll be here. If you want to send them to us for a weekend at the White House, we're down for that."

"They'd love to do that. They talk all the time about how much fun it was there."

"Then let's do it soon. My kids would love it. We'll have Abby and Ethan, too," she said of Tracy's younger kids. "Cousin-palooza."

"Thanks, guys," Angela said. "Thank you for everything."

"Anything for you, kid," Tracy said as Sam nodded.

CHAPTER SEVENTEEN

B elinda Cane lived in a Georgetown penthouse that looked out over the campus of Georgetown University and the Potomac River. It was one of the best views Freddie had ever encountered in his years on the job.

She led him and Gonzo to a sitting area by the windows and offered them refreshments.

"We're good, thanks," Gonzo said.

She had long blonde hair, big blue eyes and flawless pale skin that reminded him of Nicole Kidman, which was an odd thought. But the comparison was fitting.

"Is this about Dr. Blanchet?" she asked. "I heard about what happened to him and his family. It's such a tragedy."

"Yes, it is," Freddie said. "That's why we're here." He kept having to remind himself that Sam wasn't there to take the lead. He had to do that. "We understand you and several other women had filed suit against him for inappropriate behavior?"

"Yes."

"What can you tell us about that?"

"It's very difficult to talk about, as you can imagine."

"We're sorry to put you through it," Freddie said, "but we're trying to fill in some blanks about what might've led to six people being found dead in their home."

"I understand, and I'm so, so sorry about his family. I couldn't sleep last night. I was sick over it. That our lawsuit might've driven him to do such a thing... That's a hard thing to live with, you know?"

"We don't know for sure that's what happened," Gonzo said.

"Oh, well..."

"Now, about your lawsuit. Can you share the details with us?"

She took a sip from a glass of ice water and seemed to be trying to find the words. "He was my doctor for several years as I struggled with infertility," she said haltingly. "It's a terribly difficult journey, and he was a source of such amazing support and encouragement. My husband used to joke that I had a crush on him, and he wasn't wrong. I relied on him to get me through the hellish tests, treatments and procedures. He was so good to me. Until... One time, about a year ago, I was under light sedation, and... I thought I was dreaming when I saw him remove his penis from his pants and ejaculate on me."

Holy shit, Freddie thought as he took notes. "Did you confront him about it?"

"Not at first, because I wasn't sure it really happened or if I dreamed it. I was so confused. Had I imagined that because of my husband saying I had a crush on him? I was a mess over it, and I didn't tell anyone for several weeks. My husband thought it was the hormones messing with my emotions, so he didn't think much of it. I'd been an emotional basket case throughout the entire process, so that was nothing new.

"I decided I had to talk to Dr. Blanchet about it before I lost my mind wondering if it had really happened. So I made an appointment and went to his office. While I was in the waiting room, I sat next to another woman named Leslie. She was shaking so hard, I asked if she was all right. She burst into tears, and the story just exploded out of her, exactly the same thing that'd happened to me. I took her by the hand and led her out of the office. We went to get coffee, and I told her my story."

Belinda reached for a tissue on the coffee table and wiped tears from her eyes. "It was such a relief to know I wasn't crazy, but also revolting to realize it had actually happened. We decided to post a generic inquiry to a local infertility support group, asking patients of Dr. Blanchet to get in touch with us. We spoke to several women, and two others reported similar incidents. That's when we called the MPD."

"An investigation was conducted," Freddie said.

She nodded. "Detective Ramsey took our statements and talked to Dr. Blanchet, who denied everything. He was outraged that anyone would accuse him of such a thing when he'd been working so diligently with us to make our dreams of having children a reality. He was highly offended and dropped us as patients."

Her hands trembled as she reached for another tissue. "That was like being revictimized. Now we had to start over with new doctors who were booked almost a year out. Not that any of us wanted to go back to him, but it was just another heartbreak on top of so many others."

Freddie was glad that Sam wasn't there to hear this woman's story after everything she'd endured with infertility, including invasive treatments that hadn't yielded the hoped-for result.

"Detective Ramsey said that he investigated our claims to the best of his ability, but without evidence to support our stories, he didn't feel that a prosecution would be successful, even with four of us willing to testify."

Freddie hated to say he agreed with anything Ramsey had done, but that would've been a tough case to prove without DNA evidence.

"That's when we decided to sue Dr. Blanchet. We also reported him to the medical licensing board."

"Where do those things stand?" Freddie asked.

"We were looking forward to our day in court in a couple of weeks. The Board of Medicine had scheduled an evidentiary hearing for April. It was about to blow up big-time."

At least that would explain a motive for Blanchet to kill his family and himself to avoid the nightmare that was about to befall him—and them by extension. In fact, they could easily make that case based on what Mrs. Cane had shared. He was eager to get Gonzo's take on it.

"We're so sorry that you went through such a difficult ordeal," Freddie said.

"Thank you, but it's not over yet. I'm still waiting to see a new doctor and hoping to carry a baby to term." Her eyes filled again, requiring another tissue. "It's all I've ever wanted, you know? To be a mom... I never imagined it would be such a heartbreaking journey, made worse by a sicko doctor who preyed on me and other women desperate to be pregnant."

"Is there any chance that one of the women involved in your lawsuit might've been angry enough to kill him?"

"No! God, no. They're all too heartbroken to have the energy to kill anyone, especially children. We're devastated by our infertility... It's so hard to explain unless you've been through it."

"How about their husbands or partners?"

"I don't know them as well as I know the women, but I can't see a man struggling to have a child of his own killing someone else's children, even someone he despised."

"I hate to say that we're going to need to know where you were the night before last."

Her expression conveyed shock and anger. "I was here with my husband all night."

"Can you give us his number?"

"Is this really necessary? If I wanted Blanchet dead, I wouldn't have killed his family, too. I would've run him over with my car. His kids didn't do anything to me, and neither did his wife. I felt sorry for her."

"Your husband's number?" Freddie asked again.

She recited it through gritted teeth.

"And the numbers of the other women who were part of the lawsuit?"

"Are you going to tell them you got their numbers from me?"

"No, ma'am."

"This is a nightmare that refuses to end," she said before reaching for her phone to find the numbers of the other three women.

Freddie wrote down the information she gave him. "We appreciate you taking the time to share your story with us." Freddie handed her a business card as he and Gonzo stood to leave. "If you think of anything else that might be relevant, you can call me any time. My cell number is on the card."

She nodded and said nothing more as they let themselves out.

"Whoa," Gonzo said while they waited for the elevator. "What the actual fuck?"

"I'm leaning more toward murder-suicide after hearing that. How about you?"

"Totally."

"But we still need to fully investigate the other women involved and confirm Mrs. Cane's alibi," Freddie said.

"Would her husband tell us if she went somewhere that night, or would he protect her?"

"We could get a warrant for the security cameras in the building," Freddie said.

"Let's see what Malone says, but I tended to believe her when she said she'd run him over before she'd hurt his kids. Someone who wants kids as badly as she does isn't going to murder other people's kids, no matter how much she hates the guy."

"Agreed. I'm not feeling her for mass murder."

"Not at all."

"But we still need to dot the I's and cross the T's, as Sam would say."

"Yep."

As they rode back to HQ, Gonzo made the call to Mr. Cane, who confirmed neither he nor his wife had left their home the night before last. "He assured me that she wanted to ruin him, not kill him. If she were going to kill him, it would've happened when she first got confirmation that he'd violated her. He said she was so angry and bewildered by the episode, and when she heard other women had had the same experience, she was almost relieved to know she wasn't alone."

As they rode back to HQ, Gonzo contacted each of the other three women involved in the lawsuit. They expressed shock at the deaths of the doctor and his family.

"I was looking forward to taking him to court," one of them said. "But all I can think of is those poor children. Whatever was going on, they had nothing to do with it. How could anyone harm them?"

The refrain was similar among all the women, who expressed heartbreak over the deaths of the children.

"I'm not seeing any of them as being involved in this," Gonzo said after he'd talked to the fourth one. "They all have alibis, seemed shocked by the turn of events, and without prompting, they expressed grief for the dead kids."

"Doesn't mean they didn't kill him and his family."

"No, it doesn't, but I'm not getting any kind of buzz from them," Gonzo said. "If anything, after hearing what he did to them, I'm more convinced than ever that this was murder-suicide. His whole life was about to explode in his face. Everyone was going to find out about what he was accused of doing to those women. His practice would be ruined."

"His *life* would be ruined."

Freddie's phone rang with a call from Lindsey McNamara. "Hey, Doc."

"I know you're working it from every angle, but I wanted to make sure you saw in the autopsy report that gunshot residue was also found on Mrs. Blanchet's hand."

Freddie hadn't gotten that far in reviewing the reports. He felt the wind go out of him. How was it possible that she had residue on her hand, too, if Marcel had been the one to kill them all?

"Thanks for the heads-up. I hadn't gotten all the way through the reports yet." How did Sam do all this while being first lady and raising three kids?

"I thought that might be of particular interest."

"It is. Thank you for calling."

"No problem. I'm working on arranging a postmortem MRI for Marcel Blanchet due to your hunch. I'll keep you posted on that."

"Thanks, Lindsey." Freddie ended the call with a sinking feeling. Maybe he wasn't as ready for this moment as Sam and Gonzo had thought.

"What's the matter?"

"She was making sure I saw that there was gunshot residue on Mrs. Blanchet's hand, too."

"Oh damn."

"I haven't gotten all the way through the autopsy reports yet, or I would've seen that."

"You'd have gotten to it eventually."

"But how much time would we have spent spinning our wheels in the meantime?"

"Every spin of the wheel is progress. We just more or less ruled out four potential suspects, and we can start fresh with a closer look at the wife. I want to know what their relationship was like with those allegations about to blow their lives wide open. I bet she wasn't too happy with him. Maybe she'd hired a divorce attorney or was considering it."

"Her best friend knew nothing about it."

"Which speaks to how traumatizing it must've been for her. There was also the matter of Marcel thinking she might be having an affair."

"True. I'll finish reading the autopsy reports and go through the dump on her phone after we see McInerny."

"Sounds good, but don't work all night."

"I won't. I've got Lindsey looking at another possibility—that Marcel had something wrong with him that could've changed his personality."

"Interesting theory. It would explain why a trusted doctor suddenly became sexually aggressive with his patients."

"And why he cut back on his hours without consulting with any of the people who'd be most affected by the decision."

"That, too. Good thinking."

"We'll see if it gets us anywhere."

Dr. Rory McInerny lived in Glover Park, near the vice president's home at the U.S. Naval Observatory and close to Georgetown University. McInerny's three-story townhouse on 40th Place Northwest was only about two miles from the Blanchets' home.

Freddie rang the bell.

The man who came to the door looked like he'd been on a multiple-day bender. His light brown hair was standing on end, his face unshaven and his eyes rimmed with red.

Freddie and Gonzo showed their badges.

He pushed the storm door open. "Come in."

"I'm Detective Cruz, and this is Sergeant Gonzales. We're investigating the murders of the Blanchet family."

"I assumed that's what this was about." He led them into a kitchen where dishes were piled in the sink. It smelled like the trash had sat for days. "Sorry for the mess. We're in total shock."

"Is your wife at home?"

"She's upstairs."

"Would you mind asking her to join us?"

"Um, sure. Okay." He went to the stairs. "Hey, Brit? Can you come down? Some police are here about Marcel and the family." He came back to the kitchen. "She'll be down in a minute. Do you guys want water or anything? Not sure what else we have."

"We're fine," Freddie said. "Thanks."

A dark-haired woman with haunted brown eyes came into the kitchen, wearing an oversized Georgetown sweatshirt and sweats.

"This is my wife, Brittany."

"I'm Detective Cruz. This is Sergeant Gonzales. We appreciate your help."

"Whatever we can do," Brittany said as she sat next to Rory at the table and reached for his hand. "We're heartbroken over the loss of our dear friends and their precious kids." She blinked back tears. "They were like our kids, too. We went to every birthday party, dance recital, school play and gymnastics meet."

"Do you have children?"

Brittany shook her head. "I had uterine cancer as a younger woman and had a complete hysterectomy. We've been talking about adopting, but haven't started that process. In the meantime, the Blanchet kids were ours, too. We loved them so much. Little Gus... He was my special friend." She wiped away tears. "I just can't imagine someone hurting them."

"We're very sorry for your loss."

"Thank you," Brittany said. "It's been such an awful couple of days."

Rory moved their joined hands to his lap.

She leaned into him, resting her head on his shoulder as if it was too much for her to hold it up on her own.

If these people weren't deeply grieving, Freddie would hang up his gold shield.

CHAPTER EIGHTEEN

"I'm sorry to make a difficult time worse, but we have a few questions," Freddie said.

"It's fine," Rory said. "We understand you have a job to do."

"We heard that you and Marcel had a screaming fight in the office over his decision to cut back on his hours," Freddie said.

"Yes, we did," Rory said with a sigh. "I was furious with him for making a decision that affected all of us without even consulting with me or Oriana. Especially with the lawsuit court date coming up and the damage that was going to do to our practice. It was a lot all at once."

"Were you surprised by the allegations of the women bringing the suit?" Freddie asked.

"I was shocked. Everyone was. Marcel was my mentor. He taught me everything I know about medicine and life. I looked up to him in every possible way. It was unfathomable to me that he could've done such a thing."

"Did you believe the women?"

"At first, I thought it was bullshit, to be honest. I figured it had to be someone who hadn't gotten the result she wanted exacting revenge on the doctor who failed to make her dream come true. But there were four of them. It's hard to deny the truth when four people are saying the same thing."

"Did you confront him about it?"

"I did," Rory said. "He denied it, said it was a witch hunt by women whose procedures had failed—and he was right that all

four of them had achieved a negative result when they accused
him of inappropriate behavior. I'll admit that I found his denial to
be plausible at first, but the women were just so convincing. When
I read the lawsuit, I became very certain they were telling the
truth, and I told him so. He was furious with me, and said he
deserved loyalty from me after everything he'd done for me. It was
a terrible position for me to be in with my own reputation tied to
his, our practice in grave jeopardy…"

"Rory was sick over it," Brittany said. "He barely slept for a
month. He was so torn over his great love and affection for Marcel
and the revulsion over what he'd apparently done to vulnerable
patients. Not to mention other odd things, such as money missing
from the petty cash in the office, Marcel making off-color jokes
that made everyone uncomfortable. He was acting so strangely."

"You have to understand," Rory said. "The three of us have
devoted our professional careers to that practice. Oriana and I
came there because of our tremendous respect for Marcel. That he
could do this to those women and take us down with him is just…"
He shook his head and blew out a deep breath.

"I've never been more upset or torn over what I should do
and what I wanted to do in my life. I wanted to stand by Marcel.
He was my best friend, my longtime mentor and business
partner. Brit and I were close to his entire family. It was a terrible
predicament. For the first time in my life, I went on medication
for anxiety as my patients began to cancel appointments with me
that they'd waited months for. Word had gotten out through the
Facebook group that the women belonged to, and suddenly, our
once booming practice was radioactive—for everyone but
Marcel, that is. We were stunned that women were keeping their
appointments with him because his reputation for producing
results was unparalleled. Oriana and me, though, we were
flooded with cancelations. Ironic, huh? We needed him to keep
those appointments, to keep the money coming in so we could at
least try to keep the practice open while we weathered this
storm. And he thought that was a good time to cut back on his
hours?"

Brittany put her arm around her husband. "It was awful for
Rory and for me to see him suffering."

"I just don't understand why someone who had it all, who'd
reached the pinnacle of his profession, would do something so

stupid and ruin everything for himself and us. Oriana and I are forever tied to him. Everyone knows he was our mentor and boss."

"Will people hold what he did against you?" Gonzo asked.

"They already are. They figure we must've known what he was capable of, but we didn't. We were as shocked as anyone by the allegations. To us, he was a consummate professional, a dedicated doctor, a loving family man. And then he compounded it by cutting back on his hours right when the practice was floundering. People desperate for a baby wanted the guy with the proven track record of success, even if he was accused of unspeakable things. Once the criminal complaint fizzled, his calendar was fully booked again. We needed him to take those appointments and get things back on track. Instead, he decided to go part time without consulting with us."

"What did he say when you confronted him?"

"That he had to do what was best for his family. I asked him what about Oriana's family and mine? What about the hits we'd taken because of the accusations lodged against him? He said he couldn't believe I'd throw that nonsense in his face when he was being unfairly accused. It was the most heated exchange I'd ever had with him. It left me feeling sick to my stomach because I realized then that he was only thinking of himself."

"Was that out of character for him?" Freddie asked.

"Completely and totally. He was always so supportive of us that it came as a shock to both of us to hear him say he didn't care about us. He only cared about himself and his family. I mean, he was the one who'd put us in this position. It was galling, to say the least, to have him come right out and say he wasn't going to help us dig our way out of it."

"That must've made you angry," Gonzo said.

"The entire situation made me angry, but if your next question is whether I killed him and his family, I can save you from asking. I loved Marcel like a brother. Even after everything that happened, the love was still there. I wanted to help him find a way out of this lawsuit and get back to normal. I never could've harmed him, Liliana or the kids. I would've done anything to protect them."

"Rory has been so upset about the changes in Marcel," Brittany said. "None of it made any sense."

"Was it possible he had mental health issues?" Gonzo asked.

"Oriana and I talked about that. It had crossed our minds, but if you've ever dealt with that, you know it's difficult to confront someone with concerns about their mental health. That would surely explain a lot, like how he went from being a devoted husband, father and medical professional to preying on his patients. That will never make sense to me."

"It's clear to us that his life was about to implode in spectacular fashion." Freddie chose his words carefully. "Do you think it's possible that he might've done this to spare them the shame?"

"No," Brittany said with more fire than she'd shown yet. "Absolutely not. He *adored* them. If you could've seen him with the kids, you'd never think he could've done this." She pulled out her phone and scrolled through until she found what she was looking for. "This is him with the kids at Christmas."

Freddie took the phone and leaned in so Gonzo could watch with him as Marcel played the piano, and the kids sang "O Holy Night" with him. His delight in and affection for his kids was visibly apparent.

"That's who he was with them," Brittany said after Freddie handed the phone back to her. "Always taking pleasure in everything they did and said."

"I agree," Rory said. "He would've killed himself before he harmed his kids."

"How did his wife feel about the lawsuit and the accusations?" Freddie asked. "We spoke to her good friend Kelly, who knew nothing about it."

"Lili was extremely upset by it," Rory said. "Like the rest of us who knew Marcel well, she couldn't understand why he would do such a thing."

"So she believed the women, too?"

"She felt like I did. At first, she thought no way, but then four women came forward with the same story. What could she do but believe them? Things between her and Marcel had been tense for months since this came to light."

"We noticed tension in their texts to each other," Freddie said.

"They spoke only about the kids, as far as we knew," Brittany said. "All our usual get-togethers had come to an end. Everything was a mess."

"Can you think of anyone else who was angry enough with him to have wanted to hurt him and his family?"

"I can't think of anyone who would harm those sweet kids," Rory said as tears flooded his eyes.

"Neither can I," Brittany said. "Anyone who knew Lili and the kids loved them."

"Who was representing him in the lawsuit?" Freddie said.

"The guy's name is Ed Leery. His office is by the National Mall."

Freddie made a note of the lawyer's name and would finish going through Marcel's emails to him before reaching out to the lawyer.

"I have to ask where you two were the night before last."

"We drove down to see my folks in Roanoke for the weekend," Brittany said. "We just got back last night. I can give you their number to confirm we were there."

"That'd be great." Freddie wrote it down as she recited it. "This has been really helpful." He put his card on the table. "If you think of anything else, please call me. The smallest detail can make the biggest difference."

"We will," Rory said. "Thank you for all you're doing for them. They meant everything to us."

WHEN SHE LEFT Angela's house, Sam asked Vernon to tell the twins' detail that she'd be picking them up at school and taking them for ice cream.

Scotty had hockey practice after school, so he'd be home later.

She was looking forward to some one-on-one time with the twins during what would usually be a workday for her. This not-working thing had its benefits.

Sam waited in the car while Vernon and Jimmy coordinated with the twins' detail to get them into her car, rather than their usual vehicle. She was beginning to get annoyed by the delay when the door opened, and two beautiful little faces appeared, grinning widely when they saw who'd come to pick them up.

She embraced them in one big hug. "Who wants ice cream?"

They shrieked with excitement, and after she seat-belted them in, they proceeded to tell her everything that'd happened that day in school, including about a boy in Alden's class who ate his own boogers.

Sam remembered exactly who in her elementary classes had

been known for eating boogers, peeing their pants and puking. You never forgot that stuff.

She directed Vernon to the Capital Candy Jar, where she and her sisters used to take Ethan, Abby and Jack when they were little. When they arrived, they waited more than fifteen minutes for the agents to set up their visit while Sam tried to be patient and keep the kids entertained.

"When can we go in, Sam?" Aubrey asked, her nose pressed to the window so she could see the shop.

"As soon as the agents say it's safe."

"It's taking forever," Alden said.

"Yes, it is." She was about to get out and ask Vernon to move things along when the door opened.

"All set, Sam," he said, helping the excited kids down from the SUV.

Sam noted that the twins' agents were also there and that they'd drawn the attention of everyone in the area as they went into the store, where the shell-shocked staff waited to greet them.

"M-Mrs. Cappuano," one of the young women said. "It's such an honor to welcome you."

"Thank you for having us. Sorry for the disruption."

"Are you serious? This is the greatest thrill of my life! And Aubrey and Alden, too!"

"The kids would love some ice cream," Sam said. "What looks good to you, kiddos?"

Aubrey usually preferred anything with peanut butter, while Alden liked chocolate chip. She ended up with peanut butter crunch and Alden with chocolate chip cookie dough, both served in cups.

"What kind do you want, Sam?" Alden asked.

"I think I'll have one scoop of Heath Bar crunch," Sam said. "Do you mind if we eat it here?" she asked the woman after she had paid for the ice cream. A few other customers trickled in, which was a relief to Sam, even as they stared at her. She hadn't wanted to shut down their business in pursuit of ice cream.

"Of course not."

"Thank you."

She joined the kids at a table and sat back to enjoy the moment. For once, no one was counting on her to hunt down murderers, and she could be "just a mom" for a few hours. It was ironic that the thing she'd most wanted was the part of her life that got the least amount of time. She wished she could change that, but while she commanded the MPD's Homicide division, nothing much was likely to change. So she had to grab these moments with the kids when she could and be more mindful of taking breaks when she needed them.

After they finished their ice cream, they picked out some fudge to take home to Scotty and some chocolate-covered Oreos with images of the White House on them for Nick. They posed for a photo with the shop's staff before heading back to the car.

"Thank you for the ice cream, Sam," Aubrey said. "That was fun."

"It was fun for me, too."

"Why aren't you at work?" Alden asked, his expression serious.

"I took a day off."

"Oh. Why?"

"So I could spend more time with you."

"Will we get to see Celia today?" Aubrey asked, seeming concerned.

"Absolutely." Sam was thrilled to realize they loved Celia as much as she did. "She'll be very happy to see you when we get home."

"That's good. We like her and Shelby, too. We see her and Noah after school every day."

"Shelby's not at the White House today, so you'll see her tomorrow probably." Sam hoped Shelby would bounce back quickly from the trauma, but worried it might take a while.

"Did she take a day off, too?" Alden asked.

"She did."

"Today is weird," he said.

Sam laughed. This had been the weirdest, best day she'd had in a long time, and it had been, she realized, just what she'd needed.

FREDDIE AND GONZO returned to HQ and caught up with the rest of the squad, who reported nothing of substance from the other parents who'd commented on social media posts about Eloise.

"They were definitely bent out of shape by her bursting onto the scene two years ago, when the other girls had been together for years, but they have alibis that check out, and all of them expressed believable grief about the deaths of four innocent kids," Green said.

"I think that's a dead end," Gonzo said. "The parents resented Eloise, but they didn't kill her."

"Agreed." Freddie shared what they'd learned from the women who'd sued Dr. Blanchet and updated them on what they'd heard from his colleagues. "The autopsy report showed that Mrs. Blanchet also had gunshot residue on her hands, so we'll be digging deeper into her tomorrow."

"I'm still stuck on him jacking off on his patients," Detective O'Brien said with a cringe.

"It's disgusting," Detective Charles said. "And such a violation."

"We don't like any of them for bringing a gun to the doctor's house?" Detective Green asked.

"Not so much," Freddie said. "They were all very upset about the dead kids and had been looking forward to their day in court with the lawsuit."

"His life was about to explode," Gonzo said. "If someone killed them, how is it not related to that? What do we have on the gun?"

"It belonged to Blanchet," Charles said. "He bought it legally two years ago."

Freddie sighed. "It keeps coming back to him."

"Yes, it does, but it's still possible that's what someone wants us to believe," Green said.

"I agree," Freddie said. "Go home, everyone, and get some rest. We'll pick it up in the morning."

After the others had left, Freddie took a seat in his cubicle, determined to finish reading the autopsy reports before he left for the day.

He took a call from Elin. "Hey, babe. How was your day?"

"It's not over yet. They asked me to teach a spin class tonight because the instructor is out sick. Do you care if I'm late getting home?"

"No problem. I have to stay late, too."

"I'll pick up something for dinner and see you at home around eight?"

"I'll be there. Love you."

"Love you, too."

With time to work, Freddie got busy with the autopsy reports, reviewing everything they'd learned thus far and making notes for the next day.

"YOU NEED TO EAT SOMETHING, SWEETHEART," Avery said as he stood at Shelby's hospital bedside. Her sister had come to take Noah after he was released. The doctors were worried about Shelby's state of mind and had determined she should spend another night under their care.

She'd tried to rally for Noah's sake, but now that he was gone, the blank look in her eyes terrified Avery. It was as if her fire had gone out, and without that...

"Shelby, honey, please..." He kissed the back of her hand. "Talk to me."

She stared at the far wall without blinking. If she'd heard him, she gave no indication.

Avery's phone buzzed with a text from Sam. *How's Shelby?*

Not great. She's sort of out of it.

Bc of meds?

She's not on anything.

Oh... Are you worried?

Frantic. I don't know what to do.

Let me make a call. I'll be right back to you.

Avery had no idea who she was calling, but Sam loved Shelby and would want to help. He sat next to the bed, still in the suit he'd worn to Cleveland.

That seemed like a decade ago rather than the day before. He hadn't had so much as an update on the Bernadino case or anything else since arriving at the hospital. For all he cared, Nick's mother had walked out of jail a free woman.

He held his wife's hand in both of his and bent his head, wishing he had the words to bring her back to him.

His phone rang with a call from Sam. "Hey."

"I talked to Dr. Trulo, our department psychiatrist, who's also a friend of mine. He said he could come by to see Shelby, if that's okay. He's very good at what he does."

"I'll take whatever help I can get."

"I'll give Trulo the green light and come by myself later."

"Thank you, Sam."

"Anything for my Tinker Bell. And for you. I'll see you in a bit."

"We'll be here."

Though he didn't want to leave Shelby for any reason, he needed coffee and something to eat. He bent over the bed and kissed her forehead. "I'll be right back, love."

She had no reaction to him leaving the room.

He moved quickly to use the restroom in the hallway, splashing water on his face and combing his hair with his fingers. Then he took the elevator to the basement, grabbed a coffee and premade egg sandwich and was back in her room ten minutes after he left.

She hadn't moved.

Her unblinking gaze was still fixed on the wall.

This was all his fault. The assholes who'd taken her and Noah hostage were people he'd grappled with on the job. They'd come to his home seeking retribution and had terrorized his wife and son. Who else was out there with a beef against him that they might one day bring to his doorstep, threatening his loved ones?

More than he could count. He didn't even remember most of them, but they remembered him. They would never forget him or the cases he'd built against them that'd put them away, for years in many cases. Going forward, he would need to be notified when each of them made parole. He would move his family to a more secure residence with gates, an impenetrable fortress.

Dr. Anthony Trulo arrived an hour later.

Avery stood to shake his hand. "Thank you for coming."

"Any friends of Sam's are friends of mine."

"She told you what happened?"

"She did, and I'm sorry." He glanced at Shelby and then gestured for Avery to come with him to the hallway. "Has she been like this since they brought her in?"

"I got here a couple of hours after, and the only reaction she's had to anything was to our son. She held him and cried, but after he left with her sister, she's barely blinked. She doesn't respond to me when I speak to her. She's not eating..."

"She's traumatized. It'll take some time for her to come down from the fight-or-flight mode her brain switched into during the incident. I'd like to get her on some meds right away to help alleviate the symptoms. As soon as she's willing and able to talk, we can begin intensive therapy."

"Whatever you think is best."

"I'd like to talk to her medical doctor and take it from there."

Relieved to have a plan, Avery gave him the name of the doctor who'd been caring for Shelby.

"I know this is very upsetting, but it's a normal response to something too big for the brain to handle. Most of the time, it's a temporary condition.

Avery tried not to fixate on the words *most of the time*. He'd heard Sam say great things about Dr. Trulo and felt better knowing he was there to guide them through the trauma. But the sick feeling in Avery's stomach wouldn't subside until he had his Shelby back the way she'd been before this horrific event.

CHAPTER NINETEEN

A s Brooke put the finishing touches on the table she'd set for herself and Nate, she was so full of excitement she feared she might combust before he arrived.

That thought made her laugh. She was so silly when it came to him, but he made her feel things she'd never thought possible, until he'd come along and changed everything. Tonight, she would share the news that she'd been accepted to Princeton. She couldn't wait to tell him. They'd have all next year together before Elijah graduated and presumably moved back to DC to live closer to his siblings.

She'd have another year at Princeton after Elijah left and took Nate, his lead agent, with him. But they'd have next year together. The rest would fall into place. Or so she hoped.

Brooke wanted forever with the sexy agent who'd turned her life upside down in the best way possible. Her suitemates had left earlier in the day to drive to Florida for spring break. She'd chosen to stay in Charlottesville with Nate, who'd taken the week off to spend with her. They'd talked about going somewhere warm and might still do that, but for now, they had no plans beyond spending a whole week together.

She couldn't wait.

For the nine hundredth time that day, she checked his location, saw that he was getting close and ran for the shower. By the time she emerged from her bedroom, wearing a new red dress she'd bought with him in mind, he was two miles away.

"Take a breath, girl, before you hyperventilate."

She laughed at her own foolishness, but she hadn't seen him in a few weeks and was more than ready for a whole week with him. Right as she opened the door, he'd raised his hand to knock.

Brooke laughed as she hauled him inside.

Nate dropped his bags and pulled her into his arms for one of those hot, sexy kisses she'd become addicted to.

He groaned as their tongues collided.

The next thing she knew, his hands were cupping her ass and lifting her as he walked them toward her room without missing a beat in the kiss of all kisses. He set her down next to the bed and had her dress off so quickly, she barely had time to breathe before he was devouring her again with more of the kisses she craved.

His ability to remove clothes while making out passionately was one of his many talents.

He lowered them to the bed and came down on top of her, pulling back to study her face to make sure she was okay.

She loved how he was always worried about sparking triggers from a long-ago night she wished she could forget.

When he would've pulled back to get a condom, she stopped him. "I got the shot."

"What?"

"The birth control shot. We're good to go."

"Oh my God. So what you're saying…"

Brooke laughed at his stunned expression. "I'm saying we don't need a condom."

"I've never done it without one."

"Is this a good development?"

"The best development ever."

"Should we see what it's like?"

The sound that came from him was half groan, half whimper. "This might be quick."

"I'm good with quick." She couldn't stop staring at his gorgeous face. He had blue eyes and dark wavy hair that had caused her suitemates to nickname him McDreamy. He was that and so much more, and as he aligned their bodies and pushed into her, she was transported right back to the pleasure she'd found with him on several other occasions.

His gasp had her biting her lip to keep from laughing at the face he made as they had sex for the first time without a condom.

"Holy. *Shit.*"

"Yeah?"

"Oh my God, yes." As he closed his eyes and threw his head back, Brooke knew there would never be anyone else for her but him. He was it. The one. The only one.

True to his word, this first time was quick, but he made sure she came before he took his own pleasure. He always put her first, which was another reason to love him.

"Damn," he said after he had caught his breath. "That was amazing." He was already getting hard again as he continued to move in her. "Best thing I've ever felt."

"Me, too."

"Brooke..."

"Hmm?" She opened her eyes to find him watching her in that intense way that reminded her of what he did for a living.

"I love you. I want everything with you. I know this has been crazy, and it's probably too soon, but—"

Brooke put her hands on his face and kissed him. "I want everything with you, too. Of course I do. I love you."

"I've never been happier than I am when I'm with you—and even when I'm not with you," he said. "I just love knowing you're in my life."

"Same," she said, smiling. "I have other news." She'd planned to tell him over dinner, but couldn't wait any longer. He knew she'd applied to Princeton, but not that she'd been accepted.

"What news?"

"I got accepted to Princeton for next year."

He raised his head and stared at her. "Really?"

She nodded.

"That's the best news I've had in years," he said. "As of right now, I'm only there for another year. You've got two more years of school."

"I know. I figure we'll have next year together, and after that, we can get through my last year. As I say that, I realize I made a lot of presumptions for both of us, and maybe I shouldn't have done that."

He kissed her as tenderly as he ever had. "You made all the right presumptions. I can't wait to be with you every day. You can move into my place there. If you want to, that is."

"Would you want that?"

"God, yes, I'd want that. And let's face it, it would be stupid for you to pay for housing when we're going to want to be together all the time."

"That's true."

"Eli is planning to stay at Princeton for the summer to do an internship and take some classes, so you can come up as soon as you finish this semester. Spend the summer. And with the twins settled into a great routine with the Cappuanos, he's even talking about grad school."

"That'd be amazing."

"I didn't think so until you shared your news. Now it's the best idea he's ever had."

Brooke smiled at him. "Is this for real?"

"You bet it is."

She rested her head on his chest as he wrapped her up in his love. Now they had even more to look forward to.

"MCDOUGAL HAS ASKED FOR A MEETING," Terry told Nick first thing the next morning.

"Need I ask why the Senate majority leader wants to see me?" Nick said. "Dare I guess all Joint Chiefs, all the time?"

"Something like that."

"Don't tell me he thinks I shouldn't have thrown the book at them."

"I haven't picked up that vibe. There was nothing else you could've done, and he certainly knows that."

"Then what's he want?"

"Maybe to talk about where we go from here?"

"We've asked the secretaries of each service to nominate replacements."

"I've already heard from the Air Force and Navy. Waiting on the Army, Marine Corps, National Guard and Space Operations."

"Maybe McDougal wants to talk about how the Senate will quickly confirm your choice of the new chair."

"You take the meeting with him and see what he wants," Nick said.

"Will do."

"And tell Cox I want an update on where we stand with charges against the traitors."

"About that," Terry said. "He's getting some pushback on charging them."

"Why?"

"The thinking is that a prosecution would do more harm than good."

"They were plotting to overthrow my administration."

"But they didn't go through with it."

"Because someone tipped me off, not because they decided not to."

"I understand the outrage, and believe me, I feel it, too. However, a long-drawn-out prosecution will keep this matter alive in the press and the consciousness of the country for the length of your term."

"It's not up to us. It's Cox's decision as attorney general."

"Some of the pushback is coming from him. He's not sure there's a case. Most of the Joint Chiefs' discussions about the matter were in person, so there's no documentation. Nothing to build a case on."

"They all but admitted it to me."

"But they didn't come right out and say the words. Cox thinks it might be enough to dishonorably discharge them and hold up their pensions."

"What message does that send to the next general or admiral who doesn't approve of the president and plots to overthrow him or her?" Nick shook his head. "I know I'm supposed to steer clear of Justice Department business, but I think they should be charged. Even if they aren't convicted, the trials would send the message that there'll be consequences for plotting a military coup."

"I hear you, and I'll pass that along."

"Please let the AG know that I will fully honor and respect whatever decision he ultimately makes."

"I'll do that, too."

Nick sat back in his chair, feeling mentally and emotionally exhausted, and his day had only just begun. "What're you hearing about my mother?"

"Nothing new since the arraignment. The public defender seems to be a putz, though. Not sure he's capable of dealing with charges of this sort."

"Remind me that I'm not under any obligation to provide an attorney for her."

"You're not under any obligation to provide an attorney for her, and it would be my most strenuous advice for you to stay out of it entirely."

"Yeah, that's what I thought you'd say. And yet... I picture her sitting in jail while I'm in the Oval Office, and despite everything, I don't like how that feels."

Terry took a seat in the chair next to the Resolute Desk. "I'm sure it feels shitty, Nick, but you can't get involved in it. You just can't. This thing with the Joint Chiefs is enough of a body blow to your fledgling administration. The last thing we need is more press about the salacious charges facing your mother."

"I know." He glanced at Terry, feeling humiliated to need to have this conversation. "But let me ask you this... How will it play with mothers when she gets out of jail and tells the world that her son, the president, let her sit in jail because she couldn't afford a decent attorney with all her assets frozen?"

"That's a fair point, but I still say you steer clear. Hopefully, the mothers of America will empathize with the fact that she's never had much to do with you and thus you owe her nothing. Hell, half of them are probably in love with you."

"Stop. They are not."

"Ah, yeah, they are. Lindsey tells me that every girlfriend she's ever had from high school to college to medical school has reached out to ask if you're as hot in person as you are on TV."

"No way."

"Swear to God," Terry said with a chuckle. "We're already coordinating with the Secret Service to make sure you're not bothered by groupies at our wedding."

"So much for trying to be a serious president."

"You are a serious president, and over time, your actions in office will speak for themselves. Your record will speak for itself. It already is. The polling off the State of the Union is still outstanding. You set the perfect tone with the speech you wrote yourself."

"I'll take the good news where I can find it."

"On another note, Derek and I were talking last night about Bora Bora."

Nick sat up a little straighter. "What about it?"

"We, ah, think this might not be the time for you to jet off on *Air Force One* for a luxurious getaway in French Polynesia."

Nick's spirits took a nosedive, right when he'd thought they couldn't go any lower. He'd been counting the minutes to his week with Sam away from the gilded cage of the White House. "Come on. That's been planned for months. The Secret Service has already done the advance trip."

"I know, but, Nick... The Joint Chiefs just got caught plotting to overthrow your administration. Everyone is on edge, and you don't want to give them any more reason to question your commitment to the job."

"I'm fully committed to the job."

"You and I know that, but we think you should either postpone or cancel the trip."

"Our anniversary is March twenty-sixth."

"I know. I'm sorry to have to do this to you, but I think it's prudent for you to stay close for the next little while."

Nick groaned as he thought about breaking the news to Sam. "What about the trip to Europe?"

"Also on hold for the moment. We need to keep you right here, front and center, doing the job, being present."

"I get it," Nick said even as he boiled with rage that he'd never show Terry, who was only doing his job by sharing this advice. It was the right thing to do, but he didn't have to like it. "You can notify the Secret Service and anyone else who needs to know that we won't be going to Bora Bora after all."

"You should probably talk to Sam first. Things get out even when we try to keep a lid on them."

"Yeah, true. I'll talk to her tonight. You can tell them tomorrow."

He dreaded that conversation. They'd been counting down to the getaway for months and having to disappoint her was heartbreaking for him. He'd never hated this fucking job more than he did right then.

The desk phone intercom came to life. "I have Mr. Donnelly and Mrs. Gonzales here for you, Mr. President."

"Please send them in."

Trevor and Christina entered the room and came to join them in the chairs surrounding the desk.

"What's up, guys?" Nick asked.

"Ruskin was all over the morning shows in full support of the Joint Chiefs' efforts to save the country from an unelected president." Trevor handed him printouts of the former secretary of State's comments. "Per your request, we've come up with a statement telling the American people that Ruskin was removed from his post for engaging in inappropriate conduct while on an official diplomatic trip to Iran that put the lives of more than two dozen American citizens in jeopardy."

Nick glanced at Terry for his input. Thus far, the public had been told that Ruskin resigned along with several of former President Nelson's cabinet members, who'd chosen not to continue to serve in Nick's administration. They hadn't been told the truth, a fact that Ruskin had been playing to his advantage in the weeks since Nick fired him.

"Go ahead with the statement," Nick said. "Let him sweat whether we're going to release the pictures of him cavorting with naked women next."

"Yes, sir, Mr. President," Trevor said.

CHAPTER TWENTY

"I want to see Marcel Blanchet's mother," Freddie said to Gonzo as they began their day. "She lives in Bowie, Maryland, so we'll head out there and see what she knew about the lawsuit."

"Can I come?" Sam asked from behind them.

Freddie spun around. "What're you doing here?"

"I'm back."

"You're on a leave of absence."

"I was. That's over now."

"It was one day, Sam."

She shrugged. "Did the trick. What'd I miss?"

Freddie wasn't sure how to respond to this turn of events. Did her return mean he was no longer in charge of the case? Part of him wouldn't mind that, but the other part was sort of disappointed.

"We, ah, talked to the partner, Rory McInerny and his wife, Brittany, as well as the four women suing Dr. Blanchet."

"You can bring me up to speed on the way to Bowie," Sam said.

"I don't need to go if you're with him," Gonzo said. "I want to take a closer look at the wife and her text messages since gunpowder residue was also found on her hand."

"Interesting," Sam said. "I didn't see that coming."

"We didn't either," Freddie said. "It threw a wrench into things right when we were starting to think he had killed his family and then himself."

"What are you hearing from Crime Scene?" Sam asked. "Any

stray bullets that might indicate a struggle over the gun that would put residue on the mother's hand?"

"Still waiting for their report," Freddie said.

"You can call Haggerty," Sam said. "He'll tell you what he knows so far."

"I'll do that on the way, unless you want to take it from here," Freddie said.

"Why would I want to do that? It's your case. I'm just along for the ride."

"Oh. Okay. Well, let's go to Bowie, then."

As they approached the morgue, Lindsey came through the automatic doors and stopped short when she saw Sam. "Thought you were on leave."

"I was. I'm back."

"Good to see you. Everything all right?"

"So far so good, Doc. How are you?"

"Fine." Lindsey gave her a wary look. "You sure you're okay?"

"I'm good. I needed a break. I took one. Now I'm ready to get back in the game."

Lindsey glanced at Freddie.

He shrugged. What was he supposed to say? Sam was the boss. If she was ready to be back, so be it.

"Have a great day, Doc," Sam said.

"You, too." To Freddie, she added, "We're transporting Marcel Blanchet's body to GW for the MRI today. I'll know more soon."

"Thanks, Doc."

"Sure thing."

Freddie followed Sam to her Secret Service SUV.

Vernon jumped out of the driver's seat to hold the back door for them. "Where to, Sam?"

Sam looked to Freddie.

He recited the address in Bowie.

"GPS says about forty minutes," Vernon said.

"You can use that time to update me," Sam said to Freddie. "What's up with Marcel having a postmortem MRI?"

"Before I do that, are you sure you didn't come back too soon?"

"I'm sure."

"What did you do yesterday?"

"Spent some time with my White House people, had lunch with Nick, hung out with my sisters, took the twins for ice cream, helped Scotty with his homework, watched a movie with the kids. I feel better."

"I'm glad to hear that. I was worried about you."

"No need to worry. Everyone needs a break every now and then. I woke up this morning feeling ready to get back in the game, so here I am. Now, tell me about the MRI and the women with the lawsuit."

"The MRI is Lindsey following a hunch of mine. Everyone we've talked to has said that Marcel's behavior in the last year has often been out of character. I looked up what can cause that, beyond a midlife crisis, and read that several types of brain tumors and other physical conditions, such as various forms of dementia, can cause personality changes."

"That's a great thought and well worth pursuing."

"I'm glad you think so."

"What's up with the lawsuit?"

As Freddie conveyed the details, Sam cringed. "That's revolting."

"Indeed, and from what they told us, the crap was about to seriously hit the fan in his life."

"How can that not be related?"

"That's my thinking, too. It's just that the grandmother was so convincing in her insistence that he never could've hurt those kids. I want to know what she knew about the lawsuit before I make a final call on the murder-suicide."

"That's what I would do, too."

"I'm glad to hear I'm on the right track. It's been a bit overwhelming."

"It can be."

"Honestly? I have all-new respect for how you juggle so many things without breaking a sweat."

"I'm sweating on the inside."

"You'd never know it."

"No matter what I'm doing, there's always something else I should be doing. That weighs on me."

"I'm sure it does."

"It was funny yesterday with the twins—they said it was a 'weird day' because I picked them up at school and Shelby wasn't there. It made me realize that while I'm eating myself up with guilt over not being with them every day after school, they have a routine with Celia that works for them. And Lilia, Roni and the others in the first lady's office have things under control."

"I hope you take some comfort from that."

"I do, but I still wish it was me meeting the twins every day after school."

"All working mothers want that, but it's not practical."

"For most, it's not. They depend on the income from their jobs. That's not the case for me. I mean, the money is nice to have, but Nick makes enough to support us. He has for quite some time."

"Just because you don't need the money doesn't mean you don't need the job."

Sam smiled as she looked over at him. "That's it exactly. I need the job for myself."

"And there's nothing wrong with that. Tell me you know that."

"I do. It's just been more complicated since the kids came into my life. For so long, I dreamed about having babies, and I've come to realize that things happened the way they did because I'm not equipped to put the rest of my life on hold to tend to a newborn."

"It's interesting that you see that now."

"Having Scotty and the twins living with us has made me see a lot of things. But especially that."

"Elin and I have talked about what we'd do if or when we have a baby."

"*When*, not if. I feel it in my bones. You're going to be parents— somehow, some way. It'll happen."

"That's good to hear. We've more or less decided that she'll work weekends at the gym and be home with the baby during the week. It'll be a big financial hit, but day care would be a bigger hit."

"Ang would watch the baby for you guys and give you a deal."

"She's going to have enough on her plate already."

"She loves kids and babies. By the time yours arrived, she'd be past the early stages of intense grief and would have a routine figured out. I bet she'd love to watch your baby—and yours would keep her new little one company."

"I'm getting ahead of myself even having this conversation."

"No, you're making plans, which is smart."

Sam took a call from Assistant U.S. Attorney Faith Miller on speaker. "Hey, Faith. What's up?"

"I wanted to let you know that the preliminary hearing for

Javier Lopez has been set for a week from Monday. Thought you might want to be there."

"You thought right. Have you notified Lenore?"

"She's my next call."

"Do you mind if I call her?"

"That'd be fine with me. It's scheduled for four p.m."

"I'll let her know. Thanks for the call, Faith."

"You got it."

Sam made a call to Lenore Worthington, also on speaker.

"Hey, Sam. How are you?"

"Doing well. And you?"

"It's been a strange month. I thought finding out why Calvin was murdered would fix things, but at the end of the day, he's still dead."

"Grief group is tonight. We had to move it to Wednesday this month because Dr. Trulo had a conflict. I hope you can make it."

"I'm looking forward to it. I need it."

"I just heard from the AUSA that the preliminary hearing is a week from Monday at four at the federal courthouse."

"We'll be there."

"I'm planning to attend, too. I'll see you tonight?"

"Yes, you will. Thank you for all you do, Sam. Closing the case, hosting the grief group, following up with victims' families. It makes a difference."

"Thank you for saying so. I needed to hear that."

"Any time you need some reinforcement, call me. I'm always here."

"Will do. See you soon."

"She sounds pretty good, all things considered," Freddie said.

"As we both know, the answers don't change the reality for victims' families."

"No, they don't." He pulled out his phone. "I'm going to check in with Lieutenant Haggerty."

"Do your thing, boss man."

He rolled his eyes at her and made the call to the commander of the Crime Scene Unit, putting it on speaker so Sam could hear. "This is Detective Cruz calling about the Blanchet case."

"I heard you were heading up this one. Everything okay with Holland?"

"I'm here," Sam said. "Just giving young Freddie a chance to take the wheel."

"Ah, I see. We wrapped up our work at the house this morning, and I should have a report to you soon. The one thing that stood out was a bullet hole in the molding near the kitchen ceiling that may be indicative of a struggle for the gun."

"That would explain the gunpowder residue on the wife's hand," Freddie said.

"Possibly," Haggerty said. "Everything else was fairly straightforward, as these things go."

Meaning that four kids shot in their beds was *straightforward*. Freddie was sickened by the notion of someone surgically killing innocent kids. "Thanks for the info, LT."

"I'll have my full report to you shortly."

"Sounds good."

Freddie ended the call with Haggerty and looked to Sam for her input. "How does a reportedly loving and devoted father do that to his own children?"

"Maybe he saw it as a way to protect them from the scandal that was about to erupt," Sam said. "Imagine being in middle school and having your father accused of ejaculating on sedated patients. It would ruin their lives as much as his."

"For sure, and there were signs of a struggle in the kitchen. Mrs. Blanchet tried to get the gun away from whoever had it." After a pause, Freddie said, "If I look at it from the perspective of him wanting to protect them from the salacious scandal, I can almost envision him standing over their beds and shooting them."

"He'd have been wrecked over it. Sobbing. Apologizing."

"Were the kids awake?" Freddie asked.

After contemplating that for a second, Sam said, "No, they never saw it coming. That's how he would've wanted it."

"Wouldn't they have heard the struggle downstairs? The parents fighting over the gun? The shots fired? They would have been loud. Wouldn't the first gunshots have awakened the other kids?"

"Maybe they were drugged, or they were heavy sleepers. We joke that a nuclear bomb wouldn't wake Scotty when he's truly asleep. We won't know if they were drugged until we get the tox screen back in a few weeks."

"Heavy sleeping is a thing with kids," Freddie said. "I read about how they sleep through smoke alarms, so some people program them in the kids' mother's voices, because they hear that for some reason when they don't hear the blare of a smoke alarm."

"It's very possible they slept through it. We can't believe the chaos Scotty sleeps through. Anyway, Marcel could've killed them while she was out of the house, and when she came home, he confronted her. It's possible they were already dead when she was killed."

"Would he have told her he'd killed her babies?" Freddie asked.

"I don't think so. He wouldn't have wanted her to know that."

"That scenario makes sense to me, but I'm worried that someone wanted it to make sense to us. That he'd be so humiliated by the looming lawsuit that he'd kill his family and himself to spare them all the agony."

"That's always possible," Sam said, "but they'd have to *know* about the lawsuit for that to make sense. I don't think it was widely known yet."

Just when he thought he had a working theory... "True."

"What's the plan with the grandmother?" Sam asked.

"I want to find out what she knew about the lawsuit and go from there."

"Gotcha."

They arrived at the Bowie home of Graciela Blanchet fifteen minutes later. Freddie led the way to the front door of the woman's well-kept white ranch-style home and rang the doorbell.

"Look at that," Sam said. "Another doorbell we can't hear from the outside."

Mrs. Blanchet came to the door and seemed surprised to see them on her doorstep. She unlocked the storm door and opened it. "Have you figured out who killed my family?"

"We're still working on that," Freddie said. "We wondered if we might have a few more minutes of your time."

"Come in," she said, giving them a wary look.

She looked exhausted and ravaged by grief.

Hers was the kind of loss that made him wonder how people survived such things. "We're sorry to intrude during such a difficult time," he said.

"It's all right. You're doing your jobs." In the kitchen, she introduced them to her sisters and cousins. The table and counters were laden with food and flowers, the lilies giving off a funereal scent. Her guests gawked at Sam.

"If we could have a few minutes alone," Freddie said, "that would be helpful."

Graciela glanced at one of the women, who led the others from the room.

Sam closed the kitchen door and then sat next to Freddie at the table.

"Were you aware of a lawsuit that involved Marcel?" Freddie asked.

Graciela's brows furrowed with confusion. "What lawsuit?"

"It's come to our attention that Marcel had been sued by four former patients who accused him of sexual misconduct."

"That's not possible," she said, her expression shocked. "My son was a consummate professional. Couples waited months for appointments with him. He made their dreams come true."

"We spoke to the four women attached to the lawsuit," Freddie said. "Their stories were shockingly similar. They accused him of ejaculating on them while they were under light sedation."

Her gasp of disgust made him feel sick. He hated having to inform people who'd lost family members to violence of things they hadn't known about their loved ones.

"How could they know that if they were sedated?" she asked.

"They were in a twilight sedation," Freddie said, "where they maintain some consciousness. At first, each of them thought it had to be a weird dream or something, but when they connected with the other women, they learned that it wasn't. They reported it to the MPD's Special Victims Unit, and an investigation was conducted. The SVU detective determined there was insufficient evidence to go forward with a criminal complaint, so the four women banded together on a civil claim that was due to go to court this month."

"He said nothing about that to me," she said tearfully. "I had no idea."

"Our current theory is that he murdered his family to spare them the humiliation."

"It's just not possible," she whispered. "He loved them more than anything. All he talked about were his kids and his pride in them, how they made him laugh and think." She gave them a pleading look. "You'll never convince me that he could've done this to them. All the humiliation in the world wouldn't have caused him to harm them." She placed her hand on Freddie's arm. "I *knew* him. I knew him as well as I know myself. We talked two or three times a day, almost always about the kids and what they were up to. They were the center of his world."

Freddie was torn. He believed her. And he believed the evidence that indicated Marcel had good reason to commit an unspeakable crime. "We appreciate the added insight."

"What does that mean? Are you going to say that he did this?"

"We haven't decided anything for certain yet. We're still collecting evidence."

"Please... Don't compound this tragedy for me by blaming my son for it. He'd been under so much stress lately with wanting to be there more for his kids... He wasn't himself."

Freddie tuned in to the telling statement. "How so?"

"It just wasn't like him to ditch work to hang out with his kids. He knew how much his patients counted on him, but lately, it seemed like more of a burden to him than a calling."

Freddie wondered if that played into his hunch about a possible medical condition.

"He would've killed himself, not the kids. Never the kids."

"We're doing everything we can to get at the truth," Freddie said. "That's all we can do."

When they rose to leave, Graciela followed them to the door. "If you determine he did it, will you tell me before you make that news public?"

"I will," Freddie said. "I promise."

"Thank you."

"We're sorry if our investigation makes this tragedy worse for you. That's not our intention."

"I understand. I want the answers as much as you do. I just hope you're looking beyond the obvious."

"We are."

"Then that's all I can ask."

CHAPTER TWENTY-ONE

"I t's unbearable," Freddie said when they were in the SUV on the way back to the District.

"Yes, it is," Sam said, "but you handled her just right. You told her we're looking at every angle, including the possibility that her son wasn't who she thought he was."

"How will she live with that if it turns out he did this?"

"I don't know." She tried to imagine one day having to accept such a thing about her husband or sons and couldn't. "People hide their true selves from even those closest to them."

"I don't do that, and neither do you."

"Everyone keeps some things completely private."

"I don't. What Elin doesn't know about me, you do, and I'm sure that between Nick, me and your sisters, you're fairly well known, too."

"Granted, but some people have a whole other side to themselves that no one ever sees. Think about some of the most famous serial killers and how people close to them said they had no clue they were capable of such a thing."

"Graciela's certainty that it couldn't have been him is weighing on me."

"I know," Sam said. "Me, too. A lot of times, family members will say, you know, he was a little off lately, or things were strange or something. She's been unwavering in her conviction that he never could've done such a thing."

"But of course a mother would say her son was incapable of such a thing," Freddie said. "Mine would."

"There is that," Sam said. "She also had no idea about the pending lawsuit, which means she didn't have a full understanding of the pressure he was under or how much he might've been dreading that information going public."

"That's true. So what now?"

"This is when you start from scratch. Go through it all again from the beginning. Start with the video surveillance from the house, the text messages, emails, social media posts, autopsies, crime scene. Every time you look at it, you'll see something new or different. At least I do. Work the case, pull the threads, do what we do. And if, at the end of the day, all roads lead to Marcel, then so be it."

"I'm worried we're wasting time by looking beyond the obvious," he said.

"We have at least five murdered victims, possibly six if it wasn't him," Sam said. "It's our job to look beyond the obvious to get at the truth, whatever that might be."

Freddie nodded. "Are you still sure I'm the right one to be running such a big investigation?"

"I'm absolutely positive. Rely on your colleagues. Delegate. Be open to ideas and thoughts from everyone. You know what to do."

"It's much easier to watch you do it."

Sam, Vernon and Jimmy cracked up laughing.

"I'm sure it is," Sam said. "But I'm enjoying watching *you* do it."

"I bet you are."

"It's like raising a child you're super proud of and then sending him off to college."

Vernon chuckled as he caught Sam's eye in the mirror.

She was glad she'd come back to work. Being with Freddie—and now Vernon and Jimmy—felt like normalcy, which was what she needed. The numbness hadn't completely worn off, but she felt more engaged than she had the day before yesterday. Spending time with her loved ones had helped, and letting Freddie take the lead on the case had relieved some of the weight on her shoulders.

Sam had to take her own advice during these complicated times for her and Nick. She needed to delegate and rely on the team that would do anything for her, especially the partner she had trained and nurtured, as well as the sergeant who had the same sensibilities as she did. Outside of Nick and her sisters, Freddie and Gonzo were her closest friends, and they would have her back, no matter what.

Back at HQ, Sam and Freddie went to the conference room and dove into the stacks of paper that had already accumulated on the case.

She started with the text messages and emails for Marcel and Liliana Blanchet, beginning with the most recent ones and working her way backward. Their exchanges were fairly routine for the busy working parents of four active kids. Coordinating rides and discussing a call they'd received from their son's day care about his propensity to kick his classmates when he wore a certain pair of boots. They talked about who was picking up what for dinner and other household matters.

As she read through the messages, she noted the lack of warmth and humor like what marked every exchange she had with Nick. They were always laughing, teasing, joking. These two were all business all the time. She went back a month, looking for any sign that they were a happily married couple and not roommates who shared children.

"Freddie."

"Hmm?"

"Marcel and Liliana were barely speaking."

"Why do you say that?"

"Read the texts. It's all business about the kids, the house, the car that needs an oil change, the soccer car pool, the son's day care."

"What's wrong with that?"

"Read me your last five texts with Elin."

"What?"

"Roll with me. And don't say anything that'll scar me forever."

"Are you serious about this?"

"You read yours, and then I'll read mine, and then we'll compare them to the Blanchets'." She rolled her hand, telling him to proceed.

"From Elin last night: 'What time will you be home?' From me: 'Why? Do you miss me?' Her: 'You know it. I'm feeling much better.' Me: 'Is that right? How much better?' Her: 'Like, really, really good.' Me: 'I'm coming.' Her: 'Not yet, but soon.'"

"Spicy," Sam said. "Here are ours. From Nick last night: 'Are you still up? I'm coming home.' Me: 'I waited up for you.' Him: 'I was hoping you were awake. I need my wife after this day from HELL.' Me: 'Your wife is here for you.' Him: 'On the stairs. Get naked.'"

"You said nothing scarring!"

"How is that scarring?"

Freddie cringed.

"Listen to this now." She read through four days' worth of text messages between the Blanchets. "Do you see the difference? There's none of the suggestive, funny stuff that we do every day with our partners. They talk only about the kids, the house, food and practical matters."

"She had to know about the lawsuit, right?" Freddie asked. "It had been filed and the court date was looming."

"I'm sure she did. I'm going back through the messages, looking for the last time they were more cordial to each other." She scanned pages of messages. "Five weeks ago, she said something flirty to him about a planned date night. His mother was coming to spend the night with the kids while they went to a birthday party for a friend. Marcel asked if they should get a hotel room, and she said she was for it."

"So sometime after that, she found out about the lawsuit, and a deep chill set in."

"That's how I'm reading it."

"I want to talk to her friends." Sam shuffled through more papers, looking for text messages from other people. "Other than Kelly, there's someone named Cara that she talks to every day. I don't see specifics about the suit, but she and Cara check in every day. Her communication with her sister was almost all business about their mother with dementia. I'm not picking up on a vibe that they shared much else. Where are the call sheets for Liliana?"

Freddie handed them to her.

Sam scanned them, looking for the number attached to Cara's texts. "She called Cara almost every night and talked for more than an hour. If anyone was up on what was happening between them, it would be her. Ask Archie to track this number and figure out a last name and where she lives."

She'd no sooner finished reciting the number than she

stopped herself. "I'm sorry. This is your case. I'm not the one giving the orders here."

"It's *our* case, and you've given me a thread to pull." He got up, went to the phone in the center of the table and called Archie. "He's going to call me back."

Detective Charles knocked on the door to the conference room. "Nice to see you back, Lieutenant."

"It's nice to be back. What's up?"

"I've been going through the financials for the Blanchets, and I found something interesting."

"What've you got?" Freddie asked.

"A ten-thousand-dollar payment several months ago to the husband of one of the four women who was suing him."

Freddie glanced at Sam, looking perplexed. "That's a wrinkle I didn't see coming."

"Same," Sam said. "What would be the purpose of that?"

"Maybe he was trying to get the guy to talk his wife out of suing him?" Charles said.

"That wouldn't stop the other three from continuing the suit," Sam said.

Detective Charles handed a piece of paper to Freddie. "This is the name and address of the man who received the payment."

"Good work, Neveah," Sam said.

"Thank you. I'll keep digging and let you know if anything else pops."

The conference room phone rang.

Freddie grabbed it. "Thanks, Archie." He wrote down the information. "Let's go talk to Cara Quinn in Adams Morgan. After that, we'll see Gordon LeBlanc in Penn Quarter."

"I'm with you, Detective Cruz," Sam said, following him to the morgue.

CARA QUINN LIVED in a duplex townhouse on Belmont Road Northwest.

Freddie rang the doorbell.

When no one answered, he called Cara and put the call on speaker so Sam could hear, too.

"Hello?"

"Ms. Quinn, this is Detective Cruz with the DC Metro Police."

"What can I do for you, Detective?"

"We're working on the Blanchet case and were wondering if we might meet with you. We're currently at your house."

"I thought it was a murder-suicide."

"We haven't made that final determination yet."

"Wasn't Marcel found with the gun?"

How did she know that?

Sam rolled her hand, telling him to get to the point.

"Are you available for a conversation, ma'am?"

After a long pause, she said, "I'll be home in a few minutes."

"We'll wait. Thank you."

The line went dead before Freddie could end the call. "How could people know he was found with the gun?"

"That's a very good question. You'll want to talk to the Patrol officers who responded to make sure they didn't tell anyone."

"I will. The grandmother could've said something."

"Why would she? She's convinced he didn't do it."

"But the grandmother's neighbor knew, and maybe she told someone we were thinking along those lines, and that person mentioned it to a coworker, and so on. You know how these things travel."

"Yeah, that's possible." Sam zipped her coat. "This is the point where I'm completely sick of winter's last gasp." This time of year, it was the wind that made even the warmest of days feel chilly.

"I'm surprised it's taken this long, especially after you broke your hip when you slipped on ice."

"This year, I was sick of it earlier than usual."

"When do you go to Bora Bora?"

"March twenty-fifth. I'm counting the days, but also kind of stressed about it."

"Why?"

"People will freak out about us going to Bora Bora, even though it's something we do every year."

"Every president takes a vacation, and every president takes heat for it."

"But those presidents were elected. Mine wasn't, so everything he does is that much more fraught. And now this thing with the Joint Chiefs..."

"That's outrageous. Everyone thinks so."

"No, Freddie, not everyone thinks so. Many people think the

Joint Chiefs are patriots for trying to rid the country of a president who wasn't elected."

"A lot of people think it's outrageous, Sam. Nelson chose Nick to be his VP. The Senate confirmed him. The VP's primary role is to step in if the president dies or becomes incapacitated. He's legitimate by anyone's definition, by the Constitution's definition."

"I appreciate your loyalty to him and to me, but if he wasn't my husband and your friend, we might be outraged by how he achieved the office, too. I'm just playing devil's advocate here."

"I still say it's bullshit. I hope the Joint Chiefs are charged with treason."

"We'll see what happens. Nick said it's up to the AG as to whether they'll be charged. He has to stay out of it, so it doesn't look like he's trying to influence the Justice Department."

"Did he tell you that before or after the booty call?"

"After," Sam said with a wink and a grin. She nodded toward a woman coming toward them. "There she is."

Cara Quinn had light brown hair and a pretty face that was set in a frown as she approached her front stoop, where they waited for her. She had a multicolored knitted scarf wrapped twice around her neck.

Sam and Freddie stepped aside to let her come up the stairs and unlock the door. They followed her inside.

"We're sorry to intrude at this difficult time," Freddie said with the personal touch that always resonated with the people they met on the job.

"I'm in total shock. I just came from my therapist. I was hoping she could give me some guidance on how I'm supposed to go forward without Lili and the kids." Her voice broke as she unwrapped the scarf and removed her coat. She hung both on a hook inside the door. "They were my babies, too. I was their godmother, their adopted aunt, their friend, their cheerleader. I'm devastated."

"We're very sorry for your loss," Freddie said.

"It's unimaginable. I don't know what to do with myself."

They followed her to a cozy living room full of pillows with inspirational sayings on them, candles and framed flower artwork. Sam thought it was the kind of living room a woman would want for herself if she didn't have to accommodate anyone else's taste.

Cara curled into a chair and pulled a blanket over her lap.

Sam and Freddie settled on the sofa.

"How long had you known Liliana?"

"We met in college at UVA. We were roommates for three of our four years and for five years after college, while she went to law school at American and I went to grad school there. She was my very best friend from the day we met until..." Tears flooded her eyes and slid down her cheeks. "I lost my fiancé in an accident when I was twenty-six. I've never married, so Lili's family was like my own."

Sam's heart went out to her. She'd suffered far too much loss in her life.

"What can you tell us about her relationship with her husband?" Freddie asked.

"They were wildly in love from the minute they met through a mutual friend when we were all at UVA. They were together from that first night on. They were that couple people loved to hate, you know?"

Sam suspected she was half of one of those couples, but she wouldn't change a thing.

"The kids arrived, and things got hectic for them as they juggled careers and caring for four young kids. It was a lot. For the first time, some cracks began to appear in their relationship lately."

"How long ago did that happen?"

"About three years ago. It was the first time I ever heard her voice discontent with him. She felt he wasn't doing his share of the parenting. I would argue that he couldn't help being called out to deliver babies at all hours, but she said it was more than that. He was disconnected from her and the kids even when he was home. I'll confess to being shocked the first time she told me that. I'd never seen any sign of that in him, and I spent a lot of time with them."

"Did you consider him a close friend, too?"

"I did, but not like I was with her. She was my girl. If I had to take sides, which I never did, I would always choose her. He knew that and used to joke that I was her other spouse—the one she actually liked."

"That's a telling statement," Freddie said.

"It was. I thought it was the pressure of two high-stress jobs and four kids to manage, but I'd begun to suspect the discontent ran deeper than that. And then she found out about the lawsuit. Do you know about that?"

"We do," Freddie said.

"I've never been more shocked in my life. She was speechless, devastated, appalled, revolted. That four women were saying the same thing... She couldn't wrap her mind around it. None of us could."

"You, her and who else?"

"Her other friends. There's a group of six of us that go back to college, and she told us so we wouldn't hear it from someone else. We were stunned. Marcel had always seemed like the ultimate professional and family man, and it just didn't jibe with who we knew him to be."

"In reviewing their text messages over the last couple of months, there was an obvious chill in the air," Freddie said. "Is that how you'd describe it?"

"Definitely. They were barely speaking. After she heard about the lawsuit, she spoke to him only about the kids. And then he decided to cut back at work right when they had mounting legal fees, and she was furious. A week ago, she'd suggested he might consider finding somewhere else to live."

Sam's heart sank. Could that've been what sent him over the edge?

"Could a request like that have driven him to murder?" Freddie asked, reading her mind.

"I don't know," Cara said. "I've been thinking about nothing else but that, and I still can't bring myself around to him shooting the kids. Her? Maybe, but not them. Never them."

They now had multiple people close to Marcel saying there was no way he could've harmed his kids.

"And even with Lili, he knew everything that was happening was his fault—not hers. So I don't see him turning a gun on her either."

"Was there anyone else in their lives who might've been angry enough to do something like this?" Freddie asked.

"Only the women suing him. And maybe the parents who were so deeply resentful of Eloise's success in gymnastics. That was truly disgusting."

"Anyone in particular?"

"The Cortezes were the worst of the lot."

"We've spoken to them."

"They made life miserable for Eloise and her parents with their blatant racism and comments about Eloise not deserving to win the meets. It was very upsetting to everyone who loved her. She would ask, 'Why are they so mean?' And none of us could give her an answer other than sometimes people suck."

"Can you think of anything else that might be relevant? We often tell people that even the smallest thing can blow a case wide open, and it's true. We see it all the time."

"I've done nothing but think about that since the second I got the dreadful news, and I can't come up with anything that would've led to an entire family being slaughtered this way. I keep coming back around to the enormous pressure Marcel was under over this lawsuit that was going to ruin his practice and his life… Who knows? Maybe he did snap."

"We appreciate your help." Freddie handed her his card. "If you think of anything else, even the smallest thing, call me. My number is on there."

Cara took the card from him. "I will." She glanced at Sam. "Lili would've been so excited to meet you. She was a big fan of you and your husband. She thought it was amazing that you were keeping your job while you're first lady."

"That's nice to hear. Thank you."

"I hope you can figure out who did this, even if it was Marcel. It would help to know."

"We run a grief group for victims of violent crime," Sam said. "We usually meet the second Tuesday of every month at MPD headquarters, but we moved it to Wednesday this month, so it's tonight. You're more than welcome to join the group if or when you feel ready."

Cara walked them to the door. "Thank you for the invite. I'll keep that in mind."

"Take care of yourself," Freddie said.

"I will."

When they were outside, they walked back to the SUV in silence.

Vernon held the door for them. "Where to?"

Freddie gave him the address of Gordon LeBlanc.

"I really feel for her," Sam said when they were on the way to Penn Quarter.

"I know. It's a brutal loss for her on top of losing her fiancé years ago."

"Some people get more than their share of tragedy."

"For sure."

"I've felt that way lately," Sam said.

"No one could blame you for that."

"And yet, I live an absolutely gilded life in so many ways."

"Everyone suffers loss, no matter how great the rest of their life is."

"I guess. It's funny, though. I really needed my dad to live forever."

"So did I."

Sam smiled at him, appreciative of his deep love for her father. "What's our next move, hotshot?"

"We'll talk to the guy who received the ten grand from the Blanchets, and then I want to keep going through the paper trail. I haven't personally looked at the social media or the rest of the texts and emails yet."

"Sounds like a plan. I have to say, I'm kind of enjoying riding shotgun on this one. I need to do that more often."

"No, you don't."

"Yes, I do."

"No."

"Yes."

"Children," Vernon said. "No bickering."

"But that's what we do," Sam said.

"It's part of our charm," Freddie added.

The agents laughed.

"Whatever you guys are doing, it's working for you," Vernon said. "You get a hideous job done and manage to have a little fun along the way."

"I hope you know the irreverence is what keeps us sane," Sam said.

"Of course we do," Vernon said.

CHAPTER TWENTY-TWO

Gordon LeBlanc ran a psychology practice from an office in his home. He answered the door with a sandwich in his hand and a surprised look on his face. He was heavyset, with thinning dark hair and brown eyes that were a little too close together.

Freddie introduced himself and Sam as they showed their badges.

"I know who you are. What do you want with me?"

"We'd like to talk to you about Marcel Blanchet," Freddie said.

He scowled when he heard the name. "Do we have to?"

"I'm afraid so."

"Come in. I'm between patients, but I only have about twenty minutes."

"This won't take long."

"What do you want to know?" LeBlanc asked when they were seated in a formal living room.

"Your wife, Leslie, was one of the plaintiffs in the lawsuit against Dr. Blanchet," Freddie said.

"That's right."

Sam realized he wasn't going to volunteer anything. They'd have to pull it out of him.

"How did you feel about that?"

"Well," he said with a bitter edge to his voice, "how would you feel if some pervert doctor got off on your wife while she was sedated?"

"I'd feel pretty angry about that," Freddie said.

"I was pretty angry."

"Our research has indicated that you received a ten-thousand-dollar payment from Dr. Blanchet. Can you tell us what that was for?"

"It was a refund for what we'd paid him to help us have a baby, which is no closer to happening today than it was when we turned over our life savings to him. The ten K was a fraction of what he owed us. He promised he'd reimburse us completely."

"Did he ask you to drop the lawsuit in exchange for that payment?"

"That came up, but Leslie wasn't willing to drop it. I followed her lead. She was the one violated by that creep."

"Did it seem like he was trying to make it right with you by returning some of the money you'd spent?"

"Maybe to him it did, but to us, it was another empty gesture. We were looking forward to our day in court and then never having to talk about him again." He looked away, his jaw clenched. "You can't possibly know what we've been through."

"I do know," Sam said. "And I can't imagine the added horror of being victimized by my doctor."

"That's right," he said, glancing at her. "You've been through it, too. Then you do know."

"I'm sorry that happened to Leslie—and to you," Sam said.

"Thank you."

"I hope you understand that we have to ask where you were Sunday night," Freddie said.

He gasped. "You think I killed him and his family? That's outrageous! His disgusting behavior was about to be in all the headlines. I can't believe you're wasting taxpayer dollars looking at anyone but him."

"We're not convinced it was him," Freddie said.

He scoffed. "How could it not be?"

"We follow the evidence, and the evidence isn't leading us to him."

LeBlanc crossed his arms. "You'll never convince me that anyone but him did this."

"Fair enough, but where were you two nights ago?"

"I played poker with some buddies, and then I came home."

"What time did you get home?"

"Around eleven."

"And your wife can attest to that?"

"She can," he said, giving Freddie a frosty glare.

"We'll need the names and numbers of your friends."

"What the fuck? You're going to actually call them?"

"That's how we confirm alibis."

He made a big production of rolling his eyes and blowing out a breath to express his displeasure before he grabbed the notebook and pen Freddie offered him, took out his phone and wrote down the requested info. "Are you going to tell my friends that you think I killed the doctor who assaulted my wife—and his family?"

"We don't suspect you of that," Freddie said. "Should we?"

His gaze fairly incinerated Freddie. "No, you shouldn't. I didn't do it, but I sure as fuck didn't cry any tears of sorrow for that sick son of a bitch."

"What about for his kids?" Freddie asked. "Did you feel for them?"

"Of course I did. Whatever this was about, it couldn't have involved them. I never understand how anyone can hurt innocent kids. Or dogs. People who hurt dogs and kids make me sick."

Freddie gave him his card and went through the usual spiel about calling with anything else that might be relevant. "Thank you for your time. We appreciate it."

"If it wasn't him, I hope you catch the person who hurt those kids."

"We're doing our best," Freddie said.

"It was cool to meet you, Mrs. Cappuano."

"It's Lieutenant Holland on the job, but thank you."

"My wife thinks you're a badass for being a cop while you're first lady."

"Tell her thanks from me, and I wish you guys all the best in your fertility journey."

"Thanks. It's a bitch."

"Yes, it is."

"Are you still hoping to have a baby?" he asked her.

"Not like I was. We're very happy with the family we have."

"It's good to know there's hope."

"There's always hope," Sam said. "Best of luck to you."

"You, too. Tell your husband to keep his chin up. Plenty of people support him."

"He'll be glad to hear that."

As they walked back to the car where Vernon and Jimmy waited for them, Sam said, "I didn't like him at first, but he rallied toward the end."

"Yes, he did," Freddie said with a laugh. "My heart goes out to him and the others struggling to have babies, only to be victimized by their doctor."

"It's awful. What's next, boss man?"

"We need to talk to the lawyer who was representing Marcel on the lawsuit. Ed Leery."

"Let's do it."

LEERY'S OFFICE was located two blocks from the Capitol in a red-brick townhouse.

Freddie rang the bell and then waited while Sam looked longingly at the neighborhood she'd called home all her life—until recently. They were three blocks from Ninth Street, the closest she'd been to their home in weeks. She'd need to go there before the trip to Bora Bora to get some of her summer clothes. That was something else to look forward to. It'd been only a couple of months since they moved across town, but it felt like forever since they'd lived on Ninth.

"Why don't you call him?" Sam said.

Freddie found the number, made the call and put it on speaker.

"Ed Leery."

"This is Detective Cruz with the Metro PD. I'm outside your office and would appreciate a few minutes of your time."

"Um, sure. I'll be right there."

The man who came to the door was tall and lean, with tousled gray hair. He wore a dress shirt under a gray cashmere V-neck sweater. "Come in. Sorry about that. I keep meaning to get the doorbell fixed." When he noticed Sam behind Freddie, he said, "Oh. It's you. The first lady."

"Lieutenant Holland," she said, showing him her badge as Freddie did the same.

"What can I do for you?" he asked, his gaze set on Sam in a stare that made her uncomfortable.

Why did people have to fucking stare at her?

"We understand you were representing Marcel Blanchet in the lawsuit filed by four former patients," Freddie said.

"I was," he said, sighing as he thankfully turned his attention toward Freddie. "Come on back."

He led them to an office in which loaded bookcases occupied all the available wall space. A laptop was nearly buried under a mountain of files and papers on his desk. He cleared files from a small sofa. "Have a seat. I wondered if you would contact me. Didn't expect to get the first lady herself," he added with a small grin that Sam wished she could smack off his face.

"What can you tell us about Dr. Blanchet's state of mind in recent weeks?" Freddie asked.

Sam appreciated that he pressed on, ignoring the first-lady comment.

"He was very upset about the lawsuit, as you can imagine. He'd spent his life building an impeccable reputation that was going to be torn apart in a matter of days. I was concerned about him and said as much to him the last time I saw him."

"What did he say?"

"That he was coping as best he could and that he would vigorously defend himself against the specious allegations."

"Did you believe him when he said he was innocent?"

"I did."

"How do you explain four different women coming forward with the same story about what he did to them?"

"How to say this delicately..."

Again, he glanced at Sam with that same small smile that put her on edge.

"Women experiencing infertility are often overwrought—"

"I'm going to stop you right there." Sam had reached her limit with this guy. "They are not overwrought because of the many disappointments that can be associated with infertility. In this case, the four women are infuriated because their doctor took advantage of them when they were at their most vulnerable."

"It was their word against his."

"We believe them," Sam said, giving him her most effective cop stare.

He was the first to blink. "My job was to defend him against those allegations. That's what I was doing."

"By smearing them?" Freddie asked.

"Whatever it took to protect my client and his reputation."

"How do you sleep at night?" Sam asked.

"Quite well. Like you, I have a job to do. Is it always sunshine and roses? Hardly ever, but everyone deserves a robust defense, especially when their life's work is at stake."

"Did Dr. Blanchet indicate why he would've risked that life's work by doing what he did to those women?" Freddie asked.

"He emphatically denied ever acting in an inappropriate manner with any of his patients. He was revolted by the accusations."

"Did he seem suicidal to you?" Freddie asked.

"Not at all. He seemed determined and was looking forward to the opportunity to defend himself in court." Leery leaned forward, elbows on his desk. "Do you think he did this? That he killed his family and then himself?"

"We're investigating all possibilities."

"There's no way he would've done that. All he cared about were his kids and his wife and how this was going to affect them. He was sick over that. He loved his family more than anything, which is something he said often. I can't picture any scenario where he could be responsible for this."

"Is there anything else you can tell us that might be relevant?" Freddie asked.

"The people suing him—the women and their partners—there was a lot of anger in that group. You should take a close look there."

"We're looking at everything." Freddie handed him his card. "Call me if you think of anything else."

"I really hope you figure out what happened. I can't stop thinking about those poor kids."

"We can't either," Freddie said. "We're working it as hard as we can. We'll see ourselves out."

When they stepped out into the chill, Sam zipped her coat and took a deep breath of the fresh air. "That guy gave me the creeps."

"Why? Because he kept staring at you?"

"For one thing. That he was defending Marcel against the credible claims of four women and actually believed in him is disgusting."

"Playing devil's advocate," Freddie said, "it's his job to believe Marcel and defend him in the lawsuit."

"It's still disgusting, especially the part where he described the women as overwrought."

"I was afraid you might throat-punch him when he said that," Freddie said with a chuckle.

"I wanted to."

"I admire your restraint."

"Thank you. I do, too."

"Is the lieutenant displaying restraint?" Vernon asked as he held the car door for them.

"There was a comment about women suffering from infertility being overwrought," Freddie said.

"I bet you wanted to throat-punch him," Vernon said.

Sam laughed. "I love you more every day, Vernon."

"Likewise, Sam."

The exchange gave her a warm and fuzzy feeling that reminded her of being with her dad, which immediately made her emotional. She turned to look out the window so Freddie wouldn't see the tears in her eyes. The longer Skip was gone, the more she missed him. But she couldn't deny that the fatherly affection from Vernon helped to fill a bit of the void. Life was so crazy that way. Skip had left. Vernon had entered.

And the days went rolling on.

CHAPTER TWENTY-THREE

"Y ou okay?" Freddie asked. "I'm sure this case is triggering in some ways for you."

"I'm okay about that." She picked up her phone and typed a text to him. *Vernon hit me in the feels just now. Thinking about Skippy and how one door closes... etc.*

Vernon adores you.

Likewise. I enjoy him—and Jimmy.

They're good guys to spend the day with.

For sure. Okay, that's it. I'm over it.

LOL

"Hey, Jimmy," Sam said. "You told me you're married, but you never gave me the details. Fess up."

"Oh, um, my wife's name is Liz, and we've been together since ninth grade."

"Of course you have," Sam said. "That's very sweet. What does she do?"

"She teaches kindergarten at Malcolm X Elementary in Southeast."

"Ah, that's amazing. I need to see a picture."

He handed his phone to her. "That's us in ninth grade. The next one is our wedding, and then after that is last weekend."

Sam scrolled through the photos of the young blond couple, to a stunning bride and groom, to a third photo of a happily married couple. "You guys are adorable."

"Thanks. We're expecting our first baby this summer."

"Congratulations," Sam and Freddie said together.

"Do you know what you're having?" Sam asked.

"A boy."

"So fun. Can't wait to meet Liz and your son."

"She'd love that. She's one of your many fans."

"I have fans?" Sam asked.

The three men laughed.

"She has no clue," Freddie said.

"And I like it that way," Sam said. "What's the latest with the Joint Chiefs and Nick's mother?"

Freddie checked his phone. "Nick's mother is being held without bail. The prosecutor described her as a flight risk."

"That's a relief. I was worried about the mayhem she might unleash if they released her."

"There's some talk about the Joint Chiefs not being prosecuted, but they'll be dishonorably discharged from the military with their pensions put under review."

"How can they not be prosecuted for plotting to overthrow the president?" Sam asked as outrage bubbled up inside her.

"I guess they were smart enough not to leave a paper trail. All the conversations were in person and weren't recorded."

"But didn't they confess to it?" Sam asked.

"Not in so many words," Freddie said. "It's more that they didn't deny the rumor that was passed on to Nick."

"Wow," Sam said. "So you can do something like that and continue to walk free, but people get thrown in jail for a million lesser offenses."

She felt terrible for Nick, who'd been so badly betrayed by people who should've had his back.

"If I may..." Vernon said, glancing at her in the mirror.

"Please," Sam said. "Speak freely."

"Over time, he'll show people what he's made of. There may be bumps in the road, like this thing with the Joint Chiefs, but in the end, the people will know the truth about him."

"Thank you, Vernon. That helps."

"Every president gets put through the wringer, whether they were elected or not," Vernon said. "While this is worse than what most deal with, he's not any different that way. Any time someone reaches the pinnacle of their career, the haters are there to tear them down. You've seen that yourself."

"Yes," Sam said, "I have."

"People suck," Jimmy said bluntly.

"You're speaking my language, and I very much appreciate the support," Sam said. "Enough about the haters. Vernon, your turn to tell me about your wife and family."

"My wife, Evelyn, and I have been married twenty-six years and have four daughters ages twenty-four to seventeen."

"Whoa," Freddie said. "You must have some stories."

"I could entertain you all evening with the adventures of parenting four preteen and teenage girls at the same time."

"No wonder why putting up with me is no big deal to you," Sam said.

"You said that. Not me."

Sam laughed along with Freddie and Jimmy. A few months ago, she'd chafed against having a detail. Vernon and Jimmy had made it so bearable that she now preferred for them to drive her. Who said she couldn't learn and grow?

Back at HQ, Sam and Freddie convened in the conference room.

"I have to be honest," Freddie said.

"I wouldn't want you to be any other way."

"I feel like we're wasting time on this case that could be better spent cleaning up Stahl's mess."

Sam leaned against the conference room table. "I agree it's starting to add up that someone who was a great husband and father could've blown under tremendous pressure and done something extremely out of character."

"That's how I see it, too. The lawsuit would ruin him. It would've engulfed them all in an epic scandal. Like you said, imagine them having to explain to kids in middle school that Daddy ejaculated on his patients. They would have been taunted by their peers, and Eloise was already under enough pressure."

Sam cringed. "Pressure like that could make the sanest person crazy."

"What I want to know is why a guy who had it all would do something like that in the first place," Freddie said. "He'd dealt with the deeply personal medical issues of thousands of female patients over the years. What caused him to suddenly become a deviant?"

"I'd like to know that, too," Sam said. "The fact that we're still asking questions like that means we aren't a hundred percent sold on murder-suicide, so we keep working the case."

"Tomorrow, we'll start at his office and talk to his staff," Freddie said. "I'm willing to give it one more day and then see where we're at."

"That sounds like a good plan," Sam said.

"Do you agree that there comes a time when we have to listen to the preponderance of evidence that's pointing in a certain direction?"

Sam fanned her face.

Freddie's brows furrowed. "What's the matter with you?"

"My little grasshopper is using words like 'preponderance.'"

"Shut up. I'm being serious."

"So am I."

He huffed out an exasperated breath. "Do you agree with what I said?"

"Yes, I do."

"Why couldn't you just say that?"

"Because it's far more fun to bust your balls."

"My balls aren't interested in being busted by you."

"It's far too late to tell me that."

"Get busy reading the rest of the texts and emails, and don't talk to me again until you have something useful to say."

"Yes, sir," Sam said, saluting him.

"Eff off."

"Freddie! You almost said a swear!"

"You drive me to it."

Deputy Chief Jeannie McBride appeared in the doorway to the conference room. "Am I interrupting?"

"We were just bickering," Sam said.

Jeannie smiled. "Ah, so business as usual?"

"That's right. What's up, Chief?" It made Sam so damned proud to see her former detective wearing the deputy chief's uniform. Jeannie's pregnancy was beginning to show under her untucked white uniform shirt.

"I've been working with Green and Lucas on the Davies case."

"Refresh my memory," Sam said.

"Eric Davies was convicted sixteen years ago on rape charges. He's denied the accusations vociferously every step of the way. Stahl investigated, tied him to the crime and testified at trial.

Davies has always claimed that the evidence was manufactured to make him look guilty. With what we know now about Stahl, we're giving the case a fresh look."

"And finding irregularities everywhere we look," Cameron Green said when he joined them, holding a manila file folder. "We're unable to locate any of the so-called evidence that was used to convict Mr. Davies. The rape kit has magically disappeared, the alleged victim is 'missing,' and I found a complaint that Mr. Davies made against Stahl after a traffic incident when Stahl was in Patrol."

"Oh my God," Sam said.

"My thoughts exactly," Jeannie said. "It's unbelievable."

"I think it's time to bring the USA in on this," Cameron said.

"It's sixteen years past time for that," Sam said, feeling sick to her soul for the man who'd spent sixteen years in prison for a heinous crime he most likely hadn't committed.

"I wanted your input before I called Forrester," Jeannie said to Sam.

"Why? You're the deputy chief."

Jeannie smiled. "And yet, your opinion is still the one I want at times like these."

"My opinion is always free of charge to you. Before you call the USA, I'd brief the chief."

"Will do. And by the way, Detectives Green and Lucas did great work on the review of this case."

"Duly noted." After Jeannie left, Sam said, "Am I the only one who feels sick?"

"Nope," Green said. "I've been feeling sick since I found the complaint Davies launched against Stahl, who roughed him up during a routine traffic stop. Stahl was suspended without pay for three days."

"And exacted his revenge the minute he could," Freddie said, shaking his head.

"On rape charges, of all things," Sam added. "Other than murder, the vilest accusation there is."

"From what I can tell, Stahl persuaded a woman to seduce Davies, had a rape kit performed on her and then charged him. We believe the woman in question was facing drug charges that were suddenly dropped after she slept with Davies."

Sam heard the words he was saying, but could barely process the implications.

"This'll be another massive scandal," Freddie said.

"What will?" Malone asked as he came into the conference room.

Sam looked to Green to update the captain.

After Cameron filled him in, Malone's expression was one of shock and outrage. "Does the chief know?"

"Jeannie was going to brief him before she calls the USA's office," Sam said.

Malone sat in one of the chairs and seemed to sag into himself. "Just when we think we've seen the full extent of his depravity…"

"There's more," Sam said.

"Yeah." Malone ran his fingers through his hair. He seemed to rally all at once as he stood. "I need to talk to Joe."

FUELED BY OUTRAGE AND DESPAIR, Jake Malone walked from the detectives' pit to the chief's suite. "May I?" Jake asked Helen, the chief's admin, as he pointed to the closed door to Joe's office.

"Go ahead."

She could probably tell he was set to boil as she waved him in.

He knocked once on the door and went in. Deputy Chief McBride was seated in one of the two chairs that faced Joe's desk.

The chief glanced at Jake, his gaze full of despair. "I take it you've heard."

"I have."

Jake sat next to Jeannie. "What's the plan?"

"I was about to call Tom Forrester." Joe picked up the receiver on his desk phone and asked Helen to call Tom for him, telling her to use the word *urgent*. While they waited, the three of them sat in uneasy silence.

The phone beeped a minute later. "Tom Forrester on line one for you, sir."

Joe took the call, putting it on speaker. "Hi, Tom. I'm here with Deputy Chief McBride and Captain Malone."

"What's up?" Tom asked in the distinctive New York accent he was known for.

"We have a situation. I'll let Chief McBride brief you."

Jeannie went through the facts of what they'd uncovered in a review of the Davies case. For a full thirty seconds after she finished speaking, Forrester was silent.

"Son of a bitch," he finally said. "Let me talk to my team. I'll be back to you ASAP."

"Thank you."

"Please tell me we'll be filing additional charges against Stahl after this is dealt with," Jake said after the chief disconnected the call with Forrester.

"Hell yes," the chief replied. "Even though he's already serving a life sentence with no chance of parole, we'll still charge him for every egregious violation he committed while wearing a badge. If for no other reason than to put everyone else on notice that we won't tolerate criminal behavior in our ranks."

"How much more do you think there is?" Jake asked.

"I think we're going to find other similar cases," Jeannie said.

"Motherfucker," Jake whispered.

"At least this one happened before I was chief," Joe said, "so they can't blame me for it."

"But they will anyway," Jake said.

"No doubt, but hopefully we'll get some credit for doing the right thing when we discovered the irregularities."

"Let's hope so," Jake said as he stood. "Keep me posted on what you hear from Forrester."

"Will do," Joe said.

When Jake returned to his office, Lieutenant Archelotta was waiting for him. "What's up?"

Archie held up a flash drive. "I think I've figured out who was archiving reports for Stahl."

"Who?"

"Remember Lieutenant Gibbons?"

"Who headed IT before you? What about him?"

"I believe he gave himself captain-level access so he could do Stahl's bidding."

"And you've got proof?" Malone asked, gesturing to the drive.

"I do."

Resigned to this day going completely to hell and another former officer being charged with a crime, Malone said, "Let's see what you've got."

. . .

SAM AND FREDDIE spent the remainder of their shift going through the printouts the rest of their team had put together from the Blanchets' financial institutions, their social media and more emails and text messages from the parents' phones and computers.

"It's amazing how one couple amasses a mountain of paper, isn't it?" Freddie asked as he worked through their social media posts.

"People never think about how their messages might someday be reviewed by law enforcement investigating a crime. If so, would they text or email their true feelings about anything?"

"Probably not," he said. "It's always in the back of my head that my own words could be used against me."

"You really think about that?"

"All the time, and you should, too, since your public-facing comments and posts will be archived for history in Nick's presidential library."

As Sam cringed to let him know what she thought of that, the BlackBerry rang with a call from Nick.

"Hey," she said. "Speak of the devil. How's things?"

"Just ducky," Nick said with an edge of sarcasm in his tone that told the true story. "I'm with the kids, and we're wondering if we should hold dinner for you."

"No, go ahead. I'm going to pop into the grief group meeting before I head home."

"Oh, that's right. You told me you were doing that."

"No worries. I'm sure you've had a long day since we had that conversation."

"I'll feed them and wait to eat with you."

"Sounds good. I won't be long at the meeting. I just like to show my face in support of the effort."

"Maybe you ought to stay this time and participate."

"We'll see."

"Whatever you need, babe."

"I'll text when I'm on the way home."

"Love you."

"Love you, too."

"How is he?" Freddie asked after she put the BlackBerry back on the table.

"He sounds exhausted."

"I suppose that's to be expected when your top military officials plot to overthrow your government," Freddie said, "while your mother is in jail on racketeering charges and your disgraced former secretary of State is trashing you to anyone who'll listen."

Sam sighed. "That's a hell of a mouthful."

"It's a hell of a crap storm."

"Yes, it is. I worry about him buckling under the weight of it all."

"He won't. He's tough, and he knows how to handle himself in all situations, including these."

"I hope so."

"He's got this, Sam. You don't have to worry."

"And yet, I do."

Freddie stood to stretch and then returned to his seat. "I'm looking at Liliana's Instagram posts. They validate everything the grandmother told us." He put the printouts on the table in front of her. Marcel was shown with each of his kids, playing in the yard, pushing them on swings, painting a canvas on an easel with little Gus.

Sam zeroed in on the painting photo and then reached for the autopsy report.

"What?" Freddie asked.

"Let me see the rest of the Insta photos."

He handed them to her.

Sam sifted through them until she found one of Marcel helping Eloise with her homework. "See that?" She pointed to the hand that held the pen and then to the photo of him holding a brush.

"What about it?"

"He was left-handed. The autopsy report said there was gunpowder residue on his *right* hand." She found the reference in the autopsy report, highlighted it with a marker and then looked up at him.

"Holy crap. He was left-handed."

"We should confirm that with his mother," Sam said.

Freddie put the call on speaker and dialed the number he had written in his notebook.

"Hello?"

"Mrs. Blanchet, this is Detective Cruz. I'm sorry to disturb you, but I have a question for you. Was your son right- or left-handed?"

"He was a lefty," she said. "The only one in our family."

"That's very helpful. Thank you so much."

"Of course."

"I'll be in touch."

Freddie pushed the button to end the call. "Someone put that gun in his right hand and pulled the trigger, which eliminates the murder-suicide angle."

Sam was oddly relieved to realize Marcel hadn't turned on his wife and kids. "Now we just have to figure out who wanted them dead."

CHAPTER TWENTY-FOUR

S am met up with Dr. Trulo outside the room on the third floor where the grief group met. "How's Shelby?"

"A little better. She was talking a bit when I checked on her an hour ago, which is a marked improvement from last night."

"Thank you so much for helping her."

"I wish I could say it was a pleasure, but it's such an upsetting thing for them."

"For sure. Avery has to be reeling right along with her."

"He is. That his work could've endangered his loved ones sits heavily on him."

"I can't imagine how he must feel. I'll stop to see them after I leave here." Sam was resigned to getting home even later. "Big crowd tonight."

Trulo glanced toward the room, a buzz of voices echoing in the hallway. "Gets bigger every month. We may have to find a new place to meet at this rate."

"I hope it doesn't come to that." She liked having the meeting upstairs from the office, so it wasn't yet another place she had to go in a day.

"I'll keep an eye on it. Don't worry." He held the door for her as they entered the room and were greeted by a sea of familiar faces.

Sam was pleased to see her sisters among the attendees. She went to hug them. "Glad you made it."

"It was touch and go until the last minute," Tracy said, keeping an arm around Angela, almost as if she might bolt if Tracy let go.

"I'm not sure I'm up for this," Angela said, "but Tracy convinced me to give it a try."

"I'm glad you did," Sam said. "And if it's too much, you can leave. You're not under any obligation to stick it out."

"Good to know. Thanks."

"Anything for you."

Roni Connolly came over to say hello.

"Hey, Roni," Sam said. "You remember my sisters, Tracy and Angela."

"Of course. It's nice to see you again. Angela, would it be okay if I hugged you?"

"Sure," Ang said with a shy smile.

The two women embraced for a long time, and when they pulled back, both were in tears.

Roni took Angela by the hand. "I've got you."

Sam grasped Tracy's arm when her older sister would've followed Roni and Angela. "Let Roni take her."

"Are you sure?"

"I'm positive. Roni knows more about what Angela's dealing with than we ever will. I hope."

"It's brutal seeing her go through this." Tracy looked more exhausted than Sam had ever seen her. "Absolutely brutal."

"Who's got her kids?"

"They're with Mike at our house."

"It's good of you both to make it possible for her to be here."

"I just hope it helps."

When they took their seats, across from Roni and Angela, Sam sent Nick a quick text. *Angela showed up to grief group, so I'm going to stick around, then try to see Shelby after. Don't wait to eat.*

I'm glad she went. I've got plenty to keep me busy until my gorgeous wife gets home.

"Everything okay?" Tracy asked when Sam put the BlackBerry in her pocket.

"Yep."

Dr. Trulo stood before the group of more than fifty people seated in a tight circle. "Welcome to our monthly meeting. I wish I could say I was happy to see you here, but I'm not. I'm sorry for whatever life-changing event has brought you to us, and I hope you can find some comfort by being with people who understand."

Sam was surprised to see Cameron and Gigi come in, holding hands.

"Would anyone like to volunteer to begin?" Dr. Trulo said.

Lenore Worthington raised her hand. "Thank you, Dr. Trulo and Sam, for organizing this group. The meetings and the friends I've made here have become a bit of a lifeline for me lately." She twisted a tissue in her hands. "I've recently gotten the answers I craved for fifteen long years, and I'm finding that to be a hollow victory. I'm not sure what I thought would happen once I could put a face to the person who took my son from me, once I knew *why*, but whatever I thought would happen... Well, it's just another day without my boy. He'd be a man now," she said with a tearful laugh. "He'd be thirty-two soon. Maybe he'd have a wife and kids and a job and a mortgage. He was going places, my Calvin, and I miss him more than ever. That's all I wanted to say."

"Your courage has been an inspiration to all of us, Lenore," Dr. Trulo said. "Thank you for sharing your feelings and for giving a voice to the often-hollow victory that comes with justice."

Sam listened to a number of other people share similar experiences of long-awaited justice being less satisfying than they'd anticipated. She understood that. Knowing who'd killed her father didn't bring him back or change the reality he'd been forced to live with as a quadriplegic the last years of his life. If anything, in his case, the answers had led to more heartache.

"I want you to know, Lenore and everyone else, that I understand how you feel." Sam said the words before she'd even decided to speak. "Even as part of the team that helps get justice for your loved ones, I'm always aware that those answers won't change the fundamental reality of your loss. It didn't change anything for me. In many ways, finding out who shot and eventually killed my dad only made things worse. What does help is knowing that others get it, so thank you for that."

Lenore nodded in agreement and sent a warm smile to Sam. "I couldn't agree more. Thank you for all you did to get justice for my family and for this opportunity to grieve together. It means everything to me."

"We have a number of new people here tonight, and I'd like to offer them the opportunity to share with no obligation," Dr. Trulo said.

Sam noticed that Angela was looking down as Cam and Gigi

glanced at each other.

"I'd like to say something," Gigi said. "I'm Detective Gigi Dominguez, and I've twice been the victim of violent crime recently. I'm completely altered by what happened, first with my former boyfriend who assaulted me and then by..."

"My former girlfriend, who broke into Gigi's home and attacked her, forcing her to defend herself with deadly consequences," Cameron said, his expression grim. "I'm Detective Cameron Green."

"We're both struggling with intense feelings of guilt and regret," Gigi added, "which is a lot of pressure on a new relationship that was making us very happy until this most recent event upended everything."

"I feel horrible for having brought that woman into Gigi's life, when she was already dealing with enough after what happened with her ex," Cameron said. "Now her career is on the line as the department investigates the shooting. I'm sick over the whole thing."

"I hate that I had no choice but to kill her to save myself," Gigi said. "I don't blame Cameron for anything that happened with her, but he has enough guilt for both of us. I don't want him to feel responsible for her hurting me, but how can he not?"

As they spoke, Sam was heartened to see their hands tightly clasped together, presenting a united front even as they expressed fear for their new relationship.

"It's often very difficult to accept the consequences that result from the actions of others," Dr. Trulo said. "The important thing is to remember you weren't in control of what she did. You're only in control of how you react to it. Having some insight into both incidents beyond what you've shared here, I happen to know you did everything you could to manage both situations before they exploded into violence."

"And yet, we both feel like we could've and should've done more," Cam said.

"What else could you have done?" Dr. Trulo asked.

"That's what we lie awake at night thinking about," Gigi said.

"You have to find a way to let go of the guilt," Gonzo said from behind Sam, surprising her as she hadn't seen him come in. "I learned that the hard way, and I don't want to see anyone else I care about suffer the way I did by wallowing in things I couldn't change. Through a lot of therapy and time with our good Dr. Trulo, I've learned that guilt is like a cancer. It'll eat you up inside. And it won't change anything."

"Thank you for sharing that, Tommy," Dr. Trulo said. "I hope you don't mind me saying how proud I am of the progress you've made since the senseless murder of your partner. You're one of my star patients."

"No offense, Doc, but there're a lot of other reasons I wish you were proud of me. I'm learning to make peace with my lack of control over what happens around me."

"I'm proud of you for many reasons, Sergeant," Dr. Trulo said. "I'm most proud of you for the journey you're walking through grief and how you're leading by example."

"What do you do when you're so angry with the person who died that you can barely think of anything but the anger?" The words seemed to erupt from Angela. "What do you do then?"

Sam was taken aback by the force behind her sister's words.

"He's left me with a nightmare to deal with, two little kids, another on the way, and even knowing he was sick doesn't make it any less of a nightmare. I'm furious with him for doing this to me."

"Your feelings are completely valid, Angela," Dr. Trulo said. "You're allowed to feel any way that you do about this unimaginable loss."

"Will I be angry with him forever?"

"No," a woman Sam didn't recognize said. "I'm Hilda, and my husband was killed in an armed robbery. He was the one doing the robbing, though, so he got what was coming to him. At least that's what people said afterward. 'You play the game, you pay the price,' they said. I had three kids under the age of ten, and I was blinded by anger for years afterward. But the anger doesn't last forever. It can't. You have children to think about, and they'll show you the way out of the darkness back into the light. Follow their lead."

"Thank you." Angela gave Hilda a grateful smile. "I needed to hear that."

"I wish I could say it was my pleasure, honey, but I wouldn't wish this journey on anyone," Hilda said. "Please know you're not alone."

"I'm beginning to see that," Angela said. "It helps to know others understand."

"We do," Hilda said. "All too well."

A few others shared their recent struggles, their frustrations with the slow-moving criminal justice system and the unexpected secondary losses of friends and family members who'd faded away, as well as the blessings that had come from connecting with new people.

As always, the meeting made Sam feel uplifted and devastated all at once. She and Tracy waited to walk out with Angela.

"She has my number," Roni said when she delivered Angela to her sisters. "She's promised not to be afraid to use it."

Angela hugged Roni. "Thank you so much."

"Any time."

Roni hugged Sam and Tracy and said her goodbyes.

"It's amazing to meet someone else who's expecting her late husband's baby," Angela said, resting a hand on her protruding belly.

Both women were due in June.

"When she tells you to reach out, she really means it," Sam said. "Her Wild Widows group is incredible. I think you'd really like them."

"I'm sure I will. I'm just not ready yet. I hope you understand."

"Of course I do. You're calling the shots, Ang. Whatever you need whenever you need it."

"Thanks for bringing me tonight, Trace. It helped."

The three of them walked out of the building arm in arm. Sam hugged her sisters goodbye and promised to check in the next day.

"Sorry to keep you guys so late," Sam said to Vernon as he held the back door to the SUV for her.

"No problem at all."

"Yes, it is, and I appreciate it. I'd like to stop at GW for a few minutes on the way home."

"Of course."

When they were on the way to the hospital, Sam texted Nick. *Leaving HQ, stopping to see Shelby for a minute, and then I'll be home. Sorry to be so late.*

No worries. The twins are still up. I think they might be coming down with something...

BOTH of them?

Yep.

Uh-oh. Be there soon.

At GW, she walked through the main doors with Vernon and

Jimmy and took the elevator to Shelby's floor.

"This is the time to go places," Sam said. "No one to stare at me."

Vernon chuckled as he led her off the elevator while Jimmy followed.

As they walked toward Shelby's room, a woman came running toward them. "You're the first lady! Oh my God!"

Vernon held up his hand to stop the woman from getting any closer.

"What's wrong? I was just saying hello."

"Please step back," Vernon said.

"Oh, I see how it is," the woman said, frowning. "You're too good for regular people now."

"What?" Sam said. "You came charging at me out of nowhere. The agents are doing their jobs. How does that make me too good for regular people?"

"I just wanted to say hello," she said, seeming chastened.

"There's nothing wrong with that, but when you come charging at someone under Secret Service protection, they're going to guard their subject. Every time. Okay?"

"I'm sorry."

"Your apology is accepted."

"I'm a big fan of you and your husband."

"Thank you. We appreciate your support."

"Ma'am?" Vernon said, wanting to move her along.

"Have a good night," Sam said to the woman.

"You, too."

"I guess I spoke too soon," Sam said after they'd walked away from the woman.

"Indeed you did," Vernon said. "Thank you for defending us."

"Always."

Sam knocked on the door to Shelby's room and stuck her head in. Avery stood by Shelby's bedside, still wearing the clothes he'd been in the last time she'd seen him. He'd removed the suit coat and had rolled up the sleeves of his white dress shirt. He looked exhausted and overwhelmed, but who could blame him?

"Come in, Sam," Shelby said softly.

Sam stepped into the dimly lit room and went to Shelby's side, taking her hand. "How're you doing?"

"A little better," Shelby said. "Dr. Trulo was a big help. Thanks for asking him to come by."

"I'm glad he was able to help."

"He prescribed some meds that perked me up."

"That's great news."

"I'm trying to get Avery to go home and get some rest, but he refuses to leave."

"I'm with you, kid," he said, sounding weary.

"Is there anything I can do for you guys or Noah?"

"He's with my sister," Shelby said. "Blissfully unaware, thank goodness."

"You'll get through this, Tinker Bell. We'll all make sure of it."

Shelby nodded as her eyes filled with tears. "Thanks for coming by."

"I love you," Sam said.

Shelby squeezed her hand. "Love you, too."

"I'll check in tomorrow, okay? Let me know if there's anything at all we can do for you."

"We will," Avery said. "Thanks, Sam."

"How's she doing?" Vernon asked when Sam rejoined them in the hallway.

"A little better, but still deeply rattled, as anyone would be."

"For sure." Vernon held the elevator door for Sam. "I can't imagine what he must be feeling, too. That something from his work put his family in jeopardy like that..."

"It's something everyone in law enforcement worries about. Even more so these days when everyone is armed."

"It's a scary world," Jimmy said.

"Which makes me extra thankful for you and your colleagues who protect my family," Sam said. "At least I don't have to worry about what happened to Avery and Shelby happening to us."

"No, you don't."

"But all my colleagues do."

"Yes," Vernon said with a sigh, "they do. Maybe you should have a talk with them about ramping up security in their homes."

"I'll do that. This is a wakeup call for everyone." The thought of another of her officers being harmed because of their work was almost more than Sam could bear, especially after losing Detective Arnold so senselessly. They worked so hard to get justice for victims and to keep their community safe. But the risks were high and getting higher all the time.

CHAPTER TWENTY-FIVE

S am arrived home to find Nick in their bed with Aubrey and Alden snuggled up to him. "How are they?" she whispered.

"Finally asleep, but both are running fevers."

She rested her hand on Alden's forehead and was taken aback by the heat radiating from him. "Should we check in with Harry?"

"Already did. He was up here earlier and said he thinks it's just a virus. He prescribed Tylenol and will check on them in the morning."

"That's another way the White House doesn't suck—having a doctor in the house."

"Right?"

"Should we move them to their room?"

"We can try."

Sam took Alden, while Nick carried Aubrey. Thankfully, both children stayed asleep as they were tucked into the bed they still shared in Alden's room, even though Aubrey had her own room. They preferred to be together, which was understandable after losing their parents.

"Rough night around here." Nick rubbed the tension from his neck. "Aubrey was crying for her mommy, which broke my heart."

When they were back in their suite, Sam put her arms around him.

He dropped his head to her shoulder. "Best thing to happen since the last time I was with you."

"Thanks for stepping up for our Littles tonight. I'm sorry I wasn't here."

"You had important things to do."

"I would rather have been here."

"We know that, babe. We always know that."

"Had a decent breakthrough in the case earlier." Sam told him about realizing Dr. Blanchet was left-handed, and the gunpowder residue had been found on his right hand.

"Oh wow," Nick said. "So what does that mean?"

"That the scene was probably staged to make it look like a murder-suicide. At least we know now that it's worth pursuing other leads, but it puts us back at square one."

"I have no doubt you'll figure it out."

"I'm glad you don't." She pulled back to look up at him. "How did things go downstairs today?"

"Just another day in paradise," he said with the wry grin she loved so much.

"Are you okay?"

"I'm okay if you and the kids are okay. Tonight, our Littles are feeling poorly."

"I should stay home with them tomorrow."

"No, you need to go to work. Celia will be here with them, and she's the next best thing."

"Are you sure?"

"I'm positive, Sam. We asked her to be here with us for this very reason. So she could cover for us with the kids when needed."

They got ready for bed and met in the middle of their king-sized bed, as they did every night.

"I can't wait for Bora Bora," Sam said. "I'm counting the days."

"About that…"

"What?"

When she would've pulled back from him, he held her closer. "Terry and Derek think it's a bad time for me to be away with what just happened with the Joint Chiefs."

"*Noooooooooooo.*" She wanted to cry, but knew he was equally disappointed and didn't want to make it worse for him.

"I'm so sorry, babe. I argued with them, reminded them that presidents are allowed to have vacations, that we go every year." His deep sigh said it all. "They didn't come right out and say it, but I think they fear what might happen if I'm away."

"So no trip to Europe either?"

"Not now."

"I hate everything and everyone, except you and the people we love."

"I hate everything, too. Believe me."

"I'm sorrier for you than I am for myself. You must be going mad trapped here every day."

"A little bit."

"If we can't have Bora Bora, we need a date night soon," Sam said. "I see you every day, and yet I miss you, as strange as that sounds."

"I miss you, too, and I know just what you mean. I'll plan something for us soon."

"Not if the kids are still sick."

"I'm sure they'll be fine in a few days."

"I hope so."

"Are you going to hate me someday for messing up our perfectly lovely lives with this job from hell?" he asked.

"I'll never hate you. I hate the Joint Chiefs and your mother and everyone else who says mean things about you. I'd personally stab every one of them with my rusty steak knife if I could."

His low chuckle made her smile. "My fierce first lady is the sexiest woman in the universe."

"Nah."

"Yes, she is, and I love her madly."

"You're going to have to do a lot of making up to me over this." She pressed against him suggestively. "I've been dreaming about naked days and umbrella drinks."

"I'm happy to make it up to you as many times as needed until you forgive me."

"That's apt to take *a lot* of effort on your part."

Nick pressed his hard cock against her. "I'm more than *up* for the job."

"I can tell. Are you just going to talk about it, or can I expect some action?"

He moved so fast, she barely saw it coming before she was on her back with the sexiest man in the world poised above her, looking down at her with fire in his lovely hazel eyes.

"Well, hello there," she said.

"How you doing?"

She curled her legs around his hips and pushed her core against his erection. "Very well and getting better all the time."

"Mmm, right there with you, babe." He pushed into her in one deep thrust that was nearly enough on its own to make her come. "Not yet."

Sam released a sound that was equal parts frustration and desire. "Don't play with me."

"I love to play with you. You're my favorite playmate of this month and every month." He dipped his head, using it to push up her T-shirt to bare her breasts. His tongue stroked her nipple, which drove her mad. Of course he knew that, which was why he did it.

"I was in a meeting today about the latest jobs report, and I found myself thinking about you and this." He bit down on her nipple, drawing a sharp cry from her. "I love how you distract me even when you're nowhere near me."

He seduced her with everything he had to work with. And like always, the combination did it for her the way nothing and no one else ever had. For some reason, she thought of Angela, who now had to live without her love, and suddenly, Sam had tears streaming down her face.

"Babe... What's wrong?"

Sam reached for him. "Nothing. Don't stop."

Thankfully, he did as she asked, moving quickly to bring them both to the finish line with gasps of pleasure and words of love.

When he'd caught his breath, he raised his head and kissed the tears off her cheeks. "What is it?"

"I suddenly thought of Ang and how she's lost her Nick. It overwhelmed me for a second there."

"I'm sorry, sweetheart."

"It's like I'm watching my sister live all my greatest fears, which makes me feel selfish. It's not about me. It's about her and the kids."

"It's about you, too. The loss we both fear the most has struck very close to home. It's got us both trying to imagine the unimaginable."

"Yes, exactly," she said with a sigh of relief. He got it. He always got it.

"You're not doing anything wrong by dwelling on the what-ifs. Sometimes I think that by allowing those thoughts in, we're preparing ourselves if the worst should ever happen. Which it won't."

"We can't know that."

"No, we can't, but the odds are pretty good that two healthy people will go the distance together."

"I'm not as healthy as I could be," Sam said. "Any time I have to chase someone, I realize how out of shape I am."

"There's a gym right here in the White House."

"Shut your filthy mouth."

Laughter shook his entire body—and hers since they were still joined. "My wife is a piece of work."

"I hear that quite often, believe it or not."

"I love her just the way she is. In my eyes, she's absolute perfection."

"It's a good thing I found you again, because you're the only guy on earth who could put up with me the way you do."

He kissed her softly and tenderly. "Putting up with you is the best thing to ever happen to me."

THE KIDS WERE STILL feverish in the morning, so Sam set them up with *Paw Patrol* on TV in the sitting room of her and Nick's suite, called their school to let them know they'd be staying home and then called Freddie. "I'm going to be late, but I'll catch up later this morning."

"I'll keep you posted on where I am."

"Take Gonzo with you. I don't want anyone working alone in the field." She'd had enough of her friends and colleagues being in grave danger to last her a lifetime.

"Yes, ma'am. I woke up in the middle of the night with a thought."

"I'm so proud."

"Of what?" he asked, sounding exasperated.

"Of how you're letting the case consume you, even when you're asleep."

"There is so much wrong with that statement, I don't even know where to begin."

Sam laughed. "About your middle-of-the-night revelation..."

"Liliana's friend Kelly said there was no way she was having an affair. But she didn't know about the lawsuit, so maybe she also didn't know about the affair."

"Good point. Double back with the other friend... What was her name?"

"Cara Quinn. I didn't ask her about an affair because Kelly was so certain it wasn't happening. Maybe there were things she told one friend but not the other for whatever reason."

"Stands to reason."

"I should've asked Cara about the affair."

"You can ask her now. It's all good. I'll catch up."

"See you in a bit."

Next, Sam called Avery to check on Shelby.

"She's doing all right," he said. "They're planning to send her home today, but she doesn't want to go to our place."

"Bring her here," Sam said without hesitation. "We have plenty of room, and she can rest and relax until she feels strong enough to go home."

"Are you sure, Sam? You guys have so much going on."

"I'm positive. The White House staff will pamper her, and she needs that right now."

"Then I gratefully accept. I'm already looking at moving us somewhere much more secure."

"There's nowhere more secure than the White House, so bring her home to us until you figure out your next move."

"I will. Thanks, Sam. I really appreciate this."

"No problem," Sam said.

Nick stood in front of her knotting his tie as she said goodbye to Avery. "That's a good idea to have them come here."

"She needs to feel safe right now," Sam said. "Which is yet another perk of La Casa Blanca."

"You're seeing a lot of perks to this place lately," Nick said.

"Don't start making a list or anything."

"Would I do that?"

"Yes, you would, and then you'd use it to remind me of why you should run for reelection."

"Still not planning to run."

"Don't make any decisions yet."

He raised his brows in surprise. "What're you saying?"

"I'm saying that you don't need to be hasty in deciding anything. You've only been in the job for a couple of months."

"Which have been hellacious."

"But you're still standing. We're adjusting fine. Everything is working out, for the most part."

"Who are you, and what have you done with my cranky, difficult—albeit ridiculously sexy—wife?"

"Haha," Sam said as she put her hair up in a clip. "What can I say? I like having a doctor at my beck and call."

"You have that even when I'm not president. Harry would come running for us. You know that."

"But he'd have to *travel* to us. Here, he's in the building most of every day. That's a perk. As is the room service, the space to house any guests we want to have, someone else doing the cooking, the cleaning, the laundry while you're working just downstairs. It doesn't totally suck."

Nick came over to her and put his hand on her forehead.

"Stop," she said, laughing. "I don't have a fever."

"And yet, I'm still alarmed by this new, agreeable version of my first lady."

She went up on tiptoes to kiss him. "Enjoy her while she lasts. The regular version will be back soon, I'm sure."

"You know I love every version of her, right? The sweet, the sexy, the contrary, the bossy, the—"

Sam kissed him again. "Those are more than enough versions."

"I love them all."

"I'm thankful for that every day."

"Tonight, I want some time in the loft with my wife."

"Yes, please."

"We'll have dinner up there. I'll arrange it."

"Can't wait."

"I'm off to my daily briefing on the world's terrors. Wish me luck."

"Good luck. Have a good day. I'll text you when I leave Celia in charge."

"Tell her to call me if she needs me."

"I will, and I'll let Gideon know that Shelby, Avery and Noah will be coming to stay for a bit."

"Sounds good." He stole another kiss. "Be careful with my wife today. She's everything to me."

"Take good care of my POTUS. He's the sexiest president in the history of not-sexy presidents."

The grin that lit up his handsome face was her favorite thing ever.

"Well, there was JFK, and you said Barack was kinda hot."

"They had nothing on my POTUS."

They went to the sitting room to see the Littles, who were snuggled up together under their favorite blanket.

Nick sat next to them on the sofa, where Skippy was cozied up to them. If Scotty was at school or out of the building, the Littles were the dog's next favorite. "How're my buddies feeling?"

"Okay," Alden said.

"Hot," Aubrey said.

Sam uncovered her and fluffed the sofa pillow under her head. "How about some breakfast?"

"Can we have oatmeal?" Alden asked.

"You can have whatever you want," Sam said.

"I want Froot Loops," Aubrey said, taking full advantage of the opening to ask for the sugary cereal she wasn't usually allowed to have.

"Oatmeal and Froot Loops coming up."

Nick kissed their foreheads and told them he'd be up to check on them in a little while.

Sam called the line to the butlers to order breakfast for the twins, adding an egg-white omelet and coffee for herself. "If we can get raisins in the oatmeal, Alden would be most appreciative," Sam said.

"Yes, ma'am, Mrs. Cappuano. We'll be right up."

"Thank you so much."

"Our pleasure."

"Breakfast is on the way," she told the twins. Then she put through a call to Gideon.

"Good morning," he said.

"Hi there. I wanted to let you know that Mrs. Hill, Agent Hill and Noah will be staying with us for a bit. Can we set them up with one of the suites on the third floor?"

"Absolutely. I'll take care of that right away."

"Can you please let Dr. Flynn know that she's being discharged from the hospital—"

A knock on the door sounded, and Harry poked his head in.

"Never mind on that last part. He's here now. I'll let him know."

"I'll get things ready for them."

"She needs top-level White House pampering."

"I'll see to it that's what she gets."

"Thanks, Gideon."

"You got it."

Sam put down the phone and greeted Harry with a hug. "Thanks for coming by."

"I just saw Nick, and he told me our Littles are still under the weather."

"They are," Sam said. "Should we be worried?"

"I checked in with their school nurse, and she told me the virus has been going around. It includes a fever, body aches and general malaise, which matches their symptoms. The good news is that it only lasts a couple of days. The bad news is that it's contagious."

"Excellent," Sam said with a grimace.

"Let me just take a quick look at them," he said.

Harry proceeded to charm the Littles with his quick wit and easy manner. "You'll feel much better by tomorrow," he told them. Looking up at Sam, he added, "You can continue to alternate the Tylenol and ibuprofen every two hours to combat the fever."

"I gave them the Tylenol earlier, so I'll let Celia know." She'd also have to tell her stepmother that the twins' virus was contagious. Perhaps she'd want to take a pass on caring for them that day. "Thanks for coming by, Harry. We appreciate you."

"No problem."

Sam texted her stepmother with an update on what Harry had told her and to let her know that Shelby, Avery and Noah would be staying with them for a while.

I was with the twins yesterday, so I've already been exposed. No worries. As a crusty old nurse, I'm usually pretty bulletproof when it comes to what's going around. I'm glad to hear that Shelby and fam will be coming here. She needs to feel safe right now. I'll be down shortly to relieve you so you can get to work.

Thank you, Sam replied. *You're the best.*

Love you all to pieces.

Asking Celia to join them at the White House had been Freddie's brilliant idea, and it had worked out so well for all of them. Celia had told her recently how much the change in scenery and new routine were helping her move forward after Skip's sudden death. Celia had taken such beautiful care of Sam's dad after his terrible injury, and Sam was thankful to still have her stepmother in her daily life.

Reginald, one of the butlers, arrived with breakfast, which the kids picked at.

When they were finished eating, Aubrey reached for her, and Sam picked her up, settling the little girl on her lap for a snuggle while they watched their show. She had a million things to do and not enough hours in the day to accomplish it all, but for this moment, she was right where she belonged.

CHAPTER TWENTY-SIX

"I demand to know when I will be released from this hellhole," Nicoletta said to the guard who'd brought her breakfast, if you could call the slop on the tray "breakfast."

"You've been held without bail, which means there's no chance of you leaving for now."

"I could pay for a better lawyer."

"I believe your assets have been frozen by the U.S. Attorney as the investigations proceed."

"My son is the president of the United States! When he finds out how I'm being treated here, he'll have your jobs."

"From what I've read, he has no interest in what's happening to you."

"You'll pay for that. If it's the last thing I do, I'll make sure you pay."

"Okay," he said over his shoulder as he walked away.

The outrage was compounding with every day she spent in this miserable place. How could her son, the most powerful man on earth, allow his own mother to rot in jail when he could get her out of there with a single phone call?

They'd allowed her to shower in a trough with a bunch of other women, and she'd traded the now-ratty red silk dressing gown for an orange jumpsuit that was too small for her. She was constantly dealing with a wedgie that only added to her outrage.

"Is your son really the president?" one of the other women asked.

"He is."

"Then how come you're still here?"

Nicoletta took a seat next to the first woman in the cell who'd spoken to her since she'd been there. She was a buxom redhead with big green eyes. "We're not on the best of terms, I guess you could say."

"Still, you're his mother. He ought to have some respect."

"That's what I say, too, but what can I do from in here?"

"I know a lawyer who'd take your case for free to get the exposure."

"You do? Who is he?"

"His name is Collins Worthy, and he's an absolute shark. If you want attention for your situation, you need him on your team."

"You heard what the guard said. I was denied bail, and my assets are frozen."

"He'd take a case like yours for free for the exposure, and he can get you a new bail hearing."

"Why are you telling me this?"

"Because I'm a mother, too, and my kids don't care about me either. We have to stick together."

"Yes, we do. How can I get him on my case?"

"Ask the guards to call him for you."

"And they'll do it?"

"They have to."

"How do you know all this?"

"Not my first rodeo, sugar."

"What's in it for you?" Nicoletta asked, leery of anything that seemed too good to be true.

"Maybe you could keep a spot for me when you get back to work."

"Have you worked in the field before?"

"Here and there, but not with the success you've had."

"Did you know who I was before I mentioned my son?"

"I sure did. You're a legend in these parts."

"Is that so?" Nicoletta sat up straighter. "That's nice to hear."

"We need to get you out of here and back to doing what you were born to do."

"From your lips to God's ears. What's your name?"

"Amber Richmond."

"It's nice to meet you."

"You, as well. Tell them to call Collins for you. He'll get you out of here and make your son sorry he disrespected you."

"I'll do that."

"And when I get out of here, you'll take my call?"

"You're damned right I will."

FREDDIE BEGAN his day with a call to Cara Quinn. "This is Detective Cruz circling back with another question."

"Whatever I can do."

"You said you spoke daily with Liliana, right?" he asked, even though he already knew that from the data found on Liliana's phone.

"Yes, we rarely missed a day."

"Did she mention anything about an affair she might be having?"

After a long pause, Cara said, "No."

"It took you a long time to answer that question, Ms. Quinn. Are you sure?"

"I, uh... Lili was such a good person. The best person I ever knew. She'd do anything for anyone."

"But?"

"No buts," she said, sounding tearful now. "She was so good to everyone."

"I understand this is very difficult for you, but we're trying to figure out what happened to her and her family."

"It was Marcel. I'm sure of it."

"We've uncovered evidence to the contrary."

"What evidence?"

"I'm not at liberty to share that. I'd really like to know if Liliana was involved with someone outside of her marriage."

"If I tell you, will it be smeared all over the place?"

"I'll do my best to avoid that."

"But you can't make any promises."

"No, not in a homicide investigation."

"I'm still in denial that this has happened. How can they all be gone?"

"I'm sorry again for your loss and for compounding it by asking questions you'd rather not answer."

Her deep sigh echoed through the phone. "It wasn't a sexual affair."

"Okay..."

"It's important that you know she never slept with him."

"I'll need you to elaborate."

"She struck up a friendship with one of the dads at Gus's preschool. They met while waiting to pick up the kids. One thing led to another, and they began talking every day by phone. He's a single dad, so it wasn't as big of a deal for him. But she developed very significant feelings for him."

"Do you know his name?"

"Keenan. I don't know his last name."

"This is very helpful. Thank you."

"Please be kind to my friend in how you use this information. She was a wonderful wife and mother. The lawsuit... It wrecked her. She believed the women and had come to the realization that she needed to leave Marcel, which was devastating. They'd been so happy together for such a long time."

Freddie took notes as she spoke. "Is there anything else we should know? Anything at all?"

"Not that I can think of."

"You're sure? Because withholding information in a homicide investigation is a crime."

"I'm sure."

"Thank you again for your time."

"I hope you get justice for my friend and her children."

"We're doing everything we can."

Freddie ended the call and went looking for the dump of Liliana's phone, zeroing in on any lengthy late-night phone calls, figuring that's when busy parents would have time to talk. He was able to eliminate the numbers belonging to Kelly, Cara and Liliana's sister, Esme. That left one number unaccounted for, which he assumed belonged to Keenan.

He ran upstairs to IT. "I need a favor," he said to Archie.

"What's up?"

Freddie circled the number and handed Archie his notebook. "I need a name and address."

With a few keystrokes on his computer, Archie produced the name Keenan Coleman. "He lives in Berkley on Meadow Road."

Archie returned the notebook with the address written next to the number.

"Thanks, man."

"How's it going?"

"Slow but making progress."

"You don't think it was the dad?"

"We're all but sure it wasn't." He told Archie about Marcel being left-handed and gunpowder residue being found on his right hand.

"Wow, that's a good catch."

"Gotta give the LT credit for that."

"Is she doing okay?"

"I think so. She's back to work after the briefest leave of absence in history."

Archie grinned. "I knew she wouldn't stay gone for long."

"Same. Thanks again for the help."

"Any time."

Freddie went back downstairs to find Gonzo. "I've got a lead on a guy Liliana Blanchet was having an emotional affair with."

"What the hell is an emotional affair?"

"The kind with no sex."

"What's the point of that?"

"She was going through a rough time with the lawsuit about to blow up their lives. I guess the other guy provided support and comfort."

"Interesting. Let's go see what he has to say."

JAKE MALONE HAD BEEN AWAKE all night thinking about the dreaded task he needed to deal with first thing that morning. He ought to have someone else with him, but this was so intensely personal, he'd decided to do it himself. After he finished a second cup of coffee at home, he left the house in his MPD SUV and drove to the familiar address off Grove Street in Petworth.

He'd been there many times before for parties, poker nights and other gatherings of friends who became family when you worked together every day.

That was the part of this situation that galled him the most.

Bill Gibbons had been like family to him, Joe, Skip and many others who'd come up through the ranks with them. Gibbons had loved being in charge of IT and reminded Jake of Sam Holland and how she was perfectly content to lead the Homicide division with no desire to move up in the ranks.

That described Bill to a T. He'd balked at any suggestion of doing any other job within the department. Like Archelotta now, Gibbons had been the best at what he did, adapting to each new technological development to make things easier for the rest of them. He'd been their go-to guy any time a computer acted up at home or at work as they transitioned to the electronic age.

Gibbons had led seminars for his colleagues on how to use new technology to solve their cases.

And the son of a bitch had enabled Len Stahl's criminal activity.

With twenty-four hours to process the info Archie had given him, Jake still couldn't believe it had been Gibbons who'd archived Stahl's bogus reports on investigations that'd never happened.

But Archie's evidence was irrefutable.

He should've started with Gibbons, the department's technology wizard, the one person working there at the time the reports were archived who would've known how to give himself captain-level status, which was required to archive reports in inactive cases. That's how Stahl had buried investigations involving Calvin Worthington and Carisma Deasly, two Black teenagers who'd gotten a fraction of the attention they should have after being murdered and kidnapped, respectively.

Jake's blood boiled over the blatant racism that had led Stahl to ignore cases that could've been solved years ago, and he wanted to know what the hell Gibbons had been thinking when he enabled that son of a bitch and helped him get away with it.

He parked outside Gibbons's townhouse and stared at the door he'd passed through many a time before he worked up the energy to get out of the SUV to clean up yet another mess on behalf of the department he'd served with honor for close to thirty years. He was sick to death of the rot that kept surfacing from within the ranks, past and present.

After taking a deep breath and releasing it slowly so he wouldn't lead with rage, he rang the doorbell.

The Bill Gibbons who came to the door had gotten grayer and heavier since Jake last saw him. His face lit up with a big smile. "Hey! This is a nice surprise. Come in."

Jake followed him into the warm, cozy home he shared with his wife, Elaine. Their four kids were now grown and out on their own. Once upon a time, Jake and his wife, Val, had been there with their kids to help celebrate their birthdays and graduations. Gibbons's son Billy had dated Jake's daughter, Mel, when they were in high school. They'd joked then about sharing grandchildren one day.

"How's Val?" Gibbons asked.

"Doing great. Retired from teaching and volunteering. How's Elaine?"

"That's been a little tricky. We're spending some time apart. She's staying with her sister in Baltimore."

"Sorry to hear that."

Gibbons shrugged. "We found we didn't have much in common when it was just the two of us again."

"That's too bad."

"Thanks. It is what it is. Coffee?"

"No, thanks. Already had my two cups for the day."

Gibbons poured himself a cup. "I hope you got my note when Skip died. I felt terrible I couldn't be there for you and Joe and the family. I was in San Diego for my mother's funeral when I got the news."

"I did get your note, and I was sorry to hear about your mother."

"She made it to ninety-two and said she had no regrets."

"Good for her. She was a great lady."

"She was. We miss her. And Skip's son-in-law... What a tragedy that was."

"Indeed. Fucking fentanyl is a scourge like nothing we've ever seen before."

Gibbons shuddered. "I miss the job like crazy, but stuff like that and guns everywhere you look? Retirement is looking pretty good to me. You ought to give it a whirl."

"One of these days." Jake told himself to get on with it. What he'd come here to do wouldn't get easier with procrastination. "So, the reason I came by is we've been looking into some of Stahl's old cases and came across some irregularities."

"I heard you solved a couple of them. I couldn't believe you found Carisma Deasly."

"I couldn't believe how easy it was to find her and Calvin

Worthington's killer once we knew what Stahl had been doing with case files he no longer wanted to deal with."

Jake was watching the other man so closely that he saw the second it registered with him why Jake was there. His Adam's apple bobbed.

"You know what I'm talking about, don't you?" Jake asked, keeping his gaze focused intently on Gibbons.

"I do," he said softly.

"What I want to know is *why*? Why would you do anything to help that scumbag?"

"He had shit on me."

"What kind of shit?"

"The sort that ends marriages and causes guys to never see their kids again."

"Do better than that."

"I was seeing one of my detectives outside of work," he said as he looked down at the table. "Do you remember Trish Linney?"

Jake's mouth fell open in shock. "Wasn't she married with kids, too?"

"Yeah, hers were little when we were together. The husband was a dick, though. Didn't help her with anything."

"How long did this go on for?"

"About four years."

"And Stahl found out."

"Yeah," he said. "I never did figure out how. We were super careful."

"How'd it go from him knowing about the affair to you archiving case files for him?"

"He said he'd tell Elaine about the affair—and Trish's husband —if I didn't do what he wanted me to do."

"And you were willing to commit a crime to keep the affair a secret?"

"My kids were still at home. Trish's were babies. I was afraid we'd both lose custody if it got out, not to mention the rap I'd take on the job for dating a subordinate."

"Jesus Christ, Bill. What the fuck were you thinking?"

Gibbons dropped his head into his hands. "My marriage was shit almost from the start. I was miserable with Elaine. Trish made me happy. She gave me hope that my whole life wasn't going to suck. The thought of giving her up was unbearable. I made stupid decisions, and I admit that, but I never meant any harm."

"Well, you fucking failed at not harming anyone. Calvin Worthington's mother waited *fifteen years* for justice for her son. Carisma Deasly was trapped in *hell* all that time. If you could've seen her after she was rescued from that filthy prison she was held in... All because you didn't want your affair found out?"

Gibbons broke down into sobs. "I'm so sorry, Jake. I hated myself for it at the time, and I've been sick over it ever since, especially since the news broke about those cases being solved."

"I'm sorry to have to tell you that you have the right to remain silent. You have the right to an attorney—"

Gibbons looked up at him, his expression one of complete shock. "Wait. You're *arresting* me?"

Jake put the cuffs he'd put in his pocket earlier on the table. "You're goddamned right I am."

CHAPTER TWENTY-SEVEN

Keenan Coleman lived on the third floor of an apartment building in the Berkley neighborhood, which abutted Cathedral Heights. Freddie knocked on the door to 3C. A tall, handsome Black man came to the door, wearing AirPods and looking annoyed by the interruption.

When he and Gonzo showed their badges, Keenan said, "I'll have to call you back," and removed the AirPods from his ears.

"I'm Detective Cruz. This is Sergeant Gonzales. We wondered if we might have a few minutes of your time."

"I'm, ah, working, but yeah, sure. Come in."

They followed him into a tidy living room where toys were stacked in colorful bins against the wall. A huge computer monitor sat on a desk in the corner of the room.

"What do you do for work?"

"I sell bourbon to bars and restaurants. What's this about?"

Freddie was surprised that he acted like he didn't know. "We're here about Liliana Blanchet."

At the mention of her name, tears flooded his eyes. He sat on the sofa and dropped his head into his hands. "How did you find me? We were careful."

"She told a friend your first name," Freddie said. "From there, it wasn't hard to find you."

"I can't believe she's gone. And her kids... I begged her to leave him before he did something like this, but she wouldn't listen to me."

"She was afraid of Marcel?"

"Do you know about the lawsuit?"

"We do."

"She was afraid of what would become of them after the details went public. She was absolutely sick over what he'd done to those women. The stress was nearly unbearable."

"Did she fear that he would harm her or the kids?" Freddie asked.

"Not specifically, but she worried about what would happen to all of them when word got out about the lawsuit, which was going to happen at any minute."

"What was the nature of your relationship with her?"

"We... we met at the preschool our boys attended. We'd wait for them outside and got to talking one day. Over a few weeks, we talked every time we picked up and eventually exchanged numbers. I think she desperately needed a friend who was one hundred percent on her side, you know?" He looked up at them, seeming to seek understanding. "Even her closest friends were Marcel's friends, too. The few people who knew about the suit found it hard to believe he could've done such a thing. They kept trying to find a way to make it not true. That wasn't helpful to her."

After a pause, he added, "Can you imagine how mortifying this was to her as his wife? That he would do such a disgusting thing to his patients when they were at their most vulnerable?"

"So you were just friends with Liliana?" Freddie asked.

"It was complicated."

"How so?"

"We had feelings for each other and were hoping to make something of it as soon as she could leave her marriage."

"What was her plan?" Freddie asked.

"She'd spoken to a divorce attorney and was planning to leave Marcel and take the kids within a month. It was all in the works."

"Did Marcel know that?"

He shook his head. "She was walking a fine line of protecting herself and the kids and not throwing gasoline on a fire. When he cut back at work to spend more time with the kids while they were drowning in legal bills, I thought she would kill him. Not that she could ever do such a thing, but I think she wanted to."

"I'm going to tell you something no one else knows, and I want it to stay between us, okay?" Freddie said.

"I don't know anyone else in her life. There's no one for me to tell."

"Someone went to a great deal of trouble to make it look like Marcel killed them all and then himself. But we have proof that's not what happened. Is there any chance Liliana could've been the one to snap?"

"Absolutely not. She loved those kids more than her own life. She would've walked through fire for them. There was nothing, and I do mean *nothing*, she wouldn't do for them."

"What kind of things had she done for them?" Freddie asked, playing a hunch that there was more Keenan would say if asked the right question.

"She, ah... she had words with those hideous Cortez people who were tormenting Eloise online and in person at the meets."

"Had words when and how?"

"After the last meet. They got into it in the parking lot. She called them racist animals."

"We talked to them. They never said anything about that."

"Would you tell people that someone called you a racist animal?"

"I don't suppose I would." Freddie thought about the way Pascal Cortez had run from them, supposedly because of a hit-and-run accident. Had he been worried about being charged with a much bigger crime? "What was the outcome of the altercation?"

"The Cortezes told her to back off, or they'd call the police. She said they should go right ahead, that she'd be happy to tell them how two grown-ass adults were harassing a child."

Freddie wanted to say, *Good for her*, but he held his tongue. "Was she having trouble with anyone else in her life?"

Keenan shook his head. "The lawsuit and the bullying of her daughter by people who should've known better were more than enough. I worried about her. I tried to convince her to go ahead and leave, but she said she wasn't ready yet. She was trying to find another place for them to live, but everything was so expensive, and what she could afford was far from the kids' schools."

"Why didn't she ask him to leave?"

"She did. He refused. He said he wouldn't be separated from his children for any reason."

"He said it just like that?" Gonzo asked. "For any reason?"

"That's what she told me. When I heard the news about what'd happened to her and the kids... In a way, I wasn't as surprised as I should've been. Her life had been like a stick of dynamite lately, waiting for a place to explode. I just wish I could've gotten her and her kids out of there before it did."

Freddie gave him his card along with the usual spiel about calling with anything else that might be relevant.

"I hope you find who did this to her and her kids," Keenan said when he walked them to the door. "She was a wonderful, loving person who didn't deserve to die this way. And neither did her kids."

"Thank you for your help."

"I wish there was more I could do."

Freddie followed Gonzo down the stairs and out into the damp chill. "I don't know about you, but I want to talk to the Cortezes again."

"Right there with you, brother."

THEY KNOCKED on the door to the Cortez home twenty minutes later. Freddie gazed into the side window, looking for signs of life.

"They're gone," a woman said from the sidewalk.

Freddie spun around, recognizing her as Mrs. Gersh from the other day. She was petite and had a scarf tied around her gray hair, which was set in curlers. "Gone where?"

She shrugged. "After they came home from the police station the other day, they loaded the kids into the car and took off. Haven't seen them since."

"Did you notice if they had bags with them?"

"I saw a couple of suitcases."

"What kind of car did they leave in?"

"A cranberry-colored Nissan SUV. It was an older one they bought secondhand."

Sometimes, Freddie thought, nosy neighbors were useful.

"Do they have family within driving distance?"

"Her folks live outside Hershey, Pennsylvania. His mother is in Maryland."

"Thanks for your help," Freddie said, handing her a card. "If you see them back here, will you please let me know?"

"Are they in trouble?"

"Not necessarily. We'd just like to talk to them again."

"I'll let you know." She gave the Cortez house a side-eyed look. "There was something off about her, if you ask me."

"How so?"

"She's dissatisfied with her life or something. She's just very unhappy and wants everyone to know it. I think he's been a disappointment to her, motherhood isn't what she thought it would be, nothing has worked out the way she wanted it to. Except for her daughter's gymnastics. That was the one thing that made her sparkle when she talked about it."

If Sam were there, she might have said she felt the tingle down her backbone that happened any time a promising lead developed.

"We appreciate the insight. Thank you again for your time."

"Is your boss tough to work for?"

"What?" Freddie asked. "Not at all. She's one of our closest friends."

"Ah, good to know. I was hoping they're as real as they seem on TV."

"They are. Thanks again."

As they walked toward Gonzo's Charger, Freddie said, "Cheers to nosy neighbors, huh?"

"I was thinking the same thing."

"Do we have to go to Hershey?" That was the last thing Freddie wanted to do.

"Nah, we'll send people. That's the beauty of command. You can delegate the shit you don't want to do."

"I'm not sure how I feel about sending people after a guy who already ran from us once before."

"They can handle it."

"Who should we send?"

"Cam and Matt."

"Okay." He looked over at Gonzo. "You're sure it's okay to send them and not go ourselves?"

Gonzo stopped and turned to face him. "You have to ask yourself how our time would be better spent as the ones leading this investigation, as the ones who have the most information on the case at any given moment. Would we be best using our time by spending hours in the car driving to Pennsylvania, or would it be better if we stayed back and continued to work the case from other angles while they go after the Cortezes?"

"When you put it like that…"

"That's how you make decisions as a commander. You think of how best to use everyone's limited time and go from there."

"Thank you for that insight. It's all new to me to be viewing it through this lens. Sam makes it seem so simple to make a thousand different decisions in a day without breaking a sweat."

"Because she's been doing it for years, and it comes naturally to her by now. You'll get there."

When they were back in Gonzo's car on the way to HQ, Freddie was still thinking about what Gonzo had said about command and delegation. "Can I tell you something?"

"Anything."

"I never pictured myself in charge of anything in this job. I've always been along for the ride, one of the worker bees, not one of the bosses. I just didn't see that happening, so I never prepared for it."

"It's because there are two people above you who are only a few years older than you and not going anywhere any time soon, so you got comfortable as one of the worker bees."

"Yeah, that's it. Exactly."

"It's good to be prepared for anything on this job so you can step up if needed. I'm glad Sam gave you the opportunity to run this case. It's training you'll be glad you have later."

"I'm not sure I'd want to do this job without her with me every day."

"I get that. I'm not sure I'd want to do it without her either. But —and this is a very big *but*—there may come a point when she can't juggle everything. If something has to give, it won't be her kids or the first lady gig, you know?"

"Yeah, that's true. I just can't imagine her anywhere but right in the middle of our squad, busting balls and pulling threads and getting shit done."

"That's where she wants to be, but sometimes life gets in the way of what you want and what you have to do."

"You're kind of freaking me out."

"She's not going anywhere any time soon. It's just that we have to keep it real, you know? She's the fucking first lady of the United States. I mean, in what world did that happen?"

"Sometimes I wake up in the morning and forget that happened. Then I remember, and it's just so huge."

"Imagine how they must feel," Gonzo said as he darted between cars on the way back to HQ.

"I can't. I'm flailing around trying to run a murder investigation. How in the world is someone we know well in charge of running the *whole country*?"

"And with nothing but bullshit happening all around him."

"Yeah, for real. I don't know how he stands it."

"This thing with the Joint Chiefs..." Gonzo said. "That's a body blow in so many ways. That they would have the nerve to do such a thing is just disgusting."

"It's kind of scary to think that people hate him just for doing the job Nelson asked him to do if the worst should happen."

"I know, especially since we know that if people just gave him a chance, he could be an amazing president. He's already done such a great job so far."

Freddie tried not to think too much about the enormous pressure his best friends were constantly under. It stressed him out to realize that so many people, who would never actually know them, hated them simply because of the office Nick now held.

Back at HQ, Freddie went to the computer to track down the license plate number of the Cortezes' maroon SUV. Next, he searched for the marriage license for Pascal and Gia Cortez to get her maiden name and looked up the address of her parents in Hershey. Then he called the Derry Township Police Department, which served Hershey, Pennsylvania, to ask for a favor. "Can you please go by the house and see if this vehicle is in the driveway?" He rattled off the license plate number.

"Sure, will do. Hey, do you work with the first lady?"

"She's our commander."

"Wow. That must be interesting."

"She's the best cop I've ever worked with. Let me know what you find out?"

"Will do."

Fifteen minutes later, the sergeant from Hershey called back. "Your car is there."

"I'm sending some detectives to pick up the owners. Would you mind having someone keep a discreet eye on the car until we can get there? If they go anywhere, follow them."

"What are they wanted for?"

"I'm not sure yet. It could be anything from nothing to mass murder."

"Got it. We'll put eyes on them. Please have your detectives get in touch before they approach them. We'll provide backup."

"Will do. Thanks very much for the assist."

"No problem."

Freddie stood and went to Cam's cubicle. "I need you and Matt to go to Hershey, Pennsylvania, and pick up Pascal and Gia Cortez at this address." He caught them up on the situation and what they had so far on the Cortezes.

"Got it. Matt, let's go."

"Thanks, Cam."

"Sure thing."

"Gonzo says we're authorized for overtime on this one."

"Glad to hear it, thanks," Cam said.

"When you get there, contact this sergeant with the local police. He said they'll provide backup. In the meantime, they've got eyes on them."

Cameron took the piece of paper with the number on it. "I'll let you know when we have them in custody."

"They have kids, so be mindful."

"Will do."

After Cam and Matt left, Freddie went to the conference room, intending to look more closely at the people involved in the lawsuit.

Captain Malone appeared in the doorway a minute later. "The press is going nuts wanting an update on Blanchet. Can you brief them?"

That was another thing he'd never pictured himself doing, even if he'd done it before. Would it ever come naturally to him? Probably not. "Sure, I can do that. Let me ask you something, though."

"What's up?"

"We know for a fact that this wasn't a murder-suicide, but I shouldn't tell anyone that yet, right?"

"What's your thinking?"

"I wouldn't want to let the murderer know that we know the scene was staged."

"Exactly right."

"Okay, thanks for confirming. I'm learning to trust myself, but I'm not quite there yet."

"You're doing great."

"I've had great training."

"It shows."

"Thank you, Captain. That means a lot coming from you. I'll get outside to brief the media in a few minutes."

"Come get me. I'll go out with you."

After he walked away, Freddie took a minute to go through his notes and to summarize what he would say at the briefing. When he felt as ready as he'd ever be, he stopped to get Malone, and the two of them went outside to face the media scrum that spent most of their days waiting for news that often never came. Any time he thought his job sucked, Freddie thought of them. Their job sucked way worse than his ever would.

"Monday morning, the bodies of Dr. Marcel Blanchet, age forty-two, his wife, Liliana, also forty-two, and their four children, Eloise, twelve, Abigail, ten, Violet, six, and August, known as Gus, four, were found shot to death in their Cathedral Heights home. Dr. Blanchet was an OB/GYN infertility specialist. Mrs. Blanchet was an attorney. Their children attended DC public schools, and Eloise Blanchet was an accomplished gymnast who'd won several local and regional competitions. As we always do in these cases, we are talking to the people who knew the family best and trying to ascertain what took place in the Blanchets' home. That's all we have at this time. We'll conduct another briefing as soon as we have more to report. If anyone has information pertaining to the case, please call our tip line." He recited the number twice.

"Was it a murder-suicide?"

"Where is the first lady?"

"Do you think the murders were related to the lawsuit against the father?"

"We have nothing further to say at this time," Freddie said. "Have a good day."

"Well done," Captain Malone said when they were back inside.

"You think so?" Freddie asked.

"Wouldn't have said it if I didn't mean it."

"Thanks for the support."

"I just had to arrest former Lieutenant Gibbons for assisting

Stahl in archiving cases he didn't want to deal with." Malone rubbed the back of his neck. "A guy I've known thirty years."

"Damn," Freddie said. "How'd he take it?"

"He was shocked that I was arresting him."

"Did he say why he did it?"

"Stahl had dirt on him having a relationship with a detective who worked with him. Told him he'd expose him unless he did his dirty work for him."

"Wow. Just when we think we've seen it all where Stahl is concerned, there's more."

"I swear to God, if it's the last thing I do, I'm going to arrest any cop—past or present—who had anything to do with Stahl and his schemes."

"It's hard to believe that people helped him."

"Most of them probably did it because he was blackmailing them, but that doesn't excuse them abetting his criminal activity."

"No, it doesn't."

"I need to go update the chief on the arrest of Gibbons. I'll check in with you later."

"Thanks for the support out there."

"No problem."

When Freddie returned to the pit, he was surprised to see the lights on in Sam's office. "Hey," he said.

"Hey, yourself," she said. "How's it going?"

"Okay, I guess. Captain Malone just told me he's arrested former Lieutenant Gibbons for assisting Stahl with the archiving of case files."

"Holy shit. No way. He was Archie before Archie. My dad worked closely with him and always said he was good people."

"Apparently, Stahl blackmailed him with info about an affair with a subordinate."

"Jeez. Does Stahl's depravity know no limits?"

"Not that I've seen. How're the kids?"

"A little better. Nick came up to stay with them before I left. He's taking meetings from the residence."

"Look at you two balancing your big jobs."

"We're doing what we can for the people. Catch me up on Blanchet. Where are we?"

CHAPTER TWENTY-EIGHT

While they waited for Cam and Matt to return with the Cortezes, Freddie, Sam and Gonzo took a closer look at the women involved in the lawsuit against Dr. Blanchet. They scanned the social media accounts of each of the four women as well as those of their partners. Previously, the other detectives in the squad had gone back a month in time on each of the named principals on the lawsuit. They went back further.

"Take a look at this," Gonzo said an hour after they'd started.

Sam and Freddie stood, walked around the conference room table and leaned over to read a Facebook post from three months ago by a man named Robert Cauley, the husband of Misty Cauley, one of the four women attached to the lawsuit. *When powerful people take advantage of others, when someone chasing a dream becomes a victim, when something is so wrong, someone must make it right. Whatever it takes.*

He'd included a photo of a raised fist with the post.

"That makes him a person of interest," Freddie said.

"I had a feeling you might say that," Gonzo said.

"What do we know about him?" Sam asked.

Gonzo scanned the report Detective Charles had put together on each of the parties involved in the suit and their immediate families. "He works as an engineer for NASA at the Greenbelt, Maryland, facility."

"It might be difficult to get in to see him there."

"Difficult, but not impossible," Gonzo said. "Let's give it a whirl."

"I'll stay here and keep digging," Sam said. "I want to look closer at Liliana. We've spent a lot of time focused on Marcel. Maybe we're looking in the wrong place."

Freddie updated her on what they'd learned from Liliana's friend Keenan.

"So we were right that she was deeply upset about the lawsuit and thinking of leaving him," Sam said. "Not sure how that plays with the other stuff we know, but I'll take a look."

"See you when we get back," Freddie said.

He and Gonzo headed for Gonzo's car.

"Where are you in buying a new ride?" Gonzo asked him.

"I'm paralyzed with indecision. I want something cool but functional."

"Get one of these," Gonzo said of his Charger.

"I can't afford it."

"Yes, you can."

"Elin and I are saving up to buy a townhouse, so I can't swing a big car payment right now."

"Ah, I see. That's a good goal."

"We figure within a couple of years, we'll have enough for the down payment."

"That's great. We'll be renting forever at the rate we're going. My illness put us seriously behind the eight ball financially. Rehab ain't cheap."

"But it was worth every dime."

"It was, but it was a lot of dimes. Christina being back to work full time helps, but it'll take a few years for us to dig our way out of the hole I put us in."

"You'll get there."

"One of these years." Gonzo shrugged as he drove out of the lot and headed for the Baltimore-Washington Parkway. "Like you said, though, what choice did we have? I'm thankful every day for my sobriety, but we paid a mighty price for it in every way."

"You and Christina are solid, though, right?"

"We are, but sometimes I still catch her watching me warily, as if she's worried I'm going to slip up again. Who can blame her? I put her through hell. I put everyone who loves me through hell."

"That's not our first thought when we look at you now,"

Freddie said. "I see a man who's fought for his life, his career, his family and friends and come out on top. I see a man who works hard every day to keep himself healthy so he can be there for his loved ones and colleagues."

"That's nice to hear. Thanks."

"I mean it."

"I know you do, and I appreciate your support through all of it. You and Sam and most of the people at work were a big part of my recovery."

"Cameron told me you were a big help to him and Gigi at the grief group last night."

"I'm glad it was helpful. I hate what they're going through."

"Now you know how the rest of us felt watching you struggle after Arnold was killed."

"Yeah, I do. It's rough to watch people who always do the right thing getting caught up in stuff like what's going on with them."

"Internal Affairs will clear her, right?" Freddie asked.

"They should. Gigi killed Jaycee out of self-defense. It was a clean shot, but we both know how these things can get twisted sometimes."

The statement gave Freddie anxiety for Gigi, who was an excellent detective and person.

"Cam is eaten up with guilt over the whole thing," Gonzo added. "Even though he couldn't have stopped what happened, you can't tell him that. All he knows is that Jaycee is dead, Gigi killed her, SWAT killed Jaycee's mother, and in Cam's mind, it all leads back to him breaking up with Jaycee."

"Which he was free to do."

"Of course he was, and thank God he left her when he did, given her sinister side. But how does he live with what happened in the aftermath? That's my worry."

"He seems okay for the most part."

"That's what worries me," Gonzo said. "When people seem okay, often they're not."

"Dr. Trulo is keeping an eye on them, and so are we. We're doing what we can."

"I hope it's enough," Gonzo said.

His worries stayed with Freddie long after they arrived at the NASA facility in Greenbelt, showed their badges and asked to speak with Robert Cauley.

"What's this in reference to?" the guard asked, probably out of nosiness more than anything.

"A case we're working on. Can you direct us to him?"

"Just a minute."

While they waited, both men checked their phones and took care of a few emails and text messages.

Gonzo looked up at the guard. "We don't have all day, man."

"One more minute."

"That's about all we've got."

Fifty-seven seconds later, the guard leaned out of his hut to direct them to the building where Cauley worked. "Security will meet you there and escort you inside."

"Thank you."

The gate lifted. Gonzo accelerated through and took a right, looking for the building number they'd been given.

"I couldn't work in a place like this," Freddie said of the mostly windowless buildings. "I'd go crazy."

"Me, too."

"As much as this job sucks on many a day, at least we get to see the sun and breathe fresh air."

"People would think we're insane for preferring chasing murderers to whatever they do here," Gonzo said.

"I choose our kind of insanity over working in a cement box any day."

They'd no sooner parked and emerged from the car than a security officer approached them. "Could I please see your badges?"

They flashed their gold detective shields.

"Right this way."

The guard led them inside and asked them to surrender their weapons while they were on the premises.

Like Sam, Freddie hated to part with his weapon while on the job, but unless they wanted this trip to be a waste of time, they had no choice but to turn their guns over to security.

After they'd put the contents of their pockets through an X-ray machine and walked through the magnetometer, the security guard said, "Follow me."

He took them to a bank of elevators and pressed the Up arrow.

Cauley's office was on the third floor.

The guard pointed to a closed office door. "Here."

"Thank you," Freddie said.

"I'll wait for you by the elevators."

Freddie knocked on the office door.

"Come in."

The man inside was younger than Freddie had expected, in his early thirties at most, with brown hair, blue eyes and a face most people would call handsome.

They showed their badges and introduced themselves.

His face registered shock. "What do cops want with me?"

They stepped into the office, closed the door behind them and sat in the chairs in front of his desk, which was neat and orderly, like the man who occupied it.

"Your wife was suing Dr. Marcel Blanchet," Freddie said.

"Yes, she was."

"I assume you're aware of what happened to him and his family."

"I am," he said, his expression grave. "I can't believe he killed his whole family."

"Why do you say that?" Gonzo asked.

"Isn't that what happened?" Cauley asked, his gaze darting between them.

"We haven't established that's what happened," Freddie said.

"Oh. Well... We heard he was found with the weapon."

"Who'd you hear that from?" Freddie asked.

"One of the other people involved in the lawsuit must've told my wife. She told me."

"It's interesting because we haven't released that information to the public, so I'm not sure how anyone would know that unless they had some sort of inside knowledge as to what happened in the Blanchet home at the time of the murders."

Cauley held up his hands as if to fend them off. "Whoa! I have no insider knowledge. I simply heard a rumor that it was a murder-suicide."

"But that's not what you said," Gonzo noted. "You said, and I quote, 'We heard he was found with the weapon.' That's a very specific piece of information."

"Look," Cauley said as he began to visibly perspire, "I'm not sure what you're trying to do here."

"We're investigating a mass homicide," Freddie said, "and you just became very interesting to us."

"*What?* How? Because I passed along a *rumor* I heard?"

"Where were you Sunday night?"

"At home with my wife."

"You never left?"

"No." He moved in his chair.

Freddie wouldn't call it a squirm, per se, but he definitely shifted.

"Wait... I went to the liquor store around nine, but I came right back. My wife can attest to that. She was annoyed that I'd gone out so late to get beer."

"Where can we find your wife?"

"She works at a bank in Northwest." He recited the name of the bank and the address. "She had nothing to do with this. Neither of us did. But after what he put us through, neither of us was sad to hear he was dead."

"Can you tell us specifically what he put you through?" Freddie asked.

"You've seen the lawsuit, I presume."

"We have," Freddie said, "but we'd like to hear it in your words."

Cauley sighed as he sat back in his chair, seeming distressed now, in addition to sweaty. "He was our last hope to have a baby. We'd practically bankrupted ourselves with treatments and procedures. He came highly recommended by some people we knew who'd gone to him for fertility treatment and ended up with twins. We waited eight months for an appointment with him, and he gave us so much hope. I don't know if you have any experience with infertility, but it's devastating."

"We've experienced it through friends," Gonzo said. "We know how hard it can be."

"When Misty came home from her appointment and told me what'd happened... At first, I didn't believe her. She was sedated, after all, so how would she know? But she said it was too vivid to not have happened. She went onto a local forum for women struggling with infertility to ask if anyone else had had an odd experience with Dr. Blanchet, and that's how she connected with the other three plaintiffs. Their descriptions of the incidents were shockingly similar. I'm sure you know the details..."

"We do," Gonzo said.

"When the cop working the case said he didn't have enough to charge him, the women decided to sue. The husbands and partners have supported them every step of the way."

Freddie put the social media post that had led them to Cauley on the desk in front of him. "Can you tell us if this was related to the incident with Dr. Blanchet?"

He rubbed his jaw with a trembling hand. "It was in part. I have a beef with people in positions of power who take advantage of others in lesser positions. Like a doctor tending to women desperate to have a baby who violates them in the most disgusting way."

"It must've made you angry to hear he'd done that to your wife," Gonzo said.

"I was... enraged. She's already been through so much with four rounds of failed IVF, two miscarriages, an ectopic pregnancy. This was just too much for us."

"Were you angry enough to kill him and his family?" Freddie asked.

Cauley stared at them for a second, his mouth hanging open in shock. "I didn't kill him. And if I had, I certainly wouldn't have killed his wife and children. I can't stop thinking about those poor kids. Whatever drove someone to murder, how did it involve them?"

"What about the other plaintiffs and their husbands? Was anyone angry enough to commit murder?"

"They were more heartbroken than angry. He was seen as a last resort to many of us. That this could've happened is still surreal."

Freddie put his card on the desk and asked him to call if he thought of anything else.

"I will. I hope you find the person who did this to them."

"We will," Freddie said, channeling some of Sam's inner confidence. "Thank you for your time."

They left the office, joined the guard by the elevators and were escorted back to the security checkpoint, where they retrieved their weapons. When they were outside, Freddie glanced toward Gonzo. "Impressions?"

"I almost arrested him when he said Blanchet was found holding the gun."

"Me, too," Freddie said. "I was like, hello, slam dunk. And yet... I kind of believed him when he said he never could've harmed the kids."

"Yeah, same. But I still want to take a closer look at him. That statement really sticks out. How could he or anyone have known the weapon was found near Marcel when we've never released that detail?"

"That's a very good question."

"You know," Gonzo said, "I had a thought in there. Four women were on the lawsuit, but what if there were more of them than the ones suing him? I mean, if a guy like him does that to four women, what's to say there aren't a bunch of others out there?"

"How do we find them if there are more?"

"We put out an alert to his patients asking anyone who experienced irregularities in their dealings with him to come forward."

"That's a good idea," Freddie said, wishing he'd thought of it. "I just keep coming back around to the same thing—how could it not involve someone who was allegedly violated by him?"

"Same. Nothing else, even the thing with the Cortezes, stands out to me the way that does as a possible motive for something like this. Like, I can see some infuriated patient or their partner thinking, 'You ruined my chance to have kids, so I'll take your kids from you.' Maybe they made him watch them kill his kids."

"I'll talk to Public Affairs about putting out a request for info from other patients."

"We should also talk to his office staff."

"Let's go do that now."

CHAPTER TWENTY-NINE

S am was reviewing the mountain of reports and documents associated with the case when she received a call from Scotty's school.

"Mrs. Cappuano, we wanted to let you know we're sending Scotty home with his detail because he has a fever."

"Thank you for the call."

"We hope he feels better soon."

"Me, too."

Sam slapped the phone closed and made an executive decision. She went to see Captain Malone.

"Hey, what's up?"

"My kids are sick. I was going to work the afternoon, but now Scotty is on his way home, too. I've got some stuff I can do from there, but just telling you where I'll be."

"Thanks. I just got a call from Faith that a hearing has been scheduled to discuss recent developments in the Eric Davies case."

"That's good, I guess."

"I'm meeting with the chief and McBride to come up with a plan to circumvent the media shitstorm this will create."

"Good idea. Let me know if I can help."

"We might want you to make the statement if you're willing to let us use you shamelessly. People are so interested in you, and the feeling is that it might go down easier coming from you—someone who's had your own tangles with Stahl."

"I'll do whatever needs to be done to protect the chief and the department."

"I had a feeling you might say that."

"Keep me in the loop."

"Will do. Hope the kids feel better."

"Me, too, and I hope we don't get it. Whatever it is seems hella contagious."

"Yikes."

"I'll check in tomorrow and will text my squad."

"See you then."

On the way home with Vernon and Jimmy, Sam sent a text to her squad, updating them on her sick kids and asking them to call with any updates they might have.

As she waited for Scotty's detail to arrive at the White House, she took a call from Freddie.

"Hey," she said. "How's it going?"

"We've just come from seeing Cauley in Greenbelt." Freddie told her about what the man had said about Blanchet being found with the gun.

"How did he know that?"

"He said he heard it from his wife, who heard it from one of the others attached to the lawsuit. We believed him when he said he never could've harmed innocent kids, but that statement about the gun is sticking with us. We're taking a more in-depth look at him. I've got Charles on the financials and social media."

"What about a warrant for his phone?" Sam asked.

"I'm not sure we've got enough for that yet."

"You won't need much more. He had motive due to what happened to the wife and the social media post that broadcast his anger to the world."

"Should we go back and bring him in?"

"That's your call. You were in the room with him. You have to trust your gut."

"My gut—and Gonzo's—is saying no."

"Then go with it until you know more. But I agree with taking a deeper look at him."

"We had another thought that there might be more patients out there who aren't attached to the lawsuit but who had similar experiences with Blanchet."

"Good point."

"We're on the way to his office now to interview the staff, and we're asking Public Affairs to put out a request for info from patients."

"You're doing all the right things."

"I'm glad you think so."

"I do for sure," Sam said. "Did you hear there's a hearing scheduled for the Davies case?"

"I hadn't gotten that word, but I'm glad to hear it."

"Me, too, even if I'm worried about the fallout."

"What would your dad say?" Freddie asked.

"That you do the right thing, no matter the fallout."

"Exactly."

"Thanks for that reminder. I have to run. Scotty's detail is pulling up. Keep me posted."

"I'll text you later."

Sam closed the phone and stepped outside with Skippy to welcome their boy home. She took one look at his pale, pinched face and could tell he was seriously under the weather.

"Hope you feel better, Scotty," his lead agent, Debra, said.

"Thanks."

"Thank you, Debra," Sam said.

"No problem."

Sam took his insanely heavy backpack from him and put her arm around his shoulders. "Not feeling so hot, huh?"

"I'm feeling crazy hot."

"Just like the Littles."

"What're you doing here?"

"My kids are sick, so I came home."

"I'm glad you're here."

Sam squeezed his shoulder. "Me, too." There was nowhere else she'd rather be.

THE GEORGETOWN OFFICES OF DRS. Blanchet, McInerny and Harvey occupied the entire second floor of a building on M Street, above a row of exclusive boutiques.

"I wonder if anyone will be there with one doctor dead and the other two out of the office," Freddie said.

"Someone still needs to deal with the patients."

"I guess."

When he discovered the door to the office locked, Freddie knocked.

A few minutes later, a woman with gray hair and wearing a headset opened the door. "Help you?"

They showed their badges.

"I'll have to get back to you," she said to the person on the phone as she removed the headset. "Come in. The phones are ringing off the hook with patients wanting to reschedule. Needless to say, having all three doctors out was unexpected. This whole thing was unexpected." She brushed at tears as she said that. "I watched the Blanchet kids grow up. It's unimaginable that they're gone. Even days later, I'm in complete denial that this could've happened."

She led them into a conference room and turned on the lights. "I'd offer you something to drink, but all I have is water."

"We're fine," Freddie said. "I'm Detective Cruz. This is Sergeant Gonzales."

"You work with the first lady."

"We do. What's your name?"

"Oh, sorry. I'm Nancy Lee, the office manager."

"How long have you worked with Dr. Blanchet?"

"More than fifteen years. Since he opened his first office."

"How would you describe your relationship with him?"

"He and Lili were family to me. I've never married, and my extended family lives in Pittsburgh, so I spent a lot of holidays with them as well as kids' birthdays, school events, gymnastics meets. They treated me like a beloved aunt, and I adored them all." She took a tissue from a box on the conference room table and wiped her eyes. "I'm sorry. I'm still in shock."

"We're sorry for your losses," Freddie said.

"Thank you."

"What can you tell us about Dr. Blanchet's relationships with his patients?"

"They loved him. Well, most of them did."

"You're aware of the lawsuit?"

"Yes," she said through gritted teeth as her eyes flashed with indignation. "I'll never believe he did what they say he did. In all the years I knew him, I never saw him be inappropriate with anyone, let alone a patient. He was a consummate gentleman and professional. He helped so many couples achieve their goal of parenthood. I could give you hundreds of names of patients who'd sing his praises. We've been overrun with calls from former patients, bereft over this senseless crime." She put her hand on her heart. "As a woman, I know I'm supposed to believe the women making these charges, and I fully support their right to speak their truth. But I knew him. I knew his heart. And I just can't believe he did what they say he did."

"When four women have the same exact story," Freddie said gently, "we believe them."

"That's the thing that's always bothered me about it, though," Nancy said. "They have the same *exact* story. It's always felt manufactured to me. And I want to add... I volunteer at a rape crisis center. I'm an advocate for believing and supporting victims of sexual violence. But this..." She shook her head. "I'll never believe it."

"What would be their motive in banding together to make up such a thing?" Gonzo asked.

"I've thought long and hard about that, as I know Marcel did, too. The only thing we could think of was if they didn't get the child they hoped to have when they came to him, they wanted financial restitution."

"I assume they sign paperwork as patients absolving the doctors and practice of any liability if they should fail to conceive and carry a child to term," Gonzo said.

"Absolutely. We have ironclad forms to that effect. We aren't miracle workers. There's always a chance of failure. But that kind of failure... It does something to people. We've seen it many times over the years."

"How so?" Freddie asked.

"The disappointment is crushing," she said. "Dr. Blanchet, in particular, was known for being able to get results in even the most difficult situations. When the treatments failed, as they did for all four of the women attached to the lawsuit, the patients experience more than just failed fertility treatments. It's like the end of their dream to carry their own child. Some of them become bitter. We've seen that happen a few times. They want someone to blame, and their doctor is a handy target. It's a rare reaction, but it does happen."

While Freddie heard what she was saying, everything in him rejected the notion that failed fertility treatments would lead women to accuse Dr. Blanchet of the things they'd said he'd done to them. "I'm sorry," he said. "All due respect for the losses of people you cared about, but I can't, for the life of me, imagine anyone making up a story like those in the lawsuit because a doctor failed to do something that they knew he couldn't guarantee from the beginning."

"I was about to say the same thing," Gonzo said.

"There's no way he ever would've done the things they said he did," Nancy said more forcefully. "I knew him for fifteen years. Worked closely with him for all that time. Was close to his family. I never once saw or heard him do anything inappropriate with women. Based on my experience with the rape crisis center, I know how to identify a predator. He was not a predator."

"Did other patients ever complain about him?" Freddie asked.

"Never."

"So these were the only four patients who ever complained about him in all his years of practice?"

"The only ones I ever knew of. Did you ever meet Marcel Blanchet?" she asked in a testy tone.

"No," Freddie said for both of them.

"I saw him just about every day for the last fifteen years. If that man was a predator, I know nothing about anything. Even your own SVU detective determined there was insufficient evidence to charge him."

If anyone other than Ramsey had investigated, Freddie would've felt better about that outcome.

"We hear what you're saying and appreciate your input," Freddie said. "Can you think of anyone else who might've had a beef with Marcel or Liliana that could've led to the murders of their entire family?"

"I've done nothing but think about that since the second I heard the dreadful news." She reached for another tissue. "I can't think of anyone who would've been capable of harming those sweet kids."

He gave her his card with the usual instructions.

When they were outside, Freddie said, "I have no idea what to think about any of this."

"Right there with you. There's no way four women would make up a story like that and go public with it if it didn't actually happen."

"I mean, it is possible they made it up, but what I can't see no matter where I look is *why* they would've done it. After what just happened to us, Elin barely wanted to talk to me about it. Sam was the same after she suffered fertility setbacks. I can't see them deciding to take out their disappointment on the doctor by accusing him of such an egregious thing."

"They never would have unless it happened," Gonzo said. "I get that Nancy Lee was a devoted friend and employee of Blanchet's, but she's not objective in this matter. Like his mother, of course she's going to defend him, especially now that he's dead. They want to protect his legacy."

"I hate this case," Freddie said.

"I do, too. More than I hate most of them. Most of all, I hate that whatever happened, four innocent kids were killed."

"Yeah, me, too. Where do we go from here?"

"Let's go back to the house and regroup. We've still got the Cortez angle to further explore, so don't lose hope yet."

"I'm trying not to, but this is going nowhere fast."

"We'll catch a break. Eventually."

"Any time now."

When Freddie and Gonzo got back to HQ, Gonzo went to check in with Green and O'Brien while Freddie closed the door to the conference room to call Sam.

"How's it going?"

"I'm extremely frustrated." He updated her on the conversation with Nancy Lee.

"I agree with you and Gonzo. There's no way those women would've gone to the police with something like that unless it actually happened. Take a closer look at Ramsey's report on his investigation. It might shed some light."

"I will."

"Keep pulling the threads and doing what we do. Something will pop."

"It would be good if it could pop soon."

"I have full faith in you and the rest of our team."

"That helps. How are the kids?"

"They're doing okay, and so far no fever for me or Nick, thankfully. I'm still working my way through Liliana's emails, texts, social media posts, work stuff. I'll let you know if anything stands out."

"Thanks for the help."

"I'll see you in the morning."

"See you then."

Cameron and Matt returned to HQ with Pascal and Gia Cortez at six o'clock.

"What a charming pair," Matt said after he'd deposited them in interview one with a Patrol officer keeping an eye on them.

"They fought us every step of the way," Cam added. "Her mother said she was calling a lawyer to sue us for harassment. We told her to please go right ahead."

"Thanks for taking one for the team, you guys," Freddie said. "Did they ask for an attorney at any point?"

"Nope," Cam said. "The only mention of lawyers was by her mother about suing us for harassment. And we advised them of their rights—twice."

"Great job," Freddie said. "We'll take it from here. I'm just waiting for one of the Millers to come in before we proceed."

"I'm here," Assistant U.S. Attorney Hope Miller said.

"Great," Freddie said. "Let me call Captain Malone, and then Gonzo and I can have another chat with them."

CHAPTER THIRTY

With Malone and Hope watching from observation, Freddie and Gonzo entered the interrogation room.

"We meet again," Freddie said.

"This is total harassment," Pascal said. "We told you before we know nothing about what happened to those people."

"It's interesting that you failed to tell us how Liliana Blanchet called you racist animals a few days before they were found dead," Freddie said.

"H-how is that relevant?" Gia asked with a nervous glance at her husband.

"When we asked you before if there was anything else you could tell us about your interactions with the Blanchets, you never mentioned that incident," Freddie said.

"You've hauled us all the way back here from a visit with family to ask us about *that*?" Pascal asked.

"As we mentioned to you earlier, in a homicide investigation, every detail matters," Freddie said. "Why did you leave town the minute you were released from our custody the last time?"

"We had plans to visit Gia's mother."

"You were told to stay local," Gonzo said. "According to your neighbors, you beat a hasty retreat. They indicated you were gone within thirty minutes of arriving home."

"Because we were already leaving later than planned," Gia said.

"You left out a rather significant detail when we spoke to you,"

Freddie said. "The kind of detail that would give someone motive for murder."

"We did *not* kill them, and you're not going to pin this on us," Pascal said.

Gia's hands were shaking so hard that she removed them from the tabletop and put them in her lap. "What kind of people do you think we are?" she asked softly.

"The kind who would torment a young girl online because she was a better gymnast than your kid," Gonzo said.

"That doesn't make us *murderers*," Pascal shouted.

"It must've made you mad that Liliana Blanchet called you racist animals, especially in front of the other parents," Freddie said.

"We aren't racist," Pascal said. "We just didn't care for the way Eloise was treated as the next big thing when she hadn't put the time in with the team that the other girls had. It had nothing to do with race."

"Sure, it didn't." Gonzo opened the laptop he'd brought into the room. "I did some research on the meets in question and took a look at Eloise's performance and then compared her performances to your daughter's. Shall we take a look?"

"We've seen them," Pascal snarled.

"Humor me." Gonzo pressed Play on a video that showed a stunning, flawless performance by Eloise and a much less polished routine from Lacey Cortez. "I'd never watched a gymnastics meet in my life before this, but even my untrained eye can see that Eloise had raw, natural talent, and your daughter, while competent, isn't in the same league as Eloise was."

"Lacey is far more talented than she was!" Gia said. "Ask anyone!"

"Did you kill Eloise and her family to get her out of Lacey's way?" Freddie asked.

Pascal's eyes bugged out of his head. "No! We didn't kill anyone!"

"Do we need a lawyer?" Gia asked. "Pascal, we need a lawyer."

"Who would you like us to call for you?" Freddie asked.

"We don't know anyone," Gia said.

"We'll call the public defender's office, then," Freddie said. "It's apt to be a day or two before they get here, so we'll move you downstairs to the city jail in the meantime."

"We need to get back to our kids!" Gia said.

"Until we can complete our conversation, you'll be our guests," Freddie said. "Shall I go make that call to the PD's office?"

"Wh-what else do you want to know?" Pascal asked.

"Once you request an attorney, we can't speak to you any further about the case," Freddie said. "Am I making the call to the public defender, or do you have the name of an attorney you'd like me to call?"

"We... we don't know any lawyers," Pascal said.

"Very well, then. I'll call the PD. We'll have the Patrol officer take you downstairs until the attorney arrives."

"But our kids..." Gia said. "What about them?"

"I assume they're safe with their grandmother?"

"Yes, but—"

"No buts. Until we can confirm your whereabouts when the Blanchet family was being murdered, you're here to stay." They didn't need to know he could hold them for only forty-eight hours without charging them with a crime.

He and Gonzo left the room and met Malone and Hope in the hallway.

"What do you think?" Freddie asked them.

He'd no sooner said the words than they heard raised voices coming from inside the room. The four of them hustled into observation and turned on the sound from the room.

"What the hell are we going to do now?" Pascal shouted at Gia, who sat crumpled on a chair at the table. "Look at where you've got us—in a goddamned police station being accused of murder! You should've backed off on Eloise when I told you to last year."

"How could I when she was ruining Lacey's life?"

"She was *not* ruining her life, Gia. They're twelve, for fuck's sake. I never should've let you talk me into this."

"*Shut up,*" Gia said on a hiss. "They're probably listening."

Freddie gasped. "What the hell?"

"Good, then they can hear it was all your idea. I'll be happy to tell them all about it."

"You wouldn't dare," Gia said on a snarl. "I know where your bodies are buried."

Freddie and Gonzo exchanged glances.

"What're you talking about?" Pascal asked, seeming genuinely confused.

"Do you think I don't know about what you've been up to with Colleen?"

"What have I been up to?"

"Please, as if you don't know."

"I have no idea what you're talking about."

"You're spending all kinds of time with her, and then suddenly her husband goes 'missing'? Are you going to stand there and tell me you have no idea what happened to him?"

"I don't! I was supporting our friend during a difficult time. How is that a crime? Don't try to turn this around on me. Your sick obsession with a kid has us under suspicion with the cops!"

"I have no regrets." Gia crossed her arms and gave him a defiant look.

"Where's my gun?" Pascal asked on a hiss.

"You don't need to know."

"If that gun gets traced back to me, I'll never forgive you."

"It can't get traced back to you. It's unregistered, remember?"

"I think I've heard enough," Hope said.

"You read my mind, Counselor," Malone said. "Arrest them both on six counts of capital murder and get her prints to the lab to be checked against the gun found at the scene. Also, figure out who the hell Colleen is and what's happened with her husband."

"Yes, sir," Freddie said as he wondered if this was it. Had they found their killer?

He and Gonzo burst into the interrogation room, taking the couple by surprise.

Freddie approached Gia and had her handcuffed before she knew what hit her. "You're under arrest for the murders of Marcel, Liliana, Eloise, Abigail, Violet and August Blanchet. You have the right to remain silent. Anything you say can and will be used against you in a court of law."

By the time Gia caught up to what was happening, Freddie had recited the entire Miranda warning.

"*What is going on?*" she cried as she struggled against the cuffs. "I didn't kill anyone!"

"Do you recall Detectives Green and O'Brien reminding you that you have the right to remain silent when they brought you in?" Freddie pointed to the camera in the corner of the interrogation room. "That means at all times."

"You were *listening* to us?" Pascal said. "That was a private conversation."

"No such thing when you're in police custody, unless your attorney is with you," Gonzo said. "Who is Colleen, and what's happened to her husband?"

His mouth fell open in shock. "She... I..." His mouth snapped shut. "I'd like to speak to an attorney."

Since he wasn't under arrest, Gonzo accompanied Mr. Cortez downstairs to the city jail while Freddie took Gia to be fingerprinted, photographed and officially charged with six counts of murder.

Thanks to the insight gathered from overhearing the couple, Freddie deduced that Gia had taken Pascal's gun to the Blanchet home, forced Marcel to retrieve his weapon and kill himself with his right hand. Then she'd used his gun to kill the kids and put two extra bullets into Eloise. He wasn't sure when she'd grappled with Liliana, but it was either before or after she confronted Marcel. Before she left, she'd put his weapon next to his right hand.

Gia cried so hard, she could barely function. "I didn't do it!" she managed to say around sniffs and sobs.

"Tell it to the judge."

CAMERON GREEN RETURNED HOME after the trip to Hershey to find Gigi in the kitchen, music playing on the Bluetooth speaker and the scent of something delicious cooking on the stove. For a second, he was so stunned to see her there that he could barely find the words to say hello.

She smiled at him the way she had before disaster struck. "How was your day, dear?"

He leaned against the doorframe, taking in the sight of her silky dark hair, olive-toned skin and big brown eyes framed by extravagant lashes. A floral silk robe was knotted at her waist, and from the way the silk clung to curves, he decided she was wearing nothing underneath. "It just got a whole lot better."

Gigi came to him, put her arms around his waist and rested her head on his chest. "For me, too."

"What brought on this burst of energy?"

"I was hungry for the first time in days, so I figured I'd cook."

"I haven't gotten to the store. Where'd you get the food?"

"Instacart." She looked up at him with a saucy grin. "It's this modern invention that delivers groceries *right to your door*."

He was so relieved to see the light back in her eyes that he could barely breathe. Emotion choked him as he held her close.

"Are you okay?" she asked.

"If you are, I am."

"I decided I couldn't spend another day in bed feeling sorry for myself. What Gonzo said last night resonated. None of this was my fault or yours. We have to find a way to move on and live with what happened." She pulled back to look up at him. "Can you do that?"

"I'm trying, babe. I swear I am, but it's just so hard to accept that someone in my life put you and your career in such danger."

"I understand, and I have an idea of how that would feel if the roles had been reversed and Ezra had come for you. But I want us to try to get back to where we were before this happened, because where we were... It's the best place I've ever been, and all I want is more of that."

Cameron gazed at her sweet face, the most beautiful face he'd ever seen. "The first time I ever saw you, after I joined the squad, I felt like I'd been punched in the gut or something. In that single second, everything changed. I asked Cruz about you, and he said you'd had the same boyfriend since high school. I've never been more disappointed than I was in that moment, which was the same moment everything ended for me with Jaycee. It was never the same between us after I met you."

"You've never told me that before," she said softly.

He brushed the hair back from her face. "She knew something had changed, but she wasn't sure what'd happened. I felt awful about it. I'd been with her for a year by then, and we'd had a good time. But I didn't feel for her in a year what I felt for you in that single second."

Gigi curled her arms around his neck and kissed him.

Cameron fell into the kiss as he lifted her into his arms and turned them to press her against the wall. Nothing in his life could compare to the bliss he'd found with her, and to have her back in his arms after fearing that might never happen again was like coming home to the place he was always meant to be.

She worked a hand between them and tugged at his belt.

He came to his senses long enough to realize what she was doing. "Gigi. Are you sure?"

"Yes. Please... I want you."

That was all he needed to hear. He pulled at the button and zipper to his pants and had them down around his hips in a matter of seconds.

When she untied the silk robe, he discovered he'd been right. She had nothing on under it.

The sound that came from deep inside of him, part growl, part desperation, took them both by surprise.

Her soft giggle filled him with joy at realizing his Gigi was coming back to him.

He grasped her supple ass cheeks and lifted her onto his hard cock.

As they joined their bodies, Cameron breathed a sigh of relief. The feeling was so powerful it overwhelmed him. For days, he'd wondered if he'd ever love her like this again after the trauma of Jaycee's assault. Witnessing her determination only made him love her more than he already did.

He had to count to one hundred in his head to keep from losing it too soon. Not before she found her pleasure. Never before her.

"Cameron," she gasped. "Harder."

Holy shit on a shingle. He already had no control where she was concerned, and then she said something like that.

Their climaxes were nothing short of explosive for both of them. His legs trembled, and the rest of him hummed with the ultimate satisfaction.

She pressed her lips to his neck, sending a jolt of sensation charging through him. "I love you so much."

"I love you more."

"No way."

He held her tight against him as aftershocks had him hard again in a matter of seconds. "Yes way."

A loud ding sounded. "Dinner's ready."

They lost it laughing, and Cameron relaxed for the first time in days. If they could still laugh and love, they would find a way through this nightmare.

. . .

AFTER A DINNER of grilled cheese sandwiches for her sick kiddos, Sam joined them in the third-floor conservatory to watch *Iron Man* for the nine hundredth time, as it was the movie Alden always chose when it was his turn to pick.

"Maybe we could watch one of the other *Iron Man* movies next time," Scotty said as he snuggled with Skippy.

"I like this one," Alden said of the original.

"I knew you'd say that," Scotty said as Aubrey giggled at the face he made.

Sam took a call from Freddie. "Hey, what's up?"

"How are the kids?"

"They seem a little better tonight. They'll be home again tomorrow, though."

"Tell them I hope they feel better soon."

"I will."

"So we arrested Gia Cortez for the Blanchet murders."

CHAPTER THIRTY-ONE

S am sat up a little straighter. "Wow. Didn't see that coming."
"Me either." He filled her in on what they'd overheard
from the interrogation room. "I've sent her prints to the lab to run
against the gun and other prints found at the scene. We're waiting
for the public defender to get here before we talk to Pascal about
who Colleen is and what's up with her husband."

"That's an amazing update. How do you feel about it?"

"Uncertain."

"How come?"

"I want it to be that simple, you know? She had motive and
access to a gun that's apparently now missing. She hated Eloise
with a passion that made her unhinged."

"But?"

"I don't know. I'm not feeling the same buzz that comes with a
slam dunk, you know?"

"I get what you mean."

"All of this over a kids' gymnastics team? And how'd they do it?
Did they pull a gun on Marcel, make him get his own gun from
wherever he kept it and stage the whole thing to look like a
murder-suicide?"

"Yeah, that's a good point. I guess you wait for the lab and
decide on next steps."

"Can we talk about a few other things from today?"

"Sure."

He told her about how they'd fully investigated everyone

involved with the lawsuit. "Other than that one incendiary post from Cauley, nothing stands out for any of them. Lots of posts about the heartbreak of infertility and updates on their journey to parenthood. Two of them have gone on to adopt. Their recent posts are filled with joy and hope, which is nice to see."

Sam's gaze took in the three kids who'd made her a mom through the most unlikely of circumstances. "I can relate to that."

"I thought you might. I have to be honest. It's hard to believe the murders didn't have something to do with the father, the lawsuit, his reputation about to be ruined and his life along with it. By all accounts, his marriage was on the rocks because of this, and he was under tremendous strain. Can you imagine what it must've been like for him waiting for that bomb to go off when the lawsuit became public?"

"It must've been unbearable, especially because he knew he'd done a disgusting thing and was about to pay for it in the most public way imaginable."

"Right, and he'd want to spare his wife and kids the scandal of it."

"Except... He was left-handed."

"Yeah, and that's where all my theories go to die. Not to mention his office manager of fifteen years swore up and down that the man she knew never would've done something like what he was accused of."

"Interesting, but I'd expect the people closest to him to defend him against the charges."

"Is it weird that his wife didn't?"

"I've been thinking about her—her work, her life, her clients. Maybe we're focusing on the wrong party when looking for motive."

"Like in the Beauclair case," Freddie said, referring to the assumed name the twins and their parents had lived under after their billionaire father was threatened by a former business partner. They were murdered in a home invasion by someone the wife tangled with after a traffic accident. Throughout the investigation, they'd focused on the obvious threat to the father, until the evidence pointed them in a whole other direction.

"Yes." Sam ran her fingers through Alden's hair. "We were so sure it was related to him. Like how could it *not* be?"

"I'm going through the rest of her social media posts, texts and emails tonight."

"Sorry I didn't get to it all today."

"No worries. I'll let you know if I find anything."

"You're doing all the right things, Freddie, by continuing to follow up even though you have suspects. Just keep pulling the threads."

"For the record, it's easier when you're telling me which threads to pull."

Sam laughed. "I'm sure it is, but this is great experience for you."

"If you say so."

"I say so, and I'm the boss of you."

Next to her, Scotty grunted out a laugh.

Sam grinned at her son. "Go home and take a break. You can start fresh in the morning."

"I might just do that."

"That was an order, not a suggestion."

"You're not the boss of me after hours."

"Oh, sweet grasshopper, where did you ever get that idea?"

"Buh-bye."

Sam was still laughing when the line went dead. "He amuses me. I'm not the boss of him after hours. Whatever. I'm always the boss of him."

"And he wouldn't have it any other way," Scotty said.

"How about you? Are you okay with it?"

"Duh. I didn't have to say yes to being adopted by you. Poor Freddie didn't have a choice. He's stuck with you."

"Very funny." Sam loved him so, so much. "And I'm extremely lucky you chose to be adopted by me, even if I know it was all about my husband."

"No, it wasn't," Scotty said, dead serious now. "It was about both of you."

"Really?" Sam asked in a higher-than-usual pitch.

"Of course it was. As much as I love him, and I love him a lot, I never would've agreed to come live with him if I didn't also love his wife just as much. I can't believe you think it was all about him."

"He is pretty great," Sam said with a small smile.

"He sure is, but so are you, even when you're full of yourself, like you were just now with Freddie."

"That's just our vibe. You know that."

"I do, and for some strange reason, he loves you, too."

"I'm very lovable."

Scotty snorted with laughter that earned him a bop on the head from his mother.

"Why is that funny?"

"You hate people but say you're lovable. Sorry, Mom, but you can't have it both ways."

Equal parts horrified and amused, Sam said, "I hate people who are extra and get in my way on the job. I don't hate people in general."

"Yes, you do."

"No."

"Yes."

"Hey," Nick said when he joined them, dressed in his after-work uniform of sweats and his favorite ratty Harvard T-shirt. "What're we fighting about?"

"That Mom can't hate people *and* say she's lovable."

"That is a dilemma." Nick cast his hazel gaze her way as he took a seat next to her on the sofa. Aubrey and Alden gravitated to his lap, and he wrapped his arms around them. "On the one hand, she does hate people in general. On the other hand, an awful lot of them love her. Even more so now that she's the first lady."

Sam made a face to let him know what she thought of that even as she adored seeing him surrounded by kids who loved him. He'd waited such a long time to have the family they'd created together.

He laughed at her playful scowl. "Well, it's true."

"That's all your fault."

"True, but I can't help that people love you. I mean, if anyone understands that, it's me."

"Don't make it gross," Scotty said. "Sick children are listening."

Sam and Nick bit their lips to keep from laughing.

He waggled his brows at her over the heads of the Littles, who were looking sleepier by the minute.

When the movie ended, they ushered the kids downstairs, to vociferous protests from Scotty, who didn't think he should have to go to bed at the same time as the twins. "Age should have privileges," he said.

"You have lots of privileges," Sam reminded him as she

gestured to the dog who never left his side. "After you take Skippy out to pee, you can watch TV or read, but you need your rest so you can get better."

"Do I have to stay home tomorrow, too?"

"Yes, since you haven't been fever-free for twenty-four hours."

"Oh," he said, seeming disappointed.

"What's up with you? I thought you'd be thrilled to miss more school."

"I am, but sometimes it's fun there."

"I need a minute here," Sam said. "Nick, call Harry. Something is seriously wrong with Scotty."

Her son rolled his eyes at her.

"I'm sorry, but did you just say school is *fun* sometimes?"

"Don't make a thing of it."

"Too late. It's officially a thing. I can't believe my ears."

"Good night, Mother," he said disdainfully as he led Skippy downstairs to go outside.

They tucked in the twins, read them one story and kissed them good night.

"Hope you feel much better in the morning," Sam said.

"Do we hafta go to school?" Aubrey asked.

"Nope," Sam said. "We'll take the rest of the week at home and then the weekend to rest and recover."

"Will you be home with us again tomorrow, Sam?" Alden asked.

"I'm not sure yet, but we'll let you know the plan in the morning, okay?"

"Okay," Aubrey said as she popped her thumb in her mouth.

Nick gave her hand a gentle tug. "We're not sucking that thumb anymore, remember?"

"Oh yeah," she said with a smile as she removed her thumb and stuck that hand under her pillow.

"That's my big girl." He kissed her forehead. "Sleep well, loves."

In the hallway, Sam gave him a hug. "You know I love you all the time, right?"

"I sure hope so."

"I do, but I love you ten bazillion times more when I see you in dad mode. You're so great with them all."

"They and you are the best thing to ever happen to me."

"Are we still on for some loft time tonight?"

"It's the only thing I've thought of all day."

"That can't possibly be true. The leader of the free world certainly has other things he should be thinking about."

Nick rubbed his erection against her belly. "He thinks about you more than anything else."

"Don't let that get out," she said, smiling at him. "It'd be another scandal."

"That's one I'd welcome because it would involve my lovely wife."

"I'm already a sure thing. You know that, don't you?"

He kissed her with a whole day's worth of desire.

Sam curled her arms around his neck and fell into the sexy kiss that was interrupted when Scotty and Skippy returned from their trip outside.

"For the love of God and all that's holy, would you two please knock it off?"

"He's gonna get a girlfriend soon, right?" Nick asked against her lips.

"Or a boyfriend," Sam said. "Either is fine."

"It'd be a *girlfriend*," Scotty said with the disdain that was becoming more frequent since he'd turned fourteen, "and I've got no interest in any of that stuff right now. I have much more important things to focus on, such as hockey."

"We'll see," Nick said with a grin for his son.

"Whatever. Good night."

"Night, son," Nick said. "We love you."

"Uh-huh. Love you, too." The door slammed behind him.

"Was it something we said?" Nick asked.

"I think it was more something we *did*."

"Can we do much, much more of that thing right away?"

"Absolutely." He patted her backside to get her moving toward the stairs.

"Wait, I need to change first."

"No, you don't. The party I have planned requires no clothing."

"That's my favorite kind of party."

He extended his hand to her and headed for the third floor.

"Wait! I need to get the monitor for the twins. I'll be right back." She dashed off to their bedroom to grab the monitor so they'd know if the kids woke up. They rarely did, but since they weren't feeling well, anything was possible.

Nick was right where she'd left him and offered his hand again.

She curled her fingers around his, looking up to find his unforgettable eyes watching her every move. More than two years after they'd reconnected, she still couldn't believe how lucky they'd been to find each other twice in a lifetime.

She'd yearned for him after the first night they'd spent together, believing he'd decided not to call her when he returned from an overseas trip. They'd lost six years thanks to the manipulations of the man she'd later married. However, they'd more than made up for the time lost since they'd been back together, and neither of them would ever take the other for granted after spending so many years wishing for what they had now.

"What's running through that busy mind of yours?" he asked as they went up the stairs.

"I'm thinking about how lucky we are."

"We're the luckiest people we know."

"I'm not sure I'd go that far. I mean, look at where we're living."

"People sell their souls to the devil, literally, to live here," he reminded her. "We didn't have to do that to get the coolest address in America. And you like the perks. You said so yourself."

"I really do, but we also have to put up with a level of scrutiny most people will never experience."

"Eh," he said with a shrug. "Let them scrutinize. What do we always say? They can't touch us unless we let them."

"You're very Zen POTUS tonight."

"I've got a date with my best girl. What do I care about anything else?" He punched in the code to their special room—0326, their wedding date—and stepped aside to let her go in ahead of him. The scent of their favorite coconut candles greeted her as she took in the table set for two.

She spun around. "Someone did some prep work."

"It seemed necessary after having to disappoint you by canceling our trip."

She put the monitor down and rested her hands on his chest. "You could never, ever, *ever* disappoint me."

"Sure I could."

"No. Never. All you have to do to keep that from happening is stay married to me for the rest of our lives."

"It's that simple?" he asked, smiling as he curled a length of her hair around his finger.

"It really is. As long as I have that—and you—I'll never be disappointed."

He put his arms around her and rested his forehead on her shoulder. "I've asked so, so much of you. I wanted to give you time away from it all, just us."

"We'll have all the time in the world to run away together after this is over. Even though Eli and Candace were going to be here with them, I was feeling a little anxious about leaving the twins for a week when they're just getting comfortable here." Eli had agreed to come home for his spring break to stay with the kids while they were gone.

"I was, too."

"So there's that. We don't have to miss our kids, and I wasn't feeling right about taking off on a romantic trip when Ang is adjusting to widowhood."

"Maybe it's fortuitous that the Joint Chiefs stepped in to change our plans."

"We aren't giving them credit for anything. We hate them."

He raised his head to meet her gaze, his eyes dancing with amusement. "Yes, we do, but enough about everyone who isn't in this room."

CHAPTER THIRTY-TWO

H is lips found hers in a soft, sweet kiss that had her on tiptoes to get closer.

"First, we eat," he said. "Then we play."

"Why can't we play first?"

"Because we'll need energy to play."

"Oh, good point, and I am rather hungry. What's for dinner?"

"I asked the butlers to surprise us."

"So, um, they were in here?"

"Nope. The meal was delivered to the door, and I brought it in."

"Oh, good. They don't need to know what we're doing in here."

"I think they know, babe."

"No, they don't, and that's all we're saying about it."

"You don't want poor Reginald imagining the first lady on her hands and knees—"

Sam put her hand over his mouth. "Say another word, and you'll never see the first lady on her hands and knees again."

"That'd be a terrible shame." He cupped her ass with both hands. "That's one of my favorite views in the whole wide world."

"It's wide, all right."

"What've I told you about disparaging my wife's sexy ass?"

"Let's make it even bigger by having some dinner." She lifted the catering lid off the plate to find filet mignon with tiny potatoes and asparagus. The scent made her mouth water. "Yum."

Over dinner, he brought her up to date on the latest news

about the Joint Chiefs. "Cox will announce tomorrow that they won't be charged criminally."

"Such bullshit."

"It's the right call if he lacks the evidence to go forward with it," he said. "I'm telling myself it's enough to see them dishonorably discharged from the military and hopefully denied their pensions, if we can even get that much without much evidence tying them to the plot."

"I'm sure Cox would've loved to have charged them if he could've made the case. At any rate, it puts others on notice that they're risking a cushy retirement by plotting to overthrow the government."

"That it does."

"Any word on the other matter?" Sam refused to say the words *mother* or *Nicoletta* in his presence.

"I heard she's called a flashy local lawyer. He's all about playing to the media and will probably plead her case in the court of public opinion by stating that her son the president would rather let his mother rot in jail than offer any kind of help."

"You have to stay strong."

"That's what everyone says."

Every indication of playfulness and fun was now gone, and in its place, the wounded young boy he'd once been remained. Sam hated Nicoletta for what she'd done to him. For what she *continued* to do to him. "What do *you* say?"

He poked at the food on the plate with his fork, seeming a million miles away. "I could get her a real lawyer. I could get Andy involved." He was one of Nick's closest friends and an attorney.

Sam wanted to yell *NO!* to that, but she bit her tongue and let him talk.

"I look like an asshole for letting her sit in jail when I could help her."

She rolled her lips together to keep words that could add to his pain from spilling out.

"What do you want to say?" he asked, glancing up at her.

The hurt she saw in his eyes enraged her. "I can't tell you how to handle this situation. You have to do what you think is best." She reached across the table to take his hand. "You're the best man I've ever met."

"Skip was the best man you ever met."

Sam shook her head. "He was an amazing man, but even he did things that I didn't agree with, such as letting Cameron Fitzgerald off on murder charges while trying to protect his dead partner's widow. I mean, I get why he did it, but he shouldn't have risked his own career and reputation to protect her. You wouldn't have done that."

"We can't possibly know that."

"You always do the right thing, even by people who don't deserve it." She paused, considering her words carefully. "The only other thing I'll say is that any time you let her into your life, you regret it because you're forced to confront the fact that she cares only about herself. She will never care about you the way a mother should, and every time you have to come to that conclusion all over again, you lose a little piece of yourself. I can't stand watching that happen." She took a sip of her wine. "So yeah, that was more than I meant to say."

He smiled, but it wasn't the usual dazzling event she was used to. "You're right. As always."

"It's hard for you to ignore her because even after everything she's put you through, you're still a good and loyal son who feels like he needs to fix things for a mother who never fixed anything for him."

"That's it exactly."

"I have no idea how you managed to grow up to be the kind, thoughtful, caring, loving man you are when you were raised by wolves. She doesn't deserve you."

"No, she doesn't."

"But if you feel the need to help her, I will never judge you, and I'll never think less of you. I promise."

"Thank you for that. It matters."

"You have to be able to live with yourself."

"That's the part I'm finding difficult. Look at where I am while she's sitting in a jail cell."

"You're here because you made different choices for your life than she did—and no thanks at all to her. You went from nothing to this, thanks to your own grit and determination and years of hard work that no one ever saw. While you were doing that, she was finding ways to rob and steal and grift and shake down her only child for money, all because she thinks the world owes her something. That's the difference between you and her, and the current circumstances are what they are because of the choices each of you made."

"Yeah."

"Please tell me you know that you're not in any way responsible for her."

"I do know that, but at the end of the day, like you said, I'm her only child."

"What do you want to do?"

"I want to forget I ever met her."

"But?"

His deep sigh said everything.

Sam got up, went around the table and gestured for him to make room for her on his lap.

He wrapped his arms around her and buried his face in her hair, breathing her in.

"Do what you need to, Nick. No one who knows you well would ever question your need to help her. We know you. We know your heart. We get it."

"I hate myself for wanting to help her. What kind of masochist am I for repeatedly going back for more when I know exactly who and what she is?"

"You're not a masochist. You're a son who loves a mother who doesn't deserve him. You'd rather love than hate, even when no one would blame you for hating her."

"Thank you for understanding."

"You speak Samantha fluently. I'd like to think I speak Nicholas fluently, too."

He pulled back so he could see her face. "You do. No one has ever spoken Nicholas as fluently as you do."

"Well, I should hope not."

That earned her a genuine smile. "Thanks, babe."

"I love you so much, and I hate her enough for both of us."

He laughed as he kissed her. "My fierce little tiger."

"That's me. You do what you need to, but God forbid I ever get my claws into her."

"I'll make sure Vernon keeps a lookout so we don't have another scandal from the first lady clawing the president's mother."

Sam was relieved that he was rolling with the silliness rather than dwelling on the heartbreak of it all. His pain was hers, and she wished his mother would just go the fuck away and stop hurting him. Since that probably wasn't going to happen, she was determined to help him deal with it.

"I'm ready for the next item on our agenda."

With his arms around her, he lifted her as he stood.

"Don't throw your back out, Mr. President."

"You're a lightweight."

Her snort of laughter made him laugh, too.

"I love every soft, sexy square inch of my gorgeous wife, especially her luscious curves."

"Her curves are extra luscious since we moved in here."

"Fine by me." He set her down by the double lounger that reminded them of their resort in Bora Bora.

Sam was so sad they wouldn't be able to get there for their anniversary this year, but she understood why the timing wasn't good for him to go half a world away from home at this moment in time. She hated the former Joint Chiefs almost as much as she hated Nicoletta, but she was determined to help Nick take his mind off all his troubles.

She pulled his T-shirt over his head and pushed his sweats and boxer briefs to the floor. Then she gave his chest a gentle push to get him to sit on the lounger. When he was settled, she dropped to her knees.

"What is happening?"

Sam gave him a sly smile. "A little of this," she said, nibbling his neck, "and a little of that." She kissed along his collarbone as she nudged him to lie back.

He propped himself on his elbows as she let her gaze travel over him before she bent to kiss his chest and chiseled abdomen. "How do you stay in such amazing shape trapped in this place all the time?"

"It has one of the best gyms I've ever seen."

"When do you do that?"

"Middle of the night, mostly."

"Nick..."

"I'd rather do that than stare at the ceiling when I can't sleep."

"I'd rather you sleep, but I gotta say, the gym time is very well spent." She touched her tongue to his washboard abs. "If the women of America could see what I see, they'd be storming the gates."

"Oh, hush," he said, embarrassed as always when she complimented his extreme sexiness.

She wrapped her hand around his cock, which was so hard, it nearly touched his belly button. "I only speak the truth."

His gasp of pleasure thrilled her.

Sam loved being the only one who ever got to see him like this, who got to love him and touch him and live her life with him. She decided she ought to tell him that. "You make me feel like the luckiest girl in the world to be loved by you."

He strained against the tight hold she had on him as she stroked him. "I'm feeling like the lucky one at the moment."

Smiling, she bent to take him into her mouth.

"And getting luckier by the minute."

Sam threw every trick she had at him, loving how his fingers tangled in her hair as his hips rose and fell with the rhythm she set.

"Samantha..."

The note of warning wasn't lost on her, but rather than heed it, she doubled down until he shouted from the release that flooded her mouth and throat. She wouldn't do that for any other man on earth. But this man... There was nothing she wouldn't do for him.

WITH HIS WORLD on fire with scandal and controversy, Nick couldn't believe how she cleared his mind of everything except her and them and the love he felt for her. The second he was able to catch his breath, he drew her down on top of him and kissed her swollen lips. "Thank you for this. I literally couldn't bear the rest of my life without you and us and our family."

"Me either, and you don't have to thank me."

"Yeah, I really do." He ran the fingers of both hands through her hair. "I talked you into taking on a new senator, and look at where we ended up. I should be thanking you every single day."

She shook her head. "No need. We could've ended up on the moon, for all I care. As long as you were there with me, I'd find a way to make it work."

"I'm not sure which is worse—the moon or the White House."

Sam laughed. "The White House isn't so bad. Everyone here makes things so easy for us, and the kids have made a smooth transition. I have no complaints, and you know that's a rare thing for me. I don't love the intense scrutiny you're under all the time, but you and your amazing team are so good at dealing with it. It's all good in the hood."

"I'm glad to hear you say that. I worry all the time about when I'm going to ask too much of you."

"Never," she said, leaning forward to kiss him as she glided over his reawakened erection.

He grasped her hips and held her still as he pushed into her. Once again, his mind went completely blank of all things that weren't her and them and the intense connection that made his life complete.

Sam sat up straight and looked him in the eye as she moved over him.

As he watched her, he committed every second to memory, wanting to remember this forever. He moved his hands from her hips to her full breasts, running his thumbs over her nipples.

She tossed her head back as her internal muscles tightened around him.

They came together in an explosive moment of perfect harmony that never failed to astound him. After all this time, how could it keep getting better? Somehow it did, and as he gathered her into his embrace, he gave thanks to the universe for bringing her to him a second time.

"I really, really needed this," he said as they came down from the incredible high they found together.

"Same."

His hand made slow circles over her back. "What should we do instead of Bora Bora? We still have a week off scheduled."

"What're our options?"

"Rent a place at the beach in Delaware like we did last summer?" he asked.

"That wouldn't be as much fun in March."

"All we need is a bed and a fireplace to make it fun."

"That's true and fine with me," she said. "Do you want me to check to see if the same place is available?"

"Works for me. Maybe we could invite the family out for the second weekend?"

"That'd be fun."

"I'm thinking of a change of scenery for Ang and the kids," he said.

"Yes, definitely. Let's do that."

"That place is big enough to invite the whole crew. We should be able to get it this time of year, and the Secret Service has already approved it."

"Sounds like a plan."

"I'm sorry again about Bora Bora," he said with a playful pout.

"We have the rest of our lives to go there and anywhere else we want to go."

"I'm looking forward to the rest of our lives."

CHAPTER THIRTY-THREE

F reddie got to HQ at six the next morning to write up the details of the investigation so they could request a warrant for the Cortezes' cell phone data. If they were able to place them at the scene of the crime via their phones, that would tie up the loose ends that were still nagging at him.

Yes, Gia Cortez was a bit unhinged over the gymnastics situation and would've wanted Eloise out of the way, but he was having a hard time stretching his imagination to her killing the entire family. A murder of that sort was usually driven by some sort of intense motive, and children's gymnastics competitions didn't meet that bar, no matter how he tried to make it fit.

"How goes it?" Malone asked when he approached Freddie's cubicle.

"Okay, I guess."

"Any word from the public defender about the Cortezes?"

"Not yet." Freddie dangled a pen between his fingers as he stared at the computer screen where he'd laid out the case against Pascal and Gia Cortez, such as it was.

"What's the matter?"

Freddie looked up at the captain. "I'm not feeling it with them."

"How come?"

"The motive doesn't fly for me. Six people dead over a middle school gymnastics competition?"

"The racist-animals comment could've lit a fuse."

"I suppose," Freddie said, still not convinced. "I've got the warrant request ready to go for their cell data."

"That'll tell the story one way or the other. I'll get it submitted."

"Sounds good."

He was surprised to see Sam enter the pit. "What're you doing here?"

"Last I knew, I worked here. Nick is working from the residence this morning. What's the latest?"

Freddie updated her on the request for the warrant as well as his reservations about whether they'd found their suspects.

"The cell data will cinch it if it was them."

"Yeah, for sure. How're the kids feeling?"

"Much better today. They should be good to go back to school on Monday."

"You didn't have to come in today."

"Yes, I did. I want to support you as you see the case across the finish line."

"Thanks. I'd much rather work with you than without you."

"You mean you'd much rather have me telling you what to do than figuring it out on your own."

"That. Exactly that."

She laughed. "From all accounts, you've done an excellent job of leading a difficult, complex, emotionally draining case."

"Really?"

She grinned. "Why do you sound so surprised?"

"I don't know. I guess I still see myself as the junior detective hoping to play in the big leagues someday."

"Freddie, my little grasshopper, you've been playing in the big leagues for years now, and you're ready for this. You have been for a while, frankly." Her smile became a frown. "I worry sometimes that working with me is holding you back from moving forward in your own career."

"No, it isn't. Where is there to go from here except for your job or some other squad, which I'd hate. I love working with you and our team, and you know that."

"I do, but there may come a time when it would be better for you to go your own way."

"I don't want to talk about that. I've got enough on my plate right now without adding that to it. I like things just the way they are, and if I'm never anything more than a detective, I'll be perfectly fine."

"You could be much more than a detective, and I don't want you to miss out on opportunities because of your loyalty to me."

"I'm not missing out on anything."

"Freddie—"

"I heard you, and I appreciate your whole if-you-love-something-set-it-free speech, but I'm good right where I am. Now, we need to figure out who Colleen is and what's become of her husband."

"Let's get to it."

THEY HAD lunch delivered while they worked the phones and sifted through the paper bomb trying to figure out who Colleen was.

Sam was looking through information gathered from the Blanchet house by the Crime Scene detectives when she came upon a file folder marked "Confidential." She checked the inventory sheet the CS officers had attached to the documents they'd taken from the house. The folder it was in had been found inside a file cabinet in Marcel Blanchet's home office.

"What's this?" Sam held up the file folder so Freddie could see it. "Inventory says it was found in Marcel's home office."

"I haven't seen that. Where was it?"

"With the Crime Scene stuff."

Sam opened the folder and read through the pages inside. "Uh, did we know they had an adopted son who they rehomed after he was violent with their other children?"

"What? No. I've heard nothing about that."

As a tingle of excitement attacked her backbone, her dyslexia picked then to kick in, making the words on the page a scrambled mess to her. "Fucking dyslexia. Read this out loud." She handed the page to him.

"It's dated October 10, four years ago. By order of the District of Columbia Courts, Family Services Division, the adoption of Isaiah Blanchet (nee Wiley), age of thirteen, is voided. Isaiah Wiley is hereby remanded to Child and Family Services for foster placement. All parental rights and privileges previously granted to Marcel and Liliana Blanchet are hereby terminated."

Freddie glanced at her with a "holy shit" look on his face. "Who do we know at Child and Family Services?"

"Dolores Finklestein." She'd been the social worker assigned to the twins after their parents were murdered. Nick had called her Ms. Picklestein, and Sam had lived in fear of calling the woman that to her face.

They stared at each other for a hot second, a silent communion that came with working a case and finding a lead that might be the proverbial needle in a very big haystack.

"I'll call her," Sam said. "You talk to the grandmother." Sam was on her way out of the conference room when she stopped and turned back to him. "That is... if you approve of that plan."

"I approve. Go to it."

Sam went into her office and sat behind the desk. The name Dolores Finklestein provoked a PTSD reaction in her as she recalled the process of bringing the twins into their family and the significant roadblocks they'd had to overcome with Dolores's agency. In the end, she'd been a huge help to them, but her name brought back memories of a time Sam would rather forget.

She made the call to Dolores's personal cell phone.

"Mrs. Cappuano. This is a surprise. Is everything all right with the twins?"

"Yes," Sam said. "They're doing great. I'm calling you as Lieutenant Holland about a case."

"What can I do for you?"

"Have you heard about the Blanchet family murders?"

"I've just returned from a cruise to the Bahamas with my sisters and need to catch up on the news."

"Does the name Blanchet mean anything to you?"

"Should it?"

"A child adopted by them was returned to your custody four years ago. Isaiah Wiley."

"Oh God," she said. "Oh no."

"I take it you recognize his name?"

"I do, and I remember them, too, now that you've refreshed my memory with his name. He was a deeply troubled child who went through hell in the system before being adopted by the Blanchets. Our entire agency celebrated him finding his forever home, but the arrangement was problematic from the start. Despite intense family therapy, he resisted the rules set forth by his new parents, and when they welcomed more children into the family, Isaiah became openly hostile toward them. The Blanchets tried everything to make it work with him, but they began to fear for the safety of their other children."

Sam's heart broke for a child who'd never had a chance in life. "What became of him after he left them?"

"He lived in several foster homes before he landed in a group home. I haven't heard anything more about him in a while, but I could check with my colleague who is his case manager if you'd like."

"I'd appreciate that."

"I'll have Therese give you a call on this number?"

"That works. Thank you so much."

"No problem, and may I say... The actions of the Joint Chiefs are an outrage. They don't represent regular Americans like me, who think your husband is doing a wonderful job."

"Oh." Sam had never been more stunned, which was saying something. "Thank you for that. I'll pass it on to him. He'll appreciate it."

"Tell him to stay tough. The people are with him."

"Thank you, Dolores."

"I'll have Therese call you."

Her BlackBerry buzzed with a text from Nick. *Everyone is feeling much better today, but we're taking it easy so they don't overdo it.*

Good call, Dad. Just talked to Picklestein. She says to stay tough against the Joint Chiefs. The people are with you.

Wow. Didn't see that coming. Why were you talking to her?!

For the case.

Oh phew. You scared me for a second there.

Sorry.

No worries.

I bet Picklestein is still thinking about the day she saw you sweaty and half naked after a workout.

She is not!

She made a major deposit in the spank bank that day.

OMG, did you really just say that? Do women have spank banks? Am I really asking that question?

Hahahahahahah, yep.

Thanks for putting that image in my head.

I do what I can for my person.

LOL. Are you working a full day?

We just stumbled onto a hot new lead. Might be a while.

Take your time. I've got things covered here. Noah is playing with the Littles in the Conservatory.

Have you seen Shelby today?

Not yet.

Ok, let me know how she is when you do.

Will do. Take care of my sexy cop. She's the sun, the moon and the stars to me.

Swoon. Love you.

Love you more.

No way. Not possible.

Very possible.

Let's have this fight later, shall we?

You got it.

Smiling, Sam put down the BlackBerry and grabbed her flip phone to take a call from a 202 number. "Lieutenant Holland."

"Hi, this is Therese Andrews from Child and Family Services. Dolores asked me to give you a call."

"Thank you so much for calling."

"I understand you're asking about Isaiah Wiley?"

"Yes."

"That young man has been through hell."

"That's what Dolores said. Can you elaborate?"

"I've been assigned to his case for sixteen years. I first met him when he was a year old, in the hospital with a skull fracture, his body covered in cigarette burns."

Sam winced and closed her eyes, steeling herself for what else she might hear.

"He's been in and out of the foster care system ever since and had every terrible experience you can imagine. Sexual, physical, emotional abuse. Despite our best efforts to provide good homes for the children under our care, we can't prevent older kids from preying on younger ones or bullying that turns violent. Isaiah has had a very, very hard road."

"Can you tell me about his experience with the Blanchet family?"

Her deep sigh came through loud and clear. "They tried so hard to make it work with him, and for a while, it did. That was the happiest I ever saw him, even as he pushed back hard against the structure they tried to instill. I'd become invested in him and stayed in contact after the adoption. Everything was working out well for them until the Blanchets began having babies. They'd had Isaiah in intensive therapy from the start, and the counselor worked with him to try to temper his resentment of the children, but it just grew and grew until the Blanchets began to fear for the safety of their other kids. The counselor agreed that the adoption should be terminated."

Sam's heart ached for a young man she'd never met. "Where is he now?"

"I don't know. He left the group home where he was living a few weeks ago, and we haven't had any luck finding him."

"Do you think there's any chance he could've harmed the Blanchets?"

"I wish I could say an emphatic no, but he never got over what happened with them. He loved them and hated them at the same time."

Freddie came to the door of Sam's office.

"Can you hang on a second, Therese?"

"Sure."

Sam put her hand over the phone. "What's up?"

"The grandmother says Isaiah came to the house two weeks ago, asking for another chance to be part of their family. She said Marcel was heartbroken to have to turn him away. He said he just couldn't risk a repeat of what'd happened before."

"We need to find him." Returning to the call, Sam said, "Do you have any idea where he might be?"

"I wish I did. The MPD Patrol division has been looking for him since he went missing and hasn't had any luck."

"Do you have a recent photo of him?" It would be quicker to get it from her than to track down the officers who'd been working the case.

"I do. I'll send it to your email?"

"That'd be great." Sam gave her the address. "Do you have his cell number and the address of the place he was living?"

Therese gave her the info she'd requested.

"I really appreciate your help."

"I wish there was more I could do. I'm praying he had nothing to do with what happened to the Blanchets."

Sam was, too, but if the sinking feeling inside her was any indication, Isaiah could've had everything to do with it.

"WHAT'S THE PLAN?" Freddie asked after Sam updated him on what she'd learned from Therese.

"You're the boss."

"She said Patrol has been looking for him for a few weeks with no luck?"

"She did."

"I think I'd like to call in Jesse Best and the U.S. Marshals."

"That's what I'd do."

"Okay, then."

"Okay, then," Sam said. "Make the call."

"Like... I should call him?"

"Yes, Freddie, you should call Jesse."

"Will he take my call?"

Sam tried hard not to laugh at his wide-eyed expression. "Only one way to find out." It was all she could do not to give him a push toward his cubicle to get him moving. Thankfully, he turned on his own and went to call Jesse.

CHAPTER THIRTY-FOUR

Captain Malone came into her office. "Heard you've got a promising new lead."

Sam filled him in on what she knew so far. "Is that enough to get a warrant for his cell phone data?"

"Let's give it a try. Write it up."

Sam spent the next hour summarizing the information they'd gathered on Isaiah and then went back to edit her work as best she could before she sent it to Freddie for proofing. He was always willing to check her work, which she appreciated. Dyslexia tested her daily and always had her questioning herself when it came to written documents.

Freddie came to the door. "I just read your warrant request. What that kid has been through..."

"I know. It's horrendous. What does it say about me that I feel for him even if it's possible he killed six people?"

"Anyone with a heart would feel for what he's endured."

"This could be one of those instances where we solve the case but don't feel good about it."

"Yeah, for sure. Although, this is finally a motive that makes sense. He wanted to be part of them. They turned him away—again—and he decided that if he couldn't be part of their family, they didn't get to go on without him."

"That makes more sense than a mother flipping out and killing six people because another kid was a better gymnast than hers."

"Where are we with the warrant for the Cortez cell phone data?" Sam asked.

"Still waiting on the judge."

"Could the judge please hurry the hell up?"

"No kidding. I'll check the request for Isaiah's phone data and submit it to Captain Malone."

"He's expecting it."

"What should we do while we wait?"

"If I were running the investigation, I'd want to know everything there is to know about Isaiah Wiley, starting with the place he was living until a few weeks ago. But, of course, that's up to you."

"I was thinking about starting with the place where Wiley was living until he took off."

"See? You've got this."

They shared a smile and then went to grab their coats.

When they were in the SUV with Vernon and Jimmy, Sam gave them the Southeast address for the group home where Isaiah had been living.

"I can't stop thinking about the things his social worker told me," Sam said. "He never had a chance."

"No, he didn't."

"From everything we've learned about Marcel and Liliana, it seems like they would've tried their best to make it work with him."

"The grandmother said they were heartbroken to have to annul the adoption."

"What an impossible situation for them. I'm sure they loved him, but they were worried for the safety of their other children. Like, what if Scotty had reacted badly to the Littles? We wouldn't have been able to keep them with us even though we already loved them." Sam shuddered just thinking about such a dilemma.

Thank God and all the saints in heaven it hadn't come to that.

Some people got lucky bringing children into their lives. Others didn't. She ached for what Marcel and Lilianna must've gone through having to void the adoption of a child they must've loved long before it came to an end.

"People always say why don't you adopt if you can't have kids of your own, or if you want to bring a child into your life who needs a good home," Sam said. "No one ever talks about what happens when it doesn't work out."

"I'm trying to wrap my head around what it must've been like for them to have to remove him from their home. Mrs. Blanchet said it was a nightmare. That was the word she used."

"It had to have been. What does it say about me that I so don't want him to be the one who did this?"

"I feel the same. I don't want it to be him."

"Contact Patrol and get a handle on what they've done so far. Um... If you agree that's a wise move."

Freddie chuckled. "You're still allowed to give the orders."

"This is your case, and I want you to take it over the finish line."

"I'm going to check in with Patrol to see what they've done so far to find Isaiah."

"That's a great idea."

"You two are hilarious," Vernon said.

"We do what we can for the people," Freddie said.

"That line is trademarked," Sam said, "and you're not authorized to use it."

The three men laughed, which gave her pleasure.

Freddie's phone chimed with a text. "Lieutenant Dawkins says they've done all the usual stuff—talked to his friends, the other residents at the house, his employer at a local pizza restaurant and his teachers. No one has heard from him in several weeks."

"Did they track his phone?"

"Not yet. That was going to be their next step."

"Tell him we'll take it from here. There might be a connection to our case."

"I told him, and he sent a thumbs-up."

"I'll bet he loves having a missing foster kid off his plate." Sam had no sooner said the words than she regretted them. "Sorry. That wasn't fair. I don't know him at all. I have no idea what he cares about."

"I get where it's coming from," Freddie said. "Ever since we found out that Stahl did next to nothing while collecting a paycheck, we're wary of everyone."

"I like to save my venom for people who deserve it, like Ramsey." To Vernon, she said, "Have you guys heard any more about him being charged for ramming us?"

"The FBI is handling the case, and I expect him to be charged federally with several felonies," Vernon said.

"Excellent," Sam said. "Whatever it takes to keep him off the job and away from us."

They arrived at the Southeast address of the group home where Isaiah had lived until he went missing. She glanced out the window at the run-down house. "Why do they put kids in their custody in the most depressing-looking places in the entire city?"

"Because they're the cheapest," Freddie said.

"And what does that say about us as a society? That the most at-risk kids in our city get the shaft at every turn."

"I don't think it's just here."

"That makes me feel so much better."

They went through an iron gate that had once been black before most of the paint chipped off and up the stairs to a three-story brown rowhouse.

"Was brown the sale color at the paint store?" Sam asked as she pushed the button to summon a staff member.

"You're on fire today."

"After hearing what this kid has been through, I feel like he should be living at Buckingham Palace or something."

"Or the White House?" Freddie asked, raising a brow.

Sam would've taken him in a minute except for the pesky possibility that he might be wanted for mass murder. "Nah, I just feel for him."

"I know. Me, too."

Sam pushed the button again and banged on the door for added emphasis.

The metal door swung open to reveal an older Black man.

Sam and Freddie showed their badges.

When he took a closer look, the man did a double take as he recognized Sam.

"We're here about Isaiah Wiley," she said, cutting off any first-lady comments.

"I told the other cops that we haven't seen or heard from him in about three weeks. What's he done?"

"Nothing that we know of," Freddie said. "We'd just like to talk to him."

"I gave the other cops the names of his friends and the info about where he works. Not sure what else I can do."

"Can we see his room?"

"Do you need a warrant for that?"

"Only if you don't want to give us access to help find a minor who went missing on your watch," Sam said.

The man bristled at her. "Do you have *any idea* how difficult it is to take care of teenagers who think they don't need to be taken care of? Most of them are just killing time until they're eighteen. They think everything will be better then, but we know better, don't we? Keeps me awake at night worrying about what becomes of them after they leave us."

"I'm sorry," Sam said when she realized he was someone who cared deeply about the kids under his care. "I can't begin to know how difficult it must be to do what you do."

"Likewise," he said. "Come in. I'll show you his room."

"What's your name?" Freddie asked.

"Chuck Dempsey."

"Did Isaiah talk about his former family at all?" Freddie asked.

They followed him into the house, which smelled like fried onions, sweat and peanut butter.

"The ones that adopted him and then gave him back?"

"Yeah, them."

"Not much other than to say he still missed them. He was happy there, but he couldn't curb his impulses when it came to their other children. He said he tried to make it work, to stop thinking of them as his enemies, but he couldn't do it. It was a very sad situation all around."

"Did you know he went to their home recently and asked them to give him another chance?"

The man stopped walking and turned to them. "No, he didn't mention that. What did they say?"

"That they wished they could, but they couldn't risk the safety of their other children."

He sighed deeply. "I feel for both sides. It was a no-win situation."

"Did you hear that the Blanchets and their four children were murdered in their home earlier this week?"

"What? No... I've been so busy with the kids that I've barely glanced at the news." All at once, the implications of Sam and Freddie being there registered with him. "Do you... You think he did it?"

"We don't know," Freddie said. "We only just learned of his existence in relation to the family today."

"He loved them," Chuck said.

"And they rejected him," Sam said. "Twice. Because of violent tendencies."

"He wouldn't have harmed them. They were the only family he ever knew."

The room Isaiah had lived in lacked any sort of personal touches. There was a bed, a dresser, a closet and a desk. Sam recalled Nick telling her that Scotty hadn't been allowed to put posters on the wall in the Richmond-area home where he'd resided before he came to live with them. They'd encouraged him to put posters on the ceiling if he wanted to in his room in their home.

"May I?" she asked, pointing to the dresser.

Chuck gestured for her to go ahead.

In the drawers, she found three pairs of boxer briefs, four T-shirts, a pair of sweats and a Washington Capitals sweatshirt.

"He loves that team," Chuck said. "He watches all their games."

The closet had three polo shirts on hangers and a pair of jeans on the shelf.

"Are these all of his possessions?"

"Yes," Chuck said.

A pervasive sadness swept over her when she thought of the things Scotty treasured and enjoyed and realized that Isaiah had nothing to call his own except for some basic clothing.

"Does he carry a backpack?"

"He does," Chuck said. "That's the only thing I can tell that's missing."

"I know you gave the names of his friends to the other MPD officers," Freddie said. "But if you could give them to us, too, we'd appreciate it."

"Sure."

They left a short time later with info about Isaiah's friends, his school and his job, and spent the rest of the day trying to track him down to no avail.

"Is there a Caps game today?" Sam asked.

"Tonight at seven."

"Maybe we need to go."

"Would he be able to afford a ticket?"

"He had a job. He might have some money."

"I suppose it's worth a try, but wouldn't that be like looking for a needle in a haystack?"

"Yeah, but the Caps are the one thing Chuck said he loved besides the Blanchets."

Freddie's phone rang. "It's Jesse Best calling me back." He pressed the green button to accept the call. "Hey, Jesse."

While Freddie gave Jesse the lowdown on the case and their need to find Isaiah Wiley, Sam checked in with Nick to see how the kids were doing.

All quiet here. Watching a movie. How goes it there?

The usual frustration. Can't find a kid who may or may not have killed the family that was forced to nullify his adoption after he was violent with their other kids.

Ugh.

Yeah.

You really think he did it?

We don't know what to think. Going to hit the Caps game tonight because our subject is a big fan. Will be home after that.

You should give Vernon a heads-up that you're planning to attend a big public event.

Oh yeah...

Samantha.

I would've thought of it. Eventually.

No, you wouldn't have.

YES!

No!

Another fight to continue when I see you.

Can't wait. Be careful with my best girl. I love her madly.

Will do. Love you madlier.

That's not a word.

Nerd.

Sticks and stones...

"I gave Jesse everything we know about Isaiah and told him we're going to look for him at the Caps game later. He said they're on it." Freddie's phone rang with a call from Malone. "Hey, Captain, what's up?"

Sam watched as Freddie's brows came together in what might've been confusion. "Really? And they're sure?" After a pause, "Well, I honestly didn't expect that. Yes, sir. Will do."

He ended the call. "Both the Cortez phone numbers had pings near the Blanchet home around the time of death given by Lindsey, and Archie has located video that puts their car there the night they were killed."

"Really?"

"That's what I said, too."

"Huh."

"So that's it, then, right? They had motive—thin as it may be—and we can put them at the scene at the time of the murders."

"It's enough to charge them both. Update Hope and see what she says." The prosecutor would have to make the case in court, and it would be up to her to tell them if they needed more evidence.

While Freddie called Hope, Sam checked in with Vernon.

"We're planning to stop into the Caps game tonight to look for a missing person," Sam said.

"Uh… I don't think that's a good idea."

"It's for a case."

"We need time to prepare for something like that, to secure the location, to figure out crowd control. Is there any way you could send someone else?"

Sam wanted to snap back and tell him no, she wasn't going to ask a member of her team to do something she couldn't do herself, but she liked Vernon and appreciated that he was doing his job, which was to keep her safe.

"I'll send someone else."

"Thank you."

"You're welcome. Please remember this gesture of goodwill."

"So noted," he said.

"Are you being sassy with me by any chance?"

"Would I do that?"

"Yes, you would!"

He chuckled. "I'm a consummate professional."

"Right. I'll be out in a few to head home."

"Ready when you are, Sam."

"Thanks." She slapped her phone closed.

"Hope says we've got enough to charge Pascal, too," Freddie said. "She wants to go over everything with us tomorrow to make sure she has the full picture."

"You should go to the Caps game," Sam said. "Ask Gonzo or Matt to go with you. Let's try to find Isaiah."

"We're still going to do that?"

"Yeah, we are." Sam wanted to find Isaiah and make sure he was safe. Knowing what she did about his life, how could she move on without closing that loop? "I'm invested."

CHAPTER THIRTY-FIVE

F reddie spent the next several hours before the game writing the report that would be used to charge the Cortezes with six counts of murder and other charges. He'd texted Gonzo and Matt, both of whom had agreed to meet him at the Caps game to try to find Isaiah Wiley. That would be a huge long shot, but worth a try.

As he worked on the report summarizing the Blanchet case, he tried to ignore the nagging feeling that he'd missed something big.

But what?

They had several of the other gymnastics parents who could testify to hearing Liliana Blanchet calling the Cortezes racist animals. They had social media posts and comments tying Gia Cortez to a racially tinged campaign against Eloise Blanchet. Cell phone data put them at the scene of the crime. Their car was spotted on video in the neighborhood. In a world where slam-dunk cases were rare, this one was shaping up to be just that.

Except, he still felt like they'd missed something.

Sam called to check in. "How's it going?"

"Everything about this outcome feels wrong to me."

"The evidence doesn't lie, Freddie. That's what you have to believe in."

"I believe in it. I just can't believe someone would commit mass murder over a middle school gymnastics competition."

"I agree, it's unreal. But we've seen all sorts of crazy reasons for murder. How often does it make sense?"

"Rarely," he said with a sigh.

"You're looking for something to make sense that will never make sense to us as people who don't understand how anyone could ever commit murder, especially the murders of four innocent kids."

"Yeah."

"You did a great job. You followed the evidence to where it led you, and you've put together a case that'll hold up in court."

"I'm glad you think so."

"I do think so."

"They've informed the public defender that they'll be getting their own lawyer. I've made calls to the three they asked for. No response yet. I hate to break it to them, but they might not find a lot of lawyers willing to represent people who'd shoot kids in their beds."

"True. You did great, Detective. I'm so proud of you."

"Thanks. You know that means everything to me."

"Finish up and go home to your wife."

"Yes, ma'am."

"Talk to you in the morning."

Freddie put down the phone, feeling slightly better after talking to her. If she was pleased with the outcome, then he should be, too. He went downstairs to the city jail, where the Cortezes were being held together. Archie's team was monitoring the camera trained on their cell, as they'd hoped the Cortezes would say something to each other to further cement the case against them.

They perked up when they saw Freddie.

"Are you releasing us?" Pascal asked.

"No. I've come to tell you we're also charging you, Pascal, with the murders of the Blanchets. You'll be arraigned in the morning."

Pascal's face turned ghostly white. "That's not possible. We didn't do it!"

"We have your social media posts showing your hatred of Eloise. Thanks to your cell phone data, we can prove you were at the home, your car was spotted in the neighborhood on multiple cameras the night of the murders, and you had motive after she called you racist animals."

"How can this be happening when we didn't do it?" Gia asked on a high-pitched wail. "Tell him, Pascal! We didn't do this! What about our children?"

"I'll be back in the morning." Freddie hoped a lawyer would take their case so they could get the case into court as soon as possible. He didn't give a crap about what became of people who'd murder children in their beds.

As he walked away, Gia continued to wail and scream to be let out of there to get home to their children. Freddie ignored her and went upstairs to submit his report.

He wanted to get back to reviewing Stahl's cases, expecting to find more irregularities.

And he was eager to go to the hockey game, look for Isaiah and then get home to Elin, who was the only one who could make him forget another long, traumatic day on the job.

Collins Worthy made Nicoletta wait an entire day before he graced her with his presence.

She was put in handcuffs and leg chains to be escorted by a deputy to a private room. As she walked into the room, she nearly stopped short at the sight of a drop-dead handsome man. He'd be described as a silver fox, with a deep tan and a sharp custom-made suit that hugged his well-honed physique.

Nicoletta's mouth watered at the sight of him.

That had never happened before. She'd used men to suit her purposes since the minute she began to understand her power as a woman, back when she was still a teenager, and had never stopped manipulating them to suit her needs. Not once had she ever been truly attracted to one of them.

Until now.

And that had to happen when she was shackled and cuffed, wearing an orange jumpsuit with her hair a mess and her face devoid of makeup. She hoped the root touch-up she'd had last week was holding back the gray hair that'd started to appear right after she turned fifty.

Meeting a man who made her mouth water when she looked like something the cat had dragged home was another thing to blame on her bitch daughter-in-law.

"Have a seat," Worthy said.

Nicoletta deeply resented the clanking of the chains as she made her way to the table, where a bottle of water had been set in front of her seat. She raised her cuffed hands to open the blessedly cold water and took greedy gulps. Ice-cold water was one of her favorite things. Living without that and so many other necessities since she'd been in this hellhole had been a nightmare. She shuddered to think how her face was holding up without her nightly mask to fight wrinkles and fine lines.

"Thank you for the water."

"You're welcome." He took a seat across from her and folded his hands on the tabletop. "So, this is a fine mess you find yourself in."

"Can you get me out of here?"

"I can sure as hell try, but first, I need you to be honest with me. Are you guilty of what you're charged with?"

Nicoletta glanced at the cameras positioned in every corner of the room.

"They can see us, but not hear us. Anything you say in here is between us."

"I, um..." Honesty was not her strong suit, but as she looked up, her gaze connecting with steely blue eyes that made her mouth water all over again, she decided to level with him. "I was running the escort service because older women have a right to love and affection, too. So many of them came to me after being widowed or unceremoniously dumped by their husbands. They wanted to get back out there, and they needed to make enough to survive. I saw it as a community service."

As she spoke, he took notes with a fine-looking pen. Maybe a Montblanc. Her father had had one that he'd treasured.

"What about the money-laundering charges through the bar?"

"I'm a co-owner of Carl's Place."

"Which has a net yield of four million a year?"

"It's a popular spot."

He put down his pen and folded his hands again.

As she thought of those strong, capable hands sliding over her skin, she broke out in goose bumps.

"I'm going to be straight with you, Ms. Bernadino."

"Please. Call me Nicoletta."

"Nicoletta... You're in a world of trouble here. The state prostitution charges are misdemeanors that can be easily pled out. However, no one believes that Carl's Place makes four million a year. The feds have you—and Carl—nailed on felony racketeering charges, which is the most serious piece of the puzzle here."

"Do you know who my son is?"

"Yes, I do, but he's not going to help you. He's made it clear that he has no relationship with you and never has."

"That is not true! It's his bitch of a wife that's making him say that stuff. We've had a wonderful relationship since he was a little boy."

Worthy gave her a skeptical look. "You're being honest with me, remember?"

She felt ashamed, and shame was an emotion that didn't look good on her. "Okay, so maybe I wasn't mother of the year, but I always loved and cared for him. I made sure he was in a good home and had what he needed. He grew up to be the president. Do you think that just happens without a lot of support?"

"I've read every word that's ever been printed about him—and you—and I have a very clear picture of how that happened. You had nothing to do with it."

Suddenly, he wasn't looking quite so attractive to her.

"If you're going to come out of this with your freedom, I'd recommend you stick to the facts and stop trying to rewrite history. No one cares if your son is the president, especially your son, the president. It's certainly not in his best interest to hitch his wagon to you while you're sitting in a jail cell."

Nicoletta wished she could get up and storm out of the room. She'd slam the door if she could, too.

"I can help you, but only if you take responsibility for your crimes and agree to pay the price. You'll have to shut down your escort service, sell your stake in Carl's and make restitution for the taxes you've avoided by running money through the bar."

"How am I supposed to do that with all my assets frozen?"

"You get a legitimate job and start to pay off your debt to society."

"And how am I supposed to live while I do that?"

"The same way everyone else does. By working hard and paying your bills."

"Amber said you were a nice guy and a shark who'd make this go away for me," Nicoletta said tearfully. "I don't think you're either of those things."

His handsome face lit up with a smile. "I'm both those things, and my goal is to get you out of here with a deal that spares you a trial and gets you back home as soon as possible. I assume that's your goal, too."

"It is, but what then? I won't be able to keep my home or any of my things. What kind of life is that?"

"What kind of life are you leading in here?"

"There has to be a way that I can hang on to some of the money. Can't we make that part of the deal?"

"I can try, but ill-gotten gains are tough to hang on to."

"They're not ill-gotten. They were gotten through hard work and determination. We never made anyone do anything they didn't want to do. Everyone involved was a willing participant."

"Maybe so, but the activities in question are still against the law."

"Well, they shouldn't be."

"Take that up with your congresspeople."

"I'll do that."

"In the meantime, if you're willing to consider a plea deal, I could get you out of here within a couple of days."

The thought of starting over—again—was almost too overwhelming to consider. "I'll need some of the money. I'm willing to plead in exchange for keeping at least half of the money so I can live without struggling. That's my bottom line."

"I'll see what I can do."

He stood and put his belongings in a fine leather tote that had his initials embossed in gold. CMW. She wondered what the M stood for.

"Will you be back?"

"Yes, Nicoletta," he said with a warm smile that made her tingle in all the most important places. "I'll be back."

At least she had something to look forward to now.

WHEN GONZO and Matt arrived at HQ to go to the Caps game together, Freddie told them he wanted to make another stop before they went to the game.

"Where're we going?"

"To the Blanchets' home."

The idea had come to him an hour earlier as he'd sifted through the paperwork on the case and tried to put himself in Isaiah Wiley's position. If he had nowhere else, where would he go? Home to his mother. Would Isaiah do the same thing, even if his "mother" wasn't there anymore?

"It's a long shot, but worth looking into."

"We're with you, boss man," Gonzo said, earning an eye roll from Freddie.

Gonzo was the boss whenever the two of them were together, and everyone knew it.

Freddie appreciated everyone deferring to him as the detective in charge of the investigation, but he'd be happy to get back to normal, where he was just a detective with Sam and Gonzo telling him what to do.

He'd already obtained the entry code from Lieutenant Haggerty with Crime Scene. They put a lockbox on the door of each place they investigated until the property was returned to the owners. He wondered who would own the home now that the Blanchets and their children were deceased. Probably Marcel's mother.

Freddie directed Gonzo to park a block from the house. "Let's fan out and see if there's any sign of someone inside."

They had radios with earpieces to keep in contact with one another as they moved around the perimeter.

"I see a TV flickering at the back of the house," Matt reported.

Freddie and Gonzo went to take a look.

Adrenaline coursed through Freddie at having followed a hunch that might possibly have led them to their missing man.

"What's the plan?" Gonzo asked.

Before Freddie could answer him, a door opened in the lower part of the house, and a person stepped outside. The spark of a lighter illuminated his face and confirmed his identity. A minute later, the scent of marijuana wafted over to where they were standing.

"Is it really gonna be this easy?" Freddie asked in a whisper.

"Looks like it," Gonzo said.

"You guys go around to the other side," Freddie said. "Let's meet in the middle."

When they were in position, Gonzo said, "Ready," into the radio.

"Let's go," Freddie replied.

With his weapon drawn, he stuck close to the shrubbery to stay hidden until the last possible second.

The young man was surrounded by cops before he knew what hit him. He put his hands in the air, one of them still holding the joint.

"Put that out," Freddie said.

Isaiah extinguished the blunt in an ashtray he'd obviously used before.

"I didn't hurt them," he said. "I loved them."

"Let's go inside and have a chat," Freddie said, directing him toward the door with his weapon.

They followed him into a spacious basement and turned on the light to find that someone was obviously living there. Clothes were strewn about, fast-food containers were on the coffee table and sneakers on the floor. Isaiah was about six feet tall with broad shoulders and a handsome face. He was mixed race with light brown skin, brown eyes and curly dark hair. He had matured significantly since the boy he'd been in the photo Freddie had been given.

"How long have you been here?" Freddie asked.

"On and off for years."

"What?" Freddie asked. "We were told your adoption was voided years ago."

"It was, but I stayed close. There's a room down here they never went near. They didn't know it existed."

"Show me," Freddie said.

They followed Isaiah to a hallway that had a number of closed doors. Inside one of the rooms was a door that connected to a small space that had an air mattress on the floor. Here, they found all the personal effects that had been missing in Isaiah's room at the facility that was his official home. There were photos of him with the Blanchets taped to the wall, along with Capitals and Washington Feds posters.

"How did you get in?" Freddie asked.

"They never changed the code on the basement door and rarely used the alarm. If the alarm was on, I still got a notification on my phone from when I lived here." He gave them a wary look. "I know how this must look to you, but I loved them. I wanted to stay close to them."

"Were you here the night they were killed?"

Isaiah hesitated before he nodded.

"Did you see anything?"

"I got some of it on video."

Freddie felt light-headed at hearing that. "Why didn't you call for help?"

"It went down fast. Like, so fast it was over before it began. I was so scared. Like, more scared than I've ever been."

"But you had the presence of mind to record it?" Gonzo asked, stealing Freddie's next question.

"It's the weirdest thing, but I have no memory of starting the video. One minute, I was watching through a crack in the dining room door, and the next minute, she was dead, and I was so scared they'd find me next. So I came downstairs and hid until all the people stopped coming."

"Did you recognize the people who killed them?"

"Nah, I never seen them before."

"Show us the video," Freddie asked.

Isaiah pulled his phone from his back pocket and sat in an upholstered chair. Freddie, Gonzo and Matt surrounded him as he pushed Play on the video that showed Gia Cortez confronting Liliana Blanchet as she came in from outside, carrying grocery bags. Liliana was shocked to find Gia standing in her kitchen, holding a gun, and dropped the bags.

"What the hell are you doing here?"

"Your husband let me in."

"No way he'd let you in here."

"It's funny what happens when a man's life is threatened."

"What do you want?" Liliana asked in a trembling voice.

Gia pointed to the ceiling. "Wait for it…"

The pop, pop, pop of gunfire had Liliana screaming as she ran toward Gia.

Gia pushed her back.

Pascal appeared in the kitchen, holding another gun.

"End her," Gia said.

"What did you do to my babies?" Liliana shrieked as she tried to get the gun from Pascal.

The gun went off, but Liliana didn't even flinch. That was probably the bullet that had ended up in the crown molding around the kitchen ceiling.

Pascal pushed her off him.

Liliana fell backward.

"Did you think you could call us racist animals in front of

everyone and go on with your lives like that never happened?" Gia screamed at her. "Your husband is dead. Your children are dead. Now it's your turn."

Liliana's screams echoed through the kitchen.

"Just do it, Pascal. I've had more than enough of her."

He pointed the gun at Liliana and put a bullet in her forehead.

"Jesus," Gonzo muttered.

"We need your phone, and we'll have to put you in protective custody," Freddie said, shaken to his core.

"Why?" Isaiah asked.

"Because we'll need you to testify to what you witnessed."

"Who were those people that killed my family?" Isaiah asked tearfully.

"Their daughter was in gymnastics with Eloise," Freddie said, sickened by what he'd seen on the video. "They were angry about her success."

"For real? That's why they killed them?"

"Yeah," Freddie said.

"That's fucked up."

"It sure is."

CHAPTER THIRTY-SIX

By the time he had Isaiah placed in a safe house where he'd be kept until he testified and the paperwork completed on the latest development, it was three thirty in the morning.

He'd texted Sam earlier to let her know what had gone down with Isaiah and the video that would cement their case against the Cortezes.

Even after seeing it play out on the video, Freddie still couldn't believe that massive jealousy and a public insult had led to the murders of six people, four of them children. It was possible that mental illness in Gia had played a part as well. Who knew what drove people to such a thing?

He thought about going home, but decided to crash on a sofa in the lobby for a couple of hours. After setting his alarm for seven so he could update Graciela Blanchet before the news went public, Freddie conked out.

He woke when someone shook him, opening his eyes to Sam standing over him.

"Has it come to this? Sleeping on the lobby sofa?"

"I finished at three thirty," he said, sitting up to run a hand over his face and stretch out the kinks.

"You found Isaiah before the marshals had the chance to get started," she said with pride in her voice and expression.

"I forgot to tell Jesse."

"All set. I talked to him on the way in."

"Thanks."

"In case I forget to tell you, great job, Detective. You've made me very proud."

He took the hand she offered him and let her help him up. "Which was the only goal."

"Nah, justice for the Blanchets was the only goal."

"You had your goal. I had mine."

"You'll handle the media briefing?" she asked.

"Do I hafta?"

"Yes, you hafta. It was your case. Get out there and finish it up."

"What do I say about Isaiah?"

"That he was in the house at the time of the murders and got the killing of Liliana Blanchet on video."

"And what do I say about why he didn't try to help her?"

"He was so scared, he couldn't move. That's what your report says, right?"

"Yeah, that's what he told us. He said he doesn't remember turning on the video and that it was over before it began. It happened very fast."

"That poor kid. And he's been living in the house ever since. I can't believe Crime Scene didn't find his secret room."

"It was very well hidden, and he stayed there until everyone had left."

"Did the Cortezes find an attorney?"

"Left messages. Haven't heard back yet."

"I want to be there when you tell them there's video," Sam said.

"I'll make sure you are."

"I'm so proud," Sam said again. "So very, very proud."

"Thanks. I wish I felt better about the outcome."

"We never feel good about the outcome. It's almost always so senseless, but this one is more senseless than most."

"Yep."

"Go call the grandmother and the other family members to update them and get ready for the briefing."

"That's the plan." Freddie went to his cubicle and downed the rest of a warm soda left from the night before. He foraged in his top desk drawer and found an unopened package of his favorite powdered doughnuts and ate all six in under a minute.

Gonzo appeared next to him with a tall coffee that he put on Freddie's desk.

"God bless you, man."

"Did you sleep here?"

"Yep. The sofa in the lobby isn't too bad."

"That's a rite of passage. Congrats on your first night on the lobby sofa."

"Gee, thanks. Everything good at the safe house?"

"I checked in this morning, and they said Isaiah got some sleep and had a good breakfast."

"I was thinking we should let Chuck at the group home know that he's in our custody."

"I'll take care of that."

"Thanks."

"Let me know what else you need."

"You feel like doing a press briefing?" Freddie asked hopefully.

"Haha, nope. That's all yours."

"I had a feeling you might say that."

Deputy Chief Jeannie McBride came into the pit, beaming as she looked at Freddie. "There's the man of the hour. Outstanding work, Detective."

"Thanks, Chief."

The word was apparently out, because everyone he worked with on the regular stopped by to congratulate him as the day shift came on duty.

He answered a good-morning text from Elin.

People are stoked about me closing the case. Lots of praise coming toward your husband.

I'm so proud! We'll celebrate tonight. I'll think of something special.

I can't wait.

Missed you last night. Hate sleeping alone.

Missed you more.

No way!

WAY! See you soon.

xoxoxoxo

He sent a text to his mother to tell her he'd closed the case and would be on TV in the next few minutes.

Congratulations! Dad and I will be watching!

Making Sam, Elin and his parents proud was definitely the best part about closing the case. Well, that and getting justice for the Blanchets. With that in mind, he placed the call to Graciela.

"This is Detective Cruz with the Metro PD."

"Do you have news?"

"I do. We've arrested Pascal and Gia Cortez for the murders of your family members. Their daughter competed with Eloise in gymnastics. A few days before the murders, Liliana called them racist animals in front of several other parents. We believe that, coupled with jealousy over Eloise's success in gymnastics, anger and blatant racism were the motives for murder."

"Dear God."

"I also wanted to tell you that Isaiah has been living in a secret room in the basement, coming and going from the house when they were home and when they weren't. He witnessed Liliana's murder and got video that will help to make our case."

"Why didn't he try to help?"

"He said he was terrified and couldn't believe what he was seeing. He doesn't recall turning the phone on to record. I believe he was also concerned about being in the house without permission and how that might work against him. Not to mention, in light of his violent background, he was possibly less fazed by violence happening in front of him than another kid his age might've been and knew better than to get anywhere near it."

"He got video of it."

"He did, and he'll also testify to what he witnessed. He's in MPD custody in a safe house."

"I... I think I'd like to see him, if possible. We all loved him so much and were heartbroken over what happened with him. Maybe... maybe I could help him or something."

"I'll mention it to him and let you know."

"Thank you for all you did for us. It doesn't change the outcome, but at least the people who did it aren't out living their lives while I prepare to bury my family."

"I'm sorry again for your loss. When you're ready, don't forget about the grief group here at headquarters for victims of violent crime. I think you'd find it comforting to be with people who understand."

"I'll get there eventually."

"Call me any time if I can be of assistance to you, and I'll keep you posted about court dates."

"I hope your mother is proud of the incredible young man she raised."

"Thank you, ma'am. She is. I'll be in touch."

After he put down the phone, he marveled at Mrs. Blanchet's

generosity toward him. In the darkest moment of her life, she was full of grace.

Sam came out of her office. "The jackals are foaming at the mouth for an update. Are you ready?"

"As ready as I'll ever be." Freddie gathered his notes and grabbed his coat, zipping it in anticipation of an unusually biting March chill. "You must be getting excited for Bora Bora. This weather blows."

"We're not going."

"What? Why?"

Sam filled him in.

"Oh damn. That sucks."

"It really does, but it's the right thing to do. We don't need our vacation picked apart in the media. By the time next year rolls around, he'll have almost eighteen months in office. The timing will be better."

"You must be crushed."

"I was. I'm over it. We're going to the Dewey Beach house for a few days by ourselves, and then the family will join us. You and Elin should come out."

"We'd love to. I'm glad you found an alternative, even if it's not French Polynesia."

"As much as I love being there, that flight is a bitch, even on the swankiest of planes." They'd traveled last year on *Air Force Two*. "I'm not sorry to miss that part of it. Besides, I keep telling myself it's the company that matters, not the location."

"That's true."

At the double doors that led to the patio where the press gathered, Freddie stopped and looked at her. "Thanks for having my back out there."

"I've always got your back."

"Means everything. And back atcha."

She patted his arm. "Go get 'em."

The reporters started shouting questions the second they walked through the doors.

Freddie followed Sam's example and waited until they stopped talking before he began, methodically going through the details of the case they'd built against Pascal and Gia Cortez. "We have an eyewitness, a teenager the Blanchets had adopted when he was a child. The adoption was unfortunately later annulled due to some issues within the family.

"Unbeknownst to the Blanchets, the young man had continued to access the home through a rarely used basement door and was in the house when the killings took place."

He explained Isaiah's terror and unconscious decision to begin recording. "As a result of his actions, we have the murder of Liliana Blanchet on video as well as the Cortezes' acknowledgments of the other murders. We believe the inciting incident that led to the killings was a statement Mrs. Blanchet made to Gia Cortez in front of other parents associated with their daughters' gymnastics team in which Mrs. Blanchet referred to the Cortezes as 'racist animals.' Mr. and Mrs. Cortez will be charged with six counts of felony murder."

"Who's representing them?" a reporter asked.

"We don't have that information yet. They've contacted several attorneys but have yet to hear back from any of them. They will be arraigned as soon as they secure representation."

"I want to be sure I understand this," Darren Tabor said. "The Cortezes were unhappy with Eloise Blanchet's success as a gymnast, picked a fight with her and her parents online and then killed the family after Mrs. Blanchet called them racist animals in front of other parents?"

"That's the gist. We had the same incredulousness as the pieces began to fall together in this case. That two parents of young children of their own could be driven to mass murder because of an insult that they had more than earned with their actions. But we followed the evidence, all of which pointed to them before we were handed the slam dunk in the form of the video."

He answered numerous other questions without having to refer to his notes, and when he was finished, he thanked the reporters for their time and escaped the podium before they could hold him there all day.

"Good job," Sam said when they were back inside. "You stuck to the facts and didn't give them any openings into other areas. That's the way to do it."

His phone buzzed with a text from his parents. *We're so, so, so proud. Our son on TV! Can't wait to hear all about it.*

Thanks for watching. Dinner this weekend?

Love to!

Chief Farnsworth approached them and shook Freddie's hand. "Fine job, Detective."

"Thank you, sir."

"I understand you were here all night."

"Yes, sir."

"Finish up the reports and head home. We'll see you back here on Monday."

"Will do. Thank you again."

Freddie walked away with a huge feeling of accomplishment after leading his first investigation.

Gonzo met him in the pit. "We found Colleen. She and Pascal had an affair that ended six months ago. Her husband found out about it, left her and is living in Texas now. I just talked to him to confirm his whereabouts."

"Thanks for closing that loop."

"No problem."

Freddie went to his computer and got to work on the last of the reports, eager to get home to celebrate with Elin.

"YOU'RE BEAMING like a proud mama, Lieutenant," the chief said after Freddie walked toward the pit.

"I feel like a proud mama. He did a great job."

"He was trained by the best." After a beat, he said, "Can you come into the office for a minute?"

"Sure." Sam nodded to Helen as she followed the chief into his office and closed the door. "What's up?" She took a seat in one of his visitor chairs.

"You heard about Gibbons?"

"I did. I'm sorry. I know it's personal to you and Captain Malone."

"It's very personal. He was a close friend and colleague." He sat back in his desk chair. "I need someone to run point on this and the Davies situation with the media. Since you've already been involved in dealing with Stahl's cases, I wondered if you'd be willing."

"Of course." That would also keep him from being the face of more scandal associated with the department. "I'll take some time to get up to speed, and then I'll do a briefing."

"Thank you," he said, seeming relieved. "I think it'll mean more coming from you."

Because Stahl had twice tried to kill her and was now serving a life sentence. "I understand."

He gave her the penetrating look he did so well. "I heard you took some personal time this week. Everything okay?"

"It is now. I took care of some things in the rest of my life that needed tending to."

"How's Angela?"

"Coping. She came to grief group the other night, which I saw as a positive sign."

"I think about her and the kids all the time."

"I know. Me, too."

"I won't keep you. As for the media, tell it to them straight. No sense hiding the details at this point."

"Anything for you, Uncle Joe." She left him with a smile and went back to the pit to prep for the briefing.

She went through the reports meticulously written by Archie and Captain Malone on the Gibbons matter and Green and Lucas on the Davies case. When she felt ready, she donned her coat and went outside, taking the press corps by surprise when she appeared for a second briefing of the day.

"I'm here to update you on the status of several matters pertaining to disgraced former Lieutenant Leonard Stahl. As you already know, we've begun a review of his past cases after discovering irregularities in the Worthington and Deasly cases. From our review, we've uncovered irregularities in another case."

She went point by point through the Davies case, from the traffic stop that had led to Stahl being suspended for three days to the bogus case he'd made against Davies that had led to Davies being incarcerated for sixteen years on false charges. She went through the whole thing—the woman hired to seduce Davies, the rape kit that tied Davies to the woman and the rest of the sordid story.

A collective gasp went through the group.

"We're working with the U.S. Attorney and the U.S. District Court to overturn Davies's conviction. We hope to have more news on that matter shortly. We've also learned that in many cases, then-Detective Stahl filed reports containing information gathered from witnesses that didn't exist or were never interviewed and that many of his open cases were archived to the system reserved for closed cases."

"Would he have been able to do that himself?" a reporter asked.

"No, and that leads to part two of this briefing. Former IT division Lieutenant William Gibbons has been charged on two felony counts of obstruction of justice for his role in burying Stahl's misdeeds. We expect there to be additional charges filed against Gibbons once we complete our full review of Stahl's cases."

"Why would Gibbons do that?" another reporter asked.

"Stahl had information about Gibbons's personal life that would've resulted in problems for him at home and at work that he used to convince Gibbons to do his bidding. Detectives Cameron Green and Erica Lucas have done exemplary work on the Davies case, while Lieutenant Archelotta and Captain Malone handled the Gibbons case."

Sam looked up from her notes. "I want to emphasize the departmentwide effort currently under way to correct these transgressions by our former colleagues. Additional charges will be filed against them in these and other matters that may be uncovered as we go forward. On a personal note, I want to say that, with few exceptions, the men and women of the Metro PD work tirelessly every day on behalf of the citizens of the District. It would be a mistake to judge the entire department on the actions of a few bad actors. That's all I have. Thank you for your time and attention."

They shouted questions at her as she walked away, but she ignored them as she went inside.

"That was very well done," Chief Farnsworth said.

"Was it carried live?"

"Any time you do anything, it's carried live."

"Huh, I didn't realize that."

"You're a big deal, Lieutenant. A very big deal."

Sam hoped her disdainful expression let him know what she thought of that.

His laughter confirmed that her message had been received.

"Thanks for taking one for the team," he said.

"You got it."

CHAPTER THIRTY-SEVEN

F reddie was waiting for her when she returned to the pit. "Would you like to come downstairs with me to break the news to the Cortezes that there's a video of Pascal killing Liliana Blanchet?"

"I would love to," Sam said.

They went down the stairs to the city jail, nodded to the sergeant on duty and proceeded to the cell where the couple were being held.

"Can we go home now?" Gia asked hopefully.

"Nope," Freddie said. "You're going to be our guests for quite some time, actually."

Sam could tell that he was taking pleasure in telling them that, which was fine by her. He'd earned the right to feel pleased by the case they'd put together.

"What do you mean?" Pascal asked. "We have rights."

"Yes, you do," Freddie said, "and we will see to it that every one of them is protected. But you should know that we have video that shows you killing Liliana and talking about how you killed the others. Remember that conversation in the Blanchets' kitchen? When you told Liliana her family was dead?"

Sam enjoyed watching both of them go pale and speechless when the impact of Freddie's words registered. "Modern technology," Sam said. "You gotta love it."

"Or hate it, in this case," Freddie said.

"True," Sam said. "You should show them the video."

"I'd love to."

Seconds after Freddie pressed Play, Pascal broke into a sweat. "Where did that come from?"

"You'll find out at trial," Freddie said.

"We need to go home to our kids," Gia said with a hysterical edge to her voice.

"Yeah, that's not going to happen any time soon," Freddie said.

Sam made eye contact with Gia and made sure she didn't blink. "The thing I'll never understand is how anyone could be so upset about middle school gymnastics competitions that they'd kill six people."

"It's all so petty," Freddie added. "Their daughter was a better gymnast than yours, so you decided to try to tear her down every which way you could with a disgusting online attack full of racist overtones. It must've infuriated you when you failed to drive Eloise out of the competitions. She just kept showing up and winning gold medals fair and square."

"Lacey was a *million* times better than her," Gia said on a snarl. "She *deserved* to win. She put in the work for *years*."

"And then Liliana had the nerve to state the truth about you two in front of the other parents, and oh boy, that made you mad," Sam said.

Gia was about to snap back at her when Pascal pulled at her arm. "Don't say anything else that they can use against us."

"You should know that we couldn't believe that something as harmless as competition among gymnasts could've led to mass murder," Freddie said. "We looked everywhere else for a motive, but the evidence doesn't lie. And now your children will be raised by others, all because you couldn't stand to see a more talented Black girl winning against your child. We'll see you in court."

They turned and walked away.

"Damn, that was fun," Freddie said.

"The most fun I've had on the job in quite a while."

As they entered the pit, Lindsey was arriving from the other hallway. "Jackpot on the hunch about possible health issues with Marcel, Detective." Lindsey led them to the conference room, where she placed several printouts on the table.

"This is the MRI result that shows Marcel Blanchet had a slow-growing tumor in the frontal lobe that could account for the personality changes reported by several witnesses. The bullet completely missed it, so the tumor is intact on the MRI. According to the American Brain Tumor Association, a number of common psychiatric symptoms can be experienced by brain tumor patients, including behavior that includes physical abuse, aggression, anger, impulsivity and disinhibition, which includes acting without forethought to consequences."

"Wow," Freddie said. "That explains so much."

"Profound personality change is another one," Lindsey said, "as are violent attacks. Great call, Detective. I'm sure his loved ones will be comforted to hear that the inappropriate things he did were most likely the result of the tumor."

"Yes," he said. "They will."

"Great job, Freddie," Sam said.

"Thanks. It's good to have an explanation for the unexplainable."

"You should call his mother and his partners in the practice to update them," Sam said.

"That's the kind of investigatory information that brings comfort to grieving family members."

"I'll do that. Thanks, Lindsey."

"No problem. Interesting outcome to a perplexing case. You guys have a good rest of your day."

"You, too, Lindsey." Sam turned to Freddie. "It continues to amaze me that we can think we have the full picture of a situation at the outset, only to realize the reality is nothing like what we thought."

"This looked like a slam-dunk murder-suicide."

"Which is why we always investigate, because we've seen many a slam dunk fall apart upon further scrutiny."

"That's a fact," Freddie said. "Should I let the women attached to the lawsuit know what we found, too?"

"I think so. It might bring them closure to know that the doctor they put so much faith in was sick, not deviant, even if that doesn't lessen the horror of what happened to them. Would you like me to make those calls for you?"

"That'd be great."

"Let's get to it. I've got cousin-palooza tonight with my nieces and nephews. I can't be late, or Nick might leave me."

Freddie laughed as he went to make his calls.

．　．　．

BEFORE SHE LEFT for the day, Sam gathered her squad in the conference room. "This was a tough one," she said. "Huge props to Detective Cruz for a job very well done."

They embarrassed him with a round of applause.

"Thanks for all the support, guys," Freddie said. "There's no I in this team."

"No, there isn't," Sam said, "and I want to thank you guys for stepping up when I needed to take a break. Knowing I have such great people working with me here makes the rest of my complicated life possible."

"Complicated," Gonzo said with a snicker. "Is that the word we're using?"

Sam laughed along with the others. "Until we come up with a better word, that works. But listen, the main reason I wanted to meet with you is you're all aware of what happened with my friend Shelby Hill the other day."

They murmured their disbelief and concern for Shelby.

"She's doing okay, but that incident and the one at Gigi's home are a reminder of how quickly things can escalate, sometimes because of the many perils that come with our profession. We put people in jail, and often they blame us for that rather than taking responsibility for the consequences of their own actions. In addition to that, my new much-higher profile has put a target on you guys as a result of your association with me. I hate that, but it's a fact of life for all of us. I'm surrounded by world-class security. The rest of you are not."

She made eye contact with each of them. "I want you to take a closer look at the security arrangements at your homes. If they aren't adequate, get them there. Do whatever you need to do to keep yourselves and your families safe."

"Yes, ma'am," Gonzo said for all of them.

"If there are any costs associated with beefed up security that are prohibitive for you, come to me," Sam said. "I mean that. Please be extra vigilant in everything you do, on and off the job. Your safety is my top priority. That's all I wanted to say. Have a good night, everyone, and thanks for all you do."

"Thank you, Lieutenant," Detective Charles said as she left the room.

The others followed her, until just Gonzo and Freddie were left.

"Was that okay?" Sam asked them.

"It was a good reminder that we need to be more careful," Freddie said. "Our lease is up this fall. I'm going to look for something more secure."

"Same," Gonzo said.

"That's good," Sam said. "I'm glad to hear it. And while I have you both, I just want to say thank you again for the way you stepped up this week when I needed a minute to catch my breath. Knowing you guys are here when I can't be makes all the difference."

"We're always here for you," Gonzo said. "Like you are for us. That's how family works."

Freddie used his thumb to point at Gonzo. "What he said."

"Have a good weekend," she said as they parted company outside the morgue.

"You, too," Gonzo said.

Sam called Vernon on her cell. "I need a favor."

"What can I do for you?"

"I need to stop at one of our safe houses in a vehicle that can't be easily identified as Secret Service. Is that possible?"

"Let me make a call, and I'll get right back to you."

"Thanks."

Sam waited ten minutes for him to call her back.

"We've got a vehicle on the way. It'll be here in ten minutes."

"Thanks, Vernon."

"Sure thing."

THE VEHICLE WAS a white Mercedes SUV.

"Fancy," Sam said as she got into the back seat.

"I'm glad you like it," Vernon said. "It's mine. My wife calls it my midlife-crisis car."

Sam laughed. "I think I'd like her."

"Oh, you definitely would. And vice versa."

Saying his wife would like her, she realized, was one of the best compliments he could pay her.

"Where to?" he asked when he got into the driver's seat, next to Jimmy in the passenger seat.

Sam gave him the address that was six blocks from their Ninth Street home. "Make sure we're not followed, okay?"

"Always do."

As Vernon drove her out of the parking lot, she took a long look at the building where so much of her life had taken place and felt satisfaction from another tough case closed, another job well done by the men and women she worked with.

Did they always get it right? Not by a long shot, but as long as they continued to give each of their victims their absolute best effort while they cleaned up the messes of the past, they'd be able to sleep at night.

That was all they could ask of themselves as they showed up every day to do a job most people would find repellent. Hell, *she* found it repellent on many a day. But it was a job that needed to be done. While they put away people who'd committed the most despicable of crimes, hopefully their work also served as a deterrent to others who might commit similar crimes.

Vernon brought the car to a stop outside a familiar house. Sam recalled keeping Selina Rameriz safe there during an earlier investigation.

"I won't be long," she said to Vernon as he held the door for her.

"Take your time, ma'am."

Sam went up the stairs and showed her badge to the officer on duty.

He opened the door for her.

Inside, Sam asked another officer if she could speak to Isaiah.

"He's in the living room, ma'am. Watching a movie."

"Thank you."

Sam followed the sound of the TV and stepped into the room where the young man sat on a sofa with a bowl of popcorn next to him and a bottle of Coke on the table in front of him.

He sat up straighter when he saw her, and then his eyes widened when he realized who she was. "Damn," he said. "They sent the big boss."

"I wasn't sent," she said with a smile that she hoped would put him at ease. "I came on my own." She pointed to a chair. "May I?"

His expression was uncertain as he nodded and paused the movie. "Am I in trouble? I know I shouldn't have been in the house—"

"No, Isaiah. You're not in trouble. I came because I want to help you."

Now he looked confused. "You want to help me? Why?"

"I read your file."

"Oh."

"I'm sorry for all the difficulties you've had."

He shrugged as if it was no big deal, when it was the biggest of deals.

"Do you remember Mr. Blanchet's mother?"

"Grammy B. Yeah, I remember her. She was always nice to me."

"She said she'd like to see you and maybe offer you a place to stay while you finish school. What would you think of that?"

"She really said that?"

Sam nodded.

"She must be so sad that they died."

"She sure is, and she thought that maybe the two of you could help each other. Would you like to see her?"

He thought about it for a second. "I think so."

"I'll let her know and set up a visit."

"How long do I have to stay here?"

"We're talking to the Assistant U.S. Attorney about how we might secure your testimony in advance of the trial so we can settle you in a new home sooner rather than later. So maybe just a little while longer, okay?"

Isaiah nodded. "They want me to tell them what I saw, right?"

"Yes. Is that okay?"

"If it means the people who killed my family will go to jail."

"That's what it means."

"I still loved them, you know?"

"I do. I know that. That's why you wanted to stay close to them."

"I should've done something when I saw what was happening. I keep thinking about what I could've done."

"If the Cortezes had known you were there, they would've killed you, too."

"You think so?"

"I know so. They weren't going to leave anyone alive in that house. Your video and testimony will help us get justice for your family."

"That's good, I guess."

Sam put her business card on the table. "If you ever need anything—anything at all—I want you to call me."

He gave her a curious look. "Why?"

"Because everyone could use a few extra friends. I want to see you make something of your life, Isaiah, to take the pain of your past and create a future that looks much different than your childhood."

"That'd be cool."

"You can do it. You need to finish high school and maybe go to college or trade school or do something that interests you. Anything is still possible if you want it badly enough."

"It's really okay if I call you?"

"It's really okay."

He offered a hint of a smile. "Thanks."

"No problem. I have your number, too. I'll be checking on you."

"That's cool."

Sam stood to leave and offered him her hand. "It was nice to meet you, Isaiah."

"You, too. Thanks for coming by."

"My pleasure."

On the way out, she said to the officer inside the door, "Take good care of him."

"Will do, ma'am."

Sam emerged from the house and zipped her coat.

Vernon held the back door for her.

"Let's go home, Vernon."

"Yes, ma'am."

EPILOGUE

Sam arrived at home to madness in the residence.

Nick was timing races in the hallway with Alden, Aubrey, Jack, Ella, Abby and Ethan competing, with Noah trailing behind them on chubby toddler legs. When Nick saw Sam coming up the stairs, he warned her to watch out lest she be run over.

Jack let out a shriek and ran for her. "Bal-SAM-ic!"

Sam cracked up. "Good one, strait-JACK-et."

His giggle made her day as she picked him up to squeeze him tight. "What've you been eating? You're a load all of a sudden." It pained her to realize she wouldn't be able to pick him up for much longer.

"Mom says I'm having a growth spurt."

"I'd say so." She kissed his whole face as he screamed and tried to break free of her.

"Disgusting! Girl cooties!"

It made her heart happy to see him laughing, joking and having fun after the blow of losing his father so suddenly.

She put him down to give the others equal attention before she finally got to Nick, who gave her a quick kiss. "Where's Scotty?"

"He got invited out for pizza with a friend after hockey practice."

"Do we know this friend?"

"It's Kyle from the team. Debra assures me the parents checked out. He'll be home by eight."

"I don't like him having a life away from us."

"I think we should prepare ourselves for more of that going forward."

"Don't wanna."

Nick smiled and hooked an arm around her as he watched the kids run the length of the hallway and then back again, screaming their heads off as they chased after Ethan, who led the pack.

"What's for dinner?" she asked.

"We're doing make-your-own-pizza night," Nick said. "Reginald set us up with all the fixings. An ice cream sundae bar is on tap for dessert."

"I'm starting to really love it here."

"I'm so glad to hear that."

Avery and Shelby came down from the third floor to join them for dinner.

Sam hugged her friend. "You're looking much better, Tinker Bell."

"I feel better. It's nice to be in this fortress where no one can get near us unless we want them to."

"Whatever it takes to make you feel safe."

"Feeling safe will be a work in progress."

Avery put his arm around her. "We'll get you there, darlin'."

"Mama," Noah said as he toddled over to Shelby. "Fun. Run."

Shelby smiled as she bent to kiss her little boy. "So much fun, buddy."

Noah ran off to see what Jack, Ethan and Alden were doing. He followed the other boys around like a little puppy, and they were so good with him.

"You guys should stay with us for as long as you want," Nick said. "We're very happy to have you here."'

"We're so glad to be here," Shelby said as she leaned into Avery's embrace.

EACH OF THE kids made mini-pizzas, while the adults crafted larger ones to share along with a tossed salad. After dinner, they went up to the third-floor conservatory, where the ice cream bar had been set up.

"Oh my God," Abby said, her eyes wide as she took it in. "This place is awesome."

"It's so much fun here," Jack said with a note of authority that amused Sam. He'd recently stayed with them after his father died. "Wait until you see the bowling alley and the pool. Flot-SAM, can we swim?"

Sam giggled at the name. "Someone's been hitting the Google."

Jack's grin touched her heart. "Duh."

"And yes, you can swim."

Scotty found them in the pool after he got home from his outing. He cannonballed into the middle of the other kids, setting off wild laughter.

"What's up?" Scotty asked as the kids splashed him.

He ducked under water and pulled Jack's legs to dunk him.

Jack came up sputtering with laughter.

"This is great," Sam said to Nick as they lifeguarded from the side of the pool. "We need to do this all the time."

"Yes, we do. Nothing takes the sting out of a hellish week like a bunch of screaming kids having the time of their lives."

"That's for sure."

After the pool, they bowled until the little ones started yawning.

Ella was the first to fall asleep.

Sam carried her to a bed on the second floor that she was sharing with Abby, who would keep an eye on her younger cousin.

Jack and Ethan were assigned to the room next door.

Sam tucked them in with a bit of tickling and giggling. "Sleep tight and no shenanigans, you hear me?"

"We hear you, Jet-SAM," Jack said with a grin.

"Go to sleep, JACK-rabbit."

She leaned over him to kiss Ethan. "You're in charge, boss. Keep him out of trouble."

"I'm on it."

Sam went to kiss Aubrey and Alden good night.

"This was so much fun," Alden said. "When can they come over again?"

"Very soon." Taking Angela's kids for an overnight was something they could do to help her sister—and it would delight Sam's own kids, too. "Sleep tight, my loves."

She knocked on Scotty's door. "Is it safe to come in?"

"Yep." As usual, he was watching the Caps game.

"Did you have a good time with Kyle's family?"

"Yeah, it was cool."

"I'm glad you had fun."

"It was fun with the kids, too."

"It was great." She leaned over to kiss his forehead. "Don't stay up too late."

"It's the weekend, Mom. That's what teenagers are supposed to do."

"If you say so, sport."

"I say so."

In their suite, Sam flopped down next to Nick. "So that's what it's like to have seven kids. Eight if we count Noah."

He laughed. "He definitely counts. I loved every minute of it."

"I know. I could tell. I love seeing you surrounded by kids and family."

"Being with you guys makes me forget what it was like to have no one."

She rested her head on his shoulder. "I'm glad."

"I've been thinking a lot about our conversation the other night about my mother and the lawyer and all that."

"What about it?"

"I've decided to stay out of it. She's made her bed. She can get herself out of it, too."

Until he said that, Sam hadn't realized she'd been holding a tight knot of stress in her chest since he'd told her he was considering getting involved. She exhaled a deep breath as she raised her head to look at him. "I'm very glad to hear you say that."

"You're right that nothing good ever comes of me getting involved with her, and right now, I can't afford the hit I'd take if it got out that I was helping her."

"I agree. I think you're doing the right thing."

"I still feel sick over it, but not as sick as I did earlier in the week."

"That's good to hear."

"I want you to know... I never would've survived a week like this without you and our family to keep me grounded in what really matters."

"We're here for you in good times and bad."

"That makes everything possible," he said, kissing her and then resting his forehead on hers.

Sam's phone rang. "Sorry," she said to Nick as she took the call from Captain Malone. "Hey, Cap. What's up?"

"Sorry to bother you so late, but I thought you'd want to know that we've received notice that Jaycee Patrick's family intends to sue Cam, Gigi and the department for one hundred fifty million over the wrongful deaths of Jaycee and her mother."

"Son of a bitch."

~

I'M GOING to leave it there for now, with a new full-length book, *State of Suspense*, coming in early 2024, which will pick up where this one left off. Please join the State of Denial Facebook Reader Group at *https://www.facebook.com/groups/812746520269847/?ref= share_group_link* to discuss this book with spoilers allowed.

Make sure to turn the page to read Darren Tabor's story about Sam.

Now, about upcoming books in the series...

I'm planning to write a novella to release Christmas week 2023 called *State of Bliss* that will take us on Sam and Nick's anniversary trip to Dewey Beach, where they'll take a break from everything to spend some time alone together before the family joins them. It'll be fun to write a full-on romance story for them!

We've got lots of cool things coming up in *State of Suspense*, including court hearings on a number of cases, including Spencer's, not to mention the wrongful death lawsuit the Patrick family has filed against Cam, Gigi and the department. As always, things will get crazy for Sam and Nick, which is just the way we like it!

State of Denial is the twenty-first full-length book in Sam and Nick's story, and I'm still having the time of my life writing them. They live inside of me like real people, my closest friends and favorite characters. I've spent more time with them than any other characters in my now 101 books, and I love them like family. MUCH more to come in their story, so buckle up. We're just getting started with the First Family Series.

I'm shaking things up to say THANK YOU FIRST AND FOREMOST (rather than last but not least) the readers who love Sam and Nick's story as much as I do and are always clamoring for more books in this series. I can't thank you enough for your support and enthusiasm. It means everything to me!

A huge thank you to the amazing team that supports me

behind the scenes: Julie Cupp, Lisa Cafferty, Jean Mello, Nikki Haley, Ashley Lopez and Rachel Spencer. To Gwen Neff, who helps me with series continuity, we're proving that two brains are definitely better than one! Thank you for all you do. To my ace beta readers, Anne Woodall, Kara Conrad and Tracey Suppo, I wouldn't want do this without your involvement. Thank you for always being willing to help. That goes to my editors, too, Joyce Lamb and Linda Ingmanson, who fit me in whenever I need them. I love working with both of you!

I've been writing this series for seventeen years with the help of Captain Russell Hayes, Newport Police Department (retired), who is always available to answer a question about policing or to connect me to the various experts I need to keep the investigations as authentic as possible. I couldn't write Sam without Russ, and I appreciate him so much!

Thank you to the Fatal/First Family beta readers, who also help with series continuity, which becomes a bigger job with every new book. I appreciate the involvement of Jennifer, Mona, Maricar, Elizabeth, Karina, Kelly, Juliane, Gina, Jennifer, Ellen, Irene, Kelley, Amy and Viki.

To Dan, Emily and Jake, thank you for your unwavering support of my author career and for making the rest of my life so much fun. I love our family!

I also love my job, and to everyone who makes it possible for me to live the dream every day... thank you from the bottom of my grateful heart.

Xoxo

Marie

SAMANTHA HOLLAND CAPPUANO
Wife, Mother, Detective and First Lady.
In that order.
By: Darren Tabor

To look at her in her element, you'd never know anything had changed. Metro Police Lieutenant Samantha Holland Cappuano sits among the Homicide detectives she commands, trading thoughts and ideas as they review the case files of now-disgraced former Lieutenant Leonard Stahl—the same former officer convicted of trying to kill her twice.

Holland Cappuano, which is how she asked us to refer to her for this article, and her team are determined to review every one of Stahl's cases after discovering the imprisoned former officer cut corners that led to disastrous consequences.

"We've uncovered serious irregularities in many of his old cases," she says. "We're going to examine each one of them and do what we can to make it right."

It's just another day in the life of America's highest-profile working mom. After a full day on the job at the MPD, she goes home to the White House where she lives with President Nick Cappuano and their children, Scotty, 14, and twins, Aubrey and Alden, 6. They consider the twins' older brother, Elijah, 20 and a junior at Princeton, to be their "bonus son."

"The kids have made a smooth transition to the White House," Holland Cappuano says. "They love the pool, bowling alley and theater as well as the chocolate chip cookies that the president and I try to stay away from."

When asked how that's going, she says with a smile, "Not great. They're *so* good. The White House staff is amazing. They take such incredible care of us. They make it possible for me to continue to work as a police officer while juggling motherhood and first lady duties."

As first lady, Holland Cappuano has put her focus on working mothers, criminal justice reform, spinal cord research, infertility awareness and adoption, all subjects near and dear to her heart. Her father, former MPD Deputy Chief Skip Holland, died in October, almost four years after being shot on the job and left a quadriplegic. His plight has made her and her family much more aware of the challenges that come with spinal cord injuries.

"I watched my dad struggle to adapt to his new reality, and it made me see how spinal cord injuries impact a patient and the entire family," she says. "It's important to me to shine a light on those struggles and to encourage donations to organizations that are pursuing treatments and therapies to assist paralyzed people."

After suffering through years of well-documented infertility, Holland Cappuano has also become a vocal advocate for more research into the causes of infertility and for support for patients enduring the invasive treatments and procedures. "They're chasing a dream that comes so easily for some people," she says. "I see that in my own life. My sisters will soon have six children between them. Two of my close friends are expecting. And while I've made peace with not being able to carry a baby, that doesn't take away the heartache of the journey I and so many others have undertaken."

Being a mother to Scotty and the twins, she says, is the best thing to ever happen to her. "They've made our family complete, and we couldn't be happier to get to be their parents and guardians."

Holland Cappuano and the president took in the twins after their parents, Jameson and Cleo Armstrong, were murdered in a home invasion last fall.

"They've very quickly become an essential part of our family," Holland Cappuano says of the twins and their older brother. "We feel so fortunate to have them and Scotty in our lives."

She gives credit to White House Chief of Staff to the First Lady Lilia Van Nostrand and the rest of the Office of the First Lady staff for making it possible for her to contribute to her husband's administration while holding down a full-time job outside the White House.

Her husband's transition from vice president to president has been bumpy, to say the least, but Holland Cappuano says she's proud of the way he's risen to the moment. "The American people may not know yet how lucky they are to have Nick in the Oval Office," she says, "but I think they'll know that before much longer. Nick is one of those rare people who always does the right thing and leads with his heart. I can't wait to see what he and his team will accomplish over the next three years."

She's coy when asked about the possibility of him running for reelection. "He's already expressed his disinterest in the long-drawn-out campaign, and that hasn't changed since he became president. He's waited all his life to have a family of his own, and he doesn't want to miss anything with the kids. The next election cycle is a couple of years away, so we're not really thinking about it right now."

She laughs when she adds, "We have more than enough on our plates as it is."

In May, the National Association of Police Organizations will present Holland Cappuano with one of its TOP COPS Awards. She will also deliver the keynote address at the organization's annual gathering. When asked how she feels about the TOP COPS Award, she is visibly uncomfortable.

"There are so many amazing law enforcement officers working every day to keep their communities safe," she says. "It feels odd to be singled out, but I'm thankful for the acknowledgment of the hard work of my team. No one does a job like mine alone. I'm blessed to work with some of the best people I've ever known, and I'll accept the award on their behalf."

The first couple will soon celebrate their second wedding anniversary. When asked how she'd sum up the first two years of their marriage, she says, "It's been the most exciting time of my life —and his."

ALSO BY MARIE FORCE

Romantic Suspense Novels Available from Marie Force

The First Family Series

Book 1: State of Affairs

Book 2: State of Grace

Book 3: State of the Union

Book 4: State of Shock

Book 6: State of Bliss (Dec. 2023)

Book 7: State of Suspense (Coming 2024)

Read Sam and Nick's earlier stories in the Fatal Series!

The Fatal Series

One Night With You, *A Fatal Series Prequel Novella*

Book 1: Fatal Affair

Book 2: Fatal Justice

Book 3: Fatal Consequences

Book 3.5: Fatal Destiny, *the Wedding Novella*

Book 4: Fatal Flaw

Book 5: Fatal Deception

Book 6: Fatal Mistake

Book 7: Fatal Jeopardy

Book 8: Fatal Scandal

Book 9: Fatal Frenzy

Book 10: Fatal Identity

Book 11: Fatal Threat

Book 12: Fatal Chaos

Book 13: Fatal Invasion

Book 14: Fatal Reckoning

Book 15: Fatal Accusation

Book 16: Fatal Fraud

Contemporary Romances Available from Marie Force

The Wild Widows Series—a Fatal Series Spin-Off

Book 1: Someone Like You

Book 2: Someone to Hold

Book 3: Someone to Love

The Miami Nights Series

Book 1: How Much I Feel *(Carmen & Jason)*

Book 2: How Much I Care *(Maria & Austin)*

Book 3: How Much I Love *(Dee's story)*

Nochebuena, A Miami Nights Novella

Book 4: How Much I Want *(Nico & Sofia)*

Book 5: How Much I Need *(Milo and Gianna)*

The Gansett Island Series

Book 1: Maid for Love *(Mac & Maddie)*

Book 2: Fool for Love *(Joe & Janey)*

Book 3: Ready for Love *(Luke & Sydney)*

Book 4: Falling for Love *(Grant & Stephanie)*

Book 5: Hoping for Love *(Evan & Grace)*

Book 6: Season for Love *(Owen & Laura)*

Book 7: Longing for Love *(Blaine & Tiffany)*

Book 8: Waiting for Love *(Adam & Abby)*

Book 9: Time for Love *(David & Daisy)*

Book 10: Meant for Love *(Jenny & Alex)*

Book 10.5: Chance for Love, *A Gansett Island Novella (Jared & Lizzie)*

Book 11: Gansett After Dark *(Owen & Laura)*

Book 12: Kisses After Dark *(Shane & Katie)*

Book 13: Love After Dark *(Paul & Hope)*

Book 14: Celebration After Dark *(Big Mac & Linda)*

Book 15: Desire After Dark *(Slim & Erin)*

Book 16: Light After Dark *(Mallory & Quinn)*

Book 17: Victoria & Shannon (Episode 1)

Book 18: Kevin & Chelsea (Episode 2)

A Gansett Island Christmas Novella

Book 19: Mine After Dark *(Riley & Nikki)*

Book 20: Yours After Dark *(Finn & Chloe)*

Book 21: Trouble After Dark *(Deacon & Julia)*

Book 22: Rescue After Dark *(Mason & Jordan)*

Book 23: Blackout After Dark *(Full Cast)*

Book 24: Temptation After Dark *(Gigi & Cooper)*

Book 25: Resilience After Dark *(Jace & Cindy)*

Book 26: Hurricane After Dark *(Full Cast)*

Book 27: Renewal After Dark *(Coming 2024)*

The Green Mountain Series

Book 1: All You Need Is Love *(Will & Cameron)*

Book 2: I Want to Hold Your Hand *(Nolan & Hannah)*

Book 3: I Saw Her Standing There *(Colton & Lucy)*

Book 4: And I Love Her *(Hunter & Megan)*

Novella: You'll Be Mine *(Will & Cam's Wedding)*

Book 5: It's Only Love *(Gavin & Ella)*

Book 6: Ain't She Sweet *(Tyler & Charlotte)*

The Butler, Vermont Series

(Continuation of Green Mountain)

Book 1: Every Little Thing *(Grayson & Emma)*

Book 2: Can't Buy Me Love *(Mary & Patrick)*

Book 3: Here Comes the Sun *(Wade & Mia)*

Book 4: Till There Was You *(Lucas & Dani)*

Book 5: All My Loving *(Landon & Amanda)*

Book 6: Let It Be *(Lincoln & Molly)*

Book 7: Come Together *(Noah & Brianna)*

Book 8: Here, There & Everywhere *(Izzy & Cabot)*

Book 9: The Long and Winding Road *(Max & Lexi)*

The Quantum Series

Book 1: Virtuous *(Flynn & Natalie)*

Book 2: Valorous *(Flynn & Natalie)*

Book 3: Victorious *(Flynn & Natalie)*

Book 4: Rapturous *(Addie & Hayden)*

Book 5: Ravenous *(Jasper & Ellie)*

Book 6: Delirious *(Kristian & Aileen)*

Book 7: Outrageous *(Emmett & Leah)*

Book 8: Famous *(Marlowe & Sebastian)*

The Treading Water Series

Book 1: Treading Water

Book 2: Marking Time

Book 3: Starting Over

Book 4: Coming Home

Book 5: Finding Forever

Single Titles

Five Years Gone

One Year Home

Sex Machine

Sex God

Georgia on My Mind

True North

The Fall

The Wreck

Love at First Flight

Everyone Loves a Hero

Line of Scrimmage

Historical Romance Available from Marie Force

ABOUT THE AUTHOR

Marie Force is the *New York Times* bestselling author of more than 100 contemporary romance, romantic suspense and erotic romance novels. Her series include Fatal, First Family, Gansett Island, Butler Vermont, Quantum, Treading Water, Miami Nights and Wild Widows.  She has also written 11 single titles, with more coming.

Her books have sold more than 13 million copies worldwide, have been translated into more than a dozen languages and have appeared on the *New York Times* bestseller list more than 30 times. She is also a *USA Today* and #1 *Wall Street Journal* bestseller, as well as a Spiegel bestseller in Germany.

Her goals in life are simple—to spend as much time as possible with her young adult children, to keep writing books for as long as she possibly can and to never be on a flight that makes the news.

Join Marie's mailing list on her website at *marieforce.com* for news about new books and upcoming appearances in your area. Follow her on Facebook at *www.Facebook.com/MarieForceAuthor*, Instagram at *www.instagram.com/marieforceauthor/* and TikTok at *https://www.tiktok.com/@marieforceauthor?*. Contact Marie at *marie@marieforce.com*.